Touch of Jules

CONNIE DUNN

Cover Image Credit: Brenda A. Millard

ISBN: 978-1-4834-4607-3 (sc)
ISBN: 978-1-4834-4609-7 (hc)
ISBN: 978-1-4834-4608-0 (e)

Library of Congress Control Number: 2016901628

Lulu Publishing Services rev. date: 03/23/2016

Acknowledgements

THIS BOOK IS FOR ALL women of a certain age as we navigate through the often difficult journey of growing older. I've discovered that you're only as old as you feel, an often clichéd saying that I used to laugh at. Now I only laugh at people who don't believe it. My mother was one of those who would remind me of that, as well as many other things. We women of today are very different from our mothers and especially our grandmothers, but as they are the little voices inside our heads, we find it hard to ignore them. Sometimes they guide us, but sometimes they hinder us. This book is dedicated to all women who have silenced the voices that tell them *no*.

You may see something of yourself or of someone you know in *Touch of Jules*, but don't be alarmed. This book is totally fiction, so any familiarities are coincidental and based on universal qualities of people of every age and gender.

Making the jump from teacher of writing to writer is no easy task, and I couldn't have made the leap without a ridiculously awesome group of people behind me. My DPS Amy held my hand and trudged through the almost daily pages I'd send her. Your encouragement kept me going, girl. Becky, Kristi, and Pam cheered me on to publish this story and hurry up in writing the sequel. I'm working on it, ladies. Mandee, thank you for the extra eyes. But no one kept me going like my husband and soul mate—Kevin, you're my rock. You've been pushing me to be better for thirty-six years, and your faith in my abilities has always led me to do more.

I hope my readers enjoy *Touch of Jules*, and if it does nothing more, I hope it encourages you to never be afraid. Never be afraid to try something new. Never be afraid of living a life that is right for you.

Chapter 1

⎯⎯⎯

As she sat at the bar waiting for her bottle of water, Julia looked out the windows that made up the wall of the clubhouse at Coyote Run Golf Club. Another group was teeing off on the first hole, but she wasn't really seeing the players: she was looking through them at another time, another clubhouse, another group. She looked like she belonged here in this setting of rich, dark wood, plush carpets, and hushed conversations. This had been her world at one time, a fact her light-blue golf skirt, white polo top, matching golf shoes and visor, and freshly manicured hands made clear. What those in the club didn't know was that she only wore the outfit because, in her words, "When you play golf as badly as I do, you have to dress the part!" She'd say it with a full laugh that drew others to laugh with her. Glancing around the room, she decided that this was a group she'd not waste her joke on.

"Here's that water, ma'am. I'm sorry it took so long. That will be two dollars," the young attendant said.

Looking into the small bag she carried around her wrist, Julia noticed her sunglasses were missing. She must have left them on the cart. She put three dollars on the counter, barely registered the girl's thanks, and hurried toward the side door. Julia may not have noticed anyone else in the clubhouse, but a group definitely noticed her. As she passed, one older gentleman, knocking back bourbon and smoking a large cigar, took a long look at the pretty lady and said to his table mates, "Well, well, well…the scenery is looking up around here."

While she didn't acknowledge him directly, she murmured under her breath, "Anything beats cigar-smoking assholes." No one in the Beltone crowd heard her—but one. He was the youngest of the group at the table (if forty-five could be considered young), and he laughed appreciatively as she pushed off from the door and strode purposefully toward the cart shed. Julia Whitman was used to her share of admiring looks, compliments, and invitations from all the right people. She was also used to saying the right words, doing the right thing, and pleasing everyone—or at least she used to be. Those very things had sent her off on her own from St. Louis to Phoenix five years earlier. That time, she was escaping from a life that had her fitting right in with the group in the clubhouse. Just the unpleasant thought of being one of that crowd brought her brows together over intense blue eyes, eyes that could draw one in or warn him away.

It was with the latter look that she rounded the corner and almost collided with a young man just coming out of the golf cart shed, where a group of haphazardly parked carts waited to be serviced.

"You must be looking for these," he said easily, holding out a pair of Ray-Bans. "I saw you wearing them earlier, so I knew they had to be yours when Troy found them on the cart. Aviators, huh?"

"Thank you so much! I've managed to hang onto these for a few years, and I was sick to think I'd lost them. And yeah, aviators look good on everyone, you know," she said with a smile, taking the glasses from his hand without really looking at him as she put things back together in her bag. "I appreciate it…"

"Austin, Austin James." Julia looked up from the sunglasses to see him for the first time. He was tall, maybe six-three, with the body of a man used to working with his hands. His deeply tanned skin was set off by longer blond hair that curled down his neck almost to his broad shoulders. But what caused her to stop in her tracks were the greenest eyes she'd ever seen. As he met her gaze, his lips curled up in a smile that made her offer one of her own.

"I'm Julia, Julia Whitman." As they continued to smile at one another, she went on. "I'm not a member here. I'm just here with my client Sharon Burns. Well, not just a client. Sharon is also a dear friend, and she invited me to play a round. I haven't hit a golf ball in probably four or five years. Yes, it has been five years because that's when I came out here from St. Louis. I'm really not very good, but I enjoy the company, and when I'm with Sharon, we do as much talking as hitting the ball!" She laughed, and stopped suddenly. "Good grief! Why didn't you stop my mouth before it carried me away like that!" She laughed again. He decided that the beautiful laugh went with the beautiful lady. He also decided that she was way above his pay grade, a bit older than he was used to, out of his league.

"Well, you were pretty much a runaway horse, and I do a lot better stopping a mower," he replied. "Head groundskeeper at your disposal, ma'am. Well, assistant, but at your disposal."

"Hmmm…and I always thought those guys were more like Carl, you know, *Caddyshack* Carl?" They both laughed at the shared joke, and Austin shook his head.

"Nope. I think after Carl left for the PGA circuit, they decided to find someone less apt to blow up the course for a gopher." He smiled. "But we do have a judge, some rich old guys, and a couple of playboys roaming around." She enjoyed that laugh again.

"I own an interior-design shop. My specialty is inside and maybe a patio once in a while." Looking around and taking in the well-manicured lawns, beds of flowers, and areas of natural desert flora mixed in with carefully planted shrubs, she added, "You're really good. Making something like this so gorgeous in the middle of the desert. I'm afraid I would make a disaster if this were my job. Like I said, my specialty is interiors. Here's my card." She pulled a small, white card from her bag.

"Touch of Jules," he read. "Nice name."

A horn blasted next to the cart shed, and Julia looked up to see Sharon behind the wheel of her Cadillac. The woman could literally afford any car in the world, but no one could talk her out of her Caddy. "I really have to go. It was nice meeting you Austin, and thanks again for rescuing my sunglasses. Later!"

"See ya around," he said before she turned and almost ran to the car, her long, curly brown hair flying out behind her, her light-blue skirt hugging her tan legs and riding a little higher as she jumped into the waiting car. A short wave of her hand, and she was gone.

Austin clutched his chest with his hand in a mock heart attack and said out loud, "I think I'm in love!" He looked down at the card once again. The name of the shop was in curly letters surrounded by what looked like tiny fern-like leaves that held small yellow flowers that resembled a cluster.

Acacia, he thought. He noted the address and cell number of Ms. Julia Whitman printed in neat letters.

Thinking of the swirling skirt that just left, he smiled once again and said to himself, "Tar Heel blue."

"Sharon, what was I thinking!" Julia exclaimed as they drove away. "God! I just gave a perfect stranger my card, for heaven's sake! I *NEVER* do that! And he's, what, twenty-one? Twenty-two, twenty-three at the oldest? I'm twice his age, a divorced, middle-aged woman! He probably thinks I'm some desperate housewife looking for attention. Dammit! I need my head examined." She slunk down into the leather, crossed her arms, and started chewing on her lower lip. "Stupid, stupid, stupid," she chided herself and wondered why making a fool of herself in front of this man bothered her so much. *Why?* she conceded only to herself. *Because Julia Whitman doesn't make a fool of herself for anyone, man or woman.* She rolled her eyes and sighed in disgust.

"Well, I think he's a hottie!" Julia looked over at her sixty-five-year-old friend and had to laugh. She knew that Sharon was happily married to the love of her life and had been for more than forty years.

"Just call us a couple of cougars, Sharon," Julia retorted, still feeling the sting of letting herself be attracted to a young man. *Man?* She chided herself. *More like a boy!*

"No," Sharon insisted, "*I'm* the cougar. You're just a puma. You'll need a few more years on you to make the rank of cougar, little girl." They both laughed.

"I wish…" Julia said wistfully. "Do you remember the mess I was when I turned forty last February? God, that was a hard birthday. You know, by age forty, a woman should be happily married, have a couple of kids, and drive a minivan to soccer and dance practices—at least that's how things go in my mother's world." Julia smiled ruefully. "I don't think I could be any further from that, and hell, who wants to drive a minivan? I suppose I'm still searching for something, someone, my life."

Sharon looked over at her young friend and thought, *You don't look a day over thirty sweetie, if that. It's small wonder that young hunk would be wanting your number!* Sharon knew the journey that had led Julia to

Scottsdale and the struggle she'd had with her family, her ex-husband, and herself.

"You know what you need?" Sharon asked. "A little pick-me-up from Mary! Let's head to my pool and let Angie work her magic at the bar." A Bloody Mary was Sharon's favorite drink, and her housekeeper Angie could make them like no other.

"Good idea. I'll either have my life figured out—or I will no longer give a damn."

"That's my girl! I'll just think of that hottie back there and purr." Julia laughed as Sharon hit the gas, pointing the Caddy in the direction of the hills in the distance.

Austin finished the rest of the day in short order. It was Friday, and since he started his day at 5:00 a.m., he could clock out any time after 12:00. Looking at the desert sun beating down on the green fairways, he could almost feel the heat intensify. *It will be over one hundred degrees if it isn't already,* he thought. Between noon and four or five in the afternoon, few had the courage to play golf in the scorching sun even though the course offered half-price on everything. He had to chuckle at the tourists who had never been to Phoenix, Arizona, in the summer months and had no clue of how hot it could get. He knew that extra water was placed in coolers on all the carts, and management kept a close watch on the players. No one wanted a guest falling over from heat stroke. *Not my circus, not my monkeys,* he thought as he clocked out and headed to his car.

He opened the door to let the little black Mustang air out, and a rush of hot air hit his face. Reaching in to turn the key, Austin flipped the switch to lower the top. He watched as it rose into the air, exposing the black interior before settling into its compartment above the trunk. The car had been a graduation present from his mom and dad when he finished high school. The new car was to get him through college until he could trade up for something "More appropriate," as his mother put it. He was far from that upgrade now. He snarled his nose as he thought of that scene—the summer he had come home from North Carolina, his father's alma mater, and announced that he wasn't going back. Pre-law, he had insisted to his disbelieving parents, wasn't for him. He wanted to study

5

horticulture, with an eye on starting his own landscape construction and management company.

Yeah, he thought, *that went about as expected.* By the time the yelling, crying, threatening, and worst of all, begging were over, Austin had dug in his heels. He loaded most of his stuff into the little car and headed west to stay with a buddy in Phoenix. He knew there were hundreds of golf courses in the valley, at least 250 in the state, and he'd land a job on one of them, save up some money, and start studying at Arizona State. Three years later, he had worked his way up to assistant head groundskeeper at the Coyote Run Golf Resort. He was almost finished with his classes at Arizona State, and he hoped the university would let him intern at the prestigious Superstition Mountain Golf and Country Club. He had already spoken to Jay Reynolds, the head groundskeeper there, and with Jay's recommendation, as well as the one from his boss at Coyote Run, Austin was feeling good about his chances. If he could do a good job there, he'd make many valuable contacts for his future and gain a lot of experience.

He shook off these thoughts, stuffed the Touch of Jules business card into his front pocket, climbed into the car, and slowly pulled out onto the parking lot. As he made his way past the parked cars, the blond man with bright green eyes and confident smile turned the heads of more than one person who was loading up equipment. Pulling out onto the street, Austin shifted the car from first to second, hit the gas before shifting to third, and roared off toward home.

Chapter 2

⁓

"**H**EY, JULES! HOW WAS YOUR weekend? We had a few walk-ins on Saturday, and one of them, a Mrs. Hampton, said she'd be in sometime today to talk to you about redoing her bedroom." Lauren Reynolds rounded the corner of the shop's office and laid several messages on Julia's desk. She took in her friend's fresh tan, a sprinkling of new freckles standing out across her nose and cheeks, and relaxed posture. "Never mind. I think I know how your weekend went. You hung out at the pool, drinking Bloody Mary's and being entertained by Sharon, right?"

"Right, right, and right," Julia looked up with a smile. "It was good. Oh, and I played golf Friday!" She laughed at Lauren's shocked expression. "Yeah, the sport I signed off on long ago. I even pulled out the old matching outfit. My game went as it usually does, but I looked GOOD!" Julia laughed again at her own joke, and Lauren had to join her. She'd seen Julia's game and had been there when she joined the Lake Forest Country Club. In fact, Lauren had been there when Julia had left the country club, left the Lake St. Louis house she had shared with Keith, and left the life she'd known in Missouri. *Heck,* Lauren thought, *I've seen it all with that girl.*

The two had met at Columbia College, in Columbia, Missouri, not to be confused with the University of Missouri that dominates the town. Columbia was a small liberal arts school that offered a top-notch design program. Julia and Lauren met that first year in Basic Design 101 and soon became roommates. They had encouraged one another through the course work and internships, held one another's hair as they hugged the toilet after drunken nights out, checked out prospective boyfriends, used

7

each other's closets, graduated together, and started their own business. Using the inheritance Julia had received from her grandmother and money Lauren's wealthy family had "loaned" her, the two soon built up a reputation. While both were extremely talented, it was Julia whose sharp eye could make something amazing out of something ordinary. Lauren's business savvy soon had the venture showing a profit, and they opened a shop in Chesterfield, Missouri, called *J-L Designs*. Even though they were making decent money, they continued to share an apartment and clothes, as both women settled into building their business and lives.

It wasn't long before Keith Landry had strolled into the shop, looking for someone to help him renovate a new/old house he'd purchased in Lake St. Louis. Lauren had given him the once-over, decided he looked like a "Julia" candidate, and turned him over to her, saying that Jules would be a better match. Working on the extensive renovations, followed by decorating and arranging everything in the house, Julia and Keith quickly built a relationship that wasn't all business. One date led to another—the two were soon inseparable. Julia met his family, and he met hers. Keith proposed, Julia accepted, the massive wedding was held, and the two went off to live happily ever after.

That thought brought a massive eye roll that Lauren couldn't stop. Keith had turned out exactly as he appeared. Unfortunately for him, her friend had grown into a woman so different from the girl he'd first fallen in love with. *Same old story*, Lauren thought. Julia had grown up pleasing everyone but herself until she really didn't know who she was. Lauren thought about all she knew of her friend's early life. As an only child, Julia had been the perfect daughter—dance lessons, swim lessons, piano lessons, family darling in pink. In school, she'd been the perfect student—honor roll, student government, prom queen. In college Jules had spread her wings a bit, but at the end of the day, she'd returned to pleasing everyone else. *Heck*, thought Lauren, *her mom had been as in love with Keith as Julia had been.* She rolled her eyes again and looked at her friend now. Leaving hadn't been easy. In fact, it had taken bravery that neither Lauren nor Julia knew she had, but Julia had started changing after the babies.

Those had been dark days for Julia, losing one baby in the first trimester, the next in week fifteen, and the last and hardest, losing her baby girl after twenty weeks. Lauren knew she'd been Julia's rock during that time as the losses put a strain on Julia, Keith, and the marriage. Lauren had watched as her friend had become more agitated with her life, with her family, and with Keith. He really didn't know what to do with a woman who was changing into someone different from his ideal. Julia had begun pulling away. Soon the divide was more than the marriage could handle, but Lauren knew that her friend would probably still be in Missouri had she not been there for the final straw. Julia had confided in Lauren that she was finished pleasing everyone but herself and that she realized how short life is. She needed to get away and start over, this time for her. Keith had made it easier, but that was a time neither woman liked to think about. In five years, a lot had changed, for sure. Julia had always had Lauren's love, but now she had her admiration for the woman Julia had made of herself. Her friend's voice brought Lauren back to the present with a start.

"I did meet someone interesting Friday at the golf course." The look on Lauren's face made Julia pause. Her friend's dark brown eyes narrowed as she looked up over her reading glasses to give Jules what they called *The Look*, one Lauren used to ward off unwanted male advances, salesmen, and small children. She, too, knew the kind of men who hang around clubhouses all day. *Not* their type.

"Come on, Lauren, don't give me that look. I didn't meet him IN the clubhouse. I met him OUTSIDE the clubhouse."

"Oh, well! That makes all the difference in the world!" Lauren's eyes rolled again, and Julia had to laugh.

"Keep that up, and you'll give yourself a headache. No, this guy WORKS at the course."

"Oh, hell, what is he? Some pro? Bored playboy?" Lauren definitely had her bias.

"No, he's assistant head groundskeeper, he's about twenty-two or twenty-three, somewhere around there, he rescued my sunglasses from the cart, he does a really good job because the course looks fantastic, and I gave him my number. Well, I gave him my card that has my number on it." Julia didn't pause for breath until she'd revealed it all to her friend.

"He's HOW OLD?" Lauren jumped on the one fact Julia had hoped she would miss, and her single raised eyebrow spoke volumes. "Twenty-two? You think? What the hell, Julia! That is a twenty-year difference in age, my friend! You could be his MOTHER!!!"

9

"Shut up! And that was a low blow. I know, I know. But he was so nice, we laughed at the same things, he has the prettiest green eyes, and he's drop-dead gorgeous. I can't stop thinking about him. And isn't that a step up from an old cigar-smoking asshole?" Keith's friends had smoked cigars—in Julia's house.

"Ok, cougar, calm down. I suppose it will be okay to just play with him. I mean, you've done the whole marriage thing. And God knows you don't really date. And you haven't slept with a man in what, years? What can it hurt, right?"

"That's what Sharon says. You're right. What's wrong with a little playing around?" Julia narrowed her eyes. "And I *have* slept with a man in—well, not years!" She grinned slyly. "You do realize that usually the whole *cougar* thing is one-sided. That is, unless the catnip is looking for a mama. Eww. I just grossed myself out." She laughed. "Besides, he's a pretty boy with lots of twenty-somethings in his bed, and my card and name are probably long gone by now."

Shaking her head, Julia refused to give Mr. Green Eyes another thought. She knew enough to know that if he didn't have the number in his cell phone, it was probably lost.

Lauren looked at her friend long and hard. Jules had determined to leave most of her conventional life behind, but Lauren wasn't sure unconventional included a boy-toy.

"I'll have you know," Julia added. "I am NOT a cougar--I'm a puma." Both women laughed as they went about opening for business.

Chapter 3

———

"Dude, you're home early. No classes today?"

Austin looked at his friend and wondered who he'd had in the bed he'd just crawled out of. Matt Hollinger had been Austin's best friend since the two had met in high school. They'd played on the same basketball, football, and baseball teams. They'd spent equal time at one another's house, using the term "Mom" interchangeably at each. They'd dated most of the same girls, enjoyed the same beer, and parted only when Matt left for Arizona State. A native of Phoenix, Matt still had most of his extended family there, so the decision to return had been an easy one. As he explained to Austin, "Winter in North Carolina is for the birds, I'm ready for a change in scenery, and I can study business anywhere." Austin had helped his friend load up his car, partied one last time until dawn, and watched him drive off. Even though both had made new friends, it was Austin whom Matt called when drunk, and it was Matt whom Austin called when he decided to leave North Carolina.

In the three years since, the two had fallen into an easy arrangement based on knowing each other almost too well. As Austin looked around at the mess that was their shared apartment, he shook his head. Some things didn't change, and his buddy was one of them. Matt now stood in front of the open refrigerator, staring and rubbing his stomach. Austin peered over his shoulder and saw an opened case of beer, half jug of milk, and the take-out remnants of at least one Chinese restaurant delivery and two pizza boxes. They seldom went to the store, and when they did, it wasn't *they* but Austin who went. Of the two, he would cook every once in a while. Scrambled eggs, bacon, biscuits and gravy, and grilled cheese rounded out his skills. As for cleaning, Matt would do so only after Austin threatened bodily harm or calling his grandma. Austin smiled at the thought. Grandma Bea was something else. She would have come every week to clean and do the laundry, but Austin had put his foot down. Grandma was also the nosiest person in the world and loved to "arrange" things. She was a sweetheart, but neither of the men could find anything for two days after one of her visits. *Besides*, Austin thought, *we should be able to handle it ourselves. We are grown men, or at least one of us is.*

"Class isn't for another hour." Austin answered his friend's question before asking his own. "So? Who was she? Anyone I know?" Matt was handsome in a sloppy-boy way—tall, athletic, tan, and just enough of a bad boy that he never lacked feminine attention. Girls fell for his compliments, crooked grin, and charm. The naïve female souls always believed they could "help" him. Feed him, dress him, screw him, and make him a better man—a.k.a. marriage material—with enough love and attention. Matt used that to his advantage every chance he got. As for the improvement, nothing there. As for marriage material, far from it.

"I don't think so. You might know her. Melissa, Melanie, something like that. She hangs out at The Corner Pocket, and after I bought her a few beers and showed her how to hit the cue ball straight, I couldn't shake her. So I thought *what the hell* and brought her home. She was okay. I've had better."

Austin shook his head and looked at his friend. "Geez, man, you can't even remember the poor girl's name? Was she at least legal age?"

"Hell, yes," Matt finally turned from the fridge to rummage through the cabinets. "What do you think I am, anyway? Some perv?"

Austin's answer was a disgusted laugh that Matt ignored.

"Shit, AJ, you need to go grocery shopping man," Matt closed the last cabinet door.

"Yeah, I'll get right on that. You could call Grandma Bea and have her bring something."

"Aw, hell no! I'm hitting the shower before I head to class. And you better leave Grandma alone, man. My mess is organized."

Austin watched his friend—clad only in nylon basketball shorts—saunter down the hall, shook his head, and headed to his own room. He shut the door and stretched out on the bed. Pulling the card from his pocket where he'd kept it since she'd given it to him, he pictured the pretty lady once again. *Touch of Jules*, he read, wondering about her business, where she lived, and her. She probably had some big-ass apartment in Fountain Hills or Scottsdale, or maybe a house, a big house in the hills. He hadn't seen a wedding ring, and she hadn't acted married. You could tell when a female was married and not looking, or married and looking for a good time. Austin had his share of inviting looks from the latter. This one was different. He wondered again how old she was. He'd guess her at thirty, thirty-two, thirty-five at the very oldest. *Not too old for me*, he decided. *Okay, ten years would be stretching it a bit, but age is just a number, right? Hell, why am I even thinking about her? It's been two days.*

He looked at the address—1825 Brown Avenue. Pulling out his phone, he typed the address into his maps app and saw that Touch of Jules was one block from the historic district, Old Town Scottsdale. Upscale, he thought, very upscale. He typed the store name into Google and hit the jackpot—a website. He saw a photo of the outside, links to shop specific items, information about custom design, and finally what he was looking for on the About Us page—Julia Whitman, smiling and laughing into the camera with her arm linked with that of another pretty woman, her partner Lauren Reynolds. The Reynolds lady was the opposite of Julia with her blond hair and dark eyes. Both women were dressed in short skirts and heels and had bodies to pull it off. *Sexy, but classy, just like the lady herself,* he thought. He read through the bio information. She was a graduate of Columbia College, Columbia, Missouri, B.S. in Interior Design. No year. *Damn, that would have answered one question*, he thought. "A sought-after and well-respected member of the industry..." "known for her polished, yet exuberant style..." "embraces color and bold statements..." "renders spaces she designs timeless..." and so on. Nothing there to give him a feel for the woman, but he really hadn't expected anything.

He looked back at the photo again. There was that smile and those blue eyes looking right at him. He screen-shot the page, cropped out everything but the woman, and saved the image. Looking at the time, he realized his daydream needed to end. *School awaits*, he thought. *And a trip to the grocery store, damn Matt.*

Austin sighed, took one last look at Julia Whitman, and turned off his phone.

Chapter 4

A WEEK PASSED, THEN TWO, AND the green-eyed man was moved to the back of Julia's mind as she started two new jobs with more on the schedule. Summer was a busy time for her as the wealthy hired her to redecorate or supervise a remodeling job, paid their deposits, and headed for the cooler climate of Flagstaff. The ladies at Touch of Jules were good, and the recommendations had increased every year. Julia and Lauren made sure the jobs were completed on time and to the customer's specifications. Their rich clientele made the occasional trip back to town for baseball games or charity events or business, and one of the women was always available to make nice, give them a inspection tour, and send them back north feeling that their castles were in good hands.

June was more than half over, and in the shop, Lauren looked at photographs of their next job—a pool/guest house that the client wanted larger with more spacious guest quarters and an attached cabana. It was to be an island theme for both, and she was making a list of possible suppliers for what was needed. As she concentrated, her reading glasses slipped down her nose. *Damn, I hate these insufferable things,* she thought. The tinkling door bell roused her from the job at hand. She put a welcoming smile on her face, rose from her desk, tossed the hated glasses in that general direction, and rounded the corner to greet the customer.

The man who had entered had his back to her, as he looked over artwork for sale that was displayed on the far wall. His appearance didn't seem to match their usual customers, but in this part of town, they saw a variety of people. As he moved slowly across the showroom, Lauren couldn't help admiring the view from behind. She cocked one eyebrow and allowed her eyes to travel from the curling blond hair at his neck, down the tight t-shirt covering a muscular back, over the firm ass in khaki shorts, and finally to well-toned, tanned legs.

Well, well, well, she thought. *I sure hope I can help him find what he needs.* She smoothed her recently touched-up blond hair and started in his direction.

"Can I help you?" she asked, sauntering across the floor and putting on her special men-only smile.

"I hope so," he replied, and as he turned, she looked into a pair of green eyes that she knew could belong to only one person.

Well, crap! thought Lauren. She knew who this had to be, and she wondered how she should handle the situation. *Damn, he really is good-looking,* but she shifted her smile from sexy to friendly.

"Is Julia Whitman in?" he asked, looking around the shop and trying to peer beyond the partition where the desks stood. "She gave me a card with your shop's information, and since I need an anniversary gift for the folks, I thought I'd come by to see if she could help. That was a few weeks ago, but I thought…"

Damn, even his voice is nice. Just enough of a southern flavor to be quite tasty. Lauren's mind began to work quickly. *Should I lie and tell him Julia won't be back all day? Tell him Julia no longer works here? Tell him…? No.* Lauren knew Julia would find out and she'd assured Lauren she'd be back early. Lauren knew that her friend would forgive pretty much anything but a lie. Keith had found that out the hard way.

"I don't remember her mentioning you, but I'm sure we have something your parents would like. Oh, and I'm expecting Jules sometime this afternoon. She's meeting a client in Fountain Hills, and I'm not sure when she'll be back. Can I help?" It was just a little white lie, and Lauren wasn't lying to Julia, but to him, anyway.

"Uh, I guess…" he was stalling, and both he and Lauren knew it.

At the sound of the door, they looked up to see Julia enter with a blast of hot air.

"Oh, my god! I had to park a mile away and in this heat I think I'm melting. Don't people know it's freaking summer in Arizona? Don't they have someplace else to go? Florida? The beach? At least the Allen's house was nice and cool, even if the carpenters were making a huge mess. Thank god, I found it before Mrs. Allen comes in tomorrow. You know how she gets when…" Julia looked up to see first Lauren smiling quizzically at her and then at Austin. "Oh…" her voice trailed off.

"Jules, this nice young man is looking for a gift for his parents' anniversary. Do you think we have something around here he might be interested in?" The double entendre wasn't lost on Julia, and she turned to give her friend a warning look. *No,* she imperceptibly shook her head, but Lauren was on a roll. "I was just going to show him around, but he asked specifically for you, and since I need to return a few phone calls, he's all yours!" With that, she breezed from the room, leaving the two behind looking not a little uncomfortable.

"Of course, I'll be glad to help you," Julia recovered first. "Just let me put this stuff down, and we'll see what we can do." She dumped her messenger bag and sunglasses onto a nearby chair and looked up expectantly.

Austin stared at her as if he were wondering how he'd gotten here, what he should do now, and if he could bolt. As she continued to smile at him, he found himself relaxing, much like he did the first time he'd met her. *If anything, she's prettier today,* he thought as he looked at her short white skirt, sleeveless red top, and white sandals. She had her long hair pulled up in a loose ponytail in deference to the heat.

He recovered and found his voice. "Yeah, my mom and dad's anniversary is in a couple of weeks, and I need something kinda nice. It's their twenty-fifth, kind of a big one, I guess."

Well, that answers one question, Julia thought. *He can't be much, if any, over twenty-four.*

"Do you know how much you want to spend? That will give us a starting point, and we can go from there."

"I don't know, a couple hundred, I guess. " He looked around the store.

"No problem. Do they like original art?" She began moving around the showroom as she asked him multiple questions—What are the house colors? What do they already have? What is their lifestyle? etc. until Julia believed she had a feel for the people who'd produced the man in front of her. He came from a comfortable, if not wealthy home, had one younger brother who was in high school, and the family lived outside Charlotte, North Carolina. Austin didn't make it home often nor did he seem to be especially close to his parents, and it registered in her mind that she was closer in age to his mother than to him. She pushed that thought farther back and decided she'd take it out and deal with it later.

After he'd picked out a small painting of the desert at its prettiest during the rainy season, Julia wrapped it up. They stood looking at one another as if to ask, what now?

Austin spoke first. "Hey, I'm off Saturday, and if you aren't busy or anything, would you like to get together? Lunch, maybe? Or dinner? Or something?" his voice trailed off as he tried to maintain eye contact.

Julia hesitated. *Well, here it is,* she thought. *Go for it? Say no? Hurt his feelings? Hurt my feelings? What to do…what to do…*

"I'd love that," she heard herself saying. "I need to come in Saturday morning for a couple of hours. Pick me up here? Say noon or so?"

Austin couldn't seem to help himself as he sent his biggest smile in her direction and found his met by hers. "Awesome! I'll see you then. Oh, and you might want to take better care of those sunglasses. I may not be around to help you find them again." He pointed out the carelessly tossed Ray-Bans lying forgotten on her bag.

With a last look, he grinned and left, leaving a waft of heat that Julia found almost as warm as what was coming off her at the moment.

"Dammit, Julia! What in the HELL are you thinking!" Lauren stormed out of the back room. "For heaven's sake! You have turned down millionaires, good-looking men OUR AGE, and to do what? Go out with some KID? And what do you think is in it for him?" She rolled her eyes and continued, "A good roll in the hay with an older woman who knows what she's doing, that's what, and then he's gone, leaving you looking like the old hag who just couldn't help herself. Who just had to jump into bed with some stud half her age and…"

"Stop. Right. There." Julia's voice was low and calm, a sure sign that she was fuming. "You are my best friend, my sister, but where do you come off telling me what I should, or shouldn't be doing? When have I ever told you what to do?" She raised one eyebrow. "Did I say anything when you threw yourself at that professional baseball player? No, I kept my mouth shut and let you look stupid when he dumped you and took up with a fake-boobed, blond bimbo who was barely drinking age. Did I say *I told you so* when that ASU professor took you off on some hiking expedition to the Grand Canyon? Yeah, like you hike. Who came and got you from that? Huh? So don't be telling me what to do now." She crossed her arms and narrowed her eyes. "And HAG? You called me a HAG? What the hell? And who knows? Maybe it's ME who will screw his eyeballs out and leave him! Did you ever think of that?"

"No, I haven't," Lauren jumped on the last point, "because that isn't who you are, and you know it." Lauren's voice softened. "Jules, let's not fight about this. You're going on a date. Period. Who knows? You two might even find something to talk about, I don't know, and that may be the end of it." Lauren gave her friend a slight smile. "I'm sorry. I love you and the last thing I want is to see you doing something that I would do. Which means doing something stupid."

They had both run out of steam. Their fights could be a bit fierce at times, but they were short-lived. Julia looked at her friend and sighed.

"You could be right, but something about this guy speaks to me," Julia began. "And I haven't had that happen in, well, ever. Not even Keith could make me feel what Austin does by just looking at me. Hell, I feel about twenty-four again myself, and that's just a bit disturbing. Who knows? It's ONE date, and that could be it. We'll see."

"Yeah, we'll see, *puma*," Lauren laughed, and returned to her suppliers list, while Julia picked up the forgotten glasses and bag and headed to her own desk.

"God, you can be such a bitch," Julia said over her shoulder.

She had to admit that Austin's visit had her in a mixed-up state. *We'll see…All I see are green eyes and trouble.* She sighed.

Chapter 5

＿＿＿＿

Austin tried to be as quiet as possible as he showered and went through his closet to find something to wear for his date. *Date,* he thought, *hell.* After going through the closet and every drawer, he settled on cargo shorts and polo shirt. *It is what it is,* he thought as he carefully shaved and ran a comb through his long hair. Tucking it behind his ears, he gave up on the curl and tossed the comb in the general direction of the sink. He discarded the idea of wearing a hat. Hats were usually fine, but not for this date. As he walked from the bedroom to the kitchen, he tried to move carefully. *Let a sleeping Matt lie* was his motto. He really didn't know why because Matt had been out the previous night and was good another three or four hours in bed. For once, Austin didn't see any purse, clothing, or other indication that they were anything but alone in the apartment, and he was thankful for that, at least.

He hadn't told his friend about Julia. He knew how Matt would react, and Austin wasn't up to the sparring match and sex jokes that would surely ensue. Women didn't mean much to Matt, who would suggest Austin enjoy the sex and show her to the door. Sometimes, Austin's friend wouldn't even do that as he'd seen more than one let herself out quietly in the early morning hours. The more he thought about it, the more reluctant Austin was to introduce Julia to this part of his life. He wanted to keep her to himself. Not that Matt wouldn't find out eventually if this worked out as Austin hoped. Matt was important, heck, he was more like family, but to expose Julia to his friend was something Austin decided could wait. *She probably already thinks I'm some pup, and I don't need her thinking that Matt is the norm,* he thought, grabbing his keys.

He let himself out the door and headed for his car. *Another beautiful, cool, July, Arizona day,* he thought wryly, even though July wouldn't arrive until the next week. Average high, ninety-nine degrees and climbing every day. He aired out the little black car and decided to keep the top up and air on for the trip. It wouldn't take much for his hair to curl even more in the breeze from the open car and for sweat to start pouring off him in the sweltering sun. Wearing his ball cap was out of the question, but he looked at it longingly. Despite the sweltering temperature, there was no place Austin would rather be than the Phoenix valley in the summer. He loved it, and the heat didn't bother him at all except for when he didn't want to sweat.

As he joined the traffic on Camelback Road, Austin could feel himself tense up a bit the closer he got to Old Scottsdale. He seldom felt nervous around the opposite sex. If anything, his good looks and easy manner made him popular with the ladies anywhere he was. Lately, the nervous fawning of females his age had gotten on his nerves, and he hated that he was the nervous one now.

"It's only lunch," he spoke out loud. "Hell, you might just discover that she's a snobby bitch and you can't stand her." *Yeah, right,* whispered a small voice in his mind.

Luck was on his side as he found a parking spot just down the block from Touch of Jules. Even in the heat, tourists were walking along, peering into windows, and occasionally stepping inside an antique shop or restaurant to cool off. They all looked the same—shorts, walking shoes, sunglasses, hats, and water bottles clutched in sweaty hands. Austin chuckled and opened the shop door.

"Julia…earth to spacey Julia…" She looked up to see Lauren smirking at her from her side of the small office space. "Time is ticking away… soon he'll be here. Woo hoo, Julia's nervous. I can tell," the sing-song voice continued.

"You," Julia looked up at her friend without moving her head and set her own mouth in a hard line, "are a pig from hell."

Lauren laughed and continued, "Woo hoo! I struck a nerve! What'cha gonna do with your little friend today, huh? Go to the zoo? Or maybe to the carnival rides? Or maybe just to the park to play! Oh, yeah, that's right. Lunch…hmmm…followed by what, my pedophile friend?" and she wiggled her eyebrows up and down before bursting into laughter.

"I take that back. You are not a pig. You are a hosebeast. And an ugly one at that."

That elicited another belly laugh from Lauren. "Oh, lighten up. Laugh. Release all that pent-up tension. Geez, you'd think you were facing a confession with your mom's priest or something. Now *that* is something to tighten your butt cheeks for."

Julia wasn't nervous, per se, but more apprehensive. What she'd seen so far about this man, she'd liked, and that didn't happen often for her. Men were all too intense, too polished, too unpolished, too rich, too dumb, too something. She thought back over the dates she'd had, and with a sigh, thought to herself, *Maybe I'm just too picky.*

About that time, the door bell jingled, and both women looked up.

"I'll get it!" Lauren laughed.

"Sit!" Julia said as she stood up and pointed to Lauren's chair. "Stay." She rounded the corner, and as soon as she saw him standing just inside the door, she couldn't help smiling.

Oh. My. God. He really is pretty, she thought. Out loud she said, "Hey! You're right on time! Good to see you."

Good to see you? she thought and inwardly cringed. *How lame.*

"Hey, yourself. Ready to go?" he asked, returning her smile. "I'm not very familiar with good places to eat in this part of town, so you can recommend something, or we can go someplace else."

"Let's go to The Mission Inn," Julia suggested. "We can walk from here, and it's one of my favorite places."

"Ready when you are," Austin replied. *Wow, how good is this? Most females would have said whatever you think and then we'd have a five-minute discussion on where to go and what to eat.* He liked it. He liked her.

"I'm outta here, Lauren!" she called to the back.

"I'm good. Take your time. Heck, I won't even wait up for you."

Julia rolled her eyes at Austin, smiled apologetically, and opened the door. The heat rushed at them as they stepped onto the hot sidewalk, but neither seemed to notice. The walk was a brief one, and they soon entered the cool darkness of the restaurant. As their eyes quickly adjusted, Austin looked around at the wood tables and leather chairs to his right, only two or three of them occupied, and the brick wall behind an old-fashioned bar to his left. It was a comfortable place. He hadn't known what to expect, but this was a pleasant surprise as it was comfortable and not pretentious at all. A waiter immediately approached, calling Julia by name and greeting her warmly.

"Julia! How's the prettiest interior designer in the valley?" he said, giving her a quick hug before stepping back to eye her escort. Both men sized each other up briefly, as Julia quickly made introductions.

"Jeremy, this is my friend, Austin. Austin, meet the best waiter in Old Towne Scottsdale." She gave Jeremy a friendly smile. "Fix us up with a nice, quiet table? Somewhere cool? It's getting miserable out there," she said.

"You bet. Right this way," and he led them to a corner table set for four. Removing two of the settings, he recited the specials of the day and offered to get them drinks.

"Well," Julia started, "since we're celebrating a new friendship, how about a couple of margaritas?" She turned to Austin. "Is that okay with you?"

"Perfect," he replied. The waiter gave him a once-over, and Austin hoped he wasn't going to ask for his ID. It happened sometimes, but this was one of those times Austin would have rather the guy punch him. He met the man's stare, and the waiter blinked first. He left to put in the drink order without another word.

"It isn't very busy right now, is it?" Austin observed, looking around the room. He hoped Julia hadn't noticed the stare down he'd had with Jeremy.

"Oh, just wait," Julia said. "We're a little early, but the crowd will roll in later this afternoon."

Jeremy returned with the drinks and a basket of warm bread and butter.

"We'll let you know when we're ready to order, Jeremy. Just check back every now and then, okay?" Julia smiled at him again as Jeremy returned the smile. Austin decided he really didn't like this Jeremy guy.

"You bet. Enjoy!" He left them alone.

Austin was sitting with his back to the windows, giving him a clear view of her face. *Just as pretty as I remembered,* he thought, taking in the light blue tank, silver necklace and earrings, and dark hair once again pulled back into a low ponytail. The shirt brought out the blue of her eyes, and he couldn't seem to look away for long.

"So, how's work? I don't know how you stand it out in this heat all day. I'd be dying out there," she said, taking a roll and generously buttering it. He watched her take a bit, close her eyes in pleasure, and smile again before she pushed the basket toward him. *A woman who actually eats in front of a man,* he thought. *Thank god.*

"Well," he said, "I start around five o'clock in the morning, and by the time I finish up around noon, it's just then getting pretty hot. Class doesn't start until two, so I have time to go home, clean up, and cool off before then."

"Oh?" Julia looked surprised. "You're a student?"

She didn't as much ask the question as make a statement. He couldn't tell from her expression if his college status was a good or bad thing, but the longer she remained quiet, the more he thought it was the latter.

"Yeah," he continued, "I'm taking a couple of courses this summer so that I can intern this fall and graduate in December. I fell a little behind when I transferred out here from UNC, and I've been catching up. Once I finish, I hope to get on at one of the bigger golf courses. Get experience. Make connections. But my ultimate goal is to start my own company, a landscape design/building and maintenance company. But that will be a few years down the road, I suppose…" he ran out of steam at her continued silence.

He moved his attention to his drink and waited. Waiting for what, he didn't quite know. Wondering if he'd said something wrong, he thought back over the conversation and decided that nothing stupid had come out of his mouth.

He looked back up at Julia.

She broke the silence. "Okay, let's put it all out there. I'm wondering. You're wondering. Let's come clean. Just how old are you, Austin?" she looked up and tilted her head as she waited. It seemed to him that she was almost holding her breath or something.

"I'm twenty-three. I'll be twenty-four in August," he said. "August 13, to be exact. You?"

Now it was his turn to wait. She lowered her eyes and concentrated on the drink in front of her. She took a long swallow before straightening her shoulders to look him in the eye.

"I learned a long time ago to not play guessing games. 'How old do you think I am?' is just stupid. Everyone lies and usually on the young side to make people feel better." She took a deep breath before going on. "I'm forty. I turned forty this past February."

Damn, he stopped himself before saying it out loud. *I'd thought thirty, maybe thirty-three, at the oldest thirty-five, but forty? My mom is in her forties, maybe forty-six? So Julia is closer to my mom's age than mine.* He looked at her again. No, he couldn't picture her with his mother. Hell, he couldn't picture her anywhere but where she was. With him. Sixteen years older. No wonder she took charge. No wonder she was so confident and successful. No wonder she exuded a sexiness that had him thinking about her all the time. She did not look forty. Nothing in her face gave him that impression, and for sure what he'd seen of her body spoke of a much younger woman.

Did it matter? He didn't want to think about it. At that moment, no, it didn't matter.

"Well, Ms. Whitman, you fooled me. As for age, it's just a number, isn't it?" He looked her straight in the eye as he said it and grinned.

"Austin, I don't want you to get the wrong idea about me. I have never dated younger men. In fact, I don't even have any *friends* your age. It isn't because I'm afraid of what people will say or think. It's because I'm not in the position of even meeting anyone younger, and definitely, I'm never in this situation." She paused, and he could see her mind working. The seconds ticked away. He was beginning to get uncomfortable when she spoke again. "So this is what I think we'll do," she continued. "We'll be friends—unconventional friends. We'll have lunch, or dinner, see a movie, take a drive, catch a Diamondbacks game, whatever, and enjoy one another's company, okay? You don't have to explain me to your family and friends. I don't have to explain you to mine. No one's uncomfortable. No expectations. Just friendship. Deal?"

Friends. Yeah, that works for me, he supposed. He didn't know what he'd do with the sexual attraction because that was strong on his side, but he liked her and wanted to know more about her. Where did she come from? Has she been married? If not, why? Divorced? Although he couldn't imagine a man letting her go. If it was friendship she wanted, friendship was what he'd give her. For the time being, at least.

"Okay," he said. "But don't close the door on anything else yet, okay? We'll have fun and just see. Deal?"

She laughed at having her word tossed back at her. "Deal. Now pass some more of that bread and let's get Jeremy over here. I'm starved."

Chapter 6

_____

HE PAID. SHE TRIED TO grab the check, but he was quicker.

"Austin, you're working your way through college. Let me, please."

"Nope," he put his foot down. "You treat next time, and after that we'll go Dutch if it makes you feel better."

"All right, but I'm not happy," she said, softening her words with a grin.

They had been there two hours. She had filled him in on her life in Missouri—growing up, college, starting the business there with Lauren, starting over in Arizona, and her family. Although he could tell she was holding things back, he felt like he'd gotten a good handle on the woman in front of him by the time she had finished, and he liked her even more. He admired her intelligence and her drive. He also saw a playfulness in her that he'd like to explore further. From him, she'd learned about his family, why he'd left North Carolina, that he was an athlete in high school, that he was a huge Tar Heel fan, that his eyes lit up when he talked about his younger brother or his field of study, and that he was more mature than she could have imagined or hoped. They discovered that neither of them liked the new country music, but both loved the old. They both liked Clint Eastwood movies, _Unforgiven_ their shared favorite, action films, but not the new horror. They both drove convertibles, hers a BMW. Neither was very religious although both had been taken to church as children. They liked to hike and swim. And they liked each other.

"Well, this has been nice, Austin," Julia said as they walked down the sidewalk back to her shop. "Geez, has it gotten hotter?"

"It has been nice," he replied, "and yes, it has gotten hotter. Or maybe the drinks are making me feel it more. Glad we stopped at two."

They paused outside the door, neither wanting to end the afternoon. She spoke first.

"Hey, my friend Sharon is out of town. She and John are in Flagstaff, and I have a key to their house and the code. I say that because she has the biggest pool I know of, well outside of the one at my apartment complex. And it's always crowded on the weekend." She looked up at him and smiled. "Would you want to go? To Sharon's? To swim?" her voice trailed off as she waited for his reply. *What am I thinking? God, take it slow, dipshit,* she scolded herself.

"Sounds awesome. Just one problem," he replied.

Here it comes, she thought. *Hey, OLD friend, this was nice, but…*

"No swim trunks," and he grinned at her. "Well, I have one—several, but they're back at my place. I could go get some and meet you somewhere."

She laughed. "Is that all? No problem! The Burnses are party people who keep a stock of swim trunks, suits, whatever, for every occasion. I keep my own stuff there all the time, and I know we'd find you something. Do you want to follow me? You can leave when you want then." She was still unconsciously offering him a way out, if he wanted to take it.

While he wasn't sure about the whole borrowed swim stuff, he was sure that he didn't want the day to end. He'd endure whatever old-man look he was sure was coming from her friends' supply of clothes.

"Works for me. Uh, where's your car?" he looked around.

"Oh, I parked in the back today. I got here early enough to find an owner's space. And you're in, what?"

"The black Mustang over there. I'll follow you, my lady," and he bowed in a sweeping gesture.

"Thank you, my lord," she replied in an equally stilted manner. They both laughed, and she turned to walk along the side of the building and disappear around the corner. He watched her until she was out of sight before hurrying to his own car. He didn't want to miss her or get lost.

He no more started his engine before he saw a little red BMW—Bimmer as he later learned she called it—come down the alley and sweep onto the street. He followed close behind as she led him out of Old Scottsdale, onto the 101 Loop. After a thirty-minute drive, she turned onto Palisade Boulevard with Austin close behind. They twisted and turned on at least three more streets until he was sure they were leaving town. He didn't know where they were as they followed the road toward the several houses built on the sides of the mountains in the distance. She finally stopped at the closed gate of a winding drive that climbed up a smaller hill. He couldn't see much beyond the gate, but he knew that this had to be leading to something pretty nice.

Austin had grown up in an upper-middle-class home, where many of his friends had swimming pools and big yards. The houses themselves were the standard three- or four-bedroom variety with a couple of bathrooms and large family rooms. Patios held gas barbeque grills and six-chair table sets with big umbrellas. Theirs had been the neighborhood that most others aspired to be living in. This neighborhood could make him uncomfortable if he allowed it.

As he followed Julia up the concrete drive, Austin admired the natural, desert landscaping dotted by rustic lamps that would give off a soft light after dark. He didn't see the house until they rounded the last curve in their upward climb. It was big, probably sixty-five hundred square feet, but not the massive home he expected. The two-story house was a mix of stucco and stone with a flat roof that was set off by gently rounded arches. He could see a covered balcony and several other windows, but the desert cactus, shrubs, and acacia trees blocked a view of the first floor. Two massive chimneys stretched toward the sky, and he could see that both were in the center of the house. They rounded the last turn, and the house stood before them—more a work of art than building. The drive circled the front, where a deep-set, tile-roofed porch stretched along a quarter of the front. Large windows were set to the left of the double door, and several others were spaced out across both sides of the porch. He wondered how many rooms and what lie inside. *So, this is where her friends live,* he thought. *Yep, definitely out of my league on this one. I wonder what* her *place is like.*

While the house had him distracted, he didn't notice Julia approach until she was next to his window. She grinned at the look on his face as he got out of the car and followed her up the wide, stone walkway and onto the porch. Before she unlocked the door, she motioned for him to turn around. The view was spectacular. On one side, he could see the mountains rising along the edge of the valley. In the center lay Fountain Hills and its namesake, the spectacular fountain shooting water more than five hundred feet into the sky. He could only imagine what it would look like lit up at night. He scanned the horizon to the right to see more of the Phoenix valley stretching for miles. Austin had never seen the valley from this perspective, and he was impressed.

She unlocked the door and disarmed the security system before motioning him to follow her in. They entered a large foyer that opened to a rustic wood staircase to his left and a great room in front of them where he could see a massive stone fireplace. A dining room to the right obviously opened into the kitchen as the three rooms flowed from one to the next. Austin pictured a crowd of well-groomed, smiling, rich, successful men surrounded by their well-kept women who dripped diamonds and made a spa their second home. He couldn't quite picture Julia here, though. He shook his head to clear the image and let her lead him through the great room and into the kitchen, where she offered him something cold to drink.

"I'll take a water, thanks. You're pretty much at home here, aren't you?" he commented.

She laughed, "I guess I am. Sharon and John's son lives across the country in New York City. They only have the one child and one grandson. John Junior is divorced. I suppose I'm the daughter they never had. At least they treat me like one. Sharon gives me the run of the place whether she's here or not. When they're home, I try not to make a pest of myself and usually come by only when invited. When they're out of town, which is often, I come up here to get away, use the pool, and sit on the upstairs balcony to enjoy the view." Her voice took on a mischievous tone. "Or to use Sharon's tub. Come on," she grinned. "I'll give you the grand tour and you'll see."

By the time they finished, Austin was in love with the place. She was right about the view and the tub. *Big-ass* was the only word he could come up with for it. He'd never seen a fireplace at the end of a tub—a fireplace with a TV above it. As for the tub itself, he guessed four people could fit easily. White marble was everywhere with two counters running along the walls on either side of the tub—his and hers. He figured that bathroom was bigger than his apartment's living room and kitchen combined.

"Okay, let's go for that swim," her voice broke into his reverie. "To the pool house!"

It was about what he expected by now. This building housed a game room with a pool table and a stone and wood bar that stretched across one wall. Bar stools sat along the expanse. He could see a small kitchen through one door, a full bath through another, and a bedroom through a third. It was into the bedroom that she led him.

"Here's the swim stuff hanging in the closet," Julia said as she gathered up her own suit and a cover-up that were hanging along the closet wall. "Just go through the suits and find your size. I know Sharon keeps at least two or three of each from small to double XL, though I doubt you'll need one that big." She grinned at him again. "You can change in here or the connecting bathroom, and I'll use the bathroom out front. Meet you at the pool." She smiled and left him standing alone in the middle of the massive closet.

It didn't take him long to find a size that fit—surprisingly not an old-man style as he'd feared—as well as a t-shirt. He dressed, left his own clothes lying neatly on the bed, and made his way to find Julia. He saw her as he started out the sliding glass door that led onto the large patio surrounding the pool itself.

Holy hell, he thought, as he watched her lay towels on first one chair and then another. This was NOT some middle-aged woman trying to retain her youth. Julia splintered that stereotype. She had changed into a black bikini that was just small enough to give him a good view of long slender leg, flat stomach, rounded bottom and breasts that filled out the top nicely without being too much. He knew that she had been a swimmer and runner earlier in her life, and it showed. She stood at the edge of the pool for only a few seconds before smoothly diving into the water. She came up cleanly and swam with long strokes to the side, where she turned to look at Austin, who was still standing at the doorway.

"You gonna stand there all day? It's wonderful!" She laughed and dove back under before rising to the top to easily swim the length of the pool.

Austin made his way to the same side from which she'd jumped, made his own smooth dive into the water, and swam under to come out directly in front of her. They swam lazily for several minutes before they left the water to lounge in the sun. Neither bothered drying off as the heat and sun would do that shortly. He could see goose bumps along her skin as the water dried faster than her skin could adjust. Feeling his eyes on her, she turned to look at him, and they both stared a few seconds before she slipped on her sunglasses and laid back.

What Austin didn't know was that Julia had been looking at him, too. He was better than she had imagined, and her imagination had been working overtime. She already knew he was muscular simply because of his work, but she didn't expect him to be so...perfect. At over six feet tall, his legs stretched out the length of the chaise lounge as he lay beside her on his own chair.

"Why aren't you tan?" she couldn't resist asking. "I mean, you work outside all day, but you're not tan except for your arms, face, and neck. And your legs are a little brown. You don't look bad," she corrected herself quickly. "I just figured, you know, tan all over."

Austin laughed. "Well, if you can talk my boss into letting me shed my shirt and the cactus into keeping its stickers to itself so that I can wear shorts, I'll be very tan."

"Duh," Julia felt a little silly. "Well, friend, we'll just have to work on it on the weekends. Don't want those white legs blinding anyone. Or that white stomach. Yikes!" He wasn't really white, but she was having fun at his expense. To emphasize her point, she tossed him a can of spray-on sun block. He laughed and started liberally spraying his exposed skin.

They spent the afternoon in and out of the water, and put a big dent in the supply of bottled water and beer they found in the pool house fridge. They talked. It seemed that they never ran out of things to talk about. The afternoon melted into early evening, but neither one noticed until Austin's stomach growled.

Julia looked at him and laughed at the embarrassment on his face.

"Oh, laugh, silly. You look like you just broke something." She started to rise. "Hungry? Let's go see what Sharon left for me this time."

When the two had changed back into their dry clothes, they met in the kitchen of the big house, as Austin referred to it. Julia scrounged ham, cheese, bread, chips and cold sodas. They made sandwiches and ate at the large counter in the kitchen, laughing and making fun of a variety of things, including celebrities, that neither liked. He discovered a side of her that he instantly loved—she could be sarcastic. "Snarky" as she called it.

Austin looked out the window and noticed that the outside lights had come on.

"It's almost dark," he said. "I can't believe we've been here all day."

"Oh, I can," Julie replied. "I come up here and lose myself." She looked at him, and said mischievously, "It should be dark enough. One more thing I want to show you before we go. Follow me."

She led him up the staircase and turned left. A large balcony over-looked the foyer and great room on one side, and on the other side, double doors led to the balcony that overlooked the front of the house. She un-locked the double doors, took his hand, and led him outside.

"There. My favorite part of this house. Well, outside of the tub, of course. Isn't it just gorgeous?" she asked, her voice taking on a breathless sound.

Austin turned his eyes to the direction she was looking and caught his own breath. It was the view he'd enjoyed earlier, but this time from higher up, and the fountain was fully lit. It stood out from among the millions of lights that surrounded the water shooting into the sky and stretched out in all directions from the center. Toward the west, the sun had descended, and in its wake, the sky was orange and yellow with shades of purple and dark blue rising against the background of the mountains. Soon, the light would be gone completely and the valley nothing but twinkling lights. They stood there for several minutes, neither one speaking. Julia felt him looking at her in the dim light from the outside house lamps and turned toward him. Austin was still holding her hand, and she felt him draw her in close. She raised her face and before she could speak, he leaned in and kissed her softly.

"Thank you for a perfect day," he spoke against her lips. He drew back and looked into her face. She was standing still, lips slightly parted, and eyes luminous in the light. This time, Julia leaned in and kissed him, not softly, but deeply, drawing him closer. She wrapped her arms around his neck and pressed into him, as his arms came around and held her. The kiss deepened and neither wanted it to end. It was Julia who pulled back first.

"Wow," she whispered.

"Yeah," he whispered back.

"I guess we need to be going," Julia said reluctantly. "It's a long drive back to the city."

"Yeah," he said again. "I just want you to know that was unbelievable, and I'm not talking about the view or the day."

"I know," she smiled then. "Perhaps we'll have a repeat sometime, huh?"

"Oh, definitely, sooner than later," and he leaned in to kiss her again. When they pulled apart this time, they knew they would either leave right then, or they would be heading to one of the five bedrooms.

"Well, I'll make sure it's all straightened up downstairs. I try not to leave Angie a mess." Julia made the decision for them.

"Angie?" Austin was confused.

Julia laughed. "Angie is Sharon's maid, cook, bodyguard, and keeper. You'll meet her sometime. She makes the best Bloody Mary in the world."

The spell was broken and they turned to go inside. Julia hung the wet swim things in the laundry room to dry and be laundered later, while Austin wiped down the counter and cleaned their glasses. He was the first outside as she turned on the security system and locked the door behind her.

"Can you find your way back?" she asked.

"I'll follow you to the 101, and then I'll be okay," he replied.

"Well, okay then. And Austin, I really enjoyed my time," her voice taking on a gentleness.

"Me, too. Can I call you?" he asked.

"Of course," she replied. "Isn't that what friends do?" He could see her wink at him in the house lights. She turned to get into her car, leaving him with no recourse but to do the same. He followed her tail lights, thinking of the kiss they'd shared. He continued to think of it all the way to the Loop, where she turned left and he turned right.

"Friends, huh?" he said out loud. If this was friendship, it like no other Austin had ever known.

Chapter 7

"DUDE! I WAITED FOR YOU. Mikey and Joel scored Diamondback tickets, box seats behind home plate, all you can eat and drink. Company seats, and they were awesome!" Matt looked his buddy over and sniffed. "You smell like a chick. Is that suntan lotion? Naw...you weren't with a chick. Not our AJ!" He fell over onto the sofa, laughing at his own joke. "Oh, man, here I thought you were working and shit, and you were all hanging out with some chick." He sobered up long enough to ask, "Well? Did you get any?" and took a long swallow of his beer. By the looks of the empty cans strewn on the coffee table and his friend's red face, Austin decided his buddy had continued the baseball party all evening. A drunk Matt wasn't something Austin wanted to deal with. He gave Matt a blank-faced stare before turning toward his room.

"C'mon, man, don't be all pissy. I don't care if you found some fun. Well, I do care about the details." Austin's back was his only reply.

Matt shouted at his friend, "Well, if you didn't get any, don't use that lotion on the counter in the bathroom. It's some kind of self-tanner that Vanessa, or Valerie, or whatever her name is, dropped out of her bag. Dude, you do NOT want an orange pecker." Matt doubled over again, drunkenly laughing at his own joke as Austin turned to quip.

"You speaking from experience? Bet your dick is orange, isn't it? A little orange Cheeto," Austin laughed, and Matt was off again, laughing uncontrollably now. Austin knew that he'd come down once he stopped guzzling the booze. Austin also knew that his friend would pass out on the sofa. Matt had to work the next day, but he always seemed to get his act together, regardless of the night he'd had before. His job at Dick's Sporting

Goods gave him a limitless supply of joke material, but as Matt liked to say, it took a lot of balls to work there and it paid the bills.

Closing his door, Austin tossed his keys on his dresser, kicked off his shoes, and stretched out on his bed. The combination of sun and water made him sleepy, but he had some thinking to do.

Forty...fuck. Austin didn't use the word often, not even in his thoughts, but it was the only thing that came to his mind regarding his current situation. He really liked this lady. He could see himself spending a lot more time with her. She was easy to talk to, she shared so many interests. She made him feel good. But could he explain her to Matt? Joel? His family? And how would he fit into her world? He wasn't part of that whole country club set. Funny, but he couldn't see Julia there, either. Even when he'd first seen her at Coyote Run, she'd stood out from the rest as much by her unconcerned attitude as by her looks.

As his mind went back over the events of the day, he became sleepy and soon drifted off.

Julia was singing as she came strolling into the apartment. She could tell Lauren wasn't around by the lack of background noise. Her friend had to have either the television or the radio going all the time. *I function better* was Lauren's excuse, and Julia had learned early on to go with it. After tossing her purse onto the hall table, Julia fixed herself a glass of ice water and stretched out onto her favorite chair. She was glad for the quiet apartment and for the time alone. She had a lot to think about and didn't know where to start.

Why, oh why can't he be ten or even better, fifteen years older? She wondered for the twentieth time. For a first date, things couldn't have gone any better, and she'd been on some loser dates. It was Austin who had made the difference. Once they'd gotten the age thing out of the way and decided on friendship, the two enjoyed one another's company. The day had been more than she could have hoped for. The fact that he hadn't tried to get her into bed was an added bonus. Julia had been with some serious assholes who almost felt like she owed them something for treating her to dinner, or the theater, or wherever they'd gone—just another reason to avoid them. Miss Independent Lauren took whatever was offered, laughed in the morning, and looked for the next target. "If they want to treat me, I'll make sure I'm treated all the way," she liked to say. Her friend's promiscuity didn't bother Julia. She'd grown up with a double standard that she'd hated all her life. The last thing she would do was point fingers at Lauren or pass judgment. She couldn't bring herself to be as free-thinking as Lauren, but that was one of the few things they'd not seen eye-to-eye on. Julia had decided early on that her being married once was the difference because even though her story was complicated, marriage had never entered into Lauren's life.

That thought took Julia back to her days with Keith. She didn't like to dwell on the unpleasant past, but she couldn't help herself. *He'd never made me laugh like Austin has today,* she thought. After the babies, nothing was the same in her marriage. Julia remembered the lost feelings she'd had after each miscarriage and the grief over her last baby, that precious little girl who wasn't meant for the world. Julia's eyes filled with tears as she thought about the last child. The doctors had all told her to be patient, to wait between pregnancies, to relax. They should have been telling that to her husband and family—well, her mother at least. Keith wanted children more than anything. Looking back, Julia often wondered if it were out of love for her or out of creating the image he so loved. As for her mother, "You just try again, love. You'll have a baby soon, and oh, won't that be wonderful!" Yeah, no pressure from either one of those two. It was her father, *Daddy* Julia called him, who had held her close and simply loved her.

"Baby girl," he'd said. "God knows when you need a baby. I don't want you to let your mother or Keith make you feel like you have to produce one next week or any time. You are young and you have lots of time. And if you feel like crying, you come cry on your daddy's lap, okay?" He'd used his handkerchief to gently wipe the tears from her face, smiled at her with his own eyes full of unshed tears, and hugged her to him once again.

Telling her mom and dad about Keith's betrayal had been the hardest thing she'd ever done. Worse even than telling them that she was leaving Missouri. Shortly after the death of their little girl, Julia noticed her husband behaving differently. She could have gone down a checklist of suspicious behaviors for cheating spouses and checked off virtually every one of them. It was Lauren who helped her find out for certain who had her husband's attentions, and fortunately for Keith, Lauren hadn't bought her gun yet. It was all Julia could do to keep her friend from ripping out his throat at worst or giving him a very public tongue-lashing at best. The two women had watched him with the pretty blonde as they sat at a corner table in the small Italian restaurant they'd followed him to. He had driven there alone, so Julia held out hope he was just in a business meeting until she'd seen him for herself.

The Hill was one of Julia and Keith's favorite places to eat, and the more than twenty restaurants within the small neighborhood offered them someplace different every time. Their favorite, above all, was Rinaldi's. Crazy as it seemed, that probably hurt Julia as much as anything because it had always been their place. It was almost as if he'd brought a woman into their home. As soon as she had entered the restaurant, Julia could tell the maitre-d was uncomfortable. Julia figured everyone in there was in on the secret since they all knew her and Keith. Spotting him across the room, she and Lauren had taken a table far enough away to be unnoticed but with a clear view. They ordered glasses of wine, nibbled the bread, and watched the show. It was a good one, as the pretty young blonde sitting across the table from Julia's husband kept leaning in, exposing her cleavage and smiling provocatively. Keith buttered her bread for her and offered her a bite, bringing the two even closer. When he leaned over to kiss her, Lauren had jumped up, stated loudly that she'd had enough, and started toward the two. Only Julia's hand on her arm had kept her from making a bigger scene. The blonde had looked up innocently, but Keith had recognized that voice immediately. As his eyes met Julia's, she knew that she was done.

Keith had begged forgiveness, promised to never go out on her again, and tried to maneuver himself back into her good graces, but Julia made sure he'd done all of this from his mother's house. She and Lauren had his things packed and sitting by the door when he'd finally gathered enough nerve to venture home. He'd even enlisted her mother to try to "talk some sense into her," but that had backfired big time. That act had brought Julia's father into the fray, and neither her mother nor Keith wanted to take him on, especially when he was defending his baby girl. Within two months, the assets had been divided—Julia receiving the lion's share—and the papers had been signed. With her name changed back from Landry to Whitman, she began making plans to leave.

Lauren had been her rock during the ordeal, even moving into the big house with Julia. They both knew it was to keep Keith at a distance, and it worked. When Julia told Lauren of her plans to leave St. Louis, her friend had enthusiastically jumped onboard. It took them only a couple of months to sell off their inventory, get the word to their customers, and transfer ownership of the building to a young woman who would open a boutique in the vacated space.

Looking back, Julia couldn't believe how easy a move it had been. Lauren insisted on changing the name of the venture, and over Julia's protests, they'd settled on Touch of Jules, since as Lauren put it "Julia, you're the creative genius." They had struggled that first year, building up the business. The luckiest day came when a petite dark-haired woman bounced in and introduced herself. Sharon Burns immediately fell in love with the two younger women and took them under her wing. After Julia had completed a remodel of her pool house, the women were best friends. With hard work and Sharon's connections, Touch of Jules was soon off and running. Until now, Julia hadn't looked back.

Shaking her head to clear her thoughts, Julia looked at the time and headed to her room. Tomorrow was Sunday, and she had some work to do before meeting a new client on Monday. As she drifted off, she wasn't thinking of Keith, or St. Louis, or anything—except a handsome young man who made her feel alive for the first time in a very long while. She was smiling as sleep overtook her.

Chapter 8

⸺

Austin awoke early and his first thought was that he wanted to talk to Julia. Just to hear her voice, make sure she was real, and continue what they had started the previous day. He picked up his phone and held it in his hand for several seconds before setting it back down. *Don't come across as some love-struck teenager,* he thought. *How do you handle an older woman?* he wondered. *Do they need or want the attention these younger girls seemed to demand?* He couldn't see Julia as the why-didn't-you-call-me-immediately type, and her independence was one of her attractions. *Her many attractions*, he corrected himself.

With Matt at work, the place was Sunday-morning quiet. He turned the radio to his favorite station and spent the morning catching up on the apartment chores he and Matt had let slip all week. This consisted of collecting his roommate's stuff and tossing it into his room—some of it even hitting the bed—cleaning the disgusting kitchen, and running a vacuum on the floors. He left the most unpleasant task, cleaning the bathroom, for last, and tossed his dirty clothes into the small apartment-sized washer. Matt, the slob, could do his own laundry.

Austin forced himself to focus on reading the required chapters for his college class as he wanted to knock those out before Matt returned home and his quiet disappeared. It was mid-afternoon when his phone rang. As he looked at the caller ID, his heart sped up a bit.

"Hey, Julia!" he tried to play it cool, but that was going to be almost impossible.

"Hey, yourself!" her voice sounded as it usually did—like she was about to laugh at a shared joke. "I'm here at the shop and just finished up some stuff I need tomorrow for a new client. What'cha up to?"

"Just finished cleaning up the place and homework. Now I'm trying to figure out whether I want a nap or something to eat."

"I'll make that decision for you—come pick me up and let's go to BDubs. Coldest beer in the valley and you can catch baseball or whatever on TV. I think the Diamondbacks game starts at one o'clock, even though I'm a Cardinals girl myself and they don't play until four o'clock."

Austin laughed, "And what makes you think I'm all about the D-backs game? Did you ever stop to think that I may be a St. Louis fan, too?"

"Uh, no," she laughed. "But I think I can make a convert of you, as long as you aren't some Nancy-boy Cubs fan. That would be a deal breaker." She laughed again. "Pick me up in thirty and we'll find out if you're worthy of the Cardinals hat I might buy you."

He couldn't help laughing with her and they both hung up soon after. *This friendship just keeps getting better*, he told himself, and he hurried to take a quick shower and head out.

Julia hadn't meant to call him first. Waiting for him to call her was something her mother would have insisted on. These days, whatever Dana Whitman deemed appropriate, her daughter avoided as much as possible. This included her mother's ideas of men, women, and relationships.

I wonder what Mother would say if she knew her darling was robbing the cradle, Julia mused, as she straightened up her desk. *I'd have to call Lauren to witness that one. She loves the drama*, she thought with a laugh.

Julia had just finished touching up the little makeup she did wear and straightening her low pony tail (she'd be glad when summer gave way to cooler weather and she could wear her hair some other way again) when she heard a knock on the shop door. Looking out the front window, she saw Austin standing on the shop's stoop. Today he was in a pair of denim cargo shorts and black t-shirt. *Damn, he looks good*, she mumbled under her breath, and she turned the lock to let him in.

His unspoken sentiment echoed hers as she threw open the door and he saw her in casual shorts, khaki this time, bright red tank top with the

St. Louis Cardinals emblem front and center, and two red cardinal birds dangling from her earlobes. She really was a serious fan.

"Hey!" she greeted him with a bright smile before she grabbed him up in a brief hug. "You are Mr. Punctual, that's for sure. I need to grab my bag and we'll go. You know how those tables fill up fast." She started for her desk, leaving him in to breath in her perfume left in her wake. *Nice.* Watching her walk away, he thought of all the places she'd put that perfume and felt himself getting warm.

Stop it, he scolded himself. *Don't be an ass. Don't be Matt for Christ's sake.*

"Ready?" She looked up at him expectantly and he nodded agreement. He was looking forward to this second date. Date? It was to him, anyway. They stepped out into the bright Arizona sun and climbed into his car.

She had been right about the crowded restaurant, but they found a table inside where it was cool. They could have sat on the covered patio, but even with misters and fans, the heat would be impossible. Instead, they found themselves in a booth with a perfect view of the big screen that covered the center of the wall. Flanking it on both sides were several smaller televisions, each with a different game going. It was Sunday in the summer—MLB was playing on every set.

The next two hours were spent much as the previous day had been. They talked sports, and he found that she was as diehard about her Cardinals as he was about his Tar Heels. He wasn't really a huge MLB fan, following college action the most, and that didn't bother her at all, just as her indifference to college sports didn't bother him. They laughed, drank beer, devoured wings and nacho chips, and had as much fun as either could remember having in a long time.

"Hey," she said. "The Cards game will be on in about an hour. Would you want to come over to my place and watch it there? I have beer. I have chips. And I have more comfortable furniture. Plus, my roommate is gone to Vegas. What do you think?"

"I think that would be great," Austin replied. He'd finally get to see her place, and he wondered if it was anything like he imagined.

She paid this time, as per their deal, and they headed back to the shop for her car.

"You'll have to follow me again, I'm afraid," she said. "This time it won't be quite the journey we took to the hills yesterday. About 7 minutes without traffic, I think. Try to keep up, though," she winked and left him looking after her.

Once again he found himself following the little red car as she headed onto Osborn Road and then onto Hayden Road. It was a short distance before she turned onto Roosevelt. This was new territory to Austin. The little car slowed as they turned onto Eighty-fifth Street and stopped at the entrance to an apartment complex. Almost magically, the security gates swung open, and they drove through.

Nice, Austin thought, as he looked at the row of townhouses that lined the street, two levels of stucco with brick accents and native landscaping. The apartments all looked alike to him, but he took note of the number above the garage door of hers—1007A. The double-car door slowly rose and she pulled in. He parked his own car behind hers and got out to meet her at the short sidewalk that led to an outside entrance housing two heavy wooden doors, each with a small glass window covered with black bars. Julia took out her keys and unlocked the door to the left.

She opened the door wide and motioned for him to enter ahead of her. The entry held a staircase that disappeared upward, another door on the left that he assumed connected to the garage, and a short hallway leading to rooms he couldn't see.

"There isn't much down here except for a small office, a big laundry room, and storage," she said. "We live upstairs." She took the lead and he followed her up the carpeted steps to see that they ended in an open living area. The living room, complete with fireplace, extended to a kitchen that he could see contained stainless steel appliances and a granite counter. A breakfast bar held four stools and to the right, a small dining table and chairs sat next to a large window. Between the kitchen area and living room, he could see sliding glass doors that he assumed led to a balcony. It was all done in what he could only call designer colors—dark brown, lighter shades of the same, and accents of turquoise and coral. He looked down at the beige carpet and wondered if he should take his shoes off. *My mom would have made me*, he thought. Before he could act, Julia strode across the floor toward the kitchen, shoes intact, making the decision for him.

"Please, Austin, make yourself at home. There's a bath in the hallway," she said over her shoulder. "The remote to the television is lying on the mantel. See if you can find the Cards game, please. Channel 671, I think."

The remote was right where she said it would be, which was a change for Austin. He and Matt usually had to scrounge around in the sofa cushions and under the furniture before one of them would find it somewhere weird, like the bathroom or once in the refrigerator. It was a nice set, placed above the fireplace and angled down so that watching from the sofa, or the long chair to the right, would be comfortable. He'd no more than sat down and turned on the set when she came in carrying two Bud Lights. The one he assumed was hers was enclosed in a red St. Louis Cardinals coozie, and the can she handed him was shrouded in plain black.

He sat in the middle of the sofa and Julia took one end. She promptly turned toward him, kicked off her sandals, and stretched her legs along the length until they rested over his lap.

"You don't mind, do you?" she asked and grinned. No, he definitely didn't mind. He grinned back at her and started to tickle one foot.

"Oh, no, you don't!" she started to move, but he took her legs and put them back across his lap as they had been before.

"I'll be good, promise. This place is awesome," he said. "Much better than a college bachelor pad," he chuckled.

"You should have seen the first apartment Lauren and I rented twenty years ago in Columbia. Talk about a dump! I think it's been torn down to make way for some new mall or something. It needed to go. If my dad had ever known the crime statistics for that neighborhood, he would have moved me immediately," she laughed. "No, he probably would have bought me some big-ass gun and taught me how to shoot straight."

"You own a gun?" Austin asked.

"Nope, but Lauren does," and she laughed again. "She was so excited when Missouri passed a conceal and carry law. I think she was one of the first to take the class and start toting her Glock with her everywhere. Yeah, a 9mm in the hands of my short-tempered friend." Not knowing Lauren very well, Austin couldn't share in her humor. "Oh, don't look so stricken. She doesn't carry it all the time anymore, and she's not shot anybody. Yet. Although my ex-husband should thank God every night that she didn't have it when we were going through our divorce."

This is the first time she's referred to being married, divorced, or an ex-anything. Austin hoped she'd say more about it. When she didn't volunteer, he couldn't keep from asking.

"So, you were married before coming out here?" he asked tentatively, waiting for her to share what she wanted. He took a nervous sip of his beer.

"Yep. I was married for almost eleven years before a series of unfortunate events ended it," she said lightly. He could tell there was much more to the story than that, but he was following her lead on this one. Austin waited for Julia to continue, but she took a sip of her own drink and smiled slightly.

"Guess that's his loss and my good luck, huh?" He grinned at her and without realizing what he was doing, gently massaged the leg closest to him as he took a long drink of his beer. She left the leg where it was and didn't say anything. Austin couldn't believe any man would let this woman walk out of his life, but then, he didn't know any more than what she'd said. His experience with divorce was limited to his friends' parents or friends of his own mom and dad. These hadn't really affected him, so he'd not paid a lot of attention.

"That was around five years ago, and I moved out here right after we split up. It was a fast end. He gave me everything I asked for, I changed my name back to my family's, Lauren and I sold the business there, and we headed out West. No regrets." She frowned slightly. "I do miss my dad. I'm a Daddy's girl, big time, but when he retires in a couple of years, I look for him and mother to visit more."

This was more of her life than she'd shared, and Austin tried to hold onto all of it so that he could think about it later. *Daddy's girl—not Mama's,* he thought.

"What about you?" she asked with a mischievous look in her eye. "Any ex-Mrs. James anywhere?"

He wiggled his eyebrows up and down and said, "Well…that bit of information may cost you another beer," to which she laughed.

"Honestly, no," he said before continuing. "I graduated high school, did the family thing by enrolling in UNC, spent a year there as a pre-law major before dropping the bomb on the folks. Law isn't for me, and it wasn't a pretty scene when I told my parents, especially my dad. Matt was already out here with family, his grandma, some aunts and uncles, so I called him, loaded up the car, and headed west myself. I lost a couple of semesters, colleges don't like to accept transfer credits, and then I needed to work and pay the rent. At first, Dad didn't want to pay for school, but when he saw that I was going to do what I wanted to do, regardless, he relented and has picked up the tab for tuition and books these last two years. I haven't had a lot of time to date much, and definitely no time for a wife. And now you know…" his voice trailed off.

Julia looked at him for a few moments before turning her attention to the television. *Holy shit*, she thought. *So young that I feel like a real cougar.* She could feel his hand still rubbing her leg and decided that he couldn't be totally an innocent, fortunately for her.

"Looks like it's time for the first pitch, and I hope the Giants are ready for an ass-whoopin' today. Go Cards!" she said with a laugh and raised one arm in a salute to her team.

After that, they both settled in to watch the game and enjoy being together.

Chapter 9

*F*OUR HOURS LATER, THE GAME ended with the win Julia had predicted. They'd consumed at least a six-pack of beer before switching to wine. The pizza they had delivered was now gone except for one lonely piece. Sometime during the evening, they had changed positions and were now each seated at an end of the sofa, facing one other with their legs intertwined.

"I should go," Austin said.

"You should sober up some first," Julia replied. "Guys don't like to admit when they are no longer totally sober, do they?" She softened the insult to masculinity with a grin.

"No argument here, but I really don't feel drunk," Austin admitted. He looked like the last thing he wanted to do was move anyway. "What do you want to do then? Watch a movie?"

"Well," Julia gave him a look he hadn't seen before. He wasn't sure where she was going. "Lauren texted me during the seventh inning, and she won't be back until tomorrow afternoon. So we have the whole apartment to ourselves."

Somewhere in the exchange, her voice had changed, and Austin looked at her quizzically. His eyes travelled to their legs, still twined around one another before he looked back up to meet her eyes. She slowly moved until she was sitting up and leaning toward him. She moved to the floor to kneel next to his end, her eyes level with his. He held his breath as she began to trail kisses along his jaw and his neck before capturing his lips with her own. She tasted like wine and he pulled her closer as he deepened the kiss.

It was every bit as exciting as it had been before, and Austin didn't want it to end as he felt Julia pull away.

"You haven't seen the rest of the apartment yet." Her blue eyes grew darker as she looked at him. "Would you like to finish the tour?"

His mouth was suddenly dry. All he could do was nod his head before she took his hand and pulled him to his feet. Still holding onto his arm, Julia led him down a short hallway to the room at the end.

"This is my room," she said huskily. "Lauren laughs at the king-size bed, but I got used to it before moving out here, and I like a lot of room when I sleep."

Austin felt himself being pulled farther in, but nothing registered. Not the furniture, nor the paintings on the wall, nor the door leading to another bath. All he saw was her, and his eyes went to the huge bed behind her. He wondered if this was a bed she'd brought with her. One she'd shared with the ex-husband. Julia broke into his thoughts as she reached up to pull his attention back to her, and this kiss was deeper and more sensual than he'd ever experienced. They parted long enough to look at one another and smile in agreement.

He tugged his shirt over his head and tossed it toward a chair in the corner of the room. She gave him a slow sexy smile and a wink before doing the same to her own tank top. Julia ran her hands over Austin's chest and shoulders, places she'd only looked at before, and then still lower across his stomach. She felt his breath catch as her hands touched the top of his shorts. He began exploring on his own. He let his eyes roam from her face to her breasts spilling over the top of her bra before he slipped the straps down. He kissed her again and his hands reached behind her to unfasten the strap. Pleased with himself for getting it undone without her help, he gave her a sexy smile before replacing his roving hands with his lips. It was her turn to catch her breath as his mouth found each soft mound before going lower still.

She took his head in her hands and lifted his face to look into her eyes.

"Are you sure, Austin?" she asked. "This will change everything, you know."

"I don't think it will change a thing, Jules. I've wanted you from the time I saw you in that golf skirt." He gave her a lazy grin, his own green eyes now dark.

"But..." she started.

"Don't talk. Don't think. Just feel." He bent to kiss her again. She gave in, and they tumbled together on the bed. Friendship was the last thing on their minds.

She looked up at him and winked before moving to the center. She motioned him to follow. He rose to his knees and stared down at the woman beneath him, letting his eyes move from her face, lower to her breasts, down her stomach and then lower. He unfastened her shorts and slid them down her legs. Once they joined the pile of clothes by the chair, he began kissing her body, starting with one foot, trailing up her leg and brushing the inside of her thigh, going still higher before he moved to the other leg and began the same process. Austin heard her exhale in a low moan as he removed the last of her clothing. She was as magnificent as he had imagined, and he tasted every part of her until he heard her gasp and call out his name. He moved up to kiss her again, and it was Julia's turn to take control.

She flipped him onto his back, laughing playfully as she began to finish undressing him. Julia stopped and stared at the man lying before her. "So pretty..." she said as she leaned over and began kissing his chest, running her hands over his body while she explored. As she moved still lower, she looked up at him again and removed her mouth just long enough to give him a sexy smile and resume her journey across his body. Austin didn't realize he was holding his breath until she took him in her mouth, and he released it with a ragged sound. What she was doing to him was beyond anything he'd ever experienced before, and he didn't know if he could stand it much longer. Just when he felt himself hovering on the edge, Julia raised herself over him and slid herself down onto him. He looked up at her and saw her eyes slowly close. They found their rhythm and for them the world was contained in this time and this place. That world exploded around them. She collapsed onto Austin's chest as they caught their breath. Julia could hear his heart pounding under her ear and knew that her own was beating equally hard. The moments passed, and she lifted her head to smile at the man under her.

As for Austin, he knew that the woman lying with him was more than he could imagine. What they shared was not simply physical—it was much more. Austin moved her to his side. She pulled the bed comforter over him and then herself. They lay in a cocoon as he tucked her under his arm. Neither had ever felt so content, so happy, or so complete. Soon both were asleep.

Austin woke first, and slipping out of the warm bed, he searched for his discarded shorts and cell phone in the pocket. He found it wasn't easy to maneuver in the dark, but he soon found what he'd been looking for and carried it with him back to bed. Sometime in the night, she had turned toward the outer edge, and as he crawled back in beside her, she scooted closer as he wrapped his arms around her once again. His phone had read 3:30 a.m., so Austin knew he had a little time before he had to go. He had to be at work by five, and he had to go home and change before heading out. He wondered how long it would take to get back to his place. His phone was still in his hand, and he lifted it over Julia's shoulder. Pulling up GPS, he typed in his address and saw that he was about twelve miles from Julia's apartment, and it would take between fifteen and twenty minutes to make the drive. If he left at four, he'd have plenty of time to get home, shower, change, and make it to work on time.

Julia must have felt him stirring because she rolled over, and Austin found himself staring at her face. By the light of his phone, he watched her sleep until she slowly opened one eye. That was followed by the other. She smiled.

"What time is it?" her voice was groggy from sleep.

"Early. About three-thirty. Go back to sleep, babe."

"Hmmm….I don't want to," and she ran her hands over his back and lower.

What better way to wake up? Austin thought as he returned the favor and kissed her upturned mouth.

Thirty minutes later, they were both up. Julia talked him into taking a shower with her before heading home. They soaped each other's hair and laughed as they took turns under the warm water, each pulling, tugging, and jockeying for position. They decided that was the problem with showers—someone was always outside the warm water. Before the play got out of hand, Austin turned off the water and handed her a towel.

"I would like nothing more than to take you right back to that bed, but duty calls. I need bill money, you know."

She sighed. "I know. Me, too. And I've got a busy day. I'm meeting with a new client and managing the shop until Lauren gets back this afternoon."

Julia looked up at him, a hint of concern on her face. She hadn't given a thought to what she'd tell her roommate. *It looks like Austin will be spending a lot of nights here if I have anything to say about it. Well, Miss Lauren can just deal, can't she?* Julia decided. Austin watched the different emotions cross her face and knew with her set jaw that Julia had reached some conclusion. He hoped it wasn't that this wouldn't be a repeat. He didn't think he could stand the thought of her ending it after their night together.

"Jules," he began. "I don't know what you're thinking, but I want you to know that last night was incredible. I never dreamed it could be that way with anyone, and…"

She stopped him by putting a finger against his lips, which he gently kissed. "Hey, let's not take it out and analyze it, okay? Just know that it was pretty incredible for me, too, sweetie. And I like spending my time with you." She grinned. "In fact, why don't you come by this evening? I should be home around six or six-thirty. I'll cook for you, how's that? Then we'll do whatever."

Austin knew the kind of *whatever* he had in mind, but he only grinned and said, "It's a date. You can cook?"

"Austin, I'm forty years old. I can cook," and she snarled her lip and raised a brow, wondering about his former girlfriends and their domestic skills. She knew one that they couldn't top her in, and her imagination where he was concerned had her already thinking about their next encounter. *I'm becoming my mother's worse nightmare—a slut*, she thought. Before she could dwell on that further, he grabbed her up in a hug.

"Is there no limit to what you can do, woman?" With that, he left her to find his clothes. She watched his backside as he walked away and thought about how limitless her imagination really was before she followed him back into the bedroom.

"What time do you go to work?" he asked, his voice muffled by the shirt he was pulling over his head.

"Usually around seven or eight, but I'll go in early today."

"Hey, sorry I woke you up so early. You should still be sleeping." He crossed to where she was standing to put his hands on her shoulders.

Her towel covered everything else, but he smiled, remembering what lay beneath.

"Oh, I think you were worth a little lost sleep," she winked and crossed the room to the closet where she retrieved her robe. He enjoyed the view even though she didn't turn back around until she was cinching the belt tight around her waist.

"Do you have time for coffee?" Julia asked, as she headed down the hallway and into the kitchen. It was still dark outside, but the nightlight above the counter glowed. She flipped on a switch, and the room was bathed in bright, white light.

"I don't drink it, but I'll take a bottle of water if you've got one," Austin replied. She raised a brow at him and laughed.

"I should have figured," was her only reply. When she opened the refrigerator, he could see several bottles neatly lined up as well as an assortment of other things, before she closed the door and handed him one.

Looks like my mother's fridge, he thought. He cringed as he thought about how that would have sounded had he said it out loud. That was a comparison that he really didn't want to make. In fact, except for the tidy refrigerator, nothing about Julia was even remotely similar to his mom. *Age really is just a number*, he thought, *and this woman is living proof. This is the first time I've given it a thought.*

"I gotta run. It'll take me about fifteen minutes to get home from here, and another fifteen to get to work from there." She wondered where *home* was but didn't ask as he headed toward the door. She followed him down the stairs and opened the door for him. Austin leaned in to give her one last kiss. He raised his head just enough to kiss her nose before turning and walking out, leaving her to stand in the doorway. She watched him pull away, turned back inside, and sat down on the stairs.

"What am I doing..." she moaned. "I told myself I wouldn't do this, and not with a twenty-four-year-old boy." She thought back over the last two days and lingered on the night she had just spent with Austin. *That wasn't a boy*, she decided, *regardless of his age. God, on his BEST days, Keith was nothing like that.* "One and done" is what she called her ex-husband's performances. Keith wasn't a bad guy; he just wasn't a romantic, nor was he that great in bed. Lauren always said he was too self-centered and that the worst lovers in the world are self-centered. *She should know*, Julia thought. She considered her friend a classy slut, if there was such a thing, and laughed with her at some of her exploits. Julia had slept with a couple of men since moving to Arizona, but she was *one and done* with them, turning down future dates. They had done nothing for her, not even satisfy her sexually much less emotionally. But this wasn't the time to think about past failures. Austin had definitely not been a failure.

"As Daddy would say 'I'm burning daylight,' and I need that coffee," she said out loud. Julia turned away from the door and climbed the stairs to begin her day.

Austin quietly let himself into the apartment, hoping he could sneak in, change clothes, and sneak out again undetected. Matt was never up at this early hour, but sometimes he'd never gone to bed, opting to sack out on the sofa. Unfortunately for Austin, this was one of those nights.

"Chicks call that the walk of shame," came a voice from the direction of the sofa. "But since you're not a chick, there is no shame. Are those your panties in your pocket, or are you just glad to see me?"

"Hey, dork," Austin abandoned being quiet and let the front door slam shut. "And you're the only Nancy I know doing anything shameful around here. Don't you ever sleep like a normal person? Geez…"

Matt sat up and looked at his friend. He turned on a light, and studied him closer before getting up to stand next to Austin. He sniffed.

"Dude, that is chick soap. You've been using chick soap," Matt eye-balled his friend. "And, you haven't been home in two days. I know. I live here. I also know that look. THAT is the look of a man who's been laid. Did my AJ get hisself laid?"

"Shut up, man, just shut up," Austin was disgusted and not a little irritated at Matt's crude reference to sex. He had no intention of letting Matt make what he had with Julia into something coarse.

"Whoa…" Matt put his hands up in the air in surrender. "I see that I touched a nerve. Dude, this is epic. This is to be recorded in the history books of sex history. My best friend AJ has gotten himself laid, ladies and gentlemen. Hold the applause. We don't know yet how good it was." He lowered his voice in a mimic of a television reporter, picked up an empty water bottle and stuck it in Austin's face. "Mr. James, we have it on good authority that you had sexual relations last night. Can you elaborate on what kind of sex it was. Intercourse? Blow job? Or a simple hand job? Just how good was it? Our viewers want to know."

Austin looked at his friend and said nothing. Matt waggled his pretend microphone at Austin's face and smiled encouragingly before Austin knocked the bottle flying. "Fuck off. And get that thing outta my face, dumbass." He glared at Matt's stunned face. "And take a shower. You stink." Austin turned and started toward his room.

Matt's hand slowly lowered to his side as he watched his buddy walk away. This was something new, and Matt wasn't sure how to react. They'd gone out before and both had scored, as Matt liked to put it, and both had laughed and compared notes the next day. *Come to think of it, Austin hasn't done that in a very long time, maybe not since his first few months in Phoenix,* Matt thought. Austin had also not told him to *fuck off* in a very long time.

Something's up, my friend, Matt thought. *I'll consider this further when I'm more awake,* and he turned to go to his own room.

Ten minutes later Austin was changed and out the door. He was glad to see that Matt had taken himself to bed because he'd hate to lose it and knock him on his ass. *This is a problem,* he thought as he let himself out the door. *How do I bring Matt and Julia together? Introduce them? Keep Matt from embarrassing them both with inappropriate idiocy?* Determined to not let his friend spoil his good mood, Austin jumped into his car, turned up the radio, and watched the sun slowly rising over the tops of the distant mountains. Slipping on his favorite ball cap, he smiled. Six o'clock couldn't come soon enough—it was going to be a long day.

Chapter 10

THE SHOP WAS QUIET AND Julia had just seen her newest client out the door. Mrs. Adams knew what she wanted and had the money to buy it. Julia felt good that she had trusted Touch of Jules to do the job for her, and Mrs. Adams seemed like the type to pass the word around. *More business means more money*, Julia thought. She and Lauren did extremely well, and the settlement Julia had received from Keith and the sale of the Chesterfield shop had provided enough money to buy the building for this shop. Her car had been a gift on her thirty-fifth birthday, from Keith, so that was paid for. All she owed was monthly rent on the apartment, utilities, and living expenses.

She had her eye on a Louis Vuitton weekend bag that was ridiculously expensive. At heart, Julia was relatively conservative when it came to money, but every once in a while she'd splurge. This would be one of those times. She was in the middle of daydreaming about her new bag when she heard the door bell. Lauren breezed in on a swirl of hot air and tossed her purse on her desk before collapsing into her chair.

"Oh. My. God. What a fantastic weekend!" She closed her eyes and smiled in ecstasy. "Jules, you missed it, girl. Men, drinks, dancing, more men, more drinks, more dancing. It had it all! Oh, and thanks for holding down things here this weekend. I'll owe you one. Just say when. I did meet one interesting man, but, I don't know. The sex was fantastic, but we really didn't talk much, you know? Little talk—lotta action," Lauren ran out of steam as she leaned back and smiled at the ceiling.

Julia gave her friend an eye roll and smiled. *Better get it over with*, she thought.

"Well, I had my own interesting weekend. You left Saturday evening, and I spent the afternoon and evening with Austin. We ended up swimming at Sharon's and then yesterday we met up to watch baseball. Oh, the Cardinals won and there were more up-close shots than usual of Mike Matheny. Your most favorite manager, as you call him." Julia stopped to gauge Lauren's reaction so far.

Her friend stared hard at Julia before exclaiming, "Oh, my god! Oh, shit! You slept with him, didn't you? I leave you alone for two nights, and you sleep with the boy." She left her chair to perch on the corner of Julia's desk. Lauren leaned in closer, looking her friend in the eye.

"Something's different. I can't put my finger on it just yet, but something's definitely different about my Julia. Was he good?" Lauren leaned back and laughed. "Dumb question. He was, wasn't he? I'll bet he was mind-blowing, unbelievable, knock your socks off, blow me down, slap me silly, un-freakin-believable!"

When Julia didn't join in the banter with her usual snarky comeback regarding sexual partners, Lauren's laughter faded. She looked at Julia and narrowed her eyes.

"Oh, god, you like him, don't you? What have I told you over and over, Julia. Men are disposable napkins. You can find them anywhere. You use them once, and you toss them away. And seriously, this guy? Oh, he's beautiful and young. But really? You've only spent two days with him. Two. Damn. Days."

Julia smiled at her friend and said, "I know. Best two damn days of my life. And I intend to spend more days with him. And more nights with him. And enjoy his company until one of us, or both of us, is ready to move on." Julia's smiled faded. "I like him, Lauren. I really like him. He makes me laugh. He makes me want to throw caution to the wind and live again." Her face grew serious as she continued. "You know I haven't felt this way in a very, very long time. Probably not since before I lost the babies, and maybe not even since I was younger than Austin is now. He's good for me." Julia looked at her friend, her eyes shining, but serious. "Be happy for me, Lauren, please?"

The subtle pleading in her friend's voice stopped Lauren short. *Jules is right. She hasn't been young and fun in a very long time. Well, I'll be the last person to stand in the way of her happiness. I'll also be the first person to knock aside anyone else who tries.*

"You know I love you more than my Louboutins. Go for it. You have my blessing." Lauren smiled at her friend. "By the way, how much will he be around? You know, so I know when I can and can't parade naked around the apartment."

"You seldom, if ever, parade around naked, skank. And he's coming over tonight. I'm fixing him dinner when I get home. You're welcome to join us. In fact, I want you to. I want the two most important people in my life to get to know one another and like each other. Just be on your best behavior, okay?"

Lauren sighed. "Oh, all right. For you. But I'm not doing the damn dishes just because you're cooking. Let Loverboy do them and earn his keep." She smiled wickedly. "Of course, I'm sure he'll earn his keep in other ways. Meow..."

With that, she hugged Julia before returning to her covered desk and an afternoon of phone calls and job lists. As for Julia, she looked at the clock on her desk and decided that the day was going to really drag by. Even though she had a lot to do, she couldn't help making plans for what she was going to fix. Maybe she could talk Lauren into closing up so that she could go to the store and get home early. Turning her attention back to Mrs. Adams' plans, she thought to herself, *Life really is good.*

Despite Julia's misgivings, the day did pass at its usual pace. At six o'clock sharp, Julia heard the doorbell and ran down the stairs. Austin stood on the stoop, flowers in hand, and a smile on his face.

"Flowers! Lauren will be so pleased!" Julia teased him before pulling his head down for a quick kiss. She took the flowers and led him up the stairs.

"I didn't even ask you what you like to eat, so it's a man's meal tonight." She spoke over her shoulder. "I have steaks marinating, baked potatoes in the oven, salad, and rolls. I figured we'd wait for Lauren before firing up the grill. She's joining us if that's okay."

"Great!" Austin followed her up the stairs and to the kitchen counter, where he took a seat on one of the bar stools. "It was so miserably hot today. The boss sent us home around 11 this morning, so I was able to work ahead in my classes. It feels good to be caught up, you know?"

"Oh, I remember the feeling," Julia smiled. "I was usually okay on deadlines, but Lauren was ridiculous. I swear, that girl would be sitting up all night reading some required book, or writing a paper, or a million other things. She always gave the excuse of being better under pressure. Said she produced, as she put it, more and better. Being in business has broken her of that habit, thank goodness." As she talked, Julia arranged the flowers in a pretty hand-painted vase. Austin had seen others like it in her shop that day he was picking out his parents' gift. *It looks like Julia,* he thought, *and the daisies were a good choice.*

"There," Julia finished. "Austin, these are beautiful. How did you know I love daisies? They're one of my favorite flowers. Now in the desert, I love acacia." She laughed. "I know. It's usually just a thorny tree, but acacia has the prettiest scent, don't you think? I love them after a rain." She grinned. "If you ever do want to bring Lauren a flower, make it a rose. And make sure it's one with lots of thorns. Fits her personality." Julia laughed at the expense of her absent roommate.

All the while she'd been talking, Austin had been silently looking at her. *She has to be the most natural, self-assured woman I've ever been with. She likes to talk, but she isn't boring like so many girls. I have to be on my toes because I never know when she'll sneak in a sarcastic remark or make a joke at my expense. I learned that very quickly our first afternoon together. That seems so long ago, but only a couple of days have passed. Wow! I can't believe how close we've gotten in that short time.* Her voice brought him out of his thoughts.

"Do you want a beer? Wine? I also have some iced tea, water, and soda. Name your poison, cowboy," she laughed at his expression. "Oh, honey, you'll have to get used to my cowboy references. I was raised on John Wayne classics and Clint Eastwood's spaghetti westerns."

"A beer would be great. I've had enough water today to fill a swimming pool. I think I felt myself slosh several times."

She leaned over to grab a Bud Light from the bottom of the refrigerator, and Austin saw that she was wearing some sort of dress today. It was bright abstract colors, sleeveless, and short. He especially liked the "short" part. It suited her.

She was pouring herself a glass of wine when they heard the downstairs door open and the garage door close.

"Yoo hoo!" Lauren's sing-song voice carried up the stairs. "Everybody decent? Except Austin. You don't have to be decent, but Julia better be completely dressed."

When Lauren entered a room, everyone noticed. If it wasn't her five-foot nine-inch frame, blond hair, or striking good looks, it was her ability to draw attention just by being there. She dropped her things onto the hall table and sauntered over to take Austin's beer from his hand. She tossed back a long drink before handing it back to him. Taking in his shorts and tight t-shirt, she decided that Julia had done quite well.

"Thanks." She smiled. "I needed that. So, what are we eating tonight, Jules?" She gave Julia a quick hug before opening the refrigerator to get her own beer. "I see a salad. Yummy!" Turning back to the room, her eyes landed on the vase. "Oh, look, flowers! You shouldn't have, Austin. And next time, just so you know, my favorites are roses."

"I'll try to remember that," Austin spoke for the first time since Lauren had entered the room. Julia and Austin's eyes met and they burst out laughing.

Lauren stood looking from one to the other before asking, "What did I miss? Did I miss something? What the hell?" which made them laugh even more.

"Oh, I love you, Lauren," Julia said. "Now get out of my way. Go change clothes and behave yourself."

Lauren took her beer with her as she followed Julia's instructions. Julia checked the baking potatoes before taking her own glass and motioning for Austin to join her outside. As they walked out onto the elevated deck, the heat wasn't as bad as Austin had expected. He saw that the deck was facing the south, so the sun was indirect, and at this time of day, completely behind the building. A breeze lifted his hair from his neck, and even though the air was hot, it was pleasant. All the apartments in this section looked out over a shared courtyard. Above that, Austin could see the mountains in the distance. *That's the thing about the valley,* he thought. *Look in any direction, and the mountains provide a distant backdrop.*

While he'd been admiring the view, Julia had been firing up the grill and checking the temperature gauge. "You can hang out here if you want. I need to grab the steaks. Have a seat."

He pulled out one of four stools that surrounded a bar-high table. The glass top was still hot from the heat it had absorbed all day, so he held his cold drink and leaned back. Julia returned soon, and it wasn't long before the sound of sizzling meat and the smell of it cooking made his mouth water. He and Matt seldom grilled anything. For one, they didn't have their own, but had to share grills that were in the "yard" by the miniscule pool. They would throw burgers or a steak or some brats on once in a while, but it was too much trouble. They'd rather eat out or do without.

She looked at her watch to time the meat and perched on a stool next to him. They sat in comfortable silence, and he reached out to take her hand. He raised it to his lips and kissed each finger before turning it over to gently kiss her palm. He looked up at her and saw her eyes darken a little before she smiled and leaned over to plant a kiss of her own. *He tastes like sun and beer*, she decided. *And he smells so clean.* She'd rather smell him than cologne any day.

"How are those steaks?" he asked, bringing her out of her thoughts.

She looked down at her watch and jumped up to check on the sizzling meat.

"How do you want yours? If it's rare, yours is about done. And don't worry about anything in between because I have to practically burn Lauren's. Super well-done for her."

"Medium-rare is great, but can I help you with anything?" he asked.

"Nope. When I cook, I find it's so much easier to just do things myself rather than give instructions. I already have the table set, and Lauren will probably get the other stuff out. Almost done here."

She took up his and her steaks and covered them lightly with foil. It would be another five minutes or so for Lauren's to finish cooking. They chatted about their day and the upcoming Fourth of July that was around the corner and soon everything was done.

Julia didn't know how Lauren would behave, but she knew her friend could be as charming as she wanted to be. This night Lauren behaved. The three talked and laughed and a comfortable chemistry developed. Lauren discovered that Austin could dish it out as well as take it, and before the meal had ended, she knew exactly why Julia was so taken with this man. *He is awesome!* She thought. *And mature. More mature than I ever expected.* She relaxed and decided that she wasn't going to worry about her friend.

Julia could hold her own with this one, and he seemed to be bringing out the best in her. Lauren watched them exchange several "knowing" looks, as if they shared some secret, and decided that her evening would be better spent out. *Maybe I'll head to Houston's and enjoy some martinis.* She rose to leave them.

"Okay, kids, this has been fun, but I have plans this evening. Austin, the cleaning of the kitchen ritual is all yours tonight. You're welcome."

She grabbed her purse and keys before coming back to hug Julia. "Don't wait up. It's lemon-drop martini night at Houston's. And if I can't find my car, I'll find a ride. Love you!" She breezed down the stairs and was out the door before either Julia or Austin could react.

"Wow! Is she always like this? So..." Austin was at a loss.

"Yes, she is," Julia laughed. "She has been from the time I met her. We've been best friends for, geez, twenty-two years now. And for almost half of that time, we've lived together! Wow, it just hit me. That's crazy." Julia smiled at Austin before getting up to clear the table.

"Nope," he protested as he rose from his chair. "I've been entrusted with the honor of conducting the kitchen ritual. You. Sit. And keep me company." Austin began stacking plates.

"Ok, but I always help the honoree. You load the dishwasher and I'll put away this stuff. We'll get done so much faster."

It didn't take long with both of them working together. Soon they were standing in the clean kitchen and looking at one another.

"What time do you need to go home tonight? I know you get up really early." Julia wasn't sure what his plans were.

Austin moved closer to her, but didn't touch. He looked down at her questioning look and grinned.

"Well, Ms. Whitman, how good is your alarm clock?"

"Last time I checked, it worked just fine." Julia closed the space between them. "In fact, I dusted it off this afternoon."

"Well, we could go out, or watch television, or talk. I'm all yours," he said.

That thought made Julia's stomach jump as she looked at the man in front of her. "None of the above. I've got a treat for you." Austin didn't protest as she took his hand and led him to her room, where she shut and locked the door. "No interruptions."

Julia took charge. Austin looked at her curiously, wondering what she was up to, before he looked at the turned-down bed sheets. He grinned back at her, but she made no move in that direction.

"I was thinking about you today," she said as she moved toward him and ran her hands up his arms and across his shoulders, where she started kneading the tight muscles. "I was wondering what I could do for a man who works so hard all day, and I decided what you need is a nice massage."

Austin's eyebrow raised and he grinned at her. "You're certified in this, ma'am?"

"Oh, yeah, I have the best certification there is, sweetie. It's called experience. Now strip down and lie on the bed."

He did as he was told and soon he was lying face down with his head to one side, looking at her. Julia had lost the dress and everything under it. She stood at her dresser, gathering a couple of bottles in her hands before she joined him in the center of the big bed. He couldn't see her now, but he could feel her straddle his back. Before he could fully appreciate the feeling, something warm was dribbled across his shoulders and down his spine. The warm liquid was replaced by her hands. As she rubbed and kneaded the tight muscles in his back and neck, Austin realized just how wonderful this felt and how much he really did need it. She moved down along his arms and shoulders with the same firm massaging and kept kneading for several minutes until the tight muscles became pliant. He felt her move away and started to turn around, when he felt that same warm liquid being poured down both legs. She started on his feet, rubbing and massaging each before her hands made their way up to his calves. She took turns with each leg, squeezing and working the lower leg before moving higher to the back of his thighs. By this time, Austin was totally relaxed and his body felt much like the liquid she'd poured onto him. He wondered what else she would be massaging, and his answer came soon enough.

She straddled him once again, this time lower and began working on his firm buttocks. She'd changed her stroke a bit, and this time it wasn't relaxing him at all. He started to turn over, but she gently held him in place. *She* wasn't ready yet. "Slow down, cowboy. All in good time…all in good time…" Her hands continued what they were doing.

After a few more minutes, she instructed, "Okay, roll over now, sir. You're to get the full treatment tonight, and I need to give some attention to your front muscles." She smiled and motioned for him to move. Once he was sprawled on his back, Julia looked him up and down before straddling him once again. Austin was anything but relaxed now. Julia looked down and smiled. "Yeah, we'll take care of that later. I have a couple of other body parts that need my attention first." He was wondering what in the world the rest of his body was thinking when she poured what he now could see was oil across his chest and down his stomach. Her hands worked their magic as she gently massaged his chest, moved to apply harder pressure to his shoulders and arms before inching lower to his legs. She followed the same pattern as before, up and down each limb. As she worked, Austin couldn't take his eyes off her body as she moved over and around him. The combination of her relaxing massage and her naked body was driving him crazy.

"I think there's only one place left to work on." She grinned and winked. His wait was over. Her mouth closed over him and Austin moaned with pleasure. When he could stand it no longer, Austin pulled her up and rolled them both over until she was lying under him. He raised his head and dark green eyes met dark blue ones before he leaned in to kiss her swollen lips. His hand trailed down her body until he found her soft center. When neither could stand it any longer, they came together, their bodies molding one into the other. This time when they were both satiated, it was Austin who pulled the blankets up around her and then himself. He gathered her under his arm, and she rested her head on his chest.

"You're hired," he said.

"Was there ever any doubt?" she teased. She looked up long enough to kiss him lightly before placing her head back on his chest.

"You know that this could become a habit," he said softly. "In fact, I can't think of a single place I'd rather be right now than here with you."

"Hmmm...I feel the same," she replied. "The alarm is set for 3:30, just in case."

"Yeah, I suppose I'm that easy," he joked.

"No, you're a man, and all men are predictable when sex is involved," she chuckled.

Austin reached over her to turn off the bed-side light and wrapped his arms back around her. *Sex.* He thought about it. *I've had sex and this wasn't the same. I feel like I've been made love to. This is what I've been missing all along.* He was fighting sleep, but the long day, the big meal, and the sex/ massage had worn him out. It wasn't long his deep, even breaths signified sleep. Julia had already dozed off.

Julia didn't know what time it was when she felt herself awakened by something hard pressed into her back. She'd rolled over at some point, but now she turned back to run her hands down his back and then around to feel what had woke her up. Austin began kissing her, and in an instant she wasn't thinking of anything but how good he made her feel. This time when they finished, it was Julia who wrapped herself around Austin's back before they fell into a second deep sleep.

I do believe my days of one and done are over, she thought before her eyes closed again.

Chapter 11

A~USTIN WAS UP, SHOWERED, AND~ gone by the time Lauren rolled out of bed and staggered into the kitchen. She had never been a morning person, and the previous night's drinking didn't help. She saw the half-empty coffee pot and her favorite mug Julia had set alongside it. Feeling loved, she poured it full, added sugar, and took a big drink.

"Ow! Shit! Damn! That stuff's hot!" Lauren was blowing air in and out of her mouth as her eyes watered.

"Yeah, brainiac, it's hot coffee. I would post a sign for you, but you can't read it in the morning without your glasses," Julia looked up to laugh at her friend. Lauren was a mess in the morning. Her blond hair stuck up in all the wrong places, her eye makeup was smudged under both eyes, and she'd thrown on whatever over-sized t-shirt she could find. On her bare feet were the cat slippers she'd found at the flea market for three dollars—her best purchase ever as she called them.

"Yeah, well, some of us didn't have great sex last night. In fact, one of us here had NO sex last night. And why can't you look like shit in the morning?" She looked over at Julia. *She looks great*, Lauren thought. *How does she do that? I look like holy hell in the morning, and Jules looks, well, perfect. No, not perfect, just better than most. Better than me. At least not like crap.*

"You know I hate you sometimes," Lauren said as she turned to hop up onto one of the bar stools.

"Oh, don't blame me. Blame the good genes. My mother always looks good in the morning."

"I call bullshit," Lauren replied. "Your mom rolls out of bed an hour before everyone else and works like a dog to give herself that I-worked-an-hour-to-look-like-I-didn't look. She needs to learn to just go with it. Be natural. Get in touch with her inner ugly."

Julia looked at her friend's train-wreck appearance and laughed out loud. "Yeah, I see that you and your inner ugly are best buds this morning." She laughed again and shook her head as Lauren stuck out her tongue.

"By the way, Jules, your little boy is dreamy," Lauren said before taking a tentative sip of her drink. "In fact, I will go on record to say that I will quit calling him little boy. He's a big boy, and I think he has the potential for you to make a real man out of him. By the way, just how big a boy is he?" Lauren gave Julia a wink and a smile.

"Eat your heart out, slut," Julia replied. "That you will never know. Now, clean yourself up, hot mess, and let's get to the shop. Wanna ride together today? Austin wants to pick me up from work."

"Oh, god…another night of your being fed and bed while I settle for another night alone."

"Good grief, when are you ever alone?" Julia laughed. Lauren noticed she was doing a lot of that this morning. "In fact, who was there last night?"

"The usual crowd—Jennifer, Karen, Heidi, the gang. Oh, they send their love, by the way, and said to tell you that you suck."

Julia turned a sober look at her friend. Her relationship with Austin wasn't for public consumption and definitely not for her friends' gossip. "Just what did you tell them, may I ask?"

"Chill, sister, I only said that you'd met someone and were having a wonderful time. Nothing else. Geez…what am I?"

"Well," Julia started, "when you've had a few drinks in you, you become quite a blabber mouth. For the record, this is *my* business, okay?"

Lauren was offended. "Julia Whitman, how many secrets of yours have I kept over the years?" Julia looked at her friend's face, now serious, and nodded.

"You've kept them all, sweetie, and I'm sorry to be so touchy. I just don't know yet how to introduce Austin to my world, you know? Right now is nice, keeping him to myself, having a good time. But if we continue, and I suspect we will, I know that day is coming."

"And when it does, I'll have your back," Lauren assured her. "I'll keep the bitches in line, and you know that I can."

Julia laughed because she knew exactly how Lauren could be. Scary when she needed to be.

"I love you, girl," Julia said as she gathered Lauren up in a girl hug.

"Right back at'cha!" Lauren hugged her back. "Now, I stink and I can no longer stand myself. Give me an hour and I'll be ready to go."

"You have thirty minutes," Julia called to her friend's retreating back, knowing the best she could do was forty-five minutes.

Lauren raised her hand to flip her friend the bird over her shoulder and disappeared into her room and to her bathroom. It was the start of a typical day.

Austin picked Julia up that evening, and they ate at one of his favorite restaurants, Miner's Camp. "Best comfort food in the world outside of Mama's kitchen," Austin called it. Julia had to admit that it was wonderful. Austin ordered the Heart Attack Burger, a concoction of smoked bacon, onion rings, avocado, cheddar cheese, greens, tomato, mayo and red relish, and, of course, what looked like a half-pound burger surrounded by fries. Julia's eyes popped when she saw the huge plate set before him. Her own grilled salmon and roasted vegetables looked almost sad next to Austin's mountain of food. She laughed when, after finishing every bite on his plate, he ordered the specialty dessert—Mile-high Chocolate Cake made up of six layers of chocolate cake, chocolate fudge icing and topped with nuts.

"I hope you're ready to tackle that thing," Julia said, looking at the monstrous piece of cake, "because I couldn't hold a bite."

"No," Austin laughed, "I'm taking this back to Matt. If he knows I've been here and didn't bring him a Mile-high, he'll make me miserable."

"Speaking of your roommate, think I could maybe meet him sometime?" Julia hadn't mentioned Matt before. Austin talked about him more than he realized, and Julia was curious.

"Uh, sure, whenever," Austin looked uneasy. "But I'll warn you, Matt can be…how do I put it without being crude…an ass?"

Julia burst out laughing. "Don't worry so much, babe. I can handle asses in my sleep. I'd like to meet him." She raised one eyebrow and tilted her head before saying, "Maybe he can fill me in on all the dark secrets of Austin James."

"Yeah, my life is so mysterious, you know. My job at Coyote Run is a front. I'm really a professional bull rider, and I sneak off every other weekend to ride the bulls in Tucson, but that's only when they don't need me for the clown act. And then there's the…"

"Never mind," Julia interrupted. "I get it, Mr. Open Book."

"Yep, that's me," Austin said as he reached for his wallet.

"Oh, no," Julia stopped him. "Remember our earlier deal. We go Dutch. And put that big-ass piece of cake on your tab, please."

He laughed and set out to split the check. As they walked to his car, Austin turned to her.

"Jules, I do want you to meet Matt. You've not seen my place yet, and if you feel brave enough, why don't you come over now? Tonight?"

Julia looked at his face in the dim light. *When he's undecided about something or unsure as he is now,* she thought, *he looks so young.*

"Honey, I was born brave." She smiled when she saw that her reply had made him happy. "You realize your Matt may not be ready for *me*." She laughed. "Let's go have a look at this bachelor pad, shall we?"

He put the top down on the car now that the sun had set, and as they drove off, anyone looking at the two would have smiled at the sight of them—laughing, hair blowing in the wind, and the little black car that left a blast of hot air in its wake.

Chapter 12

Julia tried to remember the different streets they'd turned down, but she couldn't keep up. Once she saw that they were on Indian School Road, she had a good idea of the location. They passed several apartment complexes, all decent but not in the zip code of hers, not that it mattered, until he turned in at 2703 E. Indian School Road. No garages here, but the large parking lot was clean and she saw covered parking along both sides. Austin pulled into a covered spot marked 207 and stopped. She got out and waited while he put the top up and locked the car before coming around to take her arm.

"Not quite what you're used to, but it's relatively quiet, at least in this unit. On the other side are the three-bedroom apartments where all the families are. And the pool. No pool on this side, but over there is a couple of tables and grills. Community property."

She smiled at him and said, "Oh, I've lived in much, much worse. This is nice, Austin."

He led her from the parking lot to a sidewalk that ran along the front of two facing buildings. Sure enough, in the center she saw the tables and grills, as well as a good-sized grassy area and trees.

"You have grass and real trees!" She said. "I miss that sometimes, you know? I could spread a blanket out on that lawn and just lie there looking up at the stars..." Her voice drifted off.

Austin laughed. "Yeah, and soon you'd smell the aroma of fresh dog shit because pets are allowed and too many idiots don't clean up after their animals."

Julia gave him a wry grin. "Thanks for dropping me back to earth with a thud." As they walked along, she caught a whiff of what he'd been talking about. "Whew! I see what you mean. Good grief!" He laughed at her expression.

They turned into a covered stairwell and climbed the metal staircase to the second floor. Each of the doors was the same brown metal with a picture window to the right. She counted down seven where he stopped to insert his key.

"I haven't been around much, so please don't be surprised if the place is a bit messy. Ok, a lot messy."

"Stop apologizing, for heaven's sake. You're two men who have no cleaning lady to come in once a week and you, at least, are never home. Stop trying to warn me off, please," Julia said as she stepped through the door and into the cool, dark interior.

It was small, really small in comparison to what Julia was used to, but it had potential. The floors were a laminate dark wood, and the walls were painted a standard off-white. Straight ahead she could see the tiny kitchen that was separated from the living room by a bar with a couple of miss-matched bar stools pushed under the counter. To the right, she saw a sofa and a chair, both in brown, and a glass coffee table. Two floor lamps provided the light, one at the end of the sofa and one by the chair. A large area rug filled the floor space under the table and between the two pieces of furniture. The wall across from the sofa was filled with a huge television and underneath that sat an entertainment center with what she recognized as a game center and a DVD player. Scattered haphazardly on the game center and floor she saw a large assortment of video games and DVD's. At the bottom of the center sat a surround-sound receiver. She looked up and saw four small speakers, one in each corner of the room, and a larger one on the game center.

"Home sweet home," Austin said as he tossed his ball cap, sunglasses, and keys on the counter. He walked around to the refrigerator, opened it to see what Matt had left him, and put the cake box on the top shelf. She could see bottles of water, a twelve-pack of beer, a half-gallon of milk, and the usual takeout food boxes. "Do you want something to drink?"

"Water would be great," Julia said, "I'm still too full for anything else."

While he was busy getting their drinks, she looked around and saw that the kitchen held white appliances: refrigerator, stove, microwave and tiny dishwasher. On the counter was a toaster that was covered in bread crumbs and a mound of dirty dishes filled the small sink. One lone dish towel hung on the oven door handle. *This is definitely the home of two young bachelors,* she thought as she looked at the game center again. She wondered when she'd last seen one of those. *It had to be at someone else's house—someone with teenagers—but I can't remember.* She looked at the man in front of her. At times like these, Julia felt all of forty, and the difference between her and Austin felt like a gap that was more than generational. As her thoughts continued racing through her mind, Julia began to feel the first stirrings of anxiety as her stomach pitched.

What in the world am I doing here? She wondered. *What in the world was I thinking? Who am I kidding? This is a kid. Who still plays video games. Who's still in college. Who's only twenty-three. Who lives in a totally different world. And I definitely don't fit into that world.*

"I can't believe he didn't leave a bigger mess," Austin's voice brought her back to the present. "I had mentioned that I'd like to bring you over. Well, I said that I was planning on bringing *someone* over. I just wasn't specific." He grinned sheepishly.

She took a drink of her water, set it down on the counter, and gave him a questioning look.

"*Someone?* What does he know about me, Austin? Anything? Have you even told him my name? I'm certain you've never mentioned that I'm old enough to be your mom." She looked at him accusingly and saw him looking uncomfortable. *He's embarrassed by me,* she thought. *Oh, god, I've been living in a fantasy world thinking that it's all okay, and he's embarrassed to introduce his old-enough-to-be-his-mother girlfriend to his best friend. Girlfriend…even that's a stupid name to call myself. What are we, in high school? Girlfriend…Maybe fuck-buddy would be more fitting, or….whatever.* Julia looked around her again and a sick feeling came over her. *What in the hell am I doing here? I don't belong here. I feel like I should don an apron, put my hair in a bun, and start his laundry or something.* The queasiness was turning into panic. *This is wrong…something's wrong here…I don't belong here…why am I freaking out? Well, shouldn't I? This is a fresh new hell….I need to get out of here and regroup.* Taking a few deep breaths, she felt nothing but consternation. Shaking her head slightly, Julia closed her eyes.

Austin watched the emotions dancing across her face, and he didn't like what he was seeing. *I should have at least told Matt that I'm seeing someone special, but what in the world is going on with Julia?* He knew her well enough by now to know that something had her freaked out. He looked around but didn't see anything to cause her reaction. It was just a place where two guys lived temporarily.

"Austin, maybe I should go. I think maybe I ate something that didn't agree with me, and I need to go home."

"What? You were just fine ten minutes ago when we were flying down the road. You even sang along with the radio, and you only do that when you're happy." His troubled green eyes looked into her equally troubled blue ones. "Jules, what's going on? Is it because I didn't tell Matt much about you? I'm sorry if that's what's bothering you. " He started toward her, but she pulled away.

"This isn't working, Austin. I'm sorry. I can't do this." He saw that her eyes were filling with tears before she could turn away.

"Wait! What the hell, Jules? Can't do what? I can't read your mind. What. Is. Wrong." He looked at her back in bewilderment. "Is it meeting my roommate? You don't have to meet Matt tonight. Hell, you don't have to meet him at all. We can go back to your place, hang out, whatever. But what's going on?" He felt her slipping away, physically and emotionally. She slowly turned around to face him.

"Austin, I like you. I like you a lot. But we're rushing this. Too much. Seeing you in your environment has made me realize that I'm all wrong for you, and you're all wrong for me." She took a deep breath and let it out slowly, using the time to think of how to say it. "You have so many things ahead of you. School, starting your career, stuff that's all in my rearview mirror. I'm sure you think this is fun, and that it is what it is, and it will end when it ends, and until then we'll just have a lot of laughs. But I'm in a different place from you. I don't play that game anymore." Julia turned and started for the door, but before she could get there, Austin took her arm and pulled her back.

"You think that just because I'm a few years younger than you, that I'm in a different place as you put it, you think I can't handle a mature relationship? You think I'm in this for a good time, and when it runs its course that we'll kiss good-bye, go our separate ways, and stay pals? Look at me, Jules." He'd said all of this to the back of her head, and he needed to see her face to try to tell if his words were having an effect. She bowed her head but refused to turn around. Austin continued.

"I'm twenty-three years old. I'll be twenty-four in about two months. So what? Big. Damn. Deal. I have never met anyone like you, Julia. You make me see things and feel things and I like it. You hear me? I like it!" His voice wasn't pleading as much as striving to get her to understand. "We're not an age. We're a man and a woman who found each other. That's all we are—a man and a woman. I refuse to let you do this to us, to me. I refuse." As he finished, he was breathing hard and trying to contain any more of an emotional outbreak.

She turned around then, put her hand along the side of his face, and looked at his beautiful eyes. They were troubled now. "Oh, sweetie," she said. "If only life were so simple. You have no clue of what we're up against here, do you? Your friends. And your family. I don't give a damn about mine, but you aren't at that point in life yet. Austin, do you want to go around explaining me all the time? Hiding me from your friends? Correcting waiters who think I'm your mother? Apologizing, so to speak?" She shook her head and gave him a slight smile. "We are what we are, and if we'd met in another time, a time where we were close in age and at the same place in life, I would grab you up and never let go."

He could hear the "but" in her voice, and she said sadly. "But we aren't." She turned toward the door.

"I can call Lauren to pick me up. You don't have to take me anywhere..."

He hadn't expected this. He knew that they would be having *the talk* sometime, but Austin had been blindsided. He knew that Julia had always felt the age thing much more than he ever had, but this had come from nowhere.

"*No!*" His voice was raised in desperation, and he came around to block her leaving. "I've listened to you, and now it's your turn to listen to me. Do you think I don't have problems here, too?" Austin didn't usually show emotion, but he was now as he frowned into her face. "Do you think that I enjoy going to a bar and worrying that I'll be carded before I get a beer and that you'll see it all? Do you think I like wondering if I'm good enough, smart enough, good-looking enough, and yes, mature enough to make you happy? Do you think it was easy for me to be at your place? Surrounded by a lifestyle you've built and I've only dreamed of? Meeting a roommate who knows you better than I ever hope to do?" He let out a short breath and a sardonic grin pulled at the corner of his mouth. "I wonder every time we're together if I'm measuring up to the ex-husband. If I can be a man worthy of you." He ran his hand through his hair and looked up at the ceiling in frustration. "God, Julia, if I could tack on fifteen years of experience and life, I'd do it in a heartbeat. I want to be with *you*. I want to share things with you. I want to share myself with you." Austin paused and looked down at her. He took a deep breath. "I thought you wanted to be with me, too. I'm sorry if I was wrong, and I'm sorry if you think I'm wasting your time."

"Austin, I..."

"I'm not quite finished yet," he interrupted her. "I sucked it up and let you pull me in. I swallowed my pride and let you pick up the tab more than once. Hell, I deluded myself into my own little fantasy world where we are equal partners in a relationship that works because it's *our* relationship." He paused and shook his head. "I dream, Jules. And I suppose that's where we differ since you seem to have let life make you forget what it's like to follow a dream." He smiled a small smile that didn't quite reach his eyes. "I dream big, and I always go after those dreams. I haven't let anything stand in my way yet, and I don't intend to now. And you're now part of that dream, a big part. I thought you were the same after seeing what you've built for yourself. I learned that you are fulfilling your dream here. I thought that you were more interested in doing what you want rather than what someone else wants." He raised his chin. "I believed that you want me. I thought you could take me as I am." He paused and sighed. "Please," he was pleading now. "Please don't let me be wrong about you, about us. Please, Jules."

She'd heard all he had said. *Can we work it out?* She looked at the man standing in front of her. At his strong face, jaw set with determination. At his eyes flashing with emotion. *Can I walk away?* Julia weighed all that he'd said. She thought about his talk of dreams, of reaching for your dreams. *I've never felt like anyone's dream before. It's nice. And I know all about sacrificing and working to realize a dream. I wrote the book on it.* She thought about the question she'd always asked herself—*Is this worth it?* Her eyes moved over his face, and she decided. *Yes, we* are *worth it.* He knew immediately when she'd made her decision. He could read her as easily as a book, and he smiled when he saw her jaw set in determination and a small smile start in the corner of her mouth.

"You're right," she said. "You are absolutely right." She shrugged her shoulders. "Screw it. I had forgotten something very important that I'd decided four years ago. And that is I don't give a damn about what anyone else thinks. I'm going to live my life the way I want to live it and with the person I want to live it with. I guess seeing you here caught me off guard, and I was distracted by the trappings of youth, so to speak." She indicated the room by looking around once again. His eyes followed hers, and he grinned and shrugged at the scene. It did look like the home of some college boys, but what she didn't know was that the majority of the mess was Matt's stuff. He'd tell her that later. He looked back at Julia as she continued. "I'm so sorry, Austin. I'm so sorry I freaked out, that I hurt you."

He gathered her to him and held on as tight as he could without hurting her. They stood that way as the seconds ticked by and neither one cared. Finally, she pulled back.

"I need some air, sweetie," she grinned. "You realize that you've made me fall just a bit more in love with you."

"Yeah, I planned the whole thing. I'm good that way," and they both laughed. *She used the word love first. Is this love? It is for me, and now I know that it is for her, too.* Austin felt himself floating on a high that he hoped he'd never lose. He pulled her close again and leaned down to seal their decision with a kiss.

It was this scene that Matt walked in on. They both heard the door and pulled apart at the same time Matt came through it. He looked up, startled, but recovered enough to shoot Julia his best bad-boy grin and come toward her.

"Well, hello, beautiful," he began. "I can see why my bastard roommate has been hiding you. Where have you been all my life?" Matt was in his Dick's Sporting Goods shirt and khaki cargo shorts. Julia looked him up and down, working her way from the short blond hair, blue eyes, work clothes, and down to his tennis shoes. Something about him made her think that this was most definitely the owner of the game console.

Julia looked back at his face and laughed. She extended her hand. "God, please don't tell me that cliché crap works. Julia, Julia Whitman. When I give you permission, you may call me Jules. And you are..."

Matt was surprised at the woman in front of him. She was different from their usual dates, and while she was incredibly beautiful and sexy, Matt wondered what she was doing with his buddy. *Who knew AJ had it in him?* He thought, as he felt her firm handshake, covered her hand with his other, and heard himself say, "Matt. Matt Hollinger. And just so you know. I'd follow you anywhere, Princess." He grinned even bigger when Julia laughed. *I don't know where he found her, but I want one, too,* Matt thought.

"That's enough." Austin disentangled the two and pulled Julia back possessively. "Matt, meet my girlfriend, Julia. Jules, this is my brother from another mother, the pain in my ass, the sloppiest man alive, the biggest man-whore in the greater Phoenix area, the..."

"Hey, man, leave some mystery, leave some mystery," Matt interrupted him. He turned back to Julia. "Believe only half of what he tells you, sweetheart. And of that half, only a tenth is truth. He thinks he knows me, but he's fooling himself. Now, you..."

"Give it a rest, man. I didn't bring her over here for you to practice your pitiful pick-up game on. I just wanted to drop off a little something we brought you. From Miner's Camp. And it's..."

"Hot damn! Cake! I've got supper! Whoot Whoot!" Julia forgotten, Matt moved around them to the refrigerator where he found the white box sitting front and center. He opened the lid, took a deep breath, and moaned loudly. He grabbed a big chunk with his fingers and started eating. "Oh, my god, this is a little slice of heaven." Intent on the cake in his hands, he moved around them to find the sofa where he plopped down and stretched his legs out the length of it. He focused on his cake a few more seconds before he looked up at the two watching him.

"Play your cards right, angel," he said around the chunk of cake in his mouth, "and I'll let you lick my fingers...yummy..." He waggled his eyebrows up and down and offered her a wolfish grin, his teeth partially covered in chocolate.

"Tempted, but I'll pass," Julia laughed again. *He's like someone's little brother*, she thought.

"Come with me," Austin took her arm and led her into the short hallway. "I need to pick up a couple of things."

"Yeah, don't go into that den of iniquity you see on your right. My pal catches you in there, and I'm a dead man." Matt was referring to his room, and from the doorway, Julia could see that it was a disaster area.

"Like she could get through the door," Austin said over his shoulder. He didn't see his friend flip him off, but he felt it. Matt was predictable.

"And here we have my room," he said. "Functional, not fancy." She looked at the full-sized bed centered along the wall with a tiny table on the right side. On the wall to her left, she could see a window, no curtain but covered in an apartment-quality mini-blind. On the same wall as the door, she could see a tiny closet that jutted into the room, and along the right wall, a desk and chair with a dresser tucked into the corner. The walls held nothing but a calendar next to the desk, a poster depicting Tar Heels basketball players in action, and a shelf with one family photo of a man, woman, younger man, and Austin. It wasn't fancy, as he'd said, but it was neat. The bed was even made.

"Awww…you knew I was coming," Julia said as she sat on the bed to wait for him. She leaned back, propped up on her elbows, as she watched him.

He turned from the closet where he'd grabbed khaki shorts and a coral-colored shirt she recognized from the golf club. As he passed her on his way to the dresser, he looked over his shoulder to warn, "I wouldn't get too comfortable there unless you want Matt to hear things he really shouldn't."

Julia laughed and stretched her legs out provocatively. "Hmmmm…. now what could we make your pal Matt hear that he hasn't before."

"Your conversation, for one. Jesus, shut the damn door!" they heard the voice from the other room.

"Oops!" Julia laughed. "I forgot how thin apartment walls can be. I'll have to get used to that, won't I?"

If she only knew how happy it made him to hear her say that. Like they were a couple, and that she would be spending time with him in his space.

"Hey, sweetie, where's the bathroom? I know I'm taking a chance here, but I can't wait until I get home."

"Oh, it's in the hallway to your left." Austin made a disgusted face and started toward the door. "It shouldn't be too bad. Or at least it wasn't when I left it last. Want me to go in first and clean it up?"

"Oh, for heaven's sake, I'm a big girl. I've seen bad bathrooms before. Not a baby, you know." She left him standing in the middle of his room, holding his clothes. He shook his head and grabbed an old gym bag from behind the desk. She returned as he was zipping it up.

"Yep. I've seen worse," Julia said. She laughed at his expression and came over to kiss him on the lips and reach around to squeeze his ass.

"I heard that," came the voice again. "And I know what you just squeezed."

Julia laughed then and called back, "What do you have in there? Surveillance equipment?" To Austin, "Let's get out of here before Junior there on the sofa learns something new."

As she walked past Matt, she looked at him still stretched out on the sofa. Julia leaned over the sofa and peered into his face. Matt stopped breathing and tried to not look down at her cleavage. He didn't want Austin to rearrange his face. Anyway, he was too taken by the blue eyes peering at him. He could smell her perfume as soon as he could take a breath, and he almost moaned.

"Not yet, but I'm guessing he'll be in a chocolate coma in about ten minutes," she said to Austin. To Matt, "Hey, Junior, you've got brown drool running down your chin. Clean up a little more for me next time, will you?" With a grin in Matt's direction and a wink, she slowly sauntered to the door and let herself out.

Matt grabbed his chest in a mock heart attack and looked at Austin. "I think I'm in love. Seriously, that is the hottest female I have ever met in my life. Look at me. I can't even curse. She's left me curseless. Is it hot in here? I'm sweating."

Austin tossed the kitchen towel at his friend. "Wipe the drool, *Junior.* You'll see me when you see me." With that, he followed Julia out the door. Matt could hear them laughing as they passed the front window, and he knew they were laughing at his expense. He couldn't care less. *That is one hell of a woman*, he thought. *Thank god. I can curse again.* He turned his attention back to his cake and rooted around in the sofa cushions for the television remote.

"Success," he said before settling in to find a ball game. *Man,* he thought, *AJ really outran his coverage on this one. Damn!*

Chapter 13

—————

LIFE SETTLED INTO A ROUTINE the next few weeks, more or less, with both Austin and Julia busy. At the end of the day, they made time to spend with one another. Sundays would find them in bed until noon before making use of the pool. Most nights were spent at Julia's simply because the bed was bigger, but others found Austin at home studying. He told Julia he couldn't get much done when he was at her place, and she knew that to be true. She tried to keep things quiet so that he could concentrate, but he assured her that it wasn't noise that distracted him. He was there one evening, and even though Julia stayed across the room and read a book, she could feel Austin's eyes on her. When she looked up, she saw him looking at her legs. Or at her face. After the third or fourth time, she called him on it.

"Austin, you have finals tomorrow. You need to concentrate."

"I am concentrating. Just not on what I should, I guess." He shot his most charming grin in her direction, and she thought, *God, he's killing me.* "I would probably do better if I moved over there with you."

On that note, she gathered his stuff for him and practically pushed him out the door, laughing at the stricken look on his face.

"Go home. Kick Matt out. Study. Learn something. I'll be here." She took the sting from her words by grinning at him and sealed her promise with a kiss. She shook her head as she watched him lumber down the stairs, pouting as he went. Lauren was coming in as he was leaving.

"What's up your butt, Ace? Jules finally kicking you to the curb?"

"Shut up, Lauren," Julia yelled from above. "He can't study here. Now, be good and make sure he makes it out the door."

Lauren laughed and slapped Austin on the behind as he walked past her. He stopped to give her a don't-do-that-again look before he grinned and yelled up the stairs.

"Julia, Lauren touched my butt. And she liked it!" To Lauren he winked and said, "You are in so much trouble now…" They were both laughing as the door closed behind him.

"Don't touch his butt. Or any other body part for that matter." Julia grinned at her roommate as she reached the top of the stairs.

Lauren laughed. "Oh, chill. He didn't like it."

"He better not," Julia was settling into her favorite chair, her chaise, when her phone rang.

"I'll bet it's your puppy," Lauren said, "begging to be let back in." Julia gave her a look and rolled her eyes before picking up her phone. "Sharon Burns" she saw on the caller ID.

"Sharon! I've missed you! How's life in Flagstaff? Are you and John settled into the simple life?"

"Julia…" Sharon was using her sing-song voice, which never boded well. "Why do I have to hear about your bringing a man to my pool from John?"

"What?!" Julia exclaimed. "Yeah, I've been going out there, but how would John know? Did I miss him somehow? I don't always go into the big house, so I suppose I could have, but why didn't he just come out and say hi or something?"

"John hasn't been there, sweetheart, his security camera has," Sharon was back to her normal voice. "Now, I couldn't see much on the video, but the man who's been out there with you looks a lot like that golf pro or whatever that you met at the club. And if it is, why did you not tell me?"

"Ahhh…I forgot about the outside cameras. There isn't one in the pool area, is there?" Sharon could hear the worry and just a touch of embarrassment in her friend's voice.

"Yes, dear, but it only monitors the gate that leads to the grounds. No, I watched the footage from the gate and driveway cameras. And you haven't answered my question yet. Who is he?"

"You haven't given me a chance," Julia laughed. "Yes, that is the man from the golf club, and no, he isn't a golf pro. He works with the groundskeeper. You know when we started seeing each other, obviously, from the date on the recording, so you know that we've been together about six weeks."

"And?" Julia settled in to give her friend all the details because she knew how relentless Sharon could be.

Julia gave the basics—name, occupation, background—all but his age. She would rather hash that out when they saw each other.

"Tell me slower. I'm writing all this down. You've left out something here. You said he's taking college classes. I saw him that day, Julia, and my guess is that this isn't some *I always wanted to study this in my spare time* college student. Are you just playing around here? You can't be serious yet because you haven't had time," Sharon seemed to be thinking out loud at this point, which she did often. "Well, fill in the blanks."

"Ok, yes, he's in college, and yes, he's much younger than I am. Sharon, I'd really rather talk about this when I see you next. There's so much more to share, and I'd just rather wait until I see you in person, okay?" Julia was hopeful.

"*No*, it's not okay, but I suppose I'll have to drive down tomorrow and take you to dinner."

Julia already had plans with Austin, but then she always planned with him in mind. She wasn't set on putting the two together yet, at least not before she could explain their relationship to Sharon.

"Julia…" the sing-song voice was back. "You are hesitating way too long. Will you, or will you not have dinner with me tomorrow? It's a simple question, dear."

"Of course, I'd love to. Will you be at the house, or do you want to meet someplace?"

"Meet me at Vista Joya around seven, dear, and come alone." Julia laughed at that. Sharon could come across as a mean bitch, but those who knew her saw a different side. Especially those she loved, and she loved Julia like a daughter.

"I'll see you then. And get us one of those awesome tables with a view. That's my favorite part of the restaurant," Julia said.

"Always. Adios, girlie," and with that her friend was gone.

"Want me to tag along?" Lauren had been listening to Julia's side of the conversation.

"No, she said to come alone," Julia smiled. Leave it to Lauren to try to have her back even when it wasn't necessary.

"Hey, Jules, you're doing okay, you know. For some reason, this thing with Austin, it's working. Hell, I don't know why, but it does. Once Sharon knows that, she'll be in your corner, too."

"God, I don't think I need a *corner*, but thanks for the thought," Julia looked at her friend. The cynical, wise-cracking Lauren's face had softened, and she gave Julia a small smile.

"People can be stupid, you know, and they can say some nasty things about the older woman/younger man thing. But we can handle them, can't we?" Lauren replied.

"Handling people. We have before, we will now, and we will in the future," Julia laughed.

"Yep." Lauren's face brightened as she had an idea. "Hey, we have an evening of just the two of us. Let's put on our pj's, pop some popcorn, open a bottle of wine, and watch a movie! We haven't done that in ages!"

"Sounds perfect," Julia grinned at her friend. "I'm feeling a Bradley Cooper night, how about you?"

"Well, I was thinking more along the line of *How Stella Got Her Groove Back*, but I suppose *Silver Linings Playbook* will work, too." Julia was already walking toward her room, but Lauren heard her laugh and looked up in time to see Julia's middle finger in the air.

The Vista Joya was part of the Desert View Resort and Club, nestled between the third and fourth peak of the Four Peaks Mountain Range in the Sonoran Desert. It catered to the golf crowd, but Julia knew that Sharon loved it for the views and her husband's connections. One of John's best friends had help start the resort by providing the financial backing, and Julia had attended weddings and private parties there. She looked forward to the restaurant more for the spectacular views than for the food, although that was world class, too. It was a thirty-minute drive from her apartment, and she left early to allow for traffic on McDowell and the 101 Loop. She pulled up to the door a few minutes early, and a valet immediately approached to help her out of the car. Julia tipped him generously, winked, and told him to take good care of her baby. The young man was flustered for half a second before he smiled largely and wished her a "lovely evening."

Julia was still smiling as she entered the foyer and approached the maitre-d.

"Good evening, madam, how may I help you?"

"Sharon Burns," Julia replied, knowing her friend's name was the only requirement. They all knew Sharon.

"But of course, right this way." Julia followed him across the wooden floor and past several tables on their way to a prime seat next to the wall of windows. Julia looked out over the mountains and Sonoran Desert that was spread before her. "Thank you," she said, as the man pulled out her chair.

"Here you are," Sharon looked up from her martini. "And I might add that you look fantastic! Girl, I don't know what you're doing or what you're taking, but I want some."

Julia laughed. "Same old, same old. You look good yourself. So smart to escape to the mountains this time of year, you know?" She looked at her friend and smiled. Sharon really was something and neither acted nor looked anything like her age of sixty-five. No one would ever call her beautiful, but she was classy. Her short dark hair, cut in an easy pageboy with bangs combed over to one side, framed her face perfectly. She was petite and could eat most men under the table without gaining an ounce. She didn't exercise except for an occasional golf game, which was as much social as it was anything else. She only played with John when she had to, usually business-related because, according to Sharon, "Men are never bigger assholes than when they are competing in golf." When her friends would brag about their personal trainers, their Bikram yoga ("One hour in hell" as Sharon called it), or their tennis lessons, she liked to quote Joan Rivers—"If God wanted me to bend over, He would have put diamonds on the floor." She was a devout Catholic when it suited her, usually on holidays and always at weddings, funerals, and births. When she loved someone, she loved them unconditionally and fiercely. Julia, she loved.

Sharon looked around the dining room before Julia could settle into her chair. "I'm not happy." She motioned for the maitre-d, who seemed to be watching her for this moment. They did know her habits.

"I'm not happy," she repeated. "I want to be outside. Will you please move us?" As if there would be any question that her request would not be immediately met, Sharon was already gathering her purse and getting up before the man could pull her chair out for her. Julia had been through this before. She smiled sympathetically as the man gathered their menus and Sharon's drink before leading them through the double doors to the balcony and the tables situated beside its edge. A glass barrier allowed a clear view of the surrounding desert. The temperature was still very warm, but above the tables, misters released moisture that was low enough to cool the air but high enough to not soak those below. With the sun almost down, it would soon be very pleasant. Most of the tables were occupied, but the maitre-d had one ready. Removing the "Reserved" sign, he pulled out chairs for them both and soon had their table in order. The women settled in. Sharon looked around at the view, slipped the man something Julia knew was a rather large bill, and smiled. "Now, I'm happy."

Julia laughed as the maitre-d tilted his head down in Sharon's direction in a thank-you nod, discreetly pocketed the cash, and asked if he could offer drinks. Sharon ordered a fresh martini and Julia opted for wine.

"You realize this is why I love dining with you. You can be such a pretentious bitch, but you pay people so well that they never spit in your food and love you anyway."

"Oh, sweetie, it's all part of my stimulating the economy. That, and I like things the way I like them, and I have the money to do it. As for spitting in my food, I doubt anyone would have those kinds of balls," Sharon said wryly before softening her words with a grin. Her dark eyes then narrowed on Julia's face, and Julia settled herself in for the inquisition.

"Julia, do not look at me like that. Like I'm going to ground you for skipping the prom to party in a private suite at the Hilton." She paused and looked out over the mountains. "Johnny did that, you know. Turd. His dad had to pick him up at three in the morning after the manager called all in a snit. Other guests complained about the noise, underage drinking, yada, yada, yada. Anyway," she shook off the memory and fastened her eyes on Julia once again. "I'm not your mother, I am your friend. Tell me about this boy. Man. Whatever."

A waiter interrupted as he brought their drinks, and Julia had a bit more time to decide how to start. He looked at Sharon in a silent question if they wanted to order yet, and she waved him off with the hand. "Just drinks for now, but come back in a few to check on us, okay?" As if he wouldn't. *Word travels fast on good tippers*, Julia thought.

They each took a sip before Sharon prodded, "Well?"

"Well…" Julia began. As she talked about Austin, Sharon could see that Julia's blue eyes would soften or light up, depending on the story. She could tell that her friend was having a wonderful time with this man and enjoying life like Sharon hadn't seen before. Julia was always happy, easy to laugh, and sweet as could be with a tough inner quality that had drawn Sharon to her and her snarky comments. However, when talking about Austin, Julia was animated in a way Sharon hadn't seen. Soon, she wound down and Sharon spoke for the first time.

"I like him. I haven't met him, but I like him," was her brief statement.

"I'd like you to meet him. I know he's young, Sharon, and that when people find out, they'll think we're crazy, but he's got a good head on his shoulders and he knows what he wants in life. And he's not afraid to work for it. Did I tell you about his parents…" Julia was off again.

It was a drink later before the subject changed to Julia's newest design assignments, Sharon's latest trip plans, and the other people in their lives. They ordered dinner, and Julia saw the newest pictures of the grandson and Johnny, and listened to Sharon's stories of their latest trip to New York and their visit. Sharon and John flew out whenever he could get away, and their stay in the city was not limited to just family. Sharon loved Broadway shows, fine restaurants, and eating as much New York cheesecake as possible. Julia was looking at photos on her friend's phone and exclaiming over the latest images when their food arrived. They ate while never missing a beat in their conversation. Soon the food was gone, and they were winding down.

"Oh, look at the time!" Julia exclaimed. "I have loved every minute of this, you know, but I need to go."

"Date with the hottie?" Sharon teased. "Oh, don't deny it. Just enjoy yourself. For me." She smiled at Julia. "We'll be back for good around the first of September, but before then, why don't you bring Austin to Flagstaff? We always have the August *Thank God It's Over* summer bash around the fifteenth. I'll even put you up in a cabin. John's buddy Jerry owns several."

Julia laughed. "John has a buddy pretty much everywhere who owns whatever we seem to want, doesn't he?"

Sharon laughed with her. "Duh. It's what rich men do. Make money and collect friends."

Julia came around the table to lean down and kiss her friend good-bye. "Drive safely, sweetie. No more martinis until you get home. Deal?"

Sharon patted the arm Julia had laid across her shoulders. No one called her sweetie except Julia. "Deal. And kitten? I've never seen you happier."

"It's puma, and thanks," Julia smiled and turned to leave.

Sharon laughed at her retreating back and motioned for the waiter, who hovered not far from the table.

"Another drink, ma'am?"

"No, just water, please. And the check." The man nodded in acquiescence. Sharon stared out over the now dark desert and took a deep breath of desert air.

"Life is good," she said to herself.

Julia had no sooner arrived home when her phone dinged. She smiled as she looked down at a message from Austin. "I'm lonely. I had to eat Chinese with Matt. I miss you."

She laughed and typed, "You know where I am," She hit send and smiled at his image on her phone screen.

Five seconds later she read, "Don't move" and laughed again. They texted one another often during the day, but it was hit-and-miss on whether they'd get the chance to read them. He was usually out manning equipment and dodging errant golf balls, and she was usually with clients or carpenters or suppliers and couldn't divide her attention. Julia had learned as part of her communication on the job, but she wasn't big on the whole texting thing. Being with Austin had forced her to get with the program, as Lauren liked to call it. She still didn't do all the abbreviations. When she sent and received texts in her line of work, abbreviations led to misunderstandings, which led to bad things happening on a job. *Plus*, she thought, *what forty-year-old uses abbreviations.*

85

Julia saw a different message from Lauren, "Out. See you when I see you." She shook her head and turned into her bedroom to change clothes. It had been hotter than usual on the restaurant balcony, and Julia felt sweaty. Austin had the code to the security gate and a key now, so she wasn't worried about answering the door. She jumped into the shower and finished up in record time before she dressed in shorts and t-shirt. She heard him come in as she was running a brush through her hair.

She smiled at his off-key singing. The song "867-5309/Jenny" echoed off the stairway walls in Austin's baritone voice.

"God, I HATE that song! Why can't your code be 1234 or anything besides 8675! Now I'll have that earworm for the next hour."

"Because I can remember it that way, and I like that song—1981 Tommy Tutone. Hey, that was music back in *my* day, remember?" She laughed at his expression and kissed him on the cheek.

"Oh, no, woman, you can do better than that," and Austin pulled her closer for a long, slow kiss. Finishing, he leaned back, his green eyes shining, and said, "Now, that's much better."

Julia wrapped her arms around his waist and pulled him close. They stood there for a few moments.

"Hmmm...you feel so good. I love the way you smell, did you know that? You smell like sunshine," she pulled back to look up at him.

"And you smell like you just got out of the shower. You couldn't wait for me?" he teased.

"No, Sharon had to sit outside where it was a bit too warm and I was sweaty. And stinky. And gross."

Austin laughed at her. "Babe, you have never been stinky and gross. Now as for sweaty, I kinda like that..." He raised one eyebrow and gave her a lecherous grin.

"Perve," she laughed and led him into the living room.

"Guilty. Although, actually *you're* the perve, cradle robber. Here you go texting me to come over and make mad, passionate love to you. What can I do but keep you busy so you'll not corrupt other young men out there." He was in one of those moods, and Julia enjoyed it. She decided to play with him a bit, too.

"I know, I know...and they're everywhere! I have to beat them off with a stick, especially when I drive by the golf course. I literally pull out my putter and fend them off." She sighed. "So many potential lovers in the world, lots of older men, but I'm stuck with a youngster. And for the record, *you* texted *me* first," she grinned. She knew Austin would quit teasing as soon as she mentioned other men. That seemed to be a sore spot with him, and he didn't disappoint this time.

"Yeah, whatever. How did dinner go?' he asked, changing the subject. "You said it was hot, but you didn't say where you were going or anything about it. How's your buddy Sharon?"

"She's good. Asking about you and taking notes. If some private investigator comes around, it's just someone John sends." Julia laughed at his stricken look. "Don't worry, Ace, I'm joking. Although with Sharon I never know. John gives her pretty much whatever she wants, and I'm sure he has an investigator on speed dial if he needs someone." He still looked worried. "I'm joking..."

"And what did she have to say about me? About us?" Julia knew Austin was curious at how he would be received by her friends. She had yet to bring him around "the girls" but she hadn't had a good opportunity. He knew that Julia was close to Sharon and her husband John, and he hoped that they wouldn't give her grief for proverbially robbing the cradle.

"Well, after I explained that you are really just a student that I'm tutoring at the request of your mother, she was okay with it all." He looked down at her. "Joking again. Geez, lighten up, Austin. It's all good."

By this time, they had situated themselves on her chaise, Austin on the bottom and Julia resting half on him and half on the chair, her leg and arm thrown over him. She was nestled in the crook of his arm. She lifted her head to eye level before she spoke.

"She likes you, okay? Sharon likes anyone I like, and she knows that you make me happy. Satisfied?"

Austin knew that she was probably leaving out a lot, but if she said all was okay, then he believed her.

"By the way," she started, settling back down against him, "we've been invited to Flagstaff, August 15, for an end-of-summer party at their mountain place. I know it's around your birthday, but would you want to go? I didn't commit until I talked to you. She even offered a cabin just for us." At this last, Julia looked up and grinned.

"Shit. I always go home for my birthday, and my mom's been on my case. 'You never call. You never write. You never come home anymore,'" he mimicked in a high, annoying voice. He thought for a couple of minutes before looking back down at her. "Accept the invite. I'll call the folks and tell them something's come up out here and I'll see them at Thanksgiving."

"Are you sure? I don't want to be the reason you skip out on your parents. It isn't as if they're going to love me at first sight, here. Antagonizing your mom isn't at the top of my to-do list."

"Don't worry about it. She'll just have to deal. She should be used to it by now, especially with me." He chuckled and kissed the top of her head. They laid there in comfortable silence then, in their own thoughts.

Julia worried that her coming between Austin and his family could cause the couple problems down the road. She couldn't care less about hers, except for her dad, but he accepted anything his baby chose to do. She knew Austin wasn't in that place yet. He'd shown a lot of independence by going against his parents and moving to Arizona to pursue his own career, but at age twenty-four, Julia knew that family opinion still mattered. *Look what it did for me. Married to a man who met the criteria for everyone but me. Now I'm divorced. Not on good terms with my mother.* Her thoughts weren't pleasant.

Austin was working out his own thoughts, but family wasn't part of them. *What will these older, wealthy people think of one of their own slumming with a college kid? Julia may not look or act forty, but she is.* A majority of her friends were that old or older. He'd be in the middle of a bunch of rich men who already had it made, surrounded by rich women who would look at him as a kid to wait on them or a toy to play with. He'd seen it at the golf club. Austin knew he'd be okay, but would Julia? For all her independence, she still had to do business with these people. She still depended on their recommendations for Touch of Jules. He hadn't gotten to the what-do-you-wear-to-these-things point, but when he did, he mentally took inventory of his closet. He couldn't think of one single thing that would work at a party like this. *Hell,* he thought. *I really don't even know what anyone wears to these things. I'll have to ask her to help me here. Maybe even go shopping, heaven help me.* That was a fresh hell he quickly put out of his mind.

She looked up. "What'cha thinkin'?" she asked.

He chuckled and said, "You wouldn't believe me anyway."

"Try me."

"Okay, I was wondering what to wear to Burns' party."

Julia burst out laughing and he found himself joining in. She finally wiped a hand across her eyes and looked up at him.

"I adore you," she said. "You are so damn cute."

"So I've been told." He sobered then and looked at her seriously. "Jules, we're okay, aren't we? I mean, what we do, the time we spend together, it's okay with you, right? You don't miss hanging out with your other friends, and I wouldn't mind you doing that, you know. I mean," he struggled to put it right, "you already had a lifestyle here, and I don't want you changing anything for me."

She frowned at him, again eye level, and studied his face for a few seconds.

"Sweetie, where is that coming from? I'm good with us, with our life. Aren't you? Is there something you want to talk about?" She rested her hand on his chest and with her chin resting on her hand, she waited.

He paused and tried to think of how to put it. "I want to go to stuff like this with you. Hell, someday I hope I'll be rubbing elbows with people like that and making business deals with my own company. But I'm not yet. Hell, I'm a twenty-three-year-old kid to them." He had been staring up at the ceiling, but he looked down at her before continuing. "Will my being with you cause you any problems? With Touch of Jules? I want to go with you, meet John and Sharon, spend a weekend at a cabin retreat, but is it what's best for you? I couldn't stand it if someone tried to make you out as some shallow older woman just messing around with some kid."

Julia felt her heart swell as she took in what he was saying. He was worried about her and her reputation, but she wouldn't let him be.

"Austin, at the end of the day, people are people. Yes, they're older than you, wealthy, and spoiled, but most of them are also nice and decent. Plus, they're more John and Sharon's friends than mine. As for your being with me. Let's see…" She held up a hand and extended a finger as she counted. "Jerry Brinkley will be there with his twenty-five-year-old wife who he married when she was twenty-two. Oh, and she'll drag their one-year-old with them, too. Jerry is sixty. And there's Toby Middleton who's fifteen years older than the third Mrs. Middleton, who he left the second Mrs. Middleton for only three years ago. And then there's…"

"Stop. I get the picture. But are there any sixty-something females with twenty-something husbands?"

Julia laughed. "God, no! Twenty-something men don't sleep with six-ty-something women. At least I've never seen it. Well, Cher is an exception, I think, but she doesn't count because her body is probably only thirty. At least the body parts she's replaced are thirty."

Julia laughed again, but Austin shook his head. "Laugh, Julia, but I don't want anyone judging you, you know? I don't want them to look down on you or laugh at your expense. Most of all, I don't want your relationship with me to harm your business."

She sobered up when she saw how serious he was about this. "Austin, you need to know something. I. Don't. Care. I don't! Yes, I do business with a few of them, but my reputation is already built. As for them laugh-ing at me? Honey, that I really don't care about!" She put a hand along the side of his face to emphasize what she was saying. "Austin, the men will want to BE you, and the women will want to take my place." She grinned at him. "Besides, no one would dare say anything about Sharon's girl. Wait, you'll see. Now, let's quit making a big damn deal out of this thing. Do you want to go, or not? I'm with you either way." She'd moved her hand to trace a path down his jaw and along his chin, where she gently rubbed a finger over the late-day stubble.

Austin thought for a couple of minutes before he looked down and smiled. "I'm in. We have to make a public appearance some day, and this is as good a time as any. Maybe we'll get lucky and someone will make a remark around Sharon. That could be fun," he joked. "I can't wait to officially meet her."

"I can't wait for that, either. Hey, can you get away a day early? We'll go on up and enjoy a day of just the four of us before the crowd comes on Saturday."

"Let me check the schedule at work. Usually that won't be a problem this time of year. Things are slow in August. Go ahead and plan on it and I'll tell you if I can't."

"Love it! I'll call Sharon tomorrow."

They lay there a while longer before both were ready for bed. Austin decided that if Julia didn't worry, then neither would he. They both slept like babies.

Chapter 14

Austin came strolling into the shop, waving a piece of paper in front of him.

"What's up, buttercup?" Lauren asked, taking in the grin on his face.

"Jules around?" he asked. "I got something to show her."

"Yeah, she's in the storeroom. Go on back." She nodded her head in the direction of the back room. "Wait. What is it?"

"Tell you later. She needs to be first."

Lauren rolled her eyes and dismissed him by looking back at her papers. *He's such a kid*, she thought. She didn't really believe it, but she liked the sound of it.

Julia had her back to the door, the cord from earbuds draping down from her ears. She was singing to The Eagles. He recognized the song as "Life in the Fast Lane," one of her favorites. He wanted to stand there and listen to the slightly off-key rendition, but this couldn't wait. He snuck up behind her and wrapped his arms around her middle, drawing her back toward him.

"Hmmmm…nice. I hope my boyfriend doesn't catch us," she joked.

She reached up, pulled the earbuds out and leaned back into him, tucking her head under his chin.

"You smell almost as nice as he does, but I think you might be a bit stronger, and sexier." She rubbed his arms.

"I'll bet you say that to all the delivery guys." He turned her around.

She kissed him lightly before asking, "What brings you here this time of day? Not that I'm complaining or anything. Did you get fired?"

"Something like that." He handed her the paper. She read through it quickly before she looked up and smiled.

"Austin, you got it! You got the internship at Superstition!"

He picked her up and swung her around, knocking over a couple of boxes in the process. Neither of them cared.

"I am so happy for you!"

"I know, I'm happy for me, too. I know that it's still work, but it's where I think I need to be. Jules, I can learn so much from the guys there. I'll meet so many people. Make contacts. Did you know that the firm that handles all the major golf courses here in the valley, as well as all the major building projects, has one of their guys on site at that course? If I can make friends with him, work with him, let him get to know me, maybe he'll put in a good word for me there."

She shared his excitement. Austin was usually reserved when it came to emotions, at least public displays of emotion, but this was big for him.

"What the hell are you two doing back here? Destroying the inventory? What's up?" Lauren had waited as long as she could before her innate nosiness led her to the storeroom. Austin turned to grin at the newcomer.

"Austin starts at Superstition Mountain Golf Club and Resort the first of September," Julia filled her in.

"Oh, I thought someone like won a lottery or something." Julia frowned over Austin's shoulder. Lauren looked at Austin and gave him her biggest smile. "Way to go, Ace. You'll be great."

"Thanks, Lauren," Austin grinned. "I know how hard that was for you to say." He laughed and turned back to Julia.

"Celebrate! Let's go! Lauren, you, too. A buddy of mine works at the Wagon Wheel Chop House in Glendale. I know that's on the other side of the valley, but we'll get cheap drinks, most of them free, and good food. You in?"

Julia nodded her *yes* and both of them looked at Lauren.

"Wagon Wheel Chop House…Free drinks…Free drinks, huh? I'm in!" She smiled at the two, turned to leave, and said over her shoulder, "I'll get the details from Jules."

"Austin, this will be fun. Hey, is Matt coming?"

"But of course. Oh…Matt…Lauren…they've not met yet, have they?"

"No," Julia mused, "but I think it's past time they did. You realize that this could be a lot of fun, don't you?"

"I suppose fun is one way to look at it. Anyway, I've got to run. Pick you up at 6:30?"

"Sure. Do you want me to drive?"

"Naw, we'll take Matt's Jeep. It has more room. The top stays off all the time, so you might want to bring something to tie your hair back or a hat. The Jeep is different from the car. Air moves around in strange ways." He laughed.

He gave her a long kiss before ending with a short kiss on her nose, and he was gone.

This, Julia thought, *is going to be interesting.*

"God, a Jeep? Seriously, Jules? You know what my hair does in all that wind. And a roommate." She followed that with an eye roll. Lauren was in a whiny mood, and Julia was tired of it.

"Lauren, stop. Just. Stop. This night isn't about you, it's about Austin. We are celebrating Austin's news. We are going to be HAPPY for him. You are going to smile. You are going to be nice. You are NOT going to make this all about you. And you aren't going to flirt with his roommate."

Lauren looked at Julia's face and knew she was out of line. "Sorry, Jules, really I am. I promise that I will make this night about Austin. I promise that I will be happy. I will smile. I will be nice. No promises on the flirting. You know that's just part of who I am, Jules. I can't help it. Men bring it out in me. Although I usually don't flirt with boys, and from your description so far, he's a boy. Eww."

Julia studied her friend for a few seconds more. "I'm not shitting you, Lauren." Her friend knew that when Julia used this tone, Lauren was on thin ice.

Letting out a long breath, Lauren looked at Julia and assured her, "I know! I'll be good. Geez, Mom, give it a rest," and rolled her eyes again much like she had done when she was sixteen.

The doorbell rang, but before Julia could get to the stairs, she heard Austin let himself in and another masculine voice.

"Be nice!" Julia hissed at Lauren, as her friend pasted a big smile on her face.

"Hey, beautiful," Austin gave Julia a quick kiss before she got a look at Matt. Julia noted that he looked good tonight. He'd worn the usual uniform, as she called it, of cargo shorts, t-shirt, and sandals, but he'd shaved and looked like he'd made an effort. Julia wondered how much brow-beating Austin had done to accomplish that.

"Hey, yourself. Hi, Matt," Julia looked past Austin to grin in his direction. "Matt, I want you to meet your counterpart, my roommate Lauren Reynolds. She's my roommate, sister, and boil on my butt. Lauren, this is Matt Hollinger."

Julia saw Matt take one look at her roommate's beautiful face and look back at Austin, his eyes going wide. *He didn't warn him*, Julia thought. *Austin, you should have told him that she's every man's dream, but Lauren will eat him alive.*

Lauren came forward then, extended her hand toward Matt, and purred, "Well, hello, handsome. Julia never told me Austin has such a yummy roomy." She turned in Austin's direction. "Shame on you."

For once, Matt was speechless. He took the extended hand, and while Lauren's attention was turned to Austin, Julia noted that he gave Lauren the quick once-over. She saw what he saw—a tall, leggy blonde in white shorts, slender with generous curves that filled out her black tank top, the ever-present cleavage, and luminous brown eyes. *Oh*, Julia thought, *is he ever in trouble.*

"Lauren," Matt managed to say, "Nice to meet you." The cockiness was gone and in its place was a twenty-three-year-old boy who was entranced by a forty-year-old woman.

Lauren picked up her bag, tucked an arm under Matt's, slipped on her sunglasses, and said to the room, "Ready to roll?"

Those two moved ahead down the stairs, as Julia grabbed her own bag and sunglasses.

"Austin," she hissed. "You didn't warn him!"

"I tried, Jules, honest, I tried, but you know how cocky his is. He just kept saying, 'Dude, ain't a woman *out* there that ol' Matt can't handle.' And he wouldn't listen. He told me to just worry about you and let him worry about the roommate."

Julia sighed. "Here we go." She rolled her eyes at Austin. It had the potential to be a long night.

They caught up with Matt and Lauren in the driveway.

"I call shotgun," Lauren said, as Matt started to help her into the front seat of the Jeep. His eyes didn't seem to know where to go—her cleavage or her legs, her legs or her cleavage.

"No," Austin said. "I'm driving and you two get in the back."

"Good call," Julia whispered. "We'd never make it with Matt driving. He can't take his eyes off her. And look at Lauren. She eats that shit up."

The Jeep was a white, four-door, four-by-four, and they all settled in as Austin pulled out of the drive. Julia had worn her hair in the requisite pony tail, and she looked back to see Lauren pulling her hair up, too. She was taking her time as she pulled her blond hair off her neck. Matt watched every move as Lauren knew he was. Julia rolled her eyes at the hot mess in the back seat and smiled at Austin. They were soon on the Loop, and at seventy miles per hour, no one could talk over the highway noise. Julia took the opportunity to look at Austin. He'd worn his ball cap, and his blond hair was curling along his neck. His Oakley sunglasses hid his eyes, and when he turned to smile at her, all she could see were sunglasses and white teeth. He'd worn bright green this evening and dark grey shorts. Once again, all Julia could think was *He's so pretty. And he's mine.* The last made her stomach jump just a little.

The trip didn't take that long and soon they were exiting onto Glendale Avenue and turning into Westgate Entertainment District, home of the Arizona Coyotes, Arizona Cardinals, a movie theater, outlet mall, shops, and several restaurants and bars. Austin drove around to the far side and parked in the lot. The four got out and headed toward the building with a wagon and fake horses fastened high up on the side, a split rail fence along the sidewalk, outdoor tables and a barn door that served as the entrance. A waitress stopped them at the end of the fence and Austin gave her his name. She gave him an appreciative once-over and turned to lead them into the building. The waitress's rear swaying in her Daisy Duke shorts didn't seem to faze Austin, and Julia smiled at the girl's attempt at sexy. *Perhaps,* Julia thought, *heels instead of cowboy boots and clothes that leave a little more to the imagination might serve her better.* Looking around, Julia decided that this was the style, and that it looked best on twenty-year-olds than on some of the older women she spied at the bar. They were trying to pull off the same look and were failing miserably.

The waitress led them to one of the tables that surrounded a mechanical bull arena. A sign on the wall said that for five dollars anyone over eighteen could take a chance and ride the bull. *I'll have to keep an eye on Lauren's drink consumption tonight,* Julia thought, *or she'll be all over that bull.*

That thought brought Julia's attention to her roommate. Lauren was holding onto Matt's arm, and he was starting to come around to himself. She could see the cockiness and mischievous look in his eye, and Julia knew that Lauren would have her hands full tonight.

Julia looked at Austin and grinned. "This looks like a fun place. I've never been here before, but it looks like some of the other western-themed bars in the valley."

"It is," Austin said. "I know that it's out of our way, but I come out here because of Joey. That's him under the big screen, behind the bar." About that time, Austin's friend looked in their direction and gave them the guy head nod and grin before he went back to drawing a draft into a large mug.

A waitress dressed like the rest came by to introduce herself. Brittany assured them that she'd be their server and listed the specials. Austin ordered an iced bucket of beer, six to a bucket, and the Monster Platter appetizer. He settled back into his chair and draped his arm across the back of Julia's. She leaned over against him and they grinned at one another.

"Matt, honey," Lauren began. "What do you think about those two?" She indicated Julia and Austin.

"Well, I don't know, but I'm thinking he may be a bit too old for her." Lauren laughed her signature husky laugh, and Matt looked back at her with his own grin. His, though, was more puppy dog than anything else.

"Lauren," Julia said, starting to get up. "Let's go do something with our hair. We're both a mess."

Julia knew this was one way to get her friend off to the side. Vanity was Lauren's weakness, and her hand flew to her hair as she rose to follow Julia. The bathrooms were behind the bar area, and Julia could feel Lauren working it as she walked across the room, around the bar seating, and down the back hallway. Julia rolled her eyes because she knew what Lauren was leaving in her wake.

They had just gotten the door closed when Julia rounded on her.

"Just what the hell are you doing? You've got that boy out there practically drooling," she demanded.

"I'm sure I don't know what you're talking about," Lauren started to take down her hair to run her fingers through the messy blond tresses.

"Oh, yes, you do. You've draped yourself all over him, and you've made sure that he can see down your shirt every time you two talk to one another." Julia's voice took on a pleading tone. She knew how her friend led men on, wrapped them around her finger, and left them without another thought. "Lauren, please, don't do this. Don't lead him around by the nose, sleep with him, and toss him aside."

"Good grief, Julia, you make me sound like some man-eater. And if he's a *boy*, then so is Austin."

"They're not the same, and you know it. Matt likes to play at flirting and being a ladies' man, but Lauren, he doesn't have experience with women. According to Austin, his playmates are *girls*. He's not used to being with a woman, and especially not a woman like you." Julia's eyes narrowed on Lauren, who had reapplied her lipstick and was working on her hair. "Be nice, but don't make a fool out of him. I have to look at him after tonight. He lives with Austin, and those two are as close as we are. If you hurt him, you'll hurt Austin. And if you hurt Austin, you'll hurt me."

Lauren stopped fiddling with her hair and looked at her friend. She thought, *Julia is right, but this could be so fun. And Matt is a cutie. Oh, not my usual type, which makes him even more attractive. As for that bad-boy attitude he tries to perfect, that is too cute.* Lauren had been attracted to the Matts of the world when she was in college. Without knowing what she was searching for, she had allowed herself to be used by more than one—none of them had taken the time to get to know the real person underneath the pretty face. Most were looking for an arm ornament and a good-time girl. She had not come out unscathed back then, and part of her play-hard attitude had been developed during that time. Men no longer left Lauren—Lauren left them. *Perhaps*, she thought, *I wouldn't have been hurt as much if someone like me had given a few lessons to the Matts in my world. And God knows the world is filled with them—too many of them. Hell, I'll be doing him a favor.* She looked at the concerned face of her friend.

"I think you and Austin are underestimating Matt," Lauren said. "I think he's tougher than you give him credit for being, and I think that he could learn a lot from me about what's acceptable and unacceptable in his treatment of women. I'll bet he sleeps with a different girl every chance he gets. Hell, I'll bet he doesn't even remember their names, does he?" Lauren's face had taken on a hard look as she was just getting started. "He uses them for the moment, and then he carelessly tosses them aside. No numbers because he has no intention of ever calling them again. He's a lousy lover because it's all about him and his getting off. He has no respect for women because for him they're a means to an end—once again his own pleasure—or they're simply for showing off. Someday, he'll decide that it's time to get married because that's what you do, so he'll pick out some poor young thing who doesn't see him for what he is, and they'll have the big fairy-tale wedding. She'll think that he's her happily-ever-after. When all he'll really do is buy her a big house in the suburbs, make her into the perfect hostess, have her pop out a couple of brats, and spend all of his time skirt-chasing at the office or at the country club. Maybe if someone like me slaps Matt down and shows him what it feels like to be used, I'll save that poor girl the heartache."

All the while Lauren was talking, Julia's face was getting whiter and whiter. By the time she'd finished, all Julia could think was *She's talking about me. I was the stupid young girl who wanted the happily-ever-after. I was married to the skirt-chaser.* At Julia's soft gasp, Lauren realized what she'd said. She looked at Julia's stricken face and felt a rush of guilt.

"Oh, Jules, I am so sorry," Lauren hugged her close. "I didn't mean Keith, I was talking about Matt. Oh, honey, don't look like that. Please. I'm sorry."

Julia pulled away first. She'd gotten the color back into her cheeks, and the spark was returning to her eyes.

"I know what Keith was, Lauren, and I know what I was, too. I dealt with that a long time ago, and I'm fine now. In fact, I'm better than ever. Austin has finally opened my eyes to the relationship I want and can have with a man. There's a part of me that sees Keith in Matt, too. But Matt isn't Keith. You don't know what he'll become someday. You really don't." Julia paused before shaking her head and continuing. "I won't tell you what to do. I'll just ask you to keep me out of it, okay? Keep Austin out of it. Please. He and I don't need the drama that seems to gravitate to you where men are concerned."

"I won't involve you at all, I promise," Lauren said. "Now, let's fix your mess of a hairdo before we go back out there. And Julia, I'll try not to hurt your Matt too badly. I'll just play with him a little." She grinned and offered her lipstick to Julia.

Julia knew that was the best she was going to get from her friend. That is was all Lauren could promise.

The two women finished up and returned to the table, Lauren once again drawing every male eye in the room to her direction. All except one male. Julia smiled at Austin, who watched her all the way across the room.

"I thought we were going to have to send little Brittany in to see if you'd been kidnapped," Austin said as he held Julia's chair for her.

Lauren stood looking down at Matt until he figured out what she wanted. He quickly pulled out her chair and held it for her while she took her time getting settled. She turned her head toward him and smiled a thank you.

"Beer?" Lauren asked Matt.

"Oh, yeah, sure," he said as he fumbled with getting a bottle out of the ice and setting it down in front of her. Julia almost laughed as she realized what her friend was doing. She was teaching Mr. Matt some manners. She cut her eyes at Austin and could see that he'd figured out the same thing. He looked back at her and they both laughed.

"Ignore them," Lauren purred at Matt, who had paused in what he was doing to look at the other couple. "They do this shit all the time. Tell me about yourself, Matty."

Austin almost choked on his beer at her calling him Matty. No one except Matt's Grandma Bea ever called him Matty, and anyone who did was promptly jacked in the arm, or head, or whatever was in reach. Coming from Lauren's mouth, Matt lapped it up. He leaned in and began telling her all about his job, his school studies, his Jeep, his busy social life, and soon Julia could see Lauren's eyes glaze over.

"Sweetie," Lauren said, "that's all nice, but don't you want to know anything about me?"

"Uh, sure, I guess," Matt was stammering. His air of arrogance was gone when he looked at Lauren.

Yes, Julia thought, *my Lauren can teach this man a lot.*

Julia tuned the two out now and turned her attention to Austin. It was his night, after all.

"Having fun, sweetie?" She imitated Lauren's voice. Austin laughed and put his arm around her.

"I'm with you. I'm having fun," he replied.

Soon the Monster Platter arrived and the men pounced on it. Julia could see ribs, onion rings, mini burgers, chicken wings, and some kind of vegetable straws. Austin identified them as sweet potato fries and she tried one. It was too sweet for her taste, but she gamely finished it. She looked across at Lauren, who had taken a rib. Julia knew what she was up to; she'd seen Lauren pull this many times. Lauren took a small bite before closing her eyes, moaning slightly. She licked her lips and ran her tongue over each finger. She looked at Matt and smiled. He'd just started to take a bite of his mini burger when he stopped to watch the Lauren Show. Julia wanted so badly to tell him to close his mouth. She looked at Austin, who was trying not to laugh. Lauren did not affect him in the least.

Lauren continued her performance through another rib and a chicken wing before she declared herself finished with the Monster Platter. She declared to the table that she wouldn't be able to eat her dinner if she didn't stop. Lauren took a long drink of her beer and sat back to watch Matt. He was used to women watching him, and he didn't even notice. He sailed through another mini burger, munched on the onion rings, and finished off the sweet potato fries. He washed it all down with another beer and looked around the table. Julia knew that he was holding in a huge belch and laughed. Austin paid no attention at all. Lauren looked him over and leaned toward him with her napkin. She put an end of it to her tongue—he watched her every move—before she swiped it over Matt's chin. He sat frozen.

"Just a bit of sauce, sweetie. You don't mind my cleaning you up a bit, do you?" He barely nodded his head that he didn't mind. "You really should be a little neater, don't you think?" Matt nodded his head again.

They were interrupted by Austin's friend Joey, who was on his break. He put another bucket of opened beers on the table and sat down for a few minutes. Austin introduced Julia, and Joey shook her hand politely while telling her how nice it was to meet her. His smile at Austin told his friend that he approved. Lauren was introduced next, and even though Julia could tell that Joey was almost as charmed as Matt, he covered it up much better. Lauren flirted shamelessly with the bartender, and Julia could see Matt's eyes growing darker as he narrowed them in Joey's direction. Austin kicked him under the table, and shook his head "no" at his buddy. Matt looked around the room then and tried to make eye contact with several of the females. A young waitress, not Brittany, came over to ask if he needed anything, but before he could reply, Lauren turned to the girl. She leaned over Matt and looked the little brunette in the eye. Raising one eyebrow, she said, "Honey, I'll let you know if we need anything over here." The girl stuttered a "sorry" before scampering off. Lauren ignored Matt as she leaned back and turned to Joey, whose break was up.

"Uh, could I call you sometime?" Joey asked Lauren.

"Perhaps." Lauren's mouth curled up in a smile. "I know where to find you, sweetie." At this disappointed look, she leaned toward him. "It's been a real pleasure, Joey," Lauren almost purred his name. "Austin, you have the nicest friends." She looked first at Matt and then at Joey, who excused himself to get back to work.

Austin laughed and called Brittany over to take their dinner order. He looked at Julia who shook her head. This could be a long night, she seemed to say.

"Good, god, Julia, I didn't ride the bull, did I?" Lauren was drinking coffee and defending herself to Julia the next morning. "And I didn't give out my number to anybody, did I? I didn't get drunk, did I? Hell, that was the tamest night I've had in ages!"

"Yes, for you, you were good," Julia admitted. "I just wish you'd stop this Matt stuff."

"What Matt stuff? I didn't sleep with him...yet. He doesn't have my number, either. And by the end of the evening, he was almost acting like a gentleman."

Julia had to admit that Lauren had him pulling out chairs, opening doors, and waiting on her hand and foot. While it seemed that Lauren was teaching Matt how to treat a lady, this lady was bound to turn on him. Julia had seen it all before, and when she wanted to, Lauren could be a man's nightmare. However, Matt and Lauren were adults, and Julia had to admit that this was Lauren's business, not hers.

Chapter 15

⎯⎯⎯

Aᴜɢᴜꜱᴛ ᴄᴀᴍᴇ ɪɴ ᴍᴜᴄʜ ᴀꜱ July ended. Hot and dry. While Arizonans brag about the "dry" heat, it was heat just the same. As Julia put it, "Air from a hair dryer feels the same as an August Arizona breeze." It would be a couple of months before most of the natives came down from Flagstaff, and Touch of Jules was busy as the ladies hurried to finish the remodel jobs that were on the books. Julia talked to Sharon every couple of days, and they looked forward to the upcoming visit and party.

Austin had broken the news to his parents that he'd be staying in Phoenix for his birthday. He told them that with the new internship, he had a lot to do at his old job before leaving, and he couldn't get away. He wasn't ready to mention Julia yet. Had he taken the time to think about it, he would have admitted that it was more about wanting to keep her to himself than fearing what his family would say.

"But Austin, it's your birthday, and I don't know if I can stand not seeing you on your birthday," Natalie James wasn't above laying a guilt trip on her son. Not that it worked very often, but she still tried.

"I know, Mom, but it just isn't going to work this year. I'm sorry, but that's how it goes sometimes."

"Well, we can come out there. Your brother doesn't start school yet, and I'm sure your father can get away."

"Mom, give it up. Caleb has football practice. Dad has clients he'd have to reschedule, and you know that's impossible at this late date. I'll be home Thanksgiving."

"But you missed our anniversary, and it was our twenty-fifth. We had a party and everything. Everyone asked where you were, and you know how I hate to make excuses for you."

"Then don't," Austin replied. *I am so tired of this same crap every time I talk to her.* Out loud, he continued, "I'm a grown man, Mom, and I don't live with you anymore. I don't live in North Carolina anymore. People don't expect me to be at every function. You have Caleb for that."

He heard her sigh over the phone, but it wasn't having the effect she was hoping for. Austin really didn't care.

"I suppose I'll just have to wait until Thanksgiving then. Well, I know you're busy..."

"I am, Mom, but we'll talk again soon. I promise."

"Love you, baby."

"Love you, mom. Bye." Austin hit the end button on his phone and let out a deep breath. He loved his mom, but sometimes she could be a load.

He looked up to see Julia watching him. She smiled sympathetically and blew him kiss.

"Come over here and make it the real thing. I need one."

She sat on his lap and wrapped her arms around his neck before leaning in to give him a kiss. They sat with their foreheads touching for several moments before she raised her head up to look at him.

"I know how you feel, sweetie. I've been where you are now, only I was getting divorced at the same time. Double whammy. Two people trying to tell you what to do is impossible. When you're getting it from two sides, you shut down and give neither the time of day." She sighed. "I do feel like this is my fault, though."

"Don't you dare. This began when I decided to go my own way and make my own decisions. Leave the nest, so to speak. It has nothing to do with you. They just make me tired, you know?"

Julia knew exactly what he was saying. "I do know. Back in the day, when I decided to kick Keith to the curb, my mother was livid. She would come over to rant, and scream, and tell me how stupid I was for giving up as she put it 'the best thing to ever happen' to me. Even when I told her he was seeing another woman, she kept making excuses. If it hadn't been for my dad, I doubt she and I would talk much less see one another. Daddy and Lauren were my lifeboats back then. One held my mother back while the other kept me going. I've never told you much about that time, have I?"

Austin wondered if this was all she was going to say on the matter, or if she was ready to tell him more. It seemed that she was ready to talk.

"After I graduated from college, Lauren and I started a business in Chesterfield, a suburb of St. Louis, and we were doing great. Business was good, and we were renting a condo in Chesterfield, not far from our shop. Well, one day Keith Landry walks in, needing some remodeling done on a house he'd bought in Lake St. Louis. He owns his own accounting firm, so money wasn't a problem. I took his job, and we were spending a lot of time together, picking out furnishings, drapes, floors, you name it. Soon we were going to dinner, and before I knew it, we were engaged. I thought I was in love with him." Her voice grew wistful. "I guess I thought I was supposed to fall in love with him." She shook her head and continued.

"My mother was thrilled. My dad, not so much. He called me into his den one day, just he and I, and asked me point blank if marrying Keith was what I wanted to do. With the wedding only three weeks away, I told him what I thought he wanted me to say. I assured him that yes, I was ready and that yes, Keith was the one. Everything was ready for the big show, as Lauren always describes that wedding. The church, the five bridesmaids, the country club reception, and the St. Thomas honeymoon. Looking back now, I know Daddy was trying to give me a way out. I just didn't know it and he didn't say it point blank. I suppose at that time I wouldn't have taken it anyway."

Julia had risen and moved to sit on the coffee table facing Austin. This next part would be very painful.

"We had the fairytale wedding and honeymoon and moved into the big house in the fancy suburbs. I learned to cook, and Lauren took over the majority of the business. Oh, I went in and kept myself busy, but she was really running the operation. Keith said that now that I was married, I wouldn't have the time for interior design work, or for any real job. Still eager to please, I settled into my role as housewife and hostess. We were quite popular." Julia smiled wistfully but the small smile faded. "We'd been married almost five years when I had the first miscarriage."

"We'd been trying to have a baby almost from the first night. I was so frustrated. Almost every month, my mother would be calling to see if I was pregnant. We saw fertility doctors, but none of them could find anything wrong with me. Tests, more tests, more failures. When I finally got pregnant, you should have seen everybody. God, you'd think I'd discovered life on the moon or something. I was barely pregnant, but Keith immediately opened an account at a baby boutique and set my mother on buying everything we could possibly need. Why my mom? Because I was carrying his child, I shouldn't be doing anything. I lost that baby at ten weeks. We were devastated. The doctors couldn't give us a reason. Just said that it happens and that we could always try again." She shrugged a shoulder and looked down at the floor.

"I lost the second baby at fifteen weeks. That was horrible. I'd made it through the first trimester. Morning sickness was still there, but I felt great. I awoke in the middle of the night, doubled over with cramping, and by the time we got to the hospital, blood was everywhere. I'd never seen Keith so upset. He didn't blame me, at least I didn't think so at the time, but he was heartbroken. Not as heartbroken as I was. He didn't feel the baby move, which I did the day before I lost it. Just a fluttering, but it was there. It was real. I spent a long time just lying in bed. Those days are a blur because I don't think anything registered with me. Finally, the doctor put me on some anti-depression medication, and that helped." She closed her eyes for a few seconds before opening them to look at Austin.

"More years passed, and while I thought the marriage was fine, I suppose I was fooling myself. I saw less and less of Keith, and when he was home, he wasn't home, you know? Oh, we were still the perfect couple. Young, beautiful, successful, popular. All we didn't have was children. I've wondered sometimes if that wasn't pushing Keith away. The fact that I was keeping him from his dream—the perfect little family to show off to the world, like his custom Corvette, or Lake St. Louis address."

Austin wanted so badly to reach out and hold her, but he was afraid of breaking the spell. Julia was inside herself now, anyway, taken back to a time that she forgot now more than she remembered. He had to let her finish.

"Oh, you have no idea how excited I was for baby number three. I'm surprised we even conceived, we had sex so seldom by that time, but we did. This time we made it through the first trimester. We were letting ourselves believe that this was it. We were really having a baby! I was thirty-five by this time, and while that isn't old, it isn't young for a first child. I was doing everything right. No lifting, no exercising, both Keith's orders. I had a maid. I was *allowed* to cook, but that was all."

Julia snarled her nose. "My mother was over all the time, living vicariously through me, I suppose. She and Keith would be in the nursery together, discussing names, what sounded good with Landry, who the baby would look like. Yeah, pretty much all the things he should have been talking about with me."

Julia was struggling now to maintain control. Austin was not looking forward to this next part to her story because he knew what was coming. *Julia has no children*, he thought.

"Well, week twenty arrived, and everything was still okay. I had done everything everyone wanted me to do, from the doctor, to Keith, to my mother, and the same thing happened. I went to bed fine, woke up in severe cramps, this time worse than before, and blood was everywhere. Keith called an ambulance because I guess all the blood scared him. It was only a ten-minute wait for the EMT's to get there, but it was the longest ten minutes of my life. Keith held my hand and handed me tissues to wipe the tears, but we didn't say a word to one another.

"We arrived at the hospital and the doctor examined me, declared the baby dead, and prepped me for a D and C. We had a little girl. Once again there was no reason for the miscarriage. The doctor advised me to stop trying. He said that my uterus had been damaged this time and that it couldn't sustain a pregnancy, regardless of what we do.

"That was the end of the marriage. I was devastated. Keith was devastated. And my mother. God, you would think her world had come to an end." Julia's faced hardened as she spoke of her mother. "She made it my fault. I must have done something to cause this. Daddy tried to keep her mouth shut, but she still hurt me. Lauren saved my life. She brought me back into the business, gave me all the new jobs, went with me to conventions, took me shopping, and made sure I didn't have time to think or sit around and mope.

"It was Lauren who suspected Keith was involved with someone else. She followed him and saw him going places that were not where he told me he was. By then, I knew that I didn't love him. At least, not like I should. And I knew he really didn't love me."

Austin felt himself tensing up as she got to this part of her story. His thoughts were racing. *I hate this Keith. I hate him with a passion for not loving Julia like she should be loved. I hate him for hurting her.* As she began talking again, he pushed aside his disgust. *She needs me to listen and love her, not sit here hating.* He silently listened for her story to continue.

"Lauren and I followed him. He had told me that he had to stay at the office to catch up on some work and for me to not wait up for him. Not like I did anyway, but when he called to tell me that, I knew he wasn't going to be at work. I felt nothing. Not a thing. I was at the shop, so Lauren knew something was up as soon as I told her. It was her idea to follow him. She was fired up and wanting to bust some heads." Julia smiled. "Lauren can be quite protective sometimes." Her smile faded again. "We took her car because Keith wasn't familiar with it, and we followed him from the office to The Hill. That's St. Louis's Little Italy, so to speak. Rinaldi's had always been our place, so to speak, and when I saw his car parked outside the restaurant, I felt the first stirrings of anger.

"We walked in and the maitre-d looked stunned. All of the wait staff know me because, like I said, we ate there all the time. I told him that I'd pick out my own table that evening, and Lauren and I went into the dining room. It didn't take long to find Keith. He was sitting across from a very young blonde. They were pretty chummy, and when he kissed her, it was all I could do to keep Lauren from jumping on him. She would have scratched his eyes out. He heard her say something like, 'That's it!' before he looked up and saw us. Saw me. I looked at him, sitting with his baby-doll blonde, and I felt nothing. The anger just melted away. I suppose to be angry you have to care. I'd stopped caring."

Julia looked up at Austin. He could see that telling her story had taken a toll. She looked tired, and for the first time, Austin saw lines on either side of her mouth. *Laugh lines*, he thought they were called. *She isn't laughing now, but she's still so beautiful. I love her more than ever.* Julia's voice caught his attention. She was almost done.

"Keith didn't come home that night, but by the time he arrived the next evening, Lauren and I had packed up his stuff." She smiled a rueful smile. "His 'stupid shit' as she called it. One thing Keith can't stand is embarrassment and scandal. I used that to my advantage as my lawyer helped me get the lion's share—the house and furniture, a cabin at Lake of the Ozarks, half of our investments, a large cash settlement, and my car. Lauren moved into the big house with me, and it wasn't long before I made up my mind to leave St. Louis. Lauren declared that if I was going, then so was she. We looked around and decided that Scottsdale, Arizona, would suit us just fine. We'd been out here for conferences and had fallen in love with it. I sold everything in Missouri, including our business there, bought the building we have Touch of Jules in, and the rest, as they say, is history."

She'd left out the major scenes with Keith and her mother, but Julia felt like she'd told Austin enough for him to understand. Only one more thing remained.

"Austin, you know that we've never talked about birth control. No condoms, nothing."

"I just figured you're on the pill," he said. "And at first I honestly wasn't thinking about birth control. Then when you said nothing, I was sure you were. What? You're not?"

"No, and this is could be a deal-breaker for us." Her voice broke as she said, "Austin, I can't have children." Her eyes filled with tears. "That's one of the main reasons why I never wanted to get involved with you. You're twenty-four damn years old. You need kids, you want kids, your own kids. I can't do that for you." He watched as the tears spilled over her eyes and rolled down her face.

"Hey, c'mere, baby," he grabbed her up and pulled her back onto his lap. She cried harder then, and Austin sat stroking her hair and letting her cry it out. *Kids.* He'd never given a thought to kids. He wasn't even sure they were in his future, and now he didn't care.

"Jules. Julia." She looked up then. "I am so sorry that son-of-a-bitch hurt you. God, I'm so sorry you lost the babies. But you do know that this whole thing about kids. It doesn't matter." As she imperceptibly shook her head, he held her tighter. "You don't believe me now because you're upset; your emotions are in the past, in St. Louis." Austin made her face him as he looked into her eyes. "Listen to me. I don't care. I love you. I can see myself with you forever. With you."

She sniffed and wiped at her face. He smiled. She was not a pretty crier. Her eyes were puffy, her nose red, and she looked like hell. He loved her even more for the imperfection.

She took a ragged breath. "You say that now, but what about later, when you're older, a successful businessman and you have a house and all of that. It will matter then, trust me."

"Bullshit. If all of that mattered, I would have stayed at UNC, studied law and gone into partnership with my dad. I would have married some southern belle, joined the country club, and died a slow and painful death." He smiled at her then. "Jules, I'm not that man. You're not that woman. None of that works for us. I love what we have. I love that we work together. I don't know why, and I don't care enough to think about it. Baby, we work. And there isn't one single thing you've told me today that's changed that."

Julia smiled then and laughed. "I know you love me now. I'm a mess! I cry and look like hell."

"Yeah, you do," he teased, "but you clean up real good." He pulled her close again for a last hug before nudging her up. "Go wash your face. We're going for a drive. Pop the top and sail through the desert. Hey, let's head up to Canyon Lake, on up to Tortilla Flat, have a beer and make fun of the tourists."

She smiled and nodded before heading to their room to clean herself up. Austin watched her go and wondered if she'd ever realize how much he loved her.

I love her more now than ever, if that's possible. His face hardened. *And if I ever come across Keith Landry, I'll make sure the asshole is missing a few teeth when I'm finished with him.*

109

Chapter 16

"Hello, birthday boy," Lauren said when she looked up at Austin coming through the door. She was at her desk finishing up a monthly report, and Julia was at hers working on a bid proposal. Lauren knew her friend was in deep concentration because she didn't even look up. Julia hated the paperwork end of the firm, which was why Lauren did the lion's share. Julia would do it, but she hated every minute.

Austin winked at Lauren, looked over at Julia, and said, "Must be paperwork. She hates that stuff."

"I can hear you," Julia looked up then. "I know that I already told you once today, but happy birthday! One more year and your insurance rates go down!" They teased one another freely about age now, and Julia was having fun during his birthday week.

"I came by to see you before the party tonight."

"Party? There's a party and I'm just now hearing about it? What the hell? Is there cake and ice cream? Clowns?" She shuddered visibly. "No, no clowns. They creep me out," Lauren took off her reading glasses to give them her full attention and smiled brightly.

"We're not invited, Goldilocks, just the guys. It's a tradition thing, right?" Julia grinned at Austin again, and he gave her his "I'm thrilled" look. She laughed, "Good grief, you're going out with your friends, drinking, carousing, picking up women—what's not fun about that?" They'd had a conversation that morning when Julia had given him a proper birthday morning greeting, and she knew that he probably would enjoy her type of party more than this.

"I know, I know, but sometimes the guys can be too much," he leaned on the corner of her desk.

"We had this discussion this morning. You've been neglecting your friends for weeks, no months now, and you need to go out. Heck, Lauren and I are meeting the girls at Houston's. So you're not the only one out carousing." She winked in Lauren's direction, and her friend joined in. No sparing Austin just because it was his birthday.

"Yeah, I'm going to ply your girlfriend with adult beverages and see if she can pick up men without my help. It should be fun." Lauren had her flirting look on her face, and Austin wasn't too happy.

"Shut up, Lauren." He turned his attention back to Julia. "What's a tradition if it isn't broken once in a while. All they'll want to do is talk sports, drink beer, and ogle women. I'd really rather skip all of that."

"Oh, hell no, you don't. And make me some 'bad guy' here? The girl-friend shrew who keeps a short leash? Uh-uh. You're going out and you're having fun if it kills you." She stood up and moved to stand between his legs. She wrapped her arms around his neck. "Besides, I need you to come by my place now. I have a birthday gift for you." At his lecherous grin, she added, "A different gift."

"We decided no presents, didn't we? What am I, twelve?"

"You said it," came the voice from across the room. They ignored her.

"I know, but this is for me, too." Julia looked over at Lauren. "Close up tonight?"

"Sure, I have no man in my life. No date. No 'honey, I'm home' wait-ing for me. Oh, wait. I hate those things." Lauren laughed and waved them toward the door. She put her reading glasses back down and focused once more on the papers on her desk.

"Thank you, Lauren," Julia's voice was the sing-song she knew her friend hated.

"Get the hell out," came a sing-song reply, as Julia gathered her bag and followed Austin. Lauren looked up and winked before Julia turned to walk out of the shop. She'd already seen the gift and thought Austin would like it.

Austin pulled into the drive behind Julia and followed her into the house and up the stairs. He was curious about this gift. She'd gone shop-ping with him over the previous weekend, and while he'd let her buy him a shirt and pants for the upcoming party at Sharon and John's—a birthday gift she'd called it—he'd refused anything more. He hoped she hadn't gone back and bought some of the other stuff they'd looked at. He hated shopping, but he hated the thought of her buying him clothes even more. He couldn't think of anything more lame than that—letting your girlfriend dress you.

"Don't look so gloomy," she grinned at him. "Follow me, but close your eyes."

"Close my eyes? You won't run me into the wall for fun, will you?"

"I hadn't thought of that, but it does sound like fun. No, I have a surprise for you." She took his hand and led him toward her room. He knew what he was hoping for, what man wouldn't, and she must have read his mind. "Down boy, you have to be somewhere."

"No, I don't. I can be late. I can be as late as I want to be."

She ignored him. "Keep 'em closed. Almost there."

He felt her lead him into her bedroom and pull him beside her. "Open them!"

Austin was standing in front of a tall bureau with six drawers. It was made of the same dark wood as her other furniture and looked like it had always been sitting there. He looked at her and frowned.

"Okay...what's this?"

"Well," she walked to stand beside it. "You're over here a lot now, most of the time, and I've watched you carry stuff back and forth in that ugly gym bag." She looked pointedly at the bag in question. He noticed that it did look sad, lying on the floor beside the chair. "This, sweetie, is yours!" She did her best Vanna White presentation.

"Mine?" he was slow to get it.

She tilted her head, looked at him, and said, "You don't get it. You can keep some stuff over here. I started to clean out a couple of drawers in my dresser, but I've got too much stuff. So I bought this. If you don't use all of it, no big deal. I always need extra clothes room. Oh, and look here," she threw open her closet door. "Ta-da! Your own side. Well, half of one side, but you have some room in here, too. What do you think?"

Austin didn't say anything. He walked over to the bureau, pulled out the top drawer and looked it over before peering into the closet at the empty space she'd made for him. He'd seen the inside of her closet before, and it had been crammed full. He wondered what she'd done with the stuff.

"Babe..." She came up beside him. "Hey, if you're uncomfortable with any of this, just say so. I thought you'd like having some space, and it doesn't mean you're moving in, or anything. It's a gesture..." Her voice trailed off.

He looked at her then and saw that she was looking at him questioningly, thinking she'd misread their situation. He flashed the smile that was her favorite, grabbed her up, and swung her around.

"I love it!" He was still holding her as he kissed her soundly.

"Whew!" she said. "I thought I'd screwed up here. And seriously, you use it as you want. I'm really not asking you to move in with me. Not that that isn't on the table at some point," she hurried to add, "but we'll know when the time's right."

"Jules, stop talking. It's a great gift. Only you would think of something like this, and yeah, I am a little tired of living out of the old bag." He laughed at the bag in question. "I just have one thing to ask. What in the hell did you do with all of those clothes that were in your closet? I mean, that sucker was crammed full."

"I donated them to the local women's shelter. It's just something I started doing when I still lived in St. Louis, and Lauren and I have continued doing it since moving out here. You've caught me on the full closet cycle, so I needed an excuse to stop putting it off."

That sounded like her. She could be sarcastic and tough, yet loving and sweet. Perfect, he thought. He leaned in to kiss her again, but she pulled back.

"Nope, you have somewhere to be. I'll see you tomorrow afternoon at 2:00. Come by here and pick me up."

"You don't want to take your car instead?" Austin wondered how his five-year-old black Mustang would fit in with the BMWs, Cadillacs, and Porsches.

"Yes, you're driving," she laughed. "I happen to like riding in your car." She took his arm and led him toward the door.

"Wait a minute," and Austin reached down to grab his scruffy gym bag. "I need to fill this back up. At least one more time," he added, as she frowned at the bag and up at him.

She walked him out, leaned into the car to give him a quick kiss good-bye, and said, "Have fun. I'll see you tomorrow."

"Yeah, you have fun, too. And don't let Lauren get you into any trouble." He was halfway serious.

Julia laughed and stepped back. "Honey, I learned long ago to not even try to keep up with that woman." Then she winked, "I'll be a good girl, promise."

He put his ball cap and sunglasses on, backed into the street, and looked at her once more.

"Yeah, that's the problem. You're almost too good," he mumbled as he headed down the street.

"Hey, it's our old pal, Austin! Where the hell you been, man?"

Austin and Matt headed toward the small group seated by the pool tables and big screen TV's. From the outside, Cactus Joe's Sports Bar, a nondescript place located close to their apartment in Cross Point Center, looked like any other strip mall restaurant, but inside the place was fairly large. On the left side of the building were several tables and chairs in the middle of the floor with booths lining the walls. Straight ahead in the center, a bar with bar tables and two pool tables filled the space, and an eighty-inch projection TV was mounted on the wall behind the bar. To the right were more tables and another eighty-inch TV attached to that wall.

Austin came in and looked at his pals seated at a group of tables on the bar side—Joey, Ryan, Eli, and Dakota. Joey he'd seen at the Wagon Wheel, but it had been weeks since he'd seen the other three. Between work, school, and Julia, Austin hadn't spared any time for his friends. Seeing them made him realize that he'd missed them. He'd never tell them that, though.

"Hey, dude," Ryan handed him a beer. "Where the hell you been? Matt says you have an old lady now, and she keeps a tight rein." He grinned as he said it, so Austin grinned back. He knew Julia would be a topic tonight, simply because Joey knew about her.

"Hey, man," Joey pulled out a chair next to him. "How's it hanging?"

"It's all good, man, it's all good," Austin took a long drink of his beer and greeted Eli and Dakota.

"Hey, we hear you've got a real lady these days. Is old AJ out of the game?" Ryan wouldn't let it die just yet.

"Pretty much, yeah, she's something." Austin wasn't about to talk too much about Julia, and he definitely wasn't going to put her out there for their inspection.

"Oh, I heard. Joey here filled me in on all the particulars. When are you gonna bring her around? Or are you afraid of the competition?"

Austin laughed at that one. "My man, on your best day, you are no competition for this guy."

"If you think Austin's woman is good, you should see her roommate." Joey looked over at Austin and grinned. "Not that your woman isn't fine, but damn, her friend is smokin' and available." He looked around the table. "Oh man, is she fine—legs up to there, blonde, big boobs, and sexy..." As Joey was talking, Austin looked over at Matt. Matt had been keeping to himself ever since the night at the Wagon Wheel. He didn't get Lauren's number that night, but neither did Joey. That hadn't stopped him from thinking about her and he was thinking about her now. *One night...that's all I want...one night...show her that ol' Matt can screw her every which way...*

"Hey," Joey turned to Austin, "she came back in the other night with a couple of other fine females." He wasn't finished, and his words cut into Matt's thoughts. At that, Matt's eyes honed in on his pal. "They sat at the bar, knocked back a few drinks, and we had us a real nice conversation." The look on Matt's face told him that he'd struck a nerve, and Joey was going to play with him a bit. He'd watched Matt with Lauren that night, and he knew that his buddy was in lust with the woman in question.

"Like you'd have anything to say that she'd want to hear," Matt was frowning at his beer as his hand clenched around it.

"Oh, my man, you'd be surprised." Joey and the others laughed, except for Austin, who only smiled at him.

"So," Austin looked at Joey, "did you get a date?"

"Naw....she's a tough one. I tried pretty much every way I could to get a number or something out of her. Hell, she side-stepped where she works even. By the time she left, I thought, *Fuck her*, and decided she's not playing."

Hearing that, Matt relaxed a little, and the six started talking about other things. Austin was glad they'd dodged that bullet. He'd hate to see Matt start something over a woman who wasn't even interested in him. Dakota asked him a question, and he turned his attention to his friends.

Every so often, he'd think of blue eyes and miss Julia.

"JULIA!!!" Jennifer, Karen, and Heidi were already at the bar, and as they squealed her name, several people looked up.

"Hey! I've missed you!" and Julia gave each a big hug before settling in at the little table. She motioned for the bartender to send someone over.

"Where have you been? Lauren tells us nothing, and Alexis said that she saw you the other day eating with some blond hunk. Why are we finding out this stuff from Alexis the Bitch, uh? I had to put up with her ugly face, all gloating and stupid." Karen would be the first to find out simply because of her business. As a busy real estate agent, she saw everyone and made it her business to find out everything going on in her circle of friends.

The waitress came by about that time, and Julia ordered a martini before taking a deep breath. She looked at the three women, who were leaning in to not miss a word.

"Well, I am seeing someone. His name is Austin. He works at the Coyote Run Golf Club. We've been dating for a couple of months now, and yes, he is gorgeous." She added that last because she knew that's what they wanted to know.

"Yeah, but is he good in bed. The gorgeous ones usually aren't, you know. Too busy making sure they are holding the right pose, or their hair is falling just right, or whatever. You'd think a video camera was rolling, the way they act," this from Heidi.

"That, ladies, you will never know," Julia smiled and winked.

"Hey, bartender, double that drink," Heidi yelled over toward the bar. "My girl needs to loosen up her tongue."

Lauren and Julia exchanged a look. It would be a long night.

Chapter 17

———

Julia was ready when Austin came up the stairs and looked at the two bags, one big and one small. His stuff was in one. They were only staying two nights, and he wondered what in the world would be in two bags.

"I know what you're thinking. One bag is clothes and the other is shoes and makeup bag. You're giving me the same look my father does, only his is double because it was always both my mom and me. She's worse."

"Hey, did I say anything? I didn't say a word." He watched her grab her purse, keys, and sunglasses.

"Babe, did you pack a jacket? Sweatshirt? It can get chilly up there at night, even this time of year," Julia had her jacket over her arm and her favorite Cardinal hoodie in her bag.

"Yep, and yep, all packed. And it isn't that bad, what, 50 degrees or so?"

Julia laughed, "Just as it's a dry heat down here, it's a damp cold in the mountains. We'll be fine. The party will be inside and out. We'll only need jackets if we lounge on the deck under the stars." That sounded perfect to him, but first they had a party to get through.

Austin had sent Julia a text around midnight the night before, and they had conversed that way most of the night. The only reason he didn't come over was that he knew they'd be together the next three days.

The drive took them a little over two hours, as they left early enough to beat the rush-hour traffic. Austin left the top down since they'd be at Burns' house long before dark, and neither said much as they drove through the desert. Taking I-17, the little Mustang climbed into the mountains. They could feel the air getting cooler and found themselves swallowing to clear their ears. Julia saw a sign telling them they were four thousand feet above sea level, then five thousand, and finally six thousand. The air was significantly cooler than when they'd started the trip. When Mount Humphreys came into view, they knew they weren't far. A couple of miles outside of town, Julia had Austin turn onto a state road that wound its way up the mountains. He could see houses back behind the thick stands of ponderosa pine trees that kept the estates private. Soon they came upon a gated community road, and Austin turned into the entrance. A security guard in a small office building leaned out and asked for their names. Once he'd checked them on his clipboard, he gave them a big smile, wished them a nice evening, and hit the button that opened the gate.

"So this is how the other half lives," Austin grinned at Julia.

"Yeah, but you already know that from the other house," Julia replied. "Turn at the third drive on the right."

As they turned onto the winding drive, Austin could barely see the house set back into the woods. They came to a spectacular two-story structure made of log and stone. He stopped short of the three-car garage and parked the car. Before getting out, Austin looked at the estate surrounding him. The front of the house was almost all glass with the garage on the left and a covered walkway to the right. A huge stone wall came out from the house, followed along the walkway, and ended at the drive. He couldn't see what was behind it, but Julia pulled his attention back to the front door. Sharon burst out and held her arms open for Julia to run into them. Behind Sharon stood a tall, slender man with close-cropped gray hair. He had the distinguished look and carriage of someone who would own this house and the one in the valley. Julia ended her hug with Sharon, and he opened his arms for his turn. Julia reached up to put her arms around his neck—he had to be around six foot two—and he pulled her up into a bear hug as they both let out a happy laugh.

"How's my girl!" he exclaimed. "I've missed you baby doll."

"John! I've missed you, too! It's so good to see you," Julia turned and motioned for Austin to join her.

"John, Sharon, this is Austin James. Austin, these are my other parents, John and Sharon." She smiled as she presented Austin to them. He stuck his hand out to Sharon, but she ignored it and grabbed him around the neck instead.

"Austin, I am so glad to finally meet you," she said before stepping back to eye him better. "Oh, yeah, you are a cutie," and she laughed when Austin winked at her in reply. To Austin's relief, John took the offered hand. His firm handshake and welcoming smile made Austin feel better about his wife's comment. John was obviously used to his wife.

"Good to meet you, Austin. Sharon has been driving me nuts all day speculating about you. Just a friendly warning—she'll ask you a million questions. Answer only what you want and smile through the rest."

"Behave yourself, John," Sharon scolded as she put Julia and Austin on each arm and led them inside. "Don't make Austin afraid of me, for heaven's sake," she said over her shoulder. "And I'm so glad we changed our plans and you're staying with us. I said to John, 'What am I thinking? We have our girl with us so seldom, and we're sending her off to some cabin.' God knows we have the room." She and Julia started talking about the house and what Sharon wanted to do to it before next year.

John leaned up to whisper to the younger man, "Remember, Austin, her bark is worse than her bite," he laughed affectionately at his petite wife, and Austin enjoyed the relationship he sensed was there. *How awesome,* he thought, *to find someone who knows you and loves you and go through life together.*

Julia looked over her friend's head to grin at Austin and wink. It was going to be a fun weekend. Austin winked back.

As they entered the front door, Austin saw a long wooden staircase to the left that led up to an open balcony. He could see a hallway branch off and a couple of other doors along the walkway that ended in a sitting area. In front of him was a great room that stretched across the width of the house, a massive stone fireplace along one wall, and more glass across the back with French doors leading to a patio that offered a view of the mountains in the distance. Past the great room, he could see the kitchen with granite countertops, a bar with four, rough wooden stools alongside it, and stainless steel appliances and trim. None of it was as large as the Fountain Hills house, but it was more comfortable and homey with all the wood and natural stone.

Separating the kitchen from the sitting area was a long table and eight chairs. When Sharon showed him where one half-bath was, he saw what had to be the master suite off the kitchen. Julia saw him looking at it and led him into a large room with its own huge stone fireplace and a back wall of glass, broken up by French doors that led to the same huge patio. The master bath was massive with the same wood and stone theme as the house. He looked at the normal-sized garden tub and grinned at Julia. This wasn't the massive tub she loved from the Fountain Hills house.

"There's another bedroom on the other side of the great room and three more upstairs," Julia explained. "They also have a game room with a pool table, a TV room, Sharon's craft room, and John's office. Every bedroom has its own bath, too."

Sharon came up behind them and spoke, "You two use the other downstairs bedroom tonight, sweetie. It's all ready, and you'll enjoy the smaller patio on that side. John, help Austin with their bags and let's get them all settled in."

Meeting back in the great room where John mixed up drinks, they settled in to an easy conversation before dinner. Sharon had given Angie the evening off since she'd be helping the next day, and John was in charge of the grill. Burgers, potato salad, baked beans, and chocolate cake rounded out the menu.

As Julia and Austin cleaned up for dinner—Sharon had run them both out of the kitchen, saying that they were getting under her feet—he hugged her close.

"I like your friends," he said.

"I knew you would," she said, and kissed him lightly. "They like you, too."

"They aren't pretentious at all, are they?"

Julia laughed, "Oh, you haven't seen Sharon in action. She can be as pretentious as the next. But at the end of the day, she's as generous as they come. Sharon didn't come from money. In fact, neither did John. They met in high school, graduated college, married, and she helped him build a business. Investments, I think, but she taught elementary school while he was starting out. When they had Johnny, she quit and never went back. He really made a load during the 90s when the stock market was rising, and he's been making it ever since. I think it's because she didn't have money that she always looks after people. For example, in a restaurant, you'll not find another person who has to have it just a certain way, but she tips everyone so well, from the maitre-d to the busboy, they look forward to seeing her." Julia grinned. "Don't let that hard exterior fool you. She's a sweetheart underneath."

"Unless I do something to you," Austin laughed. "Then she'd rip my throat out."

Julia laughed, "You're probably right. Once she loves you, you're hers."

"Hmmm...sounds like someone else I know." He looked down at her and decided that he was another one who'd rip out the throat of anyone who hurt this woman.

"Hey, you two," Sharon called from the hallway. "Break it up and get in here. I'm hungry enough to start gnawing my arm off."

"She's classy, too, isn't she?" Austin laughed.

"Don't let her hear you call her classy," Julia laughed. "She'll gnaw on you!"

They were laughing as they joined the other two.

"Good night, kids. Big day for me tomorrow. Turn in when you want." Sharon kissed Julia good-night, waved a hand at Austin, and left them alone. John had gone back a few minutes before.

Julia was stretched out on the sofa, her feet in Austin's lap and he was rubbing them absently.

"Ummmm....that's nice," her voice low. Austin started massaging up her leg, and she gave him a slow smile. "Keep on going, and we may be in trouble."

"Then let's move this party to the bedroom." Austin's voice had taken on the husky tone that she knew was an indicator of his mood. She got up, took his hands, and they made their way to the back bedroom. Julia shut the door and walked over to the gas fireplace. She flipped a switch and fire danced behind the glass door.

She came to him then, and he gathered her into a long, slow kiss. The kiss continued, growing more intense before Austin picked her up and carried her to the bed. He laid her gently on the quilt and she saw him smiling in the firelight. Without saying a word, Austin pulled his t-shirt over his head and removed the rest of his clothes. Julia watched him from her position on the bed, her eyes growing darker in the dim light. She started to rise to remove her own when he gently pushed her back down.

"Let me do it," he whispered. She settled back and watched him as he unfastened her jeans and slid them down her legs. He tossed them aside and reached up to unbutton her shirt, slowing undoing each button before placing a kiss on the skin he was exposing. When he'd gone through them all, he pulled her forward, pushed each sleeve off and tossed the discarded shirt with the jeans. While he still had her up, he unfastened her bra, and replaced his mouth on her skin where the fabric had been. As his mouth worked across each breast, he heard her moan and tighten her hands on his shoulders. He laid her back down and slipped a finger under each side of the lace panties. In one smooth movement, he had them off and lying on the pile on the floor. His mouth replaced this fabric, too, and soon he could feel her tensing as she felt each movement.

When she couldn't take it anymore, she rose and took his face in her hands. Kissing him deeply, she could taste herself on his mouth, and that only intensified her kiss. Austin started up over her, when she pulled back and over to push him down where she'd just been. As Julia moved up and over him, Austin could feel her mouth and thought he would explode before she raised up and positioned herself over him. *In the firelight, she looks magnificent,* he thought as she arched her back and pulled her hair loose. She knew he loved her hair loose, and she leaned over to create a curtain around their faces as she kissed him again. Soon their movements quickened, and he felt her tense just before he exploded.

Julia collapsed on top of him and he rolled her onto her side. He held her close.

"Jules, let's get under the covers before we fall asleep."

"M'kay," she mumbled, as he lifted her up to pull the blanket and sheet down. When he pulled them up over them both, she opened her eyes and smiled lazily.

"I think I'm falling in love," she teased.

"I think I'm already there," he replied.

The sun was pouring through the uncovered windows as they woke up to make love again before taking a shower. It was a huge tile and glass stall that was obviously built for two.

"I should have looked closer yesterday. We could have waited until we got in here," he teased, as they scrubbed each other's backs and he leaned back to let her rinse her hair. "Of course, I'm ready again if you are."

"This is exactly why I love you younger men," Julie laughed. "But I do believe I smelled bacon before we came in here. Bacon? Food? Isn't that what drives you boys?"

"Oh, hell no," Austin leaned toward her, but she jumped out of the shower and grabbed a towel.

"Well, horn toad, it's driving ME this morning. We did work up an appetite earlier. Morning calisthenics make me hungry, especially when it's a long workout," and she grinned over her shoulder as she grabbed her toothbrush. She handed him a towel with one hand but held it out of his reach. He knew what she was doing, and he stood there with his hands on his hips, grinning at her. She liked to tease him, and in games where one or both were naked, they usually ended up back in bed.

"You really want to play that game?" he asked.

"Tempted," she said around her toothbrush before tossing the towel in his direction. He easily caught it, wrapped it low around his hips, and walked to the second sink to dig his own toothbrush out.

Finished, he leaned in to give her another kiss. For some reason, he always loved kissing her right after they'd both brushed their teeth. She laughed and gave him what he wanted.

"Aren't we a little late for fresh breath this morning?" she teased.

"Naw...both times work for me." Morning breath really didn't bother him as it did her. At least hers bothered her. When she asked, he only replied that when sex is involved, breath really isn't an issue. She'd laughed and gone with it after that.

It didn't take him long to shave and run a comb through his curling hair. He tucked it behind his ears and went into the bedroom to dig out his clothes. He came back shortly in jeans and sweatshirt with tennis shoes on his feet. He told her that he was going to walk around outside a bit and for her to join him when she finished.

"Good morning, Sunshine!" Sharon greeted Julia as she came into the kitchen a few minutes later. "My, don't you look well rested and *relaxed*," and she laughed as she said the last. "Hottie Boy was just in here and I sent him out back. Grab a mug of the good stuff and join him."

"Do you need me to do anything? To help you now? Help you tonight?"

"Oh, hell, no. I've got this, and I have a team arriving at noon to set up tables and chairs outside. Angie will have the caterer in tears by 2:00, the bartender will be here at 3:00, and everyone should start showing up around 4:00. You know this crowd, though, always fashionably late. I told them we're eating at 5:00, and if they miss the good stuff, they miss it." Sharon meant what she said.

"Arighty then," Julia had filled her mug. "I'll go join my Hottie Boy."

"Jules." Sharon's more serious tone made Julia stop and turn around. "You know that people won't think a thing about the age difference, don't you?" Sharon knew Julia well, and she was pretty certain that the opinions of others didn't bother her. This crowd was different, more like what Julia had escaped from in St. Louis, and Sharon didn't want her young friend to be uncomfortable. Heaven help anyone who made her so.

"Sharon, you know that I couldn't care less, don't you?" Julia replied.

Sharon laughed then. "That's my girl! Hey, you two come back in about fifteen minutes, and I'll have breakfast ready. Bacon, eggs, biscuits, gravy—the works. Angie would die if she suspected I could cook like this." She laughed again.

"Naw...she knows you just keep her around for the Bloody Mary's," Julia teased. "Be back in a few."

She found Austin sitting on a log bench under the tall ponderosa pines. Julia loved these trees. There were pines in Missouri, but not this massive and this beautiful. From their spot, they saw Mount Humphreys in the distance as it dwarfed other mountains stretching out on either side. Julia sat down beside him and followed the direction he was looking.

"Julia, this is heaven, isn't it?" Austin's voice was almost a whisper.

"It is. I've been up here about four or five times now, but every time I see something different. Sharon said we have about fifteen minutes until breakfast is ready."

"That's fine. I'll just start my morning with two of the most beautiful sights in the world." He took her hand, kissed the palm, and smiled his biggest smile before turning back to the mountain view. Still holding hands, they sat like that until they heard Sharon's voice calling them in.

"Well, let's get this day started," Austin stood to pull her up beside him. "It will definitely be an interesting one."

"Babe, it's just a party, and they're just people. We can exit any time."

"Exit to where, exactly?" Austin asked.

"In this big-ass place? Honey, I know lots of hidey-holes," and they were laughing as they entered the kitchen.

"I just love looking at you two together," Sharon said. "Reminds me of another couple I know. And here's the other half of it," she said as John entered the room. She blew a kiss in his direction.

The rest of the day, Julia and Austin spent in Flagstaff, looking in some of the shops—her idea—and taking a walk through Buffalo Park.

"I wish we had the time to see Sedona today. Let's drive through there on our way back home, okay? I know it's a longer drive, but it's so pretty," Julia said.

"No clue. I've never been there. In fact, I've not done much besides school and work since I made it out here. I saw the Grand Canyon when I was a kid on one of our family vacations, but I was a kid. Looked around about five minutes, got yelled at for climbing on the rocks too close to the edge, and was ready to go." Austin laughed at the memory.

"Well," said Julia, "we'll go there, too. Just not tomorrow. That's a two-day trip by itself."

They headed back to the house in the early afternoon, and the place was bustling with caterers. A rental company was setting up tables and chairs on the back patio. Sharon was directing everyone.

"Thank god, you're back. I don't need you for anything, I just wanted you to have first dibs on parking. It will be interesting. NO, not there!" She was off in the direction of the rental deliveryman. Julia laughed to think of the long afternoon ahead of all those people.

They were dressed and enjoying drinks as the first of about thirty to forty people arrived that evening. John made introductions, showed them to the bar, and moved off to welcome another couple. By 4:30, the place was almost full and Austin found himself sitting with the men while Julia was at a table of females. He caught her eye and grinned. She rolled her eyes in return. The eye roll made him chuckle. *She hates these things*, he thought, *and in a way I can see why.*

"And who is that smoking hunk of man, may I ask?" This came from Arnie, Arnette Dunklin. "Julia, did he come with *you*?" Arnie had never been shy, and she wasn't about to start now. Julia looked over at Austin, whose green shirt and khaki slacks hugged him in all the right places. His hair was curling around his neck and he had it tucked behind each ear, as usual.

"Why, yes, yes he did, Arnie," Julia smoothly replied. "Why do you ask?"

"Oh…just curious, I guess. My, my, my, he does appear to be rather young, isn't he?" Arnie hadn't taken her eyes off Austin yet. Arnie wasn't above moving past the looking part and making a play for any man she thought interesting. She was an attractive woman, and at fifty-four, she could still hold her own in the looks department. She'd made a pass at most of the husbands there, and Sharon was sure she'd been successful a time or two. Arnie spoke again, "He looks to be about my Justin's age. Does he know my Justin?" Arnie looked at Julia as she said the last, and Julia recognized the innuendo in her voice.

Sharon started to say something, when Julia whispered, "I got this," to her friend.

"Oh, I doubt it," Julia remarked. "He doesn't spend that much time around jails. Didn't your Justin recently find himself in the company of the Maricopa County Sheriff? Drunk and disorderly, or some such scandal, wasn't it?" At Arnie's shocked expression, Julia leaned toward the woman and continued in her best concerned voice. "Bless his heart, Arnie, I'm sure that had to be the absolute worst time in that poor boy's life! And poor you! Sharon, didn't I say more than once, 'God love those poor Dunklins, to have something this awful happen.' How is he these days, Arnie? And you are just so strong to make it through the storm, but I'm sure it was just an overnight stay, wasn't it?" Julia's face was filled with concern but her eyes flashed something else entirely.

Arnie didn't know whether to respond to Julia's kind words or to her veiled insult. She looked from Julia to Sharon and back to Julia. With Sharon looking over Julia's shoulder, Arnie knew which path she'd better take.

"Why, yes, Julia, it has been such a mess and we're trying everything to keep him from having a criminal record. And poor Justin was just rail-roaded, you know. That damn Joe Arpaio. Ollie tried everything he could to get that sheriff to see reason, but not Sheriff Joe." She went on a rant that both Julia and Sharon ignored.

"Well played, grasshopper, well played," Sharon whispered in Julia's ear as soon as Arnie's attention was focused on another member of the group.

Julia really didn't care what these women thought. She'd done work for more than half of them, not Arnie fortunately, and they all liked Julia. To see her channel her inner Sharon was entertainment itself.

Austin watched from across the way, and he couldn't wait to find out what Julia had said to the woman who had been staring at him. *Staring, hell,* he thought, *she looked like she wanted to eat me up for an hors d'oeuvre.* Whatever Julia said worked. The woman had looked away once Julia started speaking to her. She looked up to smile. It was her "I'm having fun at someone's expense" smile. The woman in question didn't look his way again. He grinned back and shook his head, turning his attention back to the men surrounding him.

One in particular caught his attention. Austin had been introduced to him by John, but the man's name escaped him now. He wished he could remember because he followed the man's line of vision, and it seemed to end at Julia. For a few moments, the man stared at her while Austin kept his eyes on him. Almost as if he sensed the other man, the stranger turned, looked at Austin, and walked over.

"I've been wondering about the man who captured our Julia," he said with a smile that didn't reach his eyes.

Austin's chin lifted slightly in an unconscious gesture, and he returned the gaze. "I can't imagine anyone actually capturing Julia," he replied. *Greg, that's his name. Greg Halston,* Austin thought. *Import/export business and obviously doing quite well.*

Greg chuckled and looked back at the woman in question. To say he was interested was an understatement, and Austin wondered what the relationship between two was, or had been.

"No," he said conversationally. "No, she is certainly an allusive female. But that's part of her charm, isn't it?" He gazed once more at her as she leaned in to say something to Sharon. "Yes, our Julia is quite charming, among other things." He turned to look at Austin once more. "Now that I know her type, I suppose I can understand why she turned me down so many times." He raised his glass in a slight salute. "Best of luck with that one, my young friend. You're gonna need it." Greg drained his drink before turning and walking away.

Austin's eyes followed him as he crossed the patio and disappeared into the house. He grinned. *Sore loser much?* he thought as he looked back at Julia. She gave him a questioning look that he answered with a wide grin and a shake of his head.

"Austin," John got his attention as he walked up with an older man, shorter than both of them, who looked to be about John's age. "I want you to meet someone. This is Stephen Jones of Coast to Coast Industrial and Commercial Landscaping. Steve, this is Austin James. Austin is a close friend of our Julia's and now of ours. He's finishing up school in December and is in your field."

Austin looked from John back to Stephen Jones and shook the hand the latter had extended.

"It's nice to meet you, sir. I've followed your company for several years now, and I must say that I'm a great admirer of the work you do."

"Austin will be interning at Superstition here in a few weeks," John continued.

"Oh, then you've met Jay Reynolds. Fine man. He works with our man there, Clayton Johnston."

Austin found his voice, "Yes, sir, I've met them both, and I'm eager to get started. They can teach me a lot."

Steve looked at John then and said, "I like a man who isn't afraid to admit that he's still learning." To Austin, "Son, you'll want to look me up when you're finished in December. But have you got a minute? I'd like to pick your brain about..." Steve and Austin walked toward an empty table where they sat, engaged in conversation.

Julia had seen Austin move away with the man, and she caught up with John to find out who he was.

"Baby doll, I'm just helping your man out here. That's Steve Jones, one of the biggest names in the industrial landscaping business. Steve and I have worked on several projects together, and I thought he should meet Austin."

Julia beamed at John, reached up to kiss his cheek, and said, "I love you, you know."

He patted the arm that was around his neck and said, "Right back at'cha, sweet pea."

They both turned as Sharon walked up to them. "I would be concerned, but he can't afford to divorce me now." She laughed. Julia filled her in and she, too, gave John a wink and a smile.

"This man takes care of his own," she said before moving off to tend to another group.

Later that night when everyone had gone home, Austin and Julia finally found themselves alone.

"Austin, I saw you talking with Greg Halston. Care to share what he had to say about me? I know Greg, and I know he was probably filling your ear with lots of 'Julia' gossip." Julia and Austin were in the bedroom but hadn't undressed for bed yet. Austin was sitting on the chair by the fireplace as he removed his shoes.

Austin looked up and grinned at her. "He wished me luck, I think." At her frown, he continued. "I suppose he's been chasing after you for some time, but 'our Julia' as he calls you wasn't responding as he hoped."

She laughed. "Good grief, he's a loser, isn't he? Yes, he asked me out more than once. Yes, I turned him down every time. You see, Greg is pretty much another Keith. He may be handsome and successful, but he isn't my type." She crossed the short distance between them and sat down on his lap. She wrapped her arms around Austin's neck. Looking at him, she smiled. "You have no reason to give Mr. Greg Halston, or any other man for that matter, a moment's thought. I've found my type right here."

Austin smoothed her hair back and cupped her face in his hand. "Oh, really? Good to know because I'd hate to go all caveman on some guy." He leaned in and kissed her.

He pulled back again, and Julia smiled before her expression changed as she looked at him questioningly.

"Oh, and John tells me that he introduced you to Stephen Jones. How did that go?"

Austin's face lit up as he shared with her his conversation with the man. "Jules, this guy is legend. And does he know his stuff! I could have picked his brain for hours tonight. And guess what? He wants me to come by in December and talk again. This could be exactly what I need to get my start."

She loved seeing him this excited. Austin wasn't one to let his emotions show, regardless of what they were, but with her he let his guard down. She laughed at his little-boy excitement and listened to him talk. Since neither was tired, they put on sweatshirts and she pulled a blanket from the closet so that they could sit on the patio. Stretched out on a double chaise lounge, they covered up with the blanket, and Austin talked on while she listened. She turned her eyes to the stars. *They are so clear here in the mountain air,* she thought as she listened to Austin describing what he'd like to build someday. By the time he wound down, Austin had shared with her more of his career plans than he'd ever done before.

I remember being that excited about starting something new. Something that was mine, she thought. Being with him was like living it again, only better. Neither had ever been happier.

Chapter 18

AUSTIN CAME INTO THE APARTMENT, and after dropping his keys on the counter, looked over at Lauren. She was sitting at the counter, a cup of coffee steaming beside her and a magazine spread out in front of her.

"Hey, Slick, what are you doing home? Don't you have some small child to run over or something?" When she didn't snark back, Austin asked, "What's up? Julia okay?"

"Yes, and no. Yes, she's fine. No, she got some bad news today, but I'll let her tell you. She's back in her bedroom, sitting in her chair, moping."

He went back and found her pretty much as Lauren had described.

"What's up, babe?" he leaned down to look her in the face. He saw that the two lines on either side of her mouth were prominent and felt himself getting upset. Julia only looked like this when she was stressed. He didn't like her to be anything but happy and was ready to do something. What, he didn't know, but he'd find out.

"Oh," she sighed loudly. "My mother called. She and Daddy are coming out here. Next week."

"Is that all?" Austin sat on the small footstool and faced her. He still didn't quite get the strained relationship between Julia and her parents. He understood it, having one of his own, but he didn't let his stress him out this much.

She looked at him then and raised an eyebrow. "Is that all? Is *that* all? Austin, you have no idea. For three days all I'll hear about is 'Why are you doing this?' or 'Why aren't you doing that?' 'Julia, for heaven's sake, dress like a forty-year-old woman' 'Do something with that hair, for god's sake' and my favorite 'Haven't you met some nice man out here dear? I've heard that there are so many, and they have good jobs, too.' I want to jab myself in the eye sometimes."

Austin couldn't help laughing at her expense. Julia glared.

"You have no idea, do you? Ask Lauren. This is the woman who made me feel about this tall," she held up her thumb and forefinger, an inch apart, "and just couldn't understand why I'd ever divorce Keith. Or move clear across the country. She blamed Lauren as much as possible."

"Lauren?! A bad influence? I can relate," Austin laughed again.

"I heard that," came the voice from the other room. "I'm not totally deaf, you know, especially when you don't shut your door. I just can't see."

"Yes, Lauren," Julia continued. "Mother just knew that if she hadn't been around to influence me, I'd still be in living in Lake St. Louis, on the arm of a *wonderful* man, and living the dream. *Her* dream."

"Will she be staying here? Do I need to make myself absent for a few days?" He wasn't wild about the idea, but whatever would help Julia was what he'd do.

"Oh, hell, no! Daddy always takes her to the Camelback Resort. They rent a one-bedroom condo there and he plays golf while she does the spa thing. Every evening, though, they'll be all in my face." Julia stopped herself. "Well, Daddy will be okay. He's always been behind me, whatever I wanted to do, but Mother. She's a load."

"So...do you want me to make myself scarce?" Austin was confused on what she wanted from him.

"Nope. You're part of my life. I love you, and it's time you met my family."

"God help you," came from the other room. Lauren appeared in the doorway. "I'll have your back, Junior."

"Whoa, for Lauren to have my back, this must be torture," he joked.

"Yuck, Yuck, Yuck," came from Lauren. "You'll thank me, you know. And don't look this gift horse in the mouth."

"For once, I supposed I'll appreciate the nag, uh?" Austin couldn't resist the jab.

"Keep it up, keep it up."

"Okay, you two. They won't be here for a few days, so let's not let Dana Whitman ruin this week, too."

The week passed quickly, and Austin took extra care the night he was to meet Dana and Lawrence Whitman. Julia told him to be himself—shave only if he wanted to, wear shorts and flip flops, put his cap on—but Austin had more pride than that. He dressed in the khakis and shirt Julia had bought him for the Burns' party, and he traded his sandals for loafers, no socks. After he tamed his hair the best he could, he almost threw the cap on his head but stopped himself.

Austin came out of their room—it was *their* room now—and sat at the bar counter. He watched her stir iced tea and finish up a platter of cheese and crackers. Austin smiled at Julia's appearance. He didn't know if forty-year-old women were supposed to wear their skirts that short, but he was glad Julia could get away with it. Her short navy skirt was topped off with a blue and white striped t-shirt, and she had slid her feet into white sandals. It was still hot, so she'd pulled her hair up, her long neck exposed. Austin came around the counter to lean down and plant a kiss on that neck. She stopped what she was doing, closed her eyes, and sighed.

"Keep that up, Ace, and the folks will have to show themselves in," she whispered.

Austin slapped her on the rear, and said, "Nope, that's not the first impression I'm going to make. 'Come on in folks, I'll be through screwing your daughter in about twenty minutes.'"

"Twenty minutes? That's all I get? Never mind, then," she teased. The doorbell rang, and Julia took a deep breath.

"Show time!" she said. "You, come with me."

Lauren had left before the happy reunion because as she put it, "Jules, I love you, but your mom makes my ass hurt. I'll see her just before she boards the plane home," and she left. *So much for having my back*, Austin thought as he heard the door slam behind her.

The bell rang again before Julia could make it down the stairs. "Coming!" she called out.

She threw open the door, and there stood a woman who could have been her twin had she been twenty-five years younger. The difference was that her dark hair was cut short and her face held a few lines around her eyes and beside her mouth. She was smiling, her blue eyes happy to see her only child, and she was starting to put her arms out. Behind her stood a tall, dark-haired man whose gray-tinted, receding hairline showed a tanned face and head. His blue eyes lit up as he saw his daughter, and Julia reached past her mother to jump up and hug Lawrence first. Dana turned her head to watch the two, and Austin could see her lips set in a hard line.

"My turn," her voice sang out, and Julia reluctantly let loose of her dad to give her mother a brief hug. "Julia, you look nice, sweetheart. I see you still have that long hair." She turned and spotted Austin, her brows coming together in a frown.

"Oh, Mother, Daddy, I want you to meet Austin James. Austin, these are my parents, Dana and Lawrence Whitman."

Austin extended his hand first to Lawrence, "Nice to meet you, sir," who shook it firmly. He turned to Dana and extended it in her direction. She backed up just a hint before she accepted the proffered hand, gave it a brief squeeze, and released it just as quickly.

"Come on in and let's get you something to drink. Are you hungry? I know that we're going out later, but I fixed a little snack." Julia led the way up the stairs with Austin holding back to be last.

They settled in with Lawrence and Dana on the sofa and Julia on the edge of the chaise. Austin started to pull a chair in from the dining table when Julia patted the space next to her and asked him come sit with her. The small space put them close together, as Julia placed her hand possessively on Austin's leg and leaned into his side. He almost smiled at her show of solidarity. No one could make a statement without saying a word like Julia.

"So, Mother, Daddy, how was your flight out?" For the next few minutes Dana extolled the "horridness" of commercial flying, while Lawrence simply gave an "uh-uh" in agreement when called upon.

"Daddy, aren't you getting ready to retire soon?" Julia pulled her dad into the conversation. She turned to Austin. "You remember, I told you that Daddy worked for Edward Jones in St. Louis. He started there early when the company was still young, didn't you, Daddy, and now he's a supervisor in the human resources department."

"Yep, Baby Girl, I'm hanging it up this October. I'll be sixty-seven by then, and it's time. I want to travel. Take your mother to see the world."

"Oh, Larry," and for the first time Austin saw a little tenderness in the woman." We've taken company trips all over the place."

"Yes, but this time, we decide where and when," he looked up and beamed at Julia. "Maybe my girl will want to tag along some."

"Your girl is busy these days," Julia said and filled them in on Touch of Jules and the work she and Lauren were doing there.

"Where is Lauren?" Lawrence asked. "I miss her." That drew a glare from his wife. "Well, I do!"

Julia laughed, "She's busy tonight, but she said she'd catch up with you." Julia just left out the "while you board the plane" part.

"Mother, help me get everyone something to drink. Daddy, what do you want?"

"Bud Light, my usual."

"Austin?"

"I'll have the same."

Dana followed her daughter into the kitchen, and Lawrence moved closer to the end of the sofa that faced Austin's chair. They could hear the women chatting as they worked.

"So, tell me what you do, Austin, and call me Larry." Austin filled him in on his internship and future plans with a shorthand version. "Wait, you're graduating college in December? Three months?" Lawrence eyed the young man in front of him.

"Yes, sir, and I'm hoping to work for one of the industrial landscape firms here in Phoenix before starting my own company." Austin met Larry's stare with his own.

About that time, the women returned with the drinks, and Julia set the platter on the coffee table before handing everyone a small plate and napkin.

"What? Who's graduating? What company?" Dana had heard just enough to ask.

"I am," Austin said. "In December, and as I was telling Larry here, I'll be looking for a job at one of the industrial landscape firms here before starting my own company."

"Landscape." Dana sniffed. "Isn't that mowing lawns and trimming shrubs?"

"Mother!" Julia leaned toward her, ready to pounce.

"Yes, I suppose that's part of it," Austin laid a hand on her shoulder and pulled her back. "But it's also designing the landscaping of major buildings, like around the University of Phoenix Stadium or Arizona Mills Mall. We work with the architect to make the outside of a building complement the land it sits on and the surrounding topography. It's really an important part of a development. For example, when say, Arnold Palmer decides to design a golf course. He'll work closely with the landscaping firm to make sure it all flows properly, that the natural scenery is kept intact as much as possible, and that we make all of his design work within the natural confines."

Dana simply looked at him now, mouth slightly open, as if she was confused about what this man was in front of her. Julia was smiling smugly and had put her hand on Austin's leg once again. Larry grinned at him.

"Good description, my man. Now, I'm a bit hungry. What'cha got here, Jules?"

They settled into general conversation after that, and soon they left for the restaurant. On their way out the door, Larry held Julia back to put his arm around her and whisper in her ear.

"So, how serious is the thing you have with the boy here?"

Julia frowned at the "boy" reference and replied, "I don't know, Daddy, I suppose you could say serious. We've only been together about three months, but it seems so much longer." She gave him a big smile. "Isn't he something?"

Larry looked at his girl's happy face. She'd never looked like this when she'd been with Keith, not even in the beginning. She looked younger and more carefree than she had in years.

"If he makes you happy, Kitten, he's okay by me."

"I knew you'd say that. Thank you, Daddy." She kissed his cheek. Dana witnessed the exchange out the corner of her eye but said nothing. *I'll deal with this later*, she thought.

"Austin, why don't you sit in front with Larry, and Julia can sit in the back with me," Dana gave everyone their directions as they climbed into the rental car. Austin winked at Julia and opened the rear door for her. On the short drive to Cattleman's, Austin and Lawrence chatted easily while the back seat remained uncomfortably quiet. Dana was still fuming over what she saw as Julia's irresponsible behavior. Her daughter knew her mother's moods and had no intention of initiating any conversation.

The restaurant was one of Lawrence's favorites as it boasted the best steaks in Scottsdale. It wasn't until they'd finished pre-dinner drinks that Dana began.

"Well, Julia, is your Arizona experience coming to an end soon?" Dana's chin rose as she looked at her daughter.

Julia laughed shortly before replying. "My Arizona experience, as you call it, has barely begun. Why do you ask, Mother?"

"Well, I assumed that you ran away to prove a point and that your point has been made," Dana's voice still contained its haughty air.

"Mother, my point in coming out here was to build a new life for myself. I was running away from nothing," Julia paused. "Unless you consider escaping a philandering husband and a life of tragedy to be running away. Call it what you want."

"Now, Jules, your mother doesn't mean anything. She and I are always hopeful that you'll move back to St. Louis some day, that's all," Lawrence tried to smooth the ruffled feathers.

"Daddy, I know exactly what Mother meant." Julia turned to Dana. "Now, why in the world would you want me to come back? Regardless of how much you love Keith, Mother, I will never return to him. You should know that by now."

"I simply don't want you to make irreversible decisions, and so far, your decisions have been anything but responsible. Darling, you…"

"Dana," her husband interrupted before the conversation could deteriorate further. "We have time to talk about this later. Austin and I are starved, and I'm ready to order."

Throughout the exchange, Austin had remained silent, fixing his attention on the menu in front of him. He looked up now and smiled at the other three as he reached across the short distance to find Julia's hand and give it a squeeze. Lawrence winked, Julia smiled, and Dana sniffed her disgust. She managed to maintain her silence regarding Julia's life through the main course, but as soon as dessert was set on the table, she turned to her daughter.

"So, tell me Julia, you said earlier that your little business is doing well? I'm surprised you're still dabbling in design."

Julia had been expecting the insult to her career, especially since Dana had said nothing when Julia was filling them in earlier. Dana rarely disappointed her.

"Well, Mother, yes, I still dabble in design. Fortunately, Touch of Jules has become a lucrative business. Lauren and I do quite well, thank you for your interest," Julia gave Dana what Austin liked to call her screw-you smile before she looked back down at the turtle cheesecake in front of her. She took a tiny bite before shoving it away and picking up her coffee. Austin noticed that she'd eaten little, but as tense as things were with Dana, he couldn't blame her. He'd make sure she ate something later.

Dana wasn't finished yet.

"Lauren," she said the name as her face took on an expression of distaste. "Yes, I hear that you're still hanging out with *that* woman." She shook her head. "Really, Julia, I would have thought you'd outgrow her by now. Lauren is…" she dismissed the woman with a wave of her hand. "Well, we all know what Lauren is."

Julia set her coffee cup down with a clatter, but before she could form a retort, Lawrence interrupted.

"How is Lauren? Will I get to see her this trip? She never fails to make me laugh," he grinned at Julia as he finished. Austin admired the man's smooth way of turning the conversation from uncomfortable topics to safe territory. *I need to take notes*, the younger man thought, *because I'll never have the practice that he's obviously had. Dana makes my mom small potatoes.*

"Lauren has made it her mission to entertain, hasn't she?" Austin grinned at Lawrence, Larry, as he insisted on Austin calling him. He found Julia's hand still gripping her coffee cup and put his hand on hers. At his touch, she visibly relaxed and smiled gratefully at him.

"I'll never forget the first time Julia brought her around," Lawrence regaled them with humorous stories until they'd all finished and the check had been settled.

The ride back to Julia's was much the same as before. At her invitation to come up, Lawrence was ready to accept when Dana spoke.

"Thank you, darling, but after traveling all day, my head is pounding," Dana put a hand up to her forehead to stress her discomfort. "We'll see you tomorrow."

"I completely understand, Mother, and I'll look forward to that," Julia's relief turned to disappointment as she looked at her dad. "Daddy, call me first thing in the morning, before golf, of course, and we'll make plans, okay?"

Lawrence's face reflected Julia's disappointment as he came around the car to give her a hug and kiss her forehead tenderly. Austin enjoyed watching the two interact—as uncomfortable and distant as Dana and Julia's relationship was, Larry and Julia's was close. He could easily see where Julia's personality came from.

"Thank you for dinner and the good company tonight," Austin said as he shook Larry's hand. To Dana, "Ma'am, I hope your head is better. Sometimes a good night's sleep is all that's required."

Dana gave him a half-hearted smile as Larry answered for both of them.

"It's been our pleasure, Austin. I look forward to spending more time with you before we leave."

The older man climbed behind the wheel and started the car. As they pulled away, Larry and Dana looked at the couple who still stood in the driveway. Austin's arm had come to circle Julia's waist and she leaned her head on his shoulder. Larry smiled at the image. Dana simply snarled her nose and looked out the side window. She wasn't happy. She had two more days to prevent her daughter from making a huge mistake. She hoped that she wasn't too late.

"Oh. My. God. That was the longest fifteen minutes of my life," Lauren lamented as she collapsed on the sofa.

"Fifteen minutes! Yeah, try three days. And what happened to all of that 'I've got your back' crap? Huh? You weren't around. Ever. I'll bet you even bailed when they stopped by the shop," Austin grinned at Lauren.

"Guilty. I put up with plenty before we left St. Louis, especially from Cruella Deville. She hates me. I hate her. We're even. As long as we stay away from one another, we'll stay that way."

"Well, did you see Larry at all?"

"Of course! He skipped golf one morning to take Jules and me to breakfast. He likes you, you know."

"He likes whoever Julia likes," Austin replied. "And you can't argue that one."

"True that," Lauren replied. "But he likes you even if she kicks you to the curb next week."

"I don't know if that's a compliment or a warning."

"Take it either way, Ace, but I need a drink. A nice, vodka palate cleansing from making nice with Brunhilda. How that woman sired Julia is beyond me." Lauren got up and made her way to the kitchen to dig out her Grey Goose stash.

"Jules definitely looks like her mom, but in personality, I see more of Larry in Julia than Dana," Austin mused.

"Thank. God," was the reply from the kitchen.

Just then Julia came up the stairs from having seen her parents off and sat down heavily on a bar stool. She looked at the vodka tonic Lauren was mixing up and said, "Make mine a double with extra lime."

Austin came over and started rubbing her neck. "Woman, you are tense," he observed.

"Yep, but it's over now for the next however many months. If I could just visit with Daddy and Mother would stay home, I'd be happy. That's not going to happen. Her leash is short. Very, very short."

"Oh, come on, Jules, she can't be all bad. You're dad's a great guy, and I can't see him settling for someone who makes him miserable. Or is it just her who makes other people miserable. How does it work with them?"

"You're right about Daddy being a great guy, and it's only ME who makes her miserable but only because I shook off her leash and ran away. That galls her more than anything. No control. No say-so." She sighed then and took a big swallow of her drink. "That's better." She took a deep breath and exhaled before turning to Austin. "Except this time, I think her meddling is going to be directed at you, sweetie," and she smiled weakly. "As long as we keep her in Missouri, we'll be fine. And as I always say when anything concerns my mother, 'It is what it is.'"

"I'll drink to that," and Lauren raised her glass. Just then her phone buzzed. She looked down and back up at the two in front of her. "I'll take this later."

"Huh? Take *what* later?" Julia took one look at her friend and knew something was up. "Lauren…Tell me now or tell me later. Either way, you know I'll find out."

Lauren turned around and walked into the living room, sipping on her drink. "Okay, I suppose you'll know sooner or later. I've been seeing someone lately, off and on, and we've been having a real good time." Lauren looked at Julia's face and knew when she'd figured it out. For Austin's sake she added, "It's Matt."

"WHAT?!? What the hell?!" Julia jumped up and pounced on her friend. "Since when? What do you mean by 'seeing'? What are you doing here, Lauren?"

"Well, you might as well come in and listen, too, Junior. It's a long story." She settled in to tell it.

Chapter 19

⎯⎯⎯⎯

LAUREN WAS ALONE IN THE shop the day Julia and Austin left for Flagstaff, and as she looked at the time on her phone, she figured the couple would be going through the desert and climbing into the mountains. Lauren had been with Julia a time or two when she'd gone to visit Sharon and John in Flagstaff. Flagstaff was a beautiful town, but a bit tame for Lauren's taste. She'd found a place called Sam's and enjoyed an evening or two, but half of the places were overrun with college kids and the other half by blue-hairs, as Lauren liked to call the retired club. *Not my scene*, she thought.

The door bell jingling brought her back to the present, and Lauren pasted on her customer smile and walked toward the showroom. Matt stepped through the doorway, pausing as he looked around nervously.

"Oh! What are you doing here? Need the bachelor pad updated? Not enough condom dispensers?" Lauren had switched from her customer smile to her I'm-flirting-but-don't-expect-anything smile. She'd removed her reading glasses and was glad she'd worn the short, red dress today. With red high-heeled sandals, she could look him in the eye. Lauren was tall, and she liked to look men in the eye whenever possible.

"Haha. Julia talks about this place, and I thought what the hell. Go see it for yourself. Here I am." Matt looked around before settling back on Lauren. He'd already given her the head-to-toe onceover and his eyes were back at her face.

"Here you are..." Lauren looked him up and down for a few seconds. "Nope. Use that lame reason on someone stupid. You're here to see me. Admit it, Matty," and Lauren smiled as she saw that she was on target.

She also knew that he hated being call "Matty," so she used it at every opportunity.

"Ok, I am here to see you. I thought that with Austin and Julia out of town that we could go out. Dinner, whatever. You know, with both of us at loose ends..." his voice trailed off.

Lauren laughed. "Sweetheart, I am *never* at loose ends. Now, if you're needing a sitter, I might be able to accommodate you." She lowered her head and looked at him through narrowed eyes. "What do you have in mind again? Was that a 'whatever' I heard? Who even says that, unless it's a sixteen-year-old boy."

Matt was getting irritated by this time and turned to leave. "Forget it. Try to be nice to someone and the bitch comes out."

"Not so fast," Lauren came around to stand between him and the door. She leaned in and saw him take a deep breath, her perfume surrounding him. "I didn't say I wasn't interested. I'm just not interested in 'whatever.' Matty, no woman wants an invitation like that. Now, you figure out where we'll go, and when you'll pick me up, and we'll talk. Okay?"

If he looked down, he'd see a lot of cleavage under his nose, but he made himself look at her face. Looking down would be admitting defeat with this woman, and he wasn't about to do that. His mouth was dry but his mind was working.

"Lauren, I'd like to take you to dinner. You enjoy Houston's a lot, so if you want to go with me, I'll pick you up at your place at 6:30."

"Now that's more like it," Lauren leaned back and looked him up and down. Shorts, t-shirt, sandals. "You're not wearing that, are you? Put on a pair of pants, find a shirt that doesn't say *Callahan Auto Parts*, some real shoes, and pick me up at 7:00, Tommy Boy. No tennis shoes, either."

Matt looked down at his shirt and back up at Lauren. He grinned and said, "I think I have something that will work. See you at 7:00." He was almost whistling as he left the shop.

"Shit!" The word shot from red gloss-covered lips. "Shit! Shit! Shit!" Lauren spoke out loud as she looked at the now-closed door. "I promised Julia I'd behave, but he just makes me want to...I don't know what I want to do with him." She ignored her desk and plopped down in an armchair that was to be delivered to Mrs. Hampton the next day.

"Okay, how bad can it be? I'll have dinner, drinks, and give Matty Boy another lesson in how to treat a woman. I will NOT sleep with him because he's off limits. Damn, he's cute, though." She thought a few moments about the broad shoulders, muscular chest and arms, and well-formed legs. Her mind was working its way to his other side and from the look on her face, anyone would know what she was thinking. She shook her head. "NO! He doesn't know what he's doing anyway, not really. I'll keep telling myself that, and we'll be just fine."

She pulled herself up and went back to work. It would be a long two hours until closing time.

I wonder what to wear, she thought before concentrating once more on the papers covering her desk.

At 7:00 that evening, Lauren took a last look at herself in the full-length mirror that covered her closet door. Long, straight white skirt with a slit up to her thigh that kept it from being too conservative. Coral sleeveless top that came down to partially cover her hips and was cut low enough to be tempting. Turquoise and silver belt, white sandals with more turquoise, large silver hoop earrings, and a large turquoise and silver bangle rounded out the ensemble. She wore her blond hair down and grabbed a straw cowboy hat trimmed in more turquoise beading to cover her hair on the ride in the Jeep. She was doing the turn one way and then another mirror dance when she heard the bell below. Grabbing a straw bag, she hurried down the stairs to greet Matt.

Lauren threw open the door and almost dropped her jaw. *Matty boy cleans up real nice,* she thought. He'd opted for dark blue jeans, a blue button-down shirt with the sleeves rolled up, and on his feet she saw dark brown Sperry's.

"You do listen—no tennis shoes. Well done, Matty. You ready?" she asked smiling at the man in front of her.

Matt found his voice and offered his arm as she closed the door. She made sure it was locked and accompanied him to the waiting Jeep. *Hmmm...the boy is learning,* she thought, as he helped her in, trying not to be too obviously staring at the length of leg she exposed when climbing into the car. He came around to his own side and grinned at her before slipping on his Oakleys and starting the motor.

"Wait," Lauren put her hand on his arm. "Let's skip Houston's tonight. I'm in the mood for something else. Can you follow directions?"

She couldn't see his eyes but knew that he was giving her his *whatever* look. She slipped her own over-sized Gucci sunglasses on and grinned back. "We'll see...." was all she said.

Following her directions as they drove down one unfamiliar street after another, Matt wasn't sure where they were going. About ten minutes later, they turned into a small shopping plaza and pulled up in front of a two-story white building that stood out from the surrounding area. It had wrought iron running half-way up the windows, boxes of flowers hanging over the edges and a fountain bubbling outside the front entrance. Parking was in front and on both sides, and Matt found them a spot beside the building.

"What is this place?" he asked as he got out of the car. Lauren sat and looked at him until he remembered to come around and help her out. *Sal's Ristorante e Bar* said the sign above the door. "Italian?"

"You have a marvelous grasp of the obvious, Junior." Lauren grinned at his annoyed look. "Yes, this is Sal's place, and you're going to love his pizza."

"Do you come here often?" Matt had never heard of the place.

"Yep. Sal and his wife Carina are old friends from St. Louis. They still have a restaurant on The Hill in St. Louis that their son runs now. They came out here about five years ago and started this one. Sal decided he'd had enough of Missouri winters, and their daughter lives in Tempe."

They had entered the cool lobby by this time, and a dark-haired woman of about sixty looked up to see Lauren and opened her arms for a hug.

"Bellissima, where have you been? Sal and I were just talking about you the other day." She hugged Lauren tightly before releasing her. "And who is this handsome young man? You have family in town?" Carina paused and looked over at Matt.

Lauren laughed. "No, no, cara, this is a friend of mine. Matt, meet Carina." Matt smiled and greeted the dark-haired woman. "Where's Sal?"

"Oh, you know him. He's in the kitchen ordering everyone around and getting in their way. I'll go get him. Let me get you situated first. Table by the water?"

"Perfect. You know me so well." They followed the short, full-figured Carina as she led them to a large dining area with a tall waterfall covering most of the far wall. It cascaded down blue tile to end in a blue pool that sat in a mosaic basin. Small tables hugged the area in front of the pool, and it was to one of these that Carina led the two. Matt started to sit when he saw Lauren standing beside her chair. He hurried to pull out the chair and help her get situated.

"Ah, such a nice young man," Carina smiled at him. "And now I get Sal. He will have one of his fits if I don't. Here are menus, but you take your time. Can I send over a bottle of wine?"

"Absolutely, a Ribolla Gialla would be wonderful."

Carina looked at Matt. "And your friend?"

Lauren and Matt looked at one another and almost laughed. "He's with me, cara, he's good."

Carina left them then and Matt looked around him.

"This is nice. You must be a regular, the way she treats you."

Lauren laughed, "Oh, just wait until Sal gets over here. If he's happy enough to see someone, it can be quite the scene."

Just then an older, heavy-set, balding gentleman in black pants and white shirt bellowed, "Ciao, piccola!" and Lauren rose to meet him. She was his height, Matt noted, as he grabbed her up into what could only be called a bear hug. Lauren laughed and kissed each chubby cheek before he released her to look at Matt. Matt rose and extended his hand, which Sal shook heartily, as Lauren made the introductions.

"Ah, my friend. Welcome to Sal's. You are in very good company to-night. Our Lauren is sei bellissima, is she not?"

Matt had no idea what the man was saying, but since he was saying it with a huge smile and an arm around Lauren, Matt felt safe in nodding his head in agreement. Just then a waiter brought an opened bottle of wine to their table. He poured a small amount into a glass and handed it to Lauren. She swirled the liquid around a bit, sniffed it delicately, and took a sip. She closed her eyes and gave a slight moan before she looked at Sal.

"Perfect. Your people always take good care of me, don't they?" She smiled at the older man.

"Always, always. They know what would happen if they didn't. And now, you and your young man friend, sit while I tell you what I have created this evening!" As they resumed their seats, he went on to describe what he'd prepared for that day. When he had finished, Lauren looked up.

"It sounds wonderful to me, but I don't know about my friend. You want some of this or just a pizza?" She teased.

It was friendly teasing, and Matt didn't know quite how to take this Lauren. There was no bite of sarcasm behind her eyes. He smiled back.

"I think that sounds perfect. I'll try it, too," he replied.

Once Sal made his exit, the air seemed to return to the room.

"Wow, he's something, isn't he? And you know them from St. Louis? How did a native Italian, obvious he wasn't born in Missouri, find his way to the middle of America?"

Bread had been brought to the table and as Lauren mixed her olive oil with spices and tore off a piece from the loaf, she filled him in on St. Louis's Little Italy. Matt watched her and for once started to relax in her presence. Gone was the sexy flirt. Oh, the sexy was still there, but not as much flirt. This was a side that Lauren reserved for only those in whose company she felt completely at ease. With everyone else, she held back, opting instead for the façade Matt had seen until now. She pushed the small saucer holding the oil mixture toward him and encouraged him to try it. Matt had been in Italian restaurants before, but they went by the names of Olive Garden or Macaroni Grill. This genuine stuff was new to him. His first bite of the bread dripping with spiced oil made him a convert of the real thing. He'd never look at another chain Italian restaurant again.

They drank, talked like old friends, and enjoyed the huge plates of Sal's pasta. They were almost finished. Matt's plate was empty while Lauren's had over half still uneaten. The waiter came up to ask about desert. Lauren laughed and pointed to her plate, indicating she'd need a "to-go" box.

Matt leaned back in his chair and rubbed his full stomach. "I couldn't hold another thing." The waiter smiled his understanding and left them to box up Lauren's leftover meal.

"That's good because I don't think the flowers are edible. Wow! I haven't seen a guy eat like that in, well, years!"

"That's because you're so old you've forgotten how we young men eat," Matt teased.

Lauren narrowed her eyes and lifted her chin. "Do you really want to go there, Junior?" she asked.

There she was. There was the woman Matt had started the evening out with. But even then, the bite wasn't as sharp.

"Nope. I concede. I can't win a pissing competition with you even if my equipment is better. Wanna see?" Matt winked.

At that she laughed hard enough for her to choke. Her natural laugh was a sound Matt hadn't heard before, as usually Lauren barely laughed, and when she did, it was a husky sound. This was an uninhibited, contagious laughter that had him grinning and chuckling with her. Taking a sip of water, she looked up to see Carina had come over to see if she needed anything. Once she assured her everything was good and her friend had returned to the maitre-d stand, Lauren looked at Matt. Really looked at him for the first time. *I do believe I could be friends with this little boy. Well, he isn't really little, but too immature for me. Way too young, for sure.*

To him, she said, "Well, Matty, this has been fun. We'll split the check and be on our way."

"Huh? Split what check? I asked you to dinner, lady. My treat."

Sal came up in time to hear what Matt had said. "No, *my* treat! I've missed my Lauren, and to see her have such a wonderful time makes my heart glad. You two, go along. Have more fun."

Lauren graciously accepted his generous gesture, gave him another hug and kiss on each cheek, and watched as Matt shook his hand and thanked him before subtly leaving a sizable tip on the table. Matt took Lauren's arm to lead her out, but not before she gave Carina the same good-bye.

The older woman took Matt's face in both hands and kissed him on the cheek. "You come back to see us anytime, whether Lauren is with you or not."

Matt grinned at Carina. "You'll be seeing me again soon. I promise."

Matt and Lauren walked out to the Jeep as the sun was disappearing behind the distance hills.

"Wanna take a drive? It's early," Matt offered.

"Absolutely," Lauren replied as he helped her back into the car. This time he had no trouble keeping his eyes to himself. What had changed, he didn't know. He still looked at her legs from his side of the car, but it wasn't the lascivious look of before. He was simply admiring the view.

The drive took them out of the city as they hit Superstition Freeway, past Apache Junction, and then north on Highway 88 until they passed the second one-lane bridge. Canyon Lake lay before them. Matt parked the Jeep on a scenic overlook, and they walked to the rock retaining wall to look out over the water. The sun had set and stars were popping out above them.

"I always love coming out here," Matt said. "Sometimes I'll just keep on driving past the Flats and hit the gravel road. Did you know that this is Arizona's oldest highway? Now that's where you see some beautiful terrain, up in the desert hills. I always think about the people who used to take this trail by stagecoach. When they were building the Roosevelt Dam, everything had to be hauled sixty miles over this narrow, rugged trail. Everything done by hand. Miles and miles of dirt and dust and sheer drop-offs until they reached the dam. Some of the gravel part is still only one lane with nothing but a drop-off on one side. You know, people actually died on that trail. Out in the desert, far from anyone." He stopped himself and looked at her self-consciously. In the dim light from the overhead lantern, she could see his face clearly.

Lauren started to tease, but something in his voice kept her silent. He didn't seem to expect a reply, and she leaned into him and twined her arm around his. They stood like that for several minutes. Two people who had found their footing with one another.

"I hate to break this up, but I have to open the shop tomorrow." Lauren really did hate to break it up.

"Yeah, I have to be at work by 9:00 in the morning."

"Duty calls, or something like that, uh?" Lauren smiled at him again, and they turned to make their way back to the Jeep.

Neither said anything as Matt turned the car toward the lights of Phoenix. The hour-long drive was spent in companionable silence. With the noise of the road in the open Jeep, conversation would have been difficult at best. He pulled up to the security gate, closed at this late hour, and Lauren gave him the code to open it.

"Eight six seven five, uh? You realize those are the first numbers you've given me?" he was teasing again.

He pulled into her drive, and Lauren looked at him as he helped her out of the four-by-four.

"Play those cards right, Matty, and you might be surprised at all the numbers I can give you."

He walked her to the door, where she unlocked it and stood in the doorway. She leaned over to plant a light kiss on his lips before replacing her lips with her finger.

"Be good, sweetie," and she was through the door before he could respond.

Matt got into the Jeep and sat for a few moments. *What just happened? I have no freakin' clue. Who was this person?* He thought. She certainly wasn't the siren he'd been dealing with and dreaming about for the past few weeks. No, this was a lady. An extremely sexy lady who made him want to sit up a little straighter, be a little nicer, and make a better impression. Matt had never had to impress a female in his life. They came to him, took him as he was, and didn't say a word. Of course, he couldn't remember half their names, but that had never bothered him in the past. *Lauren...* that was one name etched in his mind. *Hell*, he thought, *and she didn't even sleep with me. How did that happen?*

Lauren heard him finally start the car and drive away. She'd been peeking from the upstairs window and watched as his taillights disappeared down the street. She grabbed a water from the refrigerator and sat on the bar stool, sipping slowly. *Maybe I've figured him all wrong,* she thought. *There really is more to this kid than I first thought. All evening, and he didn't make the requisite pass or invitation for sex at the end of it. Maybe I'm slipping...*She thought that one over briefly before shaking her head.

"Nawww....I never slip," she spoke out loud before she turned to go to bed. She had no clue of what tomorrow or the next day or the next would bring, but Lauren had never worried overmuch about that. She always slept like the dead.

Chapter 20

JULIA STARED AT HER. LAUREN had finished telling her and Austin about the "date" she and Matt had taken, their texts almost every day, and how the two had developed an easy friendship. It was a friendship, Lauren assured both Julia and Austin.

"You mean to tell me, my roommate didn't put the moves on you, and he hasn't tried anything at all?" Austin was in disbelief. "I've known this guy since we were kids, and I've never seen him pass up the opportunity to come-on to a girl."

"Yeah, well, Ace, I ain't no girl," Lauren looked at Austin. "And just maybe this guy you've known for years is growing up on you. Did you think of that?"

No, he hadn't, and Austin's face said as much. "Yeah," he continued, "but to go from panting after you and talking about you and everything else he'd do while thinking about you." Lauren gave him a *don't go there* look. "I can't believe we're talking about the same Matt." Austin shook his head. "Don't worry. It's coming. When you least expect it, he'll try to get you into bed."

Lauren rolled her eyes at Austin, and said, "Big deal. Big. Damn. Deal. Did it ever occur to you that your Matt is a grown up? Yeah, he's a big boy now, and if he and I decide to have sex, it really isn't any of your business. Geez, Daddy, I only told you we're friends now because I'd just have to go through this sooner or later." She turned to Julia. "You're awfully quiet. Letting Austin do all the talking for you these days?"

Julia rolled her own eyes at Lauren and shook her head. "Just shut up before you say something we'll be fighting about here." She looked at

Austin. "You know, Matt *is* a big boy. This *is* their business, not ours. I happen to think they'll either remain friends and we'll all be one happy family, or not." Austin looked at her. "Come on, let's celebrate our freedom from Cruella and Larry, and play nice. I do want my two favorite people to play nice."

Lauren and Austin looked at one another and Austin grinned first. "Whatever. Dragon Lady here will make him or break him."

"I told you that already. No harm, no foul." Lauren got up to leave, and as she was walking off, they could see her checking her phone.

Time moved quickly for them all after that. Julia and Lauren were busy finishing up a job a day, it seemed, and meeting clients to show off the work that had been completed in their absence. The big rush would come around October, but many returned in September to enjoy a little heat before winter. Not that winter was a big deal in Phoenix, but December and January didn't have pool temperatures. Austin settled in at Superstition Golf Club, but this job found him doing more from the business end and working inside a lot of the time. Steve Jones had come around more than once and reminded him of the December meeting. John and Sharon had returned, and Austin saw John a few times as he brought clients out to play a round of golf. October turned to November, when Austin received an interesting letter. He stopped by Touch of Jules to share it with Julia.

"Hey, Sexy Beast," Lauren looked up to greet him. "Julia will be back in a few. She had to walk Mrs. Simpson around her new sunroom addition. God, that woman is a load. 'But are you sure it won't be too warm in here?' Oh, no, it's a *sun room* for Christ's sake."

Austin laughed at her imitation of a haughty snob and sat down behind Julia's desk. It was messy, as usual, but he didn't touch anything. To do so would be taking his life into his hands. She called it an organized chaos, and somehow she did know where everything was. Ask her about a particular invoice or something, and she'd lay her hands on it from under a stack of other things. About that time, the woman in mind came breezing in.

"I thought I saw a smokin' hot Mustang parked out front. Is the smokin' hot man who goes with it here?" Julia laughed at Lauren's eye roll, and plopped down on Austin's lap. Her purse and sunglasses were discarded on top of her messy desk as she leaned over to kiss him hello.

"What are you doing here?" she asked. "Not that I mind, but I didn't expect to see you until later tonight."

"Yeah, I got a letter from my mom today. I guess I've ignored her calls too long, because she sat down and actually wrote a letter." He laughed and pulled it from his pocket. Julia stood up to give him room and sat down on her desk to face him.

"Okay, what's the news from home?" she asked.

"They want me to come home for Thanksgiving. I already told her a month ago it wouldn't be possible because that time of year is the busiest at the course, but I suppose she thinks I'm lying to her. Oh, and I'm to bring you." He looked at her.

"I didn't even know you told her about me," Julia looked at him questioningly.

"I didn't. Matt said something to Grandma Bea who mentioned you to my mom last time they talked. Yeah, Grandma keeps her up to date on the boys, and now she's chomping at the bit to get a look at you."

"Good lord," was all Julia could muster. "Well, sweetie, we knew this was coming, didn't we?"

"Yep," Austin grinned at her then. "I seriously can't wait to get the two of you in the same room." He looked over at Lauren. "Sure you don't want to come along for the show?" he asked. Lauren frowned over the top of her reading glasses and flipped him off.

"I don't even like to go to *my* parents' house for holidays, much less yours. You're on your own, both of you. I have plans."

"You don't even know when we're going," Austin laughed again.

"Doesn't matter. I have plans. Big, important, unchangeable ones." She went back to her paperwork.

Julia smiled brightly and asked, "Just when are we going on this adventure? I'll have to see if my partner will cover for me. That is, unless she has big, important, unchangeable plans…"

"Nope, I can cover. I just don't do families," came the reply.

"Well, I thought we'd try to go next weekend. That's early enough that I won't have too much scheduling to change at work, and we'll get this over with."

"Whoa, next weekend? Lauren, are you good with that?"

"Yep, I'll be around. You go meet Mr. and Mrs. James." She looked up to grin at Julia.

Julia took a deep breath and let it out slowly. "Alrighty then. I've never been to North Carolina. Should I dig out that old Tar Heel t-shirt I've been sleeping in?" she teased.

"Don't bother. I'll buy you a new one when we get out there," Austin promised.

"Woo-hoo," from across the room.

"Hey, don't knock it. I look good in Tar Heel blue," Julia looked to Austin for confirmation.

"Good in, better out," he leaned up to kiss her when Lauren broke in.

"Get a room. God, you two are ridiculous."

"Yes, yes, we are," and Julia covered the remaining few inches to kiss him back.

Austin got up and Julia joined him as he crossed the room and walked toward the door.

"We'll talk more when you get home tonight. I think I'll grill some burgers. Hey, D-L, you in?" D-L was short for Dragon Lady, Austin's newest nickname for Lauren

"Yep, I'm free as a flying dragon. Make mine extra well-done. Last time it was raw, and not just pink raw, but red raw."

"Yeah, I'll be right on that." With a pat on Julia's rear, he was out the door,

"He's going to make it raw, I just know he is, and then I'll be waiting around filling up on chips while you two eat. You know he'll do it, too."

"Don't knock it. He's cooking. That's more than most men do."

Lauren thought back to Keith, who had never done a thing in the kitchen. "You're right. Keep him if for nothing more than that."

Julia grinned as she walked by and said over her shoulder, "Oh, he's good for a LOT more than that."

Chapter 21

⁓

THE PLANE LANDED SMOOTHLY, AND as it taxied up to the terminal, Julia felt a bit of unease. She and Austin had talked about his family, he telling her about his seventeen-year-old brother who was finishing up high school and living in a world of sports, school, and girls. His dad, Phillip, who was gone a lot, putting in fifty- to sixty-hour work weeks, but who still had taken the time to be there for Austin during his school years. And his mother, Natalie, who held it all together while Phil made the living and the boys filled her life with all the "mom" things.

It wasn't that Julia was afraid of these people; quite the opposite was true. She'd been around long enough to know that people are people. Julia was who she was, and they could take it or leave it. Her concern was more for Austin. After all, he was the one who had ventured out of the family fold, cut ties to North Carolina, and was keeping them at arm's length. She didn't want to be the reason for another rift in the relationship. It wasn't like she and Austin were getting married or anything, but Julia in his life would keep him from more "appropriate" young women or returning to Charlotte. Austin had never said that to her, but Julia knew enough about how moms think to know that would be going through Natalie's mind. These were the years when Austin should be working on his future. Did someone like Julia belong in the future? She shook her head at the thought. She didn't know, either. They worked and they were enjoying what they had. She smiled at Austin as they rose to exit the plane. For them, that was enough.

After going through baggage claim and picking up the rental car, they headed into traffic and toward Myers Park, a suburb of Charlotte. It would

Connie Dunn

be a twenty-minute drive to Austin's old neighborhood. He hit the Billy Graham Parkway and headed around the south side of the city. When they got closer, he pointed out his old high school, the houses of some of his old friends, and the Myers Park Country Club, where Austin had worked both the summers of his junior and senior years. He turned onto Normandy Road. The houses here were older, well-maintained, mostly two-story structures that looked like they would hold children. He pulled into the driveway of a two-story, white house with green shutters and a small front stoop. Two huge oak trees seemed to stand guard on each side of the house with smaller maples dotting the front yard. A low, green hedge followed the drive up and around to end at the attached garage. As they pulled into the front, the green door opened and a slender woman with short blonde hair came out. She was dressed in khaki slacks and a long-sleeved green sweater. As Austin stopped, she hurried down the two steps to grab him up in a hug before he'd hardly gotten out of the car. Julia watched the two as she took her time getting out on her side. She waited until Natalie James pulled back and looked at her oldest son. Green eyes met green eyes and he said, "Good to see you, Mom," before disengaging himself to turn toward Julia.

She came around the car and saw that Natalie was sizing her up much as Julia had done the older woman just moments before. Julia thought about what she'd see: slender, dark-haired woman of medium height, blue eyes, and dressed in skinny jeans, riding boots, and long, dark-gray sweater. Natalie's face gave nothing away—not approval, disapproval, surprise, or anything to indicate her first impression.

Julia held out her hand, "It's so nice to finally meet you, Mrs. James. Austin's description doesn't do you justice. You look more like his sister than his mother."

"Mom, this is Julia, Julia Whitman. Julia, my mom, Natalie."

Natalie reached her own hand out and the two women gave each other a brief squeeze before Natalie pulled away to address Austin.

"Sweetie, help Julia with her suitcase. I told your brother to get out here and help, but you know how he can be. Caleb, there you are!"

Caleb James came through the front door, rolled his eyes in his mother's direction, and he and Austin grabbed one another in a guy hug.

156

"Whoa, you're almost ready to take on your big brother, punk," Austin said affectionately. Julia already knew from hearing him talk about Caleb that he was proud of his baby brother. The six years' difference in age had encouraged Caleb to idolize his older brother and to copy pretty much whatever Austin did. Now, he looked at him through the eyes of a young man coming into his own, and the devotion was plain to see.

Austin turned to Julia. "Caleb, I'd like you to meet Julia Whitman. Julia, this is my baby brother."

Caleb came toward the hand Julia had reached out to him, but he sidestepped it and grabbed her in a hug instead. He pulled away to look her over and turned back to Austin.

"Dang, bro. You didn't tell me your Julia was a babe." To Julia. "If you ever get tired of this double bagger, give me a call." He grinned, and it was Austin's playful grin that always made her laugh.

"Well, Handsome, I'll keep that in mind," Julia smiled at Caleb, and knew that this was one member of the James family who wouldn't mind her hanging around.

"Caleb," Natalie pulled him back from staring too long. "Help your brother with their stuff." She turned to Austin. "I've got the guest room all ready for Julia, and you, of course can use your old room. Just like old times." She laughed.

"Uh, Mom, let's just get this out there. Julia and I stay together. We'll both use my old room." Natalie had stopped in mid-stride to turn and look at Austin. Her eyes moved from one to the other before they finally settled on Austin.

"Oh, of course, I wasn't thinking." She laughed nervously, but was gracious enough to turn to Julia. "You may still want to take the guest room, you and Austin. His old full-sized bed might be a bit cramped. The guest room is larger and much more comfortable. It also has its own bathroom."

"It sounds lovely," Julia knew this had to be hard for Natalie. "Your home is beautiful. I can't wait to see the rest of it."

"Well, let's get you kids inside. I fixed some sandwiches and, of course, Austin's favorite pie. You look like you've lost weight, Austin. You're working too hard at the golf course, aren't you?"

Austin followed the two women inside trailed by Caleb, and the two men set the bags down at the foot of the steps.

"Actually, Mom, my job has changed with the internship, and I almost feel lazy some days. If it's okay with you, we'll just go up and put this stuff away and be back down in a few. Okay?"

"Of course, hon. Take your time." Natalie watched the three of them go up the stairs before she remembered something and called up after them. "Austin, your dad is working, and we're going to meet him at the club around 6:00."

"No problem. Gives us more time to visit before he gets home," Austin replied over his shoulder.

At the top of the stairs, Julia saw a hallway that ran the width of the house with rooms branching off both sides. Austin passed the first door on the left. "Mom and Dad's room," he said. He stopped at the second door down the hall from his parents' room. Turning in, Julia saw a queen-sized bed against the far wall with tables on each side, a dresser on the opposite wall, a chair and ottoman in the corner, and a door leading to a private bath. The other closed door on that side was the closet. Caleb tossed onto the bed the two bags he'd been carrying, Julia's large suitcase and the Louis Vuitton bag she'd treated herself to.

"Take it easy, Hulk, you might break something," Austin admonished his brother

"Yeah, like airport baggage handlers gently set bags into the plane." He did look apologetically at Julia, who smiled.

"It's okay, Caleb, and you're right about the disrespect my bags have been getting from Phoenix to here. Nothing breakable, trust me. And thanks for bringing them up for me." She sent him a smile that had the little brother in him blushing.

"Well, I'll leave you two. And Austin, are you as surprised as I am about how cool Mom is with your sleeping arrangements? I didn't see that one coming, did you?"

Austin shrugged his shoulders. "I don't know. I'm not used to being on adult-to-adult footing with her, but yeah, she handled it good."

They exchanged a knowing smile. Their mom was usually predictable, but she still surprised them.

"Ok, then, catch you downstairs."

He closed the door behind him, and Julia and Austin stood for a moment looking at one another. He broke the gaze first, and crossed over to her. He gathered her in his arms and rocked them both gently.

"Wasn't that easy?" he asked and laughed.

"Oh, yeah," she laughed with him. "I could see her wheels turning—speculating about everything from my pedigree to my looks to the big question, my age. Now I know how the chimps feel at the zoo."

"Oh, c'mon, it wasn't that bad, was it?"

"Let's see…how did my mother look at you? Huh?" she teased.

"Before or after she decided to not simply squish me under her high-heeled shoes like some pesky insect." He laughed with her. "You're right. The microscopes are out and everyone is giving you the one-eye look over. I think you'll pass inspection, don't you?"

"But of course. Now, let's get stuff unpacked and go back downstairs before she thinks we're up here having sex." Julia crossed the room to open the door. "That will make her feel better," she added.

"Well, what if I WANT to start this visit off with afternoon sex? Did that cross your mind?"

"If I think like you, sex is always on my mind, but one of us has to have some control here, don't you think?"

About that time, Natalie knocked on the open door. She had a stack of clean towels in her arm and looked at them uncertainly.

"I'm not interrupting anything, am I?" she asked. "I brought some extra towels since you both will be using the bathroom in here."

"How thoughtful!" Julia took the stack from her hands and carried them through to the bathroom.

"Food's ready when you are," she reminded. "Take your time, though. See you in a few." And with that she turned and left them.

They made sure she was down the stairs, Austin peaking around the doorway, before they looked at one another and burst out laughing.

Well, that wasn't obvious, at all, Julia thought, as she unzipped her bag and started unpacking. *Not a bad beginning, but we'll see.*

The rest of the afternoon passed with the four chatting, eating, and getting to know one another. Austin was right about one thing—his mother wasn't used to having an adult son under her roof, and Julia could see her struggling a bit. Several times she started to say something to Austin's talk about the job and his upcoming graduation. Julia knew the look. It was the "don't you think you should instead…" look that her mother wore pretty much all the time these days. In her favor, Natalie held her tongue, giving her bonus points in Julia's book. Dana Whitman would have just blurted it out and then gotten mad when her advice wasn't taken as gospel.

They were eating dinner out that night. Phillip had called to ask about Austin's arrival and to remind them he'd see them at the club. Julia had brought sweater dresses and heels, and opted for one of those, blue with tights and high heeled black boots.

"You don't have to dress up, babe." Austin was in black denim jeans, a deep red sweater, and boots.

Julia looked at him, smiled, and said, "Oh, I think I do. At least to keep up with you. And this isn't dressed up." She indicated the plain dress. "Besides, I don't want your father's first impression of me to be some jean-clad loose woman who's made it her life's mission to corrupt his son."

"Well, I like jeans, I'm incorruptible, and I happen to like my women loose," he teased.

"Yeah, I'll remember that if I see any loose women tonight." Picking up a black pashmina shawl and her black bag, she was ready to go. Julia had started wearing her hair down ever since the weather had cooled because Austin liked it best that way. It was hanging in long, shining curls that flowed over her shoulders and down her back.

"You're gorgeous, you know. And I adore you," he kissed her lightly.

"Back at you, sweetie. Now, let's go face the lord of the manor."

They were laughing as they made their way down the stairs to meet Natalie and Caleb in the foyer.

"Wow, Julia!" Caleb couldn't help himself, but when his mother playfully smacked the back of his head, he quickly apologized.

Julia laughed. "It's all good. Thank you, Caleb. You clean up pretty good yourself." He had on dark blue jeans, a button down shirt and loafers. His blond hair was cut close to his head, but Julia could see that if it were even a half-inch longer, it would be a curly mop. *He's adorable*, she thought. Natalie had changed into white wool slacks, a black silk turtleneck sweater, and black heels. *Classy*, Julia thought. *And I see where the curly hair comes from. I'll bet if she'd lose her flat iron, her hair would be as curly as Austin's.*

"You both look wonderful, but we need to go. You know how your father hates to wait on us." Natalie turned and started out the door. Someone, Caleb probably, had pulled her car into the drive. Julia and Austin climbed into the back seat of the Mercedes SUV. Natalie drove and Caleb sat in the front with her.

As they walked into the Country Club, Natalie, Caleb, and Austin smiled and greeted virtually everyone already seated. Austin shook more than one hand, and Julia found herself presented over and over. When they finally made their way to their corner table, Julia leaned over to whisper in his ear.

"I'll never remember all of these people! Are you running for office or something?"

Austin looked down at her and laughed, "Or something."

A tall, gray-haired, distinguished man stood to meet them. He was handsome and Julia could see a lot of Austin in the man before her. All but the green eyes. Phillip James came forward to pull his son into a brief hug before turning to Julia. He fixed his eyes on hers for a brief moment before holding out his hand and shaking hers warmly.

"And you must be Julia. It's nice to meet you. Natalie didn't warn me that you would be so pretty." He smiled at his wife.

"It's nice to meet you, too," Julia smiled at the man in front of her. "I look forward to visiting with you. I just spent a lovely afternoon with Natalie and Caleb. You have a beautiful family."

As they seated themselves around the table, Austin leaned over to whisper in Julia's ear, "'Lovely afternoon'? 'Beautiful family'? Where's my girlfriend, and what have you done with her?"

"Shhh...I know what I'm doing. Years of practice, remember?" she whispered back.

By the end of the dinner, Phillip was eating out of Julia's hand, and she had distracted him enough to allow Natalie the chance to fill Austin in on the gossip of many of the people she'd met on the way in.

"Oh, before I forget," Natalie spoke to them all. "The Thanksgiving Carnival is this weekend, and we have tickets to the banquet Saturday night."

Connie Dunn

"Mom, that's mine and Julia's last night here. Are you sure about going?" Austin seemed surprised.

"Yes, darling, and it's rather informal, so don't worry about what you'll wear," Natalie smiled at them both.

"I'm sure it will be fine, Natalie, and we'll look forward to it," Julia smoothly kept Austin from saying anything more.

Once they arrived home, Caleb, Natalie, and Phillip excused themselves to bed. Julia's and Austin's bodies were still on Mountain Standard Time, so they wished everyone a good night and walked into the family room to relax.

Austin stretched out on the leather sofa as Julia took a seat farther down. She knew what he wanted, and sure enough, he kicked off his boots and plopped his feet in her lap. She laughed and started rubbing them absently, her mind working.

"What are you thinking, woman?" Austin was curious.

"Oh, I was just imagining you and Matt and your friends all lounging in here, rough housing or watching ball games. You had a great childhood, didn't you, sweetie?"

"Better than most, not as good as others. Lots of rules around here with my old man. You haven't gotten to see that side of him yet, and who knows, maybe he's toned it down a lot. He could be difficult sometimes." He chuckled. "Mom was the peacemaker."

Julia looked at him and saw that he was thinking back. She watched different emotions play across his face, noticed by her only because she knew him so well. Yes, she could see that Phillip James liked to run things his way. It probably served him well in a courtroom, but with kids it might be a bit difficult to pull off and not raise resentment. She also saw a bit of that in Natalie although Austin seemed oblivious to it.

They sat in companionable silence a while longer, when Austin suggested they call it a night. Making their way up the stairs and past his parents' door, they heard low voices. Julia wondered what they were saying about her, but Austin took her hand and pulled her along.

Once inside their room, he closed and locked the door and pulled her close.

"Oh, no," she shook her head. "I know exactly what that look means, and I am *not* having sex with you tonight with your parents right next door."

"You worry too much. There's a big walk-in closet and a bathroom between us and them. You seriously don't expect us to be celibate the whole time we're here, do you?" He put a fake horrified look on his face before he replaced that with a sexy grin. "You don't plan on being that noisy tonight, do you?" he teased, and started to unzip her dress, his hands warm where they trailed down her back.

"No, I'm not going to be noisy because there will be no reason to be," Julia pulled away and started into the bathroom to finish undressing.

Austin simply followed her. He wasn't one to give up that easily. As she took her boots off and slid the dress down to step out of it, he pulled her close again and kissed her. She resisted at first, but soon he could feel her responding. As he came up for air, he looked at her. She still had her eyes closed and licked her lips, running her tongue slowly over her bottom lip. She knew that drove him nuts.

"Are you sure we don't want to break in that bed?" he invited again. Julia opened her eyes to look at him. He was standing in front of her, grinning, and he stepped back to pull off his own sweater. He unfastened his jeans and started to slide them down when she grabbed him close.

"You really are tempting, Austin James," she whispered. "And if we can be very, very quiet, I think we might have some fun."

It wasn't long before both had their clothes strewn across the bedroom chair and were soon under the blanket. He rolled toward her, and the bed gave out a loud creak. He pulled her on top of him, and the bed let out another creak, louder than the first. To test it out, they both rolled to either side, and it creaked again. By this time, both were laughing.

"This is too funny," Julia could barely talk for laughing. "You warn *me* to be quiet and this bed could wake up the people in the next house!" She started laughing again.

Austin didn't find it that funny, and as he watched her chest rise and fall with each laughing gasp, he decided there was more than one way to handle a creaking bed. He climbed out, and the bed creaked again, causing Julia to laugh even harder. She didn't laugh when he picked up her and the blankets and laid her on the carpeted floor. He reached up to grab the pillow and settled it all around them.

"Where there's a will..." he said. He didn't finish the statement, but instead starting kissing her again. The floor made no noise, and for that they were both grateful.

Chapter 22

THEY AWOKE BACK IN THE bed. Sometime during the night, Austin had awakened and put both Julia and the bed things back on the mattress. The bed still creaked, but only until he could wrap himself around her and try to nod off. She opened her eyes once, smiled sleepily at him, and promptly dozed off again. He had lain there a few minutes more thinking about the day and evening they'd had. Things had gone much better than he'd expected, but Austin knew that his controlling parents weren't going to sit back and say nothing. Julia was wonderful, but she wasn't what either of his parents had in mind when they thought of a future daughter-in-law. Austin felt himself becoming irritated as he thought of everything wonderful about Julia that they wouldn't see because of the difference in age. He sighed, and knowing that he couldn't do anything about it in the middle of the night, he gave in to sleep.

As the sun streamed into the room through the closed window blinds, Julia rolled over and grinned at her groggy lover. "Hey," she whispered.

"Hey, yourself," Austin said, "and stop whispering, will ya? No one is listening, Jules, trust me."

She laughed and snuggled in closer. She had turned him into what she liked to call a snuggler. They would wake up, and if time allowed, hold one another close and enjoy the feel of each other's body. Of course this often led to recreational activities, but more often than not, they simply connected. All of a sudden, she looked up.

"What time is it? We don't want to lie in bed all morning. I don't care how much of a time difference there is, we shouldn't leave everyone hanging." Julia's voice held her agitation.

"I don't know, don't care," Austin really did look completely unperturbed. At that, Julia got up and looked at her phone.

"Geez, nine o'clock Eastern time! I'm taking a shower. You, stay put." She said this last as he was crawling out with his "I'm joining you" look. Austin didn't listen but followed her into the bathroom.

She laughed and rolled her eyes. "You are too much. Shave, brush your teeth, do something. I won't be long." She jumped into the shower before he could reply. Sure enough, she'd barely started the water when she felt him behind her.

"Austin, you have got to behave," Julia said as she poured shampoo and started on her hair. Austin pushed her hands out of the way and massaged her scalp as he knew she liked. When he finished, he turned her around to rinse the soap from her long hair.

"I'm not going to put the moves on you, babe. Promise," he grinned. And he didn't. They soaped each other and when they finished, dried one another's backs.

"See?" he was quite proud of himself. "I can behave."

She rolled her eyes and went into the bedroom to dress. It was North Carolina in November. She knew the high would be around sixty degrees, but coming from Scottsdale, Arizona, that would feel much cooler. Julia decided on jeans and a sweatshirt with her tennis shoes, and she watched as Austin put on much the same. As she brushed her teeth and dried her hair, she thought about what the day would bring. She wanted Austin to spend the time with his family. She saw him every day. They only saw him once or twice a year.

"Babe," she got his attention. "Why don't you plan on spending today with your folks and Caleb. I can take the car and do some shopping or look around town or something."

"Why would you do that?" He was curious.

"Because you need some time, just you and them. I'm not going to intrude on family time." Julia had finished and was making the bed.

Austin came over to help her, in his own thoughts. They finished and he came around to her side and looked down at her.

"Julia, don't you know that right now, you *are* my family? I love you so much, and my mom, dad, and Caleb can't fall in love with you if you're not around, right? You can do what you want, but I really want you to stay with me, whatever I end up doing today, okay?"

He was so sweet when he asked her, and she nodded a "yes" before they turned to head downstairs. *What am I going to do with him?* Julia thought. Then she smiled. *I think I'll just keep him.*

The day passed quickly. True to his word, Austin hardly let Julia out of his sight. When he played basketball with Caleb, he moved a chair for her to sit next to the driveway goal and asked her to keep score. When he sat in the family room talking with his mom and dad, he made sure she was on the sofa next to him. When they ate, Austin had Julia sitting beside him. It was after dinner that night when Natalie finally caught Julia alone in the kitchen as the two women cleaned up the dishes.

"My son seems to be quite taken by you, Julia," Natalie started the conversation. "You and I haven't had a moment alone."

Julia laughed. "He told me this morning that he wanted me with him all day, and I suppose he wasn't kidding." Julia looked closely at Natalie and her voice took on a friendly, yet serious tone. "What do you want to know, Natalie? I know that you have a million questions for me, don't you? Fire away." Julia wasn't going to play games with the woman. *Get it over with*, she thought.

Natalie laughed nervously, but returned Julia's look. "Well, let's see. You're obviously older than my son. Let's start there."

Neither Julia's expression nor her voice wavered. "Well, last birthday was a big one for me. I turned forty and will be forty-one this February."

She watched Natalie's shocked expression before the shock was replaced by something else as the woman mentally did the math.

"You're closer to my age than Austin's, aren't you?" she seemed to be talking to herself before she looked back at Julia. "How in the world did the two of you get together?"

Julia related the story of their meeting at Coyote Run, Austin's coming into the shop to pick out the picture that Julia had seen hanging on the wall of the sun room, some of the interesting things they'd done together, and stopped with their trip to Charlotte. While she talked, Julia could see that Natalie's mind was working. *She's probably wondering what's in it for me, or for her son*, Julia thought.

"I see that you enjoy each other's company, and Austin is obviously crazy about you, but where do you go from here?" Natalie was concerned. "Your lives are so different. My son is young, he's only twenty-four, and he hasn't really lived yet. And you? What have you done in life, Julia? What attracts you to a boy like Austin?"

Julia thought a moment before she carefully replied. She didn't want to offend this woman. She was Austin's mother, for heaven's sake, and at the end of the day, Natalie loved him, too. But she also didn't intend to satisfy this woman's curiosity just because, nor was she going to be talked to like she was doing something wrong.

"Well, your son, Natalie, is far from being a boy. When I first met him, I never thought we'd be more than acquaintances. But the more time we spent together, the less the age thing mattered, and the more the person mattered. Now, I can't imagine my life without Austin in it." Julia didn't know it, but her face had taken on a soft expression as she talked about Austin. She took a deep breath before she continued. "As for what have I done in my life? Well, let's see…I have a college degree, I have built two successful businesses, I have married once and divorced, and I have created for myself a very comfortable life that I like sharing with your son." Julia finished and stood staring at the woman in front of her. She offered a small smile. She wasn't going into any more detail about her life or herself.

Before Natalie could reply, Austin came in and put an arm around Julia. She wondered how much he had heard, but he only grinned at them both.

"Did you survive my mother's inquisition, babe?" he grinned mischievously at Natalie.

"We've had a nice chat," was all Natalie would say.

"Well, I'm going to take my girl for a drive. We'll be back later, but if we're not here by bedtime, don't wait up."

"Of course, no problem," was all Natalie said. She watched the two walk out the door before turning to find her husband in the family room. He said nothing as she sat in her recliner and stared at the television, not really watching.

"You okay?" Phillip asked.

"I will be," Natalie replied. "Phil, what do you think of this woman?"

Phillip looked at his wife. "Honestly, I haven't. I'm enjoying stress-free time with my son." He gave her a hard look. "And don't do anything to offend either one of them. It's none of our business."

"None of our business…."

"You heard me," Phillip said. "Don't make a big deal out of this. They're not married. And if they do get married, you'll have to respect your son's choice." He shrugged and sat back. "I'm thinking he could do a lot worse. She's smart, beautiful, successful…I think she's a good influence on him."

"That's fine coming from you. It was your controlling that sent him packing in the first place." She shot her husband a dirty look.

"Not true." Phillip shook his head. "My disapproval of his career choice was simply the catalyst that gave Austin the determination he needed to do his own thing. Don't blame me for that. I've thought a lot about that time. It's turned out to be the best thing to happen to him."

Neither spoke after that. A few minutes later, Natalie excused herself to bed. Phillip sat by the fireplace reading. He couldn't focus as he thought about his wife, his son, and Julia. Julia really was good for Austin, and Phillip could plainly see her influence in the man he'd become. He thought of Austin and his future, and it wasn't long before he reached his own conclusion regarding the relationship. *My wife better not try to mess this up,* he thought. *I won't be happy.*

Saturday dawned sunny and warm. Julia was glad to enjoy a pretty day because they had the Thanksgiving Carnival at the country club that night. She really wasn't looking forward to it. *Been there, done that,* she thought. *Hated it then, hate it now.*

After lunch, Austin found her in the bedroom and asked, "How do you want to spend your last afternoon here?"

Julia planted a kiss on his cheek, and smiled happily. "I don't know, don't care. I'm all yours to do whatever."

"Well…" and Austin wiggled his eyebrows up and down and looked pointedly at the bed. They hadn't tried to use it since that first night. Julia wasn't about to now.

She laughed, "Not on your life! That bed is a menace to my sex life!"

"Yeah, but thank god for floors and showers," Austin laughed with her. "Let's take a walk and I'll show you around the old neighborhood."

'I'd love that! I feel like we've done nothing but eat and talk," Julia replied.

They strolled from one street to another with Austin describing who lived where, different things he'd done in this house or that house. He even showed her the home of an old girlfriend from high school. He was a bit reluctant to tell her that they'd been pretty serious at one time. Well, as serious as eighteen-year-olds can be. Julia laughed and told him that she's glad he'd had a bit of practice before her.

"Practice, huh?" Austin pulled her to his chest. "Should I take you to the old football field and show you what practice is? I think they still have the old bleachers."

Julia just laughed. "Yeah, like anyone ever had sex behind football field bleachers. You boys make that shit up all the time to impress one another, don't you?"

"You think I'd lie about that?" Austin pretended to be hurt.

"Yep, all day long," Julia laughed.

Late in the afternoon, they strolled into the house and went up to change for the evening's dinner. Julia decided on the black long-sleeved dress and black heels. She knew that Austin had brought some wool slacks, and he changed into those and a dark green sweater.

"I love that color on you. Your eyes pop, you know," Julia looked over at Austin and smiled.

"What exactly does that mean? You women say it all the time, but I've never figured out what it means. Do my eyes get bigger like a frog? Do they protrude?"

Julia laughed. "Never mind. Let me try again. You're eyes are greener and deeper in that color." She moved closer to him. "A woman could look into your eyes and lose herself." She reached up to put her arms around him. "It's no wonder you pulled me in like you did. Those bedroom eyes are irresistible." With that she kissed him.

When they pulled apart, Austin looked at her and said, "Why didn't you say that to begin with?"

"Austin!" Natalie knocked on their door. "We're leaving now. Are you riding with us or taking your own car?"

Austin opened the door to see his mother standing there in her coat.

"We'll drive ourselves. Thanks."

"Well, follow us over, please. We need to all come in together."

At that, Austin turned to Julia and rolled his eyes. Without realizing it, he had picked up the habit from Julia and Lauren. Over his back he said, "Right behind you." He grabbed his leather jacket and turned to help Julia on with hers. Natalie stood at the door until they followed her down the hallway.

They all pulled up to the brightly lit country club, and Julia was already feeling her stomach drop. She still attended functions similar to this one but only because of her job. This wasn't her idea of pleasure. Her face must have revealed something as Austin looked over at her and took her hand. He squeezed it before putting it to his lips to place a kiss on her palm.

"You okay?" he asked.

"Not a problem in the world," Julia assured him as it was their turn to exit the car and turn it over to the valet. She hated these things. At least it wasn't a black tie affair. Those were the worst. A boy of high school age opened Julia's door, and he didn't hide his perusal of a pretty lady. She grinned at him as he helped her get out of the car, and they joined his parents on the steps. Caleb looked like he'd love to jump into the nearest vehicle and escape. Natalie's hand under his arm kept that from happening.

"Isn't this fun?" she said to the group, and they trooped in.

Once again, Julia felt herself on display as they moved from group to group, chatting and laughing until they found their table.

"Oh, look," Natalie said. "We're sitting with the Millers." She turned to Julia. "We've been old friends of Charlie and Sue since, well, since before the kids were born. I do hope they bring Allison tonight. In fact, I know she'll be here. Austin, how long has it been since you've seen Allison? You two were so sweet together."

Austin gave his mother a hard look before answering, "I'm sure I don't remember, Mother. Probably since we graduated from high school, don't you think?"

"Julia," Natalie wasn't finished. "Austin and Allison were just the cutest couple back then. Why, they were practically engaged! Austin, remember when you took Allison to the prom and..."

"Natalie," Phillip interrupted her. "I think Cheryl Lane is trying to get your attention. Why don't you go see what she needs?"

As Natalie made her way over to her friend, Phillip looked at Julia.

"I'm sorry about my wife's blatant attempt at whatever it is she's attempting with Allison." He turned to Austin. "Son, you know your mother. I hate that she's dragging the girl here. Leave whenever you want to, and I'm sorry if she's made tonight a pain."

Caleb spoke up for the first time then. "Can I leave? I think tonight is a pain." He looked hopefully at his dad.

"No, but you can leave when Austin and Julia do. That's the best you're gonna get. I, on the other hand, am stuck." The three laughed at Phillip's expression, but at Natalie's return their eyes were fixed on the girl with her. She was a twenty-something strawberry blonde, whose face brightened upon seeing Austin. *Allison*, Julia thought. *That's the name of the old high school sweetheart if my memory serves me correctly. Natalie, Natalie...you really shouldn't be playing these games.* Julia painted a smile on her face and looked at the girl first and Natalie's smug face second.

"Look who I found," Natalie's voice raised in a sing-song tone.

"Hello, Mr. James, Caleb, Austin," her eyes settled on the latter. She smiled hopefully at him, and Julia felt Austin's displeasure without looking at him. To his credit, Austin smiled politely and took Julia's hand, giving it a gentle squeeze.

"How's it going Allison? Long time..."

"Great! I hear you're in Arizona these days. School?" she asked. Julia could tell from the way her blue eyes honed in on Austin that she wasn't paying any attention to the girlfriend. *Probably hoping I'll disappear if she ignores me long enough*, Julia thought, her smile never wavering. Julia could play nice when the occasion called for it.

"Yep, graduating next month." Austin broke eye contact and pulled Julia closer. "Allison, this is my girlfriend, Julia. Julia, this is Allison, an old family friend and former classmate of mine. I think I pointed out her house today." Austin looked down and smiled at Julia, making sure Allison knew where his attention lay. He winked at Julia, and her fake smile turned to a grin and she winked in return before she looked back at the girl.

"Nice to meet you, Allison," Julia said smoothly, her fake smile back in place. "I've had a wonderful time seeing where Austin grew up and meeting people from his home town. It's nice to meet an old friend." Neither woman reached out a welcoming hand.

"Allison, where are your folks?" Phillip asked.

"Like I told Natalie, Daddy had an unexpected business trip and Mother went with him. It's just me tonight."

"Well, let's sit and see what's on the menu," Phillip held Julia's chair, while Caleb pulled out Allison's. Because Austin didn't trust himself to get too close to his mother, Natalie was left to take care of her own chair, but no one seemed to notice. Phillip looked down at the card sitting at his place and put on a pair of reading glasses. "Oh, look, the usual. Rubber turkey roast and dressing with cold veggies and salad. At least dessert is cheesecake." He grinned as he finished, and the table laughed at his fitting description. It was a charity event, and prime rib wasn't in the budget.

Throughout the meal, Julia saw Allison's eyes stay on Austin, but he didn't seem to notice and looked at her only when the conversation at the table moved in her direction. Natalie said nothing. The look on her face spoke volumes, and as soon as dinner ended, she excused herself to find a friend who she needed to speak to. Phillip looked at Julia. He smiled and asked, "Well, Julia, have you enjoyed your little visit here this weekend?"

Julia returned his smile. "More than you know. I'm so glad we were able to come. Seeing Austin in his natural habitat, so to speak, has been wonderful. And Caleb alone was worth the flight." She looked at the little brother, who had sat silently throughout the meal, ignoring everyone and everyone ignoring him.

"Right back at'cha," Caleb grinned at Julia. She always made him feel good.

"Well," Allison said. "I'm sorry Mother and Daddy couldn't make it tonight. Austin, they'll be sorry they missed you." She looked at him and caught his eye.

"Yeah, give them my best and tell them I said 'Hi,'" he said. "It's been good to see you, Allison." Austin probably didn't mean to, but his words and tone of voice seemed to dismiss her.

It isn't the poor girl's fault that Natalie has dragged her into an uncomfortable situation, Julia thought. She felt badly for the girl and couldn't let her leave awkwardly, even though the young woman who now stood to go would have liked nothing more than to be leaving with Austin.

"Allison?" she looked at Julia. Julia smiled a genuine smile now. "It was really nice meeting you. I hope to see you again next trip."

"Oh," Allison was surprised at Julia's attitude. "Sure, nice meeting you, too." She walked away.

They watched her back as she made her way through the crowd, and as she disappeared, Caleb spoke up. "Well, that wasn't stupid at all. What the hell was Mom thinking, dragging her over here, anyway?"

"Language, son," Phillip looked at Austin and Julia. "I apologize. I really don't know what my wife thought to accomplish, but you handled it like a pro." He smiled at her. "Julia, I for one am glad Austin brought you home. I think you're very good for my son." He looked at Austin. "Please, bring him back soon."

"I will," Julia assured softly. "Phillip, you won't mind if we take Caleb and go, will you? I know there's this dance and…"

"Uh, no," Austin interrupted. "I am here with the prettiest woman in the room. I intend to dance with her and make every other man here want to be me."

"No, son, you will share the pretty lady, especially with your dad."

"And brother," Caleb piped up. "It's not every day I'm with a knock-out." He grinned at Julia.

"For that, Caleb James, you get the first dance. Let's go." Julia took his hand and Caleb followed her out to the dance floor as the band began playing.

"Son," Phillip started to speak.

"Dad, not your fault. You know how Mom is. She wants to control things. She has this little fantasy where I bring home the princess that she's chosen for me, we have the fairy tale wedding and live happily ever after. Next door to her, of course." Austin laughed, then sobered and looked at his dad, "Question, why haven't you said anything to me? About my job? Julia? Living in Arizona?" Austin grinned at his dad. "You are always the one to have an opinion to give me."

Phillip laughed. "I guess I'm getting older. And wiser. When you left, son, I was at first angry, then disappointed, and then just hurt. It wasn't long before I realized that I was taking something personally that had nothing to do with me. I watched you take control of your life, work hard, and accomplish what you set out to do. I can't help admiring that."

"Thanks, Dad, I didn't expect to hear that from you." Austin realized what he'd just said. "Sorry."

Phillip laughed. "No apology necessary. I love you, son, and I want you happy. I see you with this woman, and she really does that, doesn't she? Make you happy?"

"That's obvious," Austin replied. "She makes me better. Don't ask me how, but I am. She's introduced me to a world out there that I've only seen from the outside. And she's just so awesome." Phillip smiled at his son's use of the word "awesome." He hadn't heard that in a long time, and it reminded him of when Austin was a boy living at home.

"The age issue? Son, you have to think about it, whether you want to or not. She has a biological clock that's ticking. She's been married before. Where do you see this going?" Phillip was concerned about these issues.

"Kids aren't a priority with me, Dad, sorry. I've never thought about them and really don't feel a need for one. As for the first marriage, let's just say that from all accounts, Julia tried. She and her ex weren't cut out for each other and married for the wrong reasons. As for where we're going. Who knows? Right now, we work. What we have works. If things change down the road, we'll deal. She's happy. I'm happy. I wish everyone else would just chill out, you know?"

"I do, son. I do. I'm glad for you. And don't worry about your mother. I'll take care of her," Phillip's tone hardened at the thought of his wife and her middle school antics. He laughed then. "What in the hell was she thinking? And poor Allison."

"Language, Dad," Austin teased. "Allison is a big girl, and she'll be just fine. In fact, I'll bet she leaves here with a new prospect. I'm just surprised she didn't earn that MRS degree before she left UNC." Austin laughed and Phillip joined him.

They were still chuckling when Caleb and Julia returned. They looked at the father and son questioningly, but neither asked.

"Phillip, would you like to be next?" Julia held out her hand.

"I'm tempted, but I better look for my wife. I don't think it would be a good idea for her to look up and see me dancing with another woman." Phillip was teasing, but Julia caught the serious undertone. After all, she was more his contemporary than Austin's.

"Hello? Remember me? I'm the guy who brought you," Austin stood up. "Next dance is mine as is every one after that."

Julia laughed as they headed for the dance floor. Caleb had spotted a pretty redhead that he was going to talk to. Before he left his dad, he asked. "Really, Dad, what do you think?"

"I think I'm through worrying. What do you think?" Phillip asked his youngest.

"I don't think—ever. Thank god," and Caleb was off.

Chapter 23

JULIA AWOKE BEFORE DAWN. *Our final morning here,* she thought. *Too bad it feels like the night never ended.* She hadn't slept well, or at all, simply because she was mad. Mad that Natalie James tried to manipulate Austin, Allison, and her. *Why does this bother me so much?* Julia thought as she lay there looking at the ceiling. *Good grief, I've watched my mother manipulate my life through school, a bad marriage, and pretty much any other way she could.* Then she realized that's why Natalie's behavior had made her so mad. Natalie was pulling a "Dana," and Julia no longer put up with Dana's antics. She wasn't about to put up with Natalie's either. Julia knew that she wouldn't sleep anymore, and she slid as quietly as she could out of the noisy bed, slipped on her jeans and sweatshirt, and quietly pulled the door shut behind her.

I'll see about making some coffee and maybe sitting out in the sunroom, she thought to herself as she made her way down to the kitchen. Julia had fixed up her mug and settled into a rocking chair by the window when she heard someone else stirring in the kitchen. Figuring it was Natalie or Phillip, Julia stayed where she was. She really had no desire to talk to anyone at that moment. Besides, she was enjoying the darkness outside the windows as it slowly turned to light. She rocked her chair gently back and forth and sipped her coffee. The combination was calming. Unfortunately, that calm was broken by the entrance of another person. Julia looked up to see Natalie standing in the doorway.

"Mind if I join you?" she asked, as she came into the room and took a seat in the other rocker that made up the pair by the window. Between them stood a small round table, and she set her mug onto the glass surface.

Julia didn't even glance over, but shrugged her shoulders and said, "Your house." She refused to make conversation easy and would have preferred no conversation at all. Then she changed her mind.

"In fact, this *is* your house, and if you came in here to talk about last night, you may want to rethink that." Julia's face had taken on the hard look of Dana Whitman. She didn't know it, but at times like these, the mother came out in the daughter.

"Yes," Natalie began, "I think I do need to discuss last night. What you and Austin did to that poor girl was almost inexcusable." Raising an eyebrow in disbelief, Julia turned to look at Natalie, but said nothing, yet. "She was embarrassed beyond belief. I expect something like that from Austin, he's still young, you know, but from you I did expect a little more. You two excluded her and made her feel totally out of place. It was almost mean the way you wouldn't let Austin carry on a conversation with his old friend. The girl is young enough to be your daughter, and I would hope that…"

Julia cut her off at that point.

"That's enough. The only person in the wrong last night was you, and we all know it, including your sons and husband." Julia had set her own mug onto the table and sat up in her chair. "But we're not going to talk about that, Natalie. No, we're going to talk about the reason why you dragged that poor girl into dinner last night to practically throw her in Austin's face. We're going to talk about your sneaking around behind Austin's back to try to undermine our relationship. We're going to talk about your pretending to be friendly with me when we both know that you are tolerating me at best. We're going to talk about the fact that you are unable to either come between Austin and me or to get the best of me." Julia had turned around in her chair and was looking at the woman straight on.

"I came here with the intention of starting a relationship with you and Phillip, a friendly relationship that would help mend some fences between you and your son. Did he tell you that I talked him into coming? No, I can tell he didn't." Julia leaned forward. "But he did tell you that he and I are together. That, Natalie, isn't going to change, regardless of how many asinine, childish pranks you try to pull." She paused, one side of her mouth drawn up in a disgusted smirk. "Seriously, did you think bringing the old flame back around was going to make him wake up, realize that I am all wrong for him, and send him off into the sunset with the girl you think is best for him? Do you even know your son?" Julia stopped there before she said something that she would later regret.

Natalie drew herself up and returned Julia's amused look with a glare.

"I know my son, better than you do, and I *do* know what's best for him. You, Julia Whitman, are not that person. You're too experienced, too smooth, and too old. He's nothing more than someone for you to play with and show off to your friends. As for a future, what, you going to marry him? Give him a baby? At your age? You, my dear, are living in a fantasy world you've built around my son, and I won't stand for it. I won't!" As she finished, Natalie slapped the arm of her chair and almost snarled.

Julia couldn't help herself. She laughed. She looked at the woman's expression and thought about the ridiculous things she'd just said. She leaned back in her chair and what started out as a chuckle soon turned into what she called a belly laugh. Julia laughed until she gasped and fought for control. Julia had lived with Dana Whitman. This woman was nowhere near her league, and Julia found that her attempt at intimidation was too funny. It wasn't all about the humor she saw in Natalie's behavior, but it was a release of tension for Julia. She'd needed an outlet for her pent-up emotions, and the woman had given her one. Natalie was not happy to see Julia laughing at her expense, and while she said nothing, her mouth was set in furious lines and her eyes were flashing. Julia finally regained control of herself.

"The fantasy, Natalie, is in your mind. You can't control him any more than you can control me. And you can't control me. As you like to remind me, I'm too old for that."

Julia was serious again. "I'm not going to fight with you. You're not worth it. But here's what we're going to do. We're going to call a truce. I've said what I wanted to say. Whether you have or not is totally irrelevant to me at this point." Natalie started to say something, but Julia held up a hand to stop her. "This isn't about us. It's about Austin, and I refuse to let you drag me into a war when he's going to be the only casualty. We are going to be polite when we are around each other. That's all. You will be welcome to visit us in Arizona, but I will not be back unless you personally invite me. And before that happens, you'll have to make some changes in your attitude. As you'd like to say, I'm too old, and you're right about that. I'm too old to put up with your shit. I've put up with shit from a lot of people most of my life, and unfortunately for you, from a woman who could give the devil lessons. No, Natalie, you don't intimidate me, or frighten me, or any of the other things you'd love to do."

Natalie looked at Julia as if she were something totally foreign. She was speechless. Julia realized that she might have come on too strong and had probably hurt the woman's feelings. She didn't care. If Julia was going to be around Austin's mom in the future, they had to get some things settled now.

"You think about this little war you're trying to start, Natalie. It isn't necessary. Your son is a man. Accept it. Move on. Men don't always do what their mommies want them to. Your son is no different." Julia softened just a bit now. Her initial temper had subsided. "You did something right, Natalie, because your boy is a special man. He didn't do that all by himself. He's special enough to completely change my mind about a lot of things." Julia's eyes were boring into Natalie's. She continued. "After my divorce, I decided that I was not interested in a relationship with any man, and I was never again going to be some malleable little woman. And I haven't. Life has taught me a lot, and most of it was at a high price. But I didn't survive; I thrived." She leaned toward the other woman. "I have found few men in this world who I consider my equal, but I do Austin. Have faith in the job you've done in raising him. Have faith in your son."

Julia was finished. Here she had thought that Austin's biggest problem with his family was his dad. Having it turn out to be his mother bothered Julia more than she would ever let her know. If life had taken a different turn, Julia would have been a mother. She would have been the one protecting her child. But at some point, that child no longer needs or wants that kind of protection. Natalie's time to figure that out with her son was now.

"Well, tell me how you really feel, Julia." Natalie had found her voice. "You may hold all the cards right now, but he'll get tired of you. Today he's infatuated with the attention you give him. And with the connections you've provided him. Your looks, which will eventually leave you. Oh, he'll move on, Julia, he'll move on."

"I don't think so, Mom," Austin's voice came from the doorway. Natalie's head whipped around toward the door, a frightened looked spreading across her face.

"Austin, I'm so sorry," Julia stood and walked toward him. "I never intended to have you witness this. I would have filled you in later, but your mom and I had some things to straighten out."

Austin looked at her and smiled. "I know, Jules, and I'm surprised you didn't say all this last night." He looked at his mom then, and he was angry. "Whatever Julia said to you, Mother, know that she speaks for us both. I don't know exactly what your problem is because you've never pulled anything like it before, but know this. You don't run my life. I'm not going to talk to you right now, because there's nothing for me to add. Julia and I are going upstairs to finish packing and make our flight." He took Julia's arm and led her from the room, through the house, and up the stairs. He didn't say anything until they were back in their room.

"Austin, I really am sorry. I feel like such a female, making a big damn deal out of something that really didn't bother me. I should have just kept my mouth shut, but when I started thinking, which never leads to anything good, I felt lied to. I thought she and I were getting along fine. That she was starting to like me even. Last night's little scene was just that. A stupid little scene. I should have laughed and passed it off. But I also know that if she tries to manipulate us now, it will never end unless we stop it. God knows I've had enough of that with my mother."

"It's all good, Jules." He interrupted her. "Really. We are going home. We're going to let her stew, and maybe I'll see them at Christmas, maybe not. You're right."

"We good?" Julia asked.

"We good," Austin replied and pulled her tight against him. "Now, we have a car to return, a flight to catch, and our lives to resume."

"Let's do it." They made good use of the shower one last time, gathered the rest of their stuff in companionable silence, and were standing in the foyer when Caleb and Phillip joined them.

"Son," Phillip hugged Austin first before turning to Julia and pulling her close, too. "When will we see you again?"

"Well, come on out next month for my graduation if you want. You, Caleb, Mom."

"Send me the date and I'll make it happen." He turned to Julia then. "Take care of my boy." He smiled as he said it.

"That's almost too easy," Julia teased. "But I'll do my best."

She turned around then to hug a sleepy Caleb. He hugged her back, and whispered, "Remember, if you ever get tired of my idiot brother, I'm right here waiting."

Julia laughed and kissed him on the cheek. "I'll keep that in mind. Until then, don't drive the girls too crazy, okay?"

"Where's Mom?" Austin looked past his dad.

"Oh, she said that she'd talked to you earlier, and she's nursing a headache. I tried to get her to come out, but she insisted she can't get out of bed right now."

"Yeah, we said all we needed to earlier," Austin said. He could tell that his dad knew the truth. Phillip's wife had said nothing, but Phillip was too intelligent to not read between the lines.

The men loaded the car. Austin and Julia pulled away and turned to wave at the two men standing on the stoop. Neither of them saw the woman standing at the upstairs window watching them drive off.

Chapter 24

"OH, MY GOD, JULES, YOU actually said that to his mother?" Lauren and Julia were catching up and were alone. Austin had returned to his apartment to check on things, as he put it. "You actually said all that shit to his *mother*?" She gave a fake sniff and wiped imaginary tears. "I'm just so proud..."

Julia tossed one of the small sofa pillows at her head and both laughed. They were drinking their favorite wine and were curled up in their pajamas. It had been a while since they'd done this. It felt good.

"Yep, and the best part was Austin. Lauren, he backed me up one hundred percent without blinking an eye. He didn't even know everything I'd said, but that didn't stop him from telling her that I spoke for us both." Julia grinned at her friend. "It was really kinda sexy." They both laughed.

"That's it Jules. Have a fight with his mother and turn it into hot sex with the son. That's my girl!"

"Speaking of sex, which is the extent of your love life, what's up?" Julia was curious.

"Well, nothing new. Same old, same old, really. Matt and I hang out some, and before you get that look on your face, we're buds. He makes me laugh. I still make him horny. It's a good relationship."

"Lauren, just don't mess around. Talk about awkward..."

"It's all good. Trust me."

Julia would try.

Thanksgiving was spent at Grandma Bea's for them all. Lauren thought about going home, but decided she'd rather go at Christmas. Matt's grandma treated them like her own, and they passed a pleasant day eating too much, watching football with the guys, playing cards, eating again, and falling into a food-induced coma. Everyone decided it was one of the best Thanksgivings they'd had in a long time.

Julia and Lauren opened the shop on Black Friday even though their business wasn't like others. They had a few who came in for original art pieces and ideas, but it wasn't a mad rush. The day passed quickly, and they headed out on time. Austin would be at the apartment when they got home. It was a different arrangement than what most people would be comfortable with. Many would think that Lauren would feel like a fifth wheel, but that wasn't the case. The townhouse was bigger than many houses, so the space wasn't crowded. Lauren was out most nights, and Austin was back and forth between Julia's and his place. Just like the May-December relationship Austin and Julia shared worked, so did the three-way friendship.

Shortly after Thanksgiving, they'd finished up dinner one night when the doorbell rang. Julia looked at Austin and Lauren who shrugged her shoulders and headed down the stairs to see who was there.

"Could be Matt," Lauren said over her shoulder. Julia and Austin continued cleaning up the mess until they heard a male voice. Julia paused and listened closer.

"Hey, Jules," Lauren called up the stairs. "You might want to come down here." Julia didn't like the sound of her friend's voice. It was the voice Lauren reserved for times when she was holding in her temper just before she let it go in someone's direction.

Julia looked at Austin, raised one shoulder in confusion, and headed down the stairs. As she reached the bottom, she looked up and stopped suddenly. Keith Landry.

"Keith, what are you doing here?" She remained on the last step. She had no idea of why he would be standing on her front porch.

"Julia, want to call off the Rottweiler, please? I'm not here to fight, just to talk."

Lauren growled in her throat and simply stood between Keith and Julia. It really was a good thing her revolver was upstairs.

Touch of Jules

"Lauren does what she wants to do. You should know that by now, but I don't need a guard dog for you. What do you want, Keith?"

"Well, I'm out here in Phoenix on business, and I thought I'd drop by to see if you want to go out for a drink? Just talk? We aren't enemies, are we Jules?"

Julia remained silent, and she felt Austin come down behind her. He'd heard the male voice and the man's name. The thought of him asking Julia out for a drink had Austin seeing red. He put a hand on her shoulder in silent question: Did she need him to step in? The thought made Julia smile and she reached up to put her hand on his. The action drew Keith's attention to the man standing behind his ex-wife. They sized one another up quickly. Keith spoke first.

"I suppose I should have called instead. Are you going to ask me in? Introduce me to your friend? Or is this Lauren's friend?" Keith asked. For some reason, he was playing dumb and Julia didn't like it.

She drew a deep breath, brought Austin next to her, and they both moved to the door. Lauren stepped back and stood glaring at Landry.

"I don't think you're coming in is a good idea, but yeah, I'll introduce you. Keith, this is Austin James. Austin, this is my ex-husband Keith Landry."

"Keith…" Austin extended a hand that Keith took. Each was still sizing the other up. Neither smiled.

"Austin…" Keith pulled his hand back first.

"Okay, once again, Keith, why in the world would you think of paying me a visit? If you haven't realized by now, we're not friends. We don't exchange Christmas or birthday cards. Hell, I haven't heard a word from you since we parted ways at the courthouse. So, I ask again, what are you doing here?" Julia's attitude was rude. "I doubt you're that thirsty." She didn't care how rude she was being. This didn't make any sense.

Keith had the courtesy to look a bit embarrassed. Julia wondered if he truly was or if he was just playing his part, like always.

"Really, I'd rather talk inside than standing in your doorway." Keith grinned at her then. "I know your mother raised you better than this." The smile quickly faded at the look on her face.

"Dammit!" Julia exclaimed. "She sent you here, didn't she? My mother called you and told you to hurry out to Arizona and straighten out her

185

daughter, didn't she? Good god, you and she are still quite the team. Well, news flash, Ace, I'm not playing." Julia was about to close the door in his face, when Keith reached out to place a hand on it. Both Lauren and Austin started to move forward then, but Julia beat them to it. She had her hand on the door latch and stood there between Keith and the other two.

"Julia, please," Keith had on his appealing face. "I need to talk to you about some things. Alone, if you don't mind."

Julia's chin rose as she looked at him. She really didn't want to give in, but she was curious. She wanted to know what the hell Dana Whitman had told this man to get him all the way out here, and after all these years. Was it worth her aggravation of talking to her ex alone if she could find out what Dana was up to? When dealing with her mother, knowledge was power. You paid a price for ignorance, as Julia had learned.

"Okay, I'll talk to you, Keith. Tomorrow. Come by the shop around noon. We'll talk then."

Realizing that he'd gotten all he would from her, Keith smiled. "Thanks, Jules. I'll see you tomorrow. Austin. Lauren." With that, he turned and walked back to the car parked in her drive. She saw that his rental was a BMW. Obviously, that was one thing about Keith that hadn't changed—his expensive taste.

She closed the door and turned to face the frowning two who had maintained their silence throughout the exchange. As expected, Lauren spoke first.

"What the FUCK was that all about? What could he possibly want?" Lauren didn't usually drop the f-bomb unless she was beyond upset. "And that fucking Dana!" She continued. "God, Jules, how you ever came from that woman is totally beyond me. Dammit!" She stomped up the stairs, and Julia heard her slamming open and shut cabinet doors. It would be a vodka night for Lauren.

Austin said nothing. He knew exactly what Keith Landry was up to. Show Julia what she was missing in settling for the youngster. Put them side by side and perhaps Julia would run back to Landry. He also knew immediately who had sent him. Dana Whitman. He looked down at Julia and grinned. Austin knew she had nothing to do with this, and if he could ease some of the tension in her face, he'd try.

"Austin, I swear, I have no clue of what that was all about except that it has my mother written all over it.That's the only reason I'd consider meeting with him. I need to know what my mother has been saying and what she did to get him out here."

"I know, baby. Meet with him tomorrow, get it over with, and move on, right?" Austin pulled her along as they headed back up the stairs. "It would seem that my mother isn't the only one to send in reinforcements in the 'Separate Austin and Julia' campaign."

She laughed. Austin was hiding his feelings well. Julia knew that instead of shaking his hand, Austin would have rather punched him in the throat. No need. She was flattered by the jealousy she'd seen in him. *What woman wouldn't be*, she thought. Regardless of how mature, secure, or loved a woman was, seeing her man show a bit of possessiveness was a compliment.

That night when they were alone in bed, their lovemaking took on a different tone. It was more intense. Austin was more loving than he'd ever been, and Julia hadn't complained before. She wondered how much of this change had to do with their visitor. *If that's the case*, she thought, *Keith can drop by anytime.* She snuggled in closer and drifted off to sleep.

Austin remained awake, thinking. *So that's Keith Landry.* He pictured again the tall, athletically built man with blue eyes, closely cropped hair, clothes from a GQ advertisement. Julia had never said, so Austin guessed his age to be late forties, maybe early fifties, and the fine lines around his eyes and mouth supported that assumption. Successful. Everything about the man screamed success, confidence, charm. Austin tried to picture Julia with Keith at a country club, like his parents' club, or a fancy restaurant. It bothered him that he could. He hated the way "Jules" slid off the man's tongue. But when he thought of the woman who threw on old jeans and tennis shoes to go hiking with him, or who pulled her hair into a ponytail as they flew across the desert in Matt's Jeep, he couldn't see that woman with a Keith Landry. Austin wasn't jealous of this guy, but he was worried. Landry had hurt her before, and Austin hoped he didn't have the power to hurt her again.

He wrapped his arms a little tighter around Julia. He knew his girl, and she was a lot tougher than Landry would remember her being. Then he smiled at the thought.

If all else fails, we'll sic the dog on him.

A few minutes before twelve, Lauren heard the door open and looked up to see Keith walking into the shop. He paused inside the door to look around, taking in the different displays, the walls of original art, the furniture groupings, and finally Lauren's face. She stood leaning against the partition that separated the office area from the rest. Her arms were crossed, head tilted to one side, and brown eyes flashing as she looked him up and down before staring straight into his eyes. Keith had dressed down on this Saturday, if creased black Docker slacks, white polo (the real deal with the horse and rider over the left breast), and black Sperrys could be considered casual. His only jewelry was the silver Rolex that Lauren knew Julia had bought him for Christmas their last year together. She smirked at his attempt to be cool and casual. *Tough to find your casual when you're always concerned with maintaining the GQ aura, Keith,* she thought. *Good try, though.* She wouldn't say out loud what she really wanted to. *Let him start something,* she thought, *and then I get to finish.* The longer she glared at him, the more she noticed his unconcerned air start to waver.

Keith broke the silence first. "Hello, Lauren. You're looking lovely today, as usual."

If he thought a compliment would break her stare or silence, he was wrong. She continued staring at him.

"Is Julia out?" He tried again. He didn't like Lauren. Never had and never would. In his opinion, Lauren wasn't a good influence on Julia when they were married, and he knew that if it weren't for Lauren, Julia would probably still be living in Missouri. In their Lake Saint Louis home. Going to dinners and parties with him. Sharing his bed at night. And not out here decorating houses and sleeping with college boys. He was trying to maintain a friendly attitude toward the blonde in front of him because he knew Lauren could undermine anything he tried to accomplish.

"So, it's the silent treatment for ol' Keith, huh?" he smiled at her again. "I suppose that probably is better than how we left things, isn't it? What was it you said just before leading my wife out of the courtroom?"

Before Keith could answer his own question, Lauren helped him out. "I believe I called you what you are. 'Fucking douchebag,' followed by

'Eat shit and die' if my memory serves me correctly." Lauren said it all in a low monotone, which was more effective than if she had stressed any of the terms she'd used.

"You always had a way with words, didn't you, Lauren? But, I'm not here for you, am I? Did Julia forget our appointment?"

"God, I hope so, but she's meeting a client and will be rolling in any minute. I'd offer you a chair, but I assume you'll just lean back on that pole stuck up your ass. By the way, how's Buffy, or Bitsy, or whatever the name is of your paramour? Did you two get married and pop out a kid or two? That was always your goal. Round out the image with two point three babies, or whatever the national average is these days."

"Not that it's any of your business, but Courtney and I ended things a few months after Julia left Missouri. No marriage. No babies."

"That's right, Courtney. I sure hope things ended well because she worked for you, didn't she? And I'm talking about a legit job like file clerk or secretary, or something, right? How did the sex discrimination case go? She did sue your ass for sexual harassment, didn't she? I sure as hell would have."

Lauren was finally getting under his skin, and the realization made her almost smile. Almost. She was shooting in the dark on her harassment remark. *Hmmm...I wonder*, she thought and almost smiled again. Before she could pursue that line, they both heard the back door open and shut, and Julia came into the room. Keith's irritation with Lauren was in an instant replaced with delight at seeing Julia walk in. For her part, Julia looked from Lauren to Keith and back to her friend in a silent question. It was never good to leave these two alone for more than a few minutes.

"Jules, Keith here was just telling me all about his sexual harassment case when he and his little sweet thing split up. I was just settling in for all the juicy details when you interrupted us." Lauren's voice was dripping sweet, and Julia knew she was trying to get a rise out of the man.

"I'm sure he was," Julia said to her friend. She had no intention of inquiring about their conversation. Julia turned to Keith. "You're a little early. I had an appointment I needed to take, and I thought I had left in plenty of time."

189

"I am a bit early," Keith smiled at her. "No harm. Lauren and I were just catching up." He turned the smile in Lauren's direction. To his credit, it never wavered.

"Well, there's a small city park across the street. Let's sit over there and you can tell me what you came to say," Julia started across the room to the front door.

"I thought we'd have lunch," Keith said. "I saw several small restaurants in the area. Aren't you hungry?" He turned on the charm, vintage Keith.

"No, I'm meeting Austin here in a while, and we're heading out to Fountain Hills for a late lunch. The park is fine." She looked at Lauren before she led Keith out the door. "If Austin gets here a little early, let him know that I won't be long."

"Will do," Lauren would be happy to relay the message. The look on Keith's face was priceless in her book. He wasn't used to not getting his way, and he wasn't happy. But when Julia turned to look at him, the charming smile was back in place.

"I'll follow you wherever," he said brightly. Lauren was rolling her eyes as the two made their way out the door. She went to the window to watch them cross the street. She was glad to see Keith try to take Julia's arm and her friend deftly avoid the contact as she hurried ahead.

There had been a time when Julia would have let him and been grateful for the gesture. Lauren grinned to see that wasn't the case any longer. She had been a little concerned the night before when Julia agreed to meet Keith. She remembered how he and Dana had controlled Julia and had her dancing to whatever music they played.

I'd wish you good luck this time around, Keith, but I don't, Lauren thought as she turned from the window and sat down in her chair. *I really wish you'd just stayed away.*

Julia led them to a bench that sat under one of the sweet acacia trees. Off to the left was a small playground area where children could be heard screaming and laughing as they scooted down the slide or whirled on the merry-go-round. She sat at one end of the bench and motioned for him to take the other. Between them she dropped her bag, marking what was her side and what was his. She had placed her sunglasses back on her face, and she turned to look at him now. His eyes were also hidden behind sunglasses, so neither could really tell what the other was thinking.

"Well? You asked, Keith, and I agreed to this little meeting. I truly don't know what we could have to say to one another. Not now. Not after all of this time has passed." Julia waited a few seconds, and when he didn't reply, she continued. "I hope you and my mother haven't cooked up some reunion scene and expect me to play my role. Won't happen." He could see her mouth harden into a straight line.

"You still wear the Ray-Bans I bought you on our trip to Mexico. They always looked so good on you, Jules."

"Yep, and isn't it ironic that these same sunglasses are the reason Austin and I met? You know how I can never keep up with the things, and when I left them on a golf cart, he made sure I got them back." Julia smiled at the pleasant memory.

"That's right, your little friend is a groundskeeper or something there, huh? You surprise me, Julia."

He could see her brows coming together over the top of her sunglasses and hoped he'd touched a nerve. She needed to see this kid for what he was—a kid.

"You want to talk about Austin, Keith? You want to go there?" Julia's voice was low.

"No, I'm sorry. I don't. Not at this time. Instead, I have some things that I always wanted to tell you, but I never had the chance. Between your dad and Lauren, I couldn't get a moment alone with you after the divorce."

"Newsflash, Keith. I'm the one who kept you away from me. They simply assisted." Her patience was waning. "Say your piece, and let's move on, shall we?"

Keith looked at her and removed his glasses. He wanted to ask her to do the same, but he knew that if he asked, she'd leave them on until hell froze over. He had rehearsed what he would say, but here with her now, he was struggling.

"Julia, I never really apologized for what happened between us."

"Yes, you did. You stood in the foyer of our home, surrounded by your stuff, and apologized about fifty times. Don't you remember?"

"I remember, but I'm not talking about that. I never apologized to you for letting you down."

He could feel her mood shift as she took that in. He wasn't sure what she was feeling, but her vitriol when she spoke caught him off guard.

"Letting me down? Which time Keith? When you totally blew off my career, thinking my place was at home as your beck-and-call girl? When you began to control almost every aspect of my life like making the 'appropriate' friends, joining the 'right' club, hosting the perfect business parties, and even making sure I dressed like the rest of the wives and drove my own luxury car?" Julia paused before continuing and looked down at her hands clinched into fists in her lap. "Or how about the time I lost the first baby and you totally ignored our losing that precious soul to start planning the next child? Or was it when I lost the second baby and watched you and my mother console one another by yes, once again planning the next?"

She stopped and raised her chin. "Oh, I know, it must be when with baby number three, you decided that I should become an invalid and lie on the couch while you and my mother, again, took over everything that should have been mine. Like decorating the nursery, picking out names, or planning the wonderful future our child would have." Julia leaned toward him as she continued her rant. "I know. How about this one? The time you let me down by leaving me at home alone while you found consolation with someone else. Help me out here, Keith, because I really can't keep up with all the times you let me down." At the end of her tirade, Julia sat back and crossed her arms. Sometime in the middle of her speech, she'd removed her sunglasses, and he could see the blue fire that shot from her eyes.

Keith wisely said nothing. He had no idea where all of this venom had come from, but he wasn't expecting it. When he did speak, he used his most reasonable tone, as if he could calm her down.

"I had no idea you felt that way, Jules. I know that we both struggled when the pregnancies failed, but I didn't know you felt so strongly about the rest of it. Why didn't you say something then?"

"I did. Over and over and over. You didn't want to hear what I had to say unless it was confirmation of your own thoughts." She sighed. "Keith, I wish I could say that this walk down Memory Lane is fun, but it isn't. You make me tired. You and my mother are both good at that, you know. I have plans and we need to wrap this up." She looked at her cell phone and back up at him. She'd replaced the sunglasses and he no longer could read her expression. If he had, he would have seen a woman on the verge of irritated. He, too, sighed and leaned back on the bench. The sun was warm and the sound of the children echoed across the park.

"Jules, how different do think it would have been if you hadn't lost the babies?" He never heard himself when talking to her. It was still her fault.

"Well, if *we* hadn't lost the babies, I'm sure lots of things would be different. Who knows, Keith? At some point, I'm sure I would have disappointed you in some other way, and you would have used that as the excuse to chase some young skirt. The difference would have been that you would have been hurting another person besides just me—you would have hurt a child who didn't deserve it anymore than I. Would I have left? Probably, but it would have been harder to do." She turned toward him and leaned forward a bit. "I'll ask one more time. Why are you here now? If I don't think you're telling me the truth, I'm walking back to my shop. If I do that, you are not to follow me. You are not to come to my home. You are to leave Scottsdale and forget all about me."

Keith hesitated and watched her rise to leave. Before she could walk away, he blurted out.

"I still love you, Jules, and I want to try again. Do you know why I didn't fight you on the house, the money, the divorce? It's because I loved you then. I love you now. And I'm so proud of what you've built here. I really am, Jules."

Julia sat back down and turned her head away from him. She was trying to absorb his words, but they were just so absurd that she wondered if she'd heard him correctly. *I should have seen this coming*, she thought. *I forgot how this man doesn't like to lose. Wow, he'll say anything to get into my good graces. He's never been proud of me one time unless he was being complimented by his friends on his beautiful wife. But why now? I wonder what my mother said to him to galvanize him to action*, she thought as she stared out across the park. She could see Touch of Jules from this vantage. She still didn't know what Dana had been saying, and that was her reason for the meeting.

"Keith, just what did my mother say to get you to come all the way out here? We've been divorced for what, almost five years now, and you've never once reached out. Why now?" Julia hoped for an honest answer, but with this man, she never knew.

"Well, you know that she and I have remained friends since you left. I knew that she and your dad were going to see you in September. As soon as they returned, she called and invited me to dinner. Just her and me. We met at the club and she filled me in on your life. Your mother tells me that you aren't doing well out here on your own. I knew that you hadn't been seeing anyone seriously since coming out here, but she said that you were now and that the guy was just using you and you were too infatuated to see it. According to Dana, you need me more now than ever since you left me. She said that if I still loved you and cared about you that I'd get myself out here and take care of you. She wouldn't elaborate or tell me anything more, and I didn't know if you were in financial trouble, or sick, or what." Keith paused here, not really sure about what to say or not to say. "What is she talking about, Julia? Are you okay?"

This tone was Keith's sincere voice, and she was moved by his concern, a little. She thought about Dana and what she meant when she said that Julia was in trouble. Austin. Her mother was pissed because Julia was with Austin and not Keith or some other man Dana approved of.

Julia looked at Keith, thought about what he'd been saying, thought about her mother and her "concern," and she couldn't help it. Her shoulders started shaking, and soon she'd thrown her head back and was laughing. She sobered up a moment to see Keith's angry face, and his expression sent her off into another burst of laughter.

"Do you mind?" he said through clinched teeth. "I don't care to be laughed at Julia, and you know that." At his angry words, she tried to stop, but it was such a ridiculous situation.

"I'm sorry," she said as she tried to catch her breath. "I really am, but you are such a putz." With that, she was off again. When she collected herself, she looked over at him, but he couldn't see that she really did feel sorry for him.

"Keith, you've just been played by Dana Whitman, my friend. She doesn't give a shit about me other than she's pissed that I'm not falling into line and listening to Mother. You were the only weapon in her arsenal, and you fell right into her hands. Seriously? You want me back. You're all sorry, but you don't even know for what. You come out here thinking I'll have cooled off by now and be ready to meekly come home and take my place at your side. That, Keith, is just so much bullshit. I don't love you.

There. I said it. I don't love you and probably didn't the last couple of years that we were married. You lose, Keith. You lose this time. But even better, Dana Whitman loses. Be sure you tell her that when you report back to her, okay?"

He had leaned forward now, his hands dangling between his knees and legs sprawled apart. Keith Landry never sat like this, and Julia felt a little sorry for him. A little. He had asked for this.

"Julia, I didn't make it a competition to win or lose. I love you."

"Just stop, Keith. Just. Stop. See yourself for what you are for once in your life. Oh, this has always been about winning, Keith, always."

As he remained quiet, Julia stood up and picked up her bag to leave.

"Take care of yourself, Keith. I don't want you to contact me again, please. We've said all we needed to say, and if nothing else, I have closure now. Well, better closure than tossing your things into the foyer of the house." She smiled. "That was fun."

Keith wasn't sure who this person was. This wasn't his Julia. His Julia wouldn't have laughed in his face. She wouldn't have thrown his love back in his face. She wouldn't have made him feel stupid. As he thought about how he'd been played, he started getting angry. With Dana not there, he turned his anger toward the woman standing in front of him. How dare she toss his love back into his face? How dare she laugh at his expense?

Keith stood up and pulled himself to his full six foot two inch height. He leaned in closer to Julia and forced her to look up at him.

"How dare you?" he asked. "Just who do you think you are? You're a nobody who wouldn't have a business or even a roof over her head if it hadn't been for my money. Yes, sweetheart, *my* money. You think you're Miss Independent, you and your blonde guard dog, but you're nothing and would still be nothing if not for me. Laugh all you want. But don't laugh at me."

Keith had grabbed her arm and pulled her hard against him as he finished this last. Julia was outmatched in physical strength, but she raised her chin in a clear challenge.

"*Your* money? Oh, Keith, I earned every penny of whatever you *think* you gave me. Now, get your hand off me," she said in a steely voice. "You do not touch me."

195

"You think?" Keith tightened his grip a little more. He was probably leaving a mark, but he was too angry to care. "You think? If I wanted to touch you, sweetheart, I'd touch you. And there's not a thing you could do about it."

Neither saw that someone else had joined them. Keith looked over Julia's head and found his eyes locked with a pair of dark green ones. Austin had gotten there early, and Lauren had told him where to find Julia. They both had been watching the two from the shop window, and when Keith rose to stand over Julia, Austin had shot out the door. He now stood behind her and he wasn't happy.

"I think the lady told you to take your hands off of her. I suggest you do it or I'll do it for you." Austin's tone was low, and Julia knew that he was as angry as she'd ever seen him.

Keith locked eyes with him and a few seconds went by before he dropped her arm and stepped back, raising both of his hands in surrender.

"No harm, no foul, here Junior. We were just finishing our conversation, weren't we, Jules?" Keith took a step back.

Austin listened to that *Jules* drip off the other man's tongue and thought he would explode. Before she could stop him, Austin grabbed Keith by the front of his shirt and had backed him into the tree. The two men were the same height, but the older man was clearly outmatched by the much younger.

"Listen, asshole, if you know what's good for you, you'll listen to the lady. Don't call her, don't try to see her. Stay away from her. And so help me if I ever see you lay a hand on her again, I'll break your hand, your arm, and your neck. Are we clear?"

Keith stared back at Austin, and Julia wondered if this would end here. A moment or two passed and Keith shook his head.

"You're welcome to her, pal. You do know that you could do better, don't you? You really shouldn't settle for someone like her. But I suppose a sugar-momma can keep a boy happy at least for a little while."

Austin wanted to smash his fist into the guy's pretty white teeth, but he felt a soft hand on his arm.

"Austin, this pile of shit simply isn't worth it. Let him go. He's finished here." Julia's calm voice kept him at bay. He released Keith's shirt and smoothed it out before leaning in.

"Remember what I said." With that, Austin turned to take Julia's hand and walk away. They didn't say anything as they crossed the street to return to the shop.

Lauren met them at the door, and when Julia looked down at what her friend had in her hand, she couldn't help herself. She pointed so Austin could also see, and they both laughed.

"What the hell's wrong with you two? And why did you let the son-of-a-bitch just walk away? I was on my way over to let him know that he might be a big man, but my little friend is a hell of a lot bigger!" Lauren waved her .38 special toward the door, and Julia stopped her before she could make her exit. The sight of the tall blonde, in skirt and high heels, eyes flashing, and hand waving a gun around had the two laughing again. They needed that nervous release, and Lauren was providing it.

"Put that thing down before you shoot one of us," Julia wiped her eyes and used her own hand to lower her friend's arm. "Here, give me that." She took the gun and laid it on Lauren's desk. "I swear, one of these days, you really will shoot somebody."

"Yeah, and the asshole will deserve it," Lauren was almost laughing now. At least, she was until she looked at Julia's arm. "Sweetie, look at that bruise. Please, I can still catch him. Just one shot in his nuts. That's all I want. And from close range, I can hit him square."

Julia held her arm out and up so that she could see what Lauren was talking about. Austin stepped up and gently ran a finger over the blue spots. It looked like a thumb mark and a couple of finger marks beside it on the inside of her upper arm where the skin was softest.

"For once, Blondie, I have to agree. I think you just might be able to get to him if you leave now."

"Austin, stop egging her on," Julia was afraid Lauren would try. "It's a little bruise, and it will go away. Just like Keith has gone away."

"You know him better than I do. Will he stay away?" Austin's adrenaline was still high, and Julia tried to reassure him.

"Yes, absolutely. He's a bully. He's lost and not happy about it, but he'll not bother me again." Julia leaned into Austin, and as he held her he could feel his breathing slowing down. She looked up at him. "You okay?"

"Yeah, I'm fine. How about you?"

"Still a little shaky. I've never seen that side of Keith before. He never laid a hand on me like that the entire time we were married. I don't get it."

"People change, Jules, and sometimes not for the better. I'm glad I got here a little early."

She smiled up at him then. "Me, too. I am not usually a damsel in distress, but he was a little frightening. Thanks for stepping in."

"Yeah, thanks, Austin, for taking away my one chance to do the world a favor," Lauren was still pouting. "All I would have done is scare him a little. Maybe make him piss himself." She laughed then. "That would have been rich—Keith Landry pissing his pants!" and she was off in a fit of laughter. At the picture she'd painted—Lauren holding her little .38 in Keith's crotch as he peed himself—the other two joined in.

"Lauren, close up shop, please. I need to go home and take a shower. Maybe I can get the asshole stench off me," Julia said as she finally had breath to talk. "Oh, that's right, we rode together. Here's my keys."

"Sure thing, girl. I'll catch up with you two later."

As Austin and Julia walked out, Lauren collapsed into her chair.

"Damn," she muttered. "Maybe next time."

Chapter 25

AUSTIN WAITED UNTIL HE HEARD the shower running before he picked up Julia's phone and scrolled through her contacts. Finding the number he wanted, he hit "send" and waited.

"Julia! I thought you'd forgotten your old friends now that you've taken up with a hottie."

"Hey, Sharon, it isn't Jules. It's Austin."

The laugh that came through was throaty and totally unembarrassed. "Well, hey Hottie! What's up?"

"Are you doing anything this afternoon?"

The pause was momentary before Sharon answered, "Not really. What do you need? Is everything all right, Austin?" Sharon knew when something was up.

"Yes, and no. Julia's had a rough day, and I thought it would help if we could drive out and visit you."

Austin had never called Sharon much less asked for anything. "Absolutely. You two kids come right on. Have you eaten? I'll have Angie fix you a late lunch."

It must be a Mother thing, he thought, *to fix life's problems with food.* They had skipped their lunch date, and he was starved.

"That sounds great. And Sharon? Have Angie mix up some of those Bloody Mary's you two love so much."

"Done. See you in a few, sweetie." He looked down and the call had already ended.

"What's with the phone? Did I miss a call?" Julia had changed and was towel drying her hair as she came into the living room. Tossing the towel aside, she curled up on Austin's lap and leaned her head on his shoulder. Putting an arm around her, he pulled her close and kissed the top of her wet head.

"That was Sharon. It's been a while since we've seen her and John, and I thought this afternoon would be a good time to drive out there. Angie is whipping up lunch and Sharon's favorite drink."

Julia lifted her head and looked at him for a moment. Then she smiled and kissed his cheek.

"You know just what I need, don't you? I won't be ten minutes." She hopped up and he knew that he had made a good decision. He took out his own phone and called Lauren.

"Hey, Blondie, I'm taking Julia out to Sharon and John's. Why don't you close up shop early and join us?"

"Say no more. Done and done. Outside of a couple of phone calls, it's been dead around here. Bloody Mary's for everyone?"

Austin laughed. "What's with you women and those tomato juice drinks?"

"What's with you men and your stinky feet? Some things only Mother Nature can explain, Junior." He heard her laugh. "See you out there in about an hour." She ended the call before he could reply. Lauren loved having the last word.

Julia came into the room.. She'd opted for a shirt with longer sleeves, and when he thought of the reason why, Austin felt his head getting warm. *If he ever shows his face around me again, I'll bust his chops just because,* he thought. Julia could read his mind, it seemed, because she crossed her arms and gave him what he called The Look. When she was finished with nonsense, this was the expression on her face. *She would have been a great mom,* Austin thought. *She already has that face down pat.*

"What?" He thought it best to play innocent.

"Nope. We're not going there. I'll share the events with Sharon and John, but after that, we're putting it behind us. Okay?"

"You have one more person that you need to talk to, you know. Your dad. If I were him, I'd want to know what your mom's been up to. And I'd also want to know what kind of man my wife has been hanging out with. Call him tonight, call him tomorrow, but call him. Okay?"

Julia rolled her eyes and took a deep breath. "You're right. You do know that my father will react much the same way you did. I don't want Daddy arrested for assaulting an asshole, so I'll call him tonight and let him cool down before Keith gets back to St. Louis. And as for my mother, well, she's on her own. He won't be happy."

"She deserves whatever she gets. Now, I'm starved. Let's head out."

November in Scottsdale, Arizona, has weather that is almost perfect. Even late in the month, the highs would be in the seventies, and with the hot sun, it was far from cool. Some of the snow birds had already started to arrive, but they wouldn't take over the valley until after Christmas. From then until May, the population swelled. Taking advantage of the sunshine, Austin lowered the top of the Mustang, handed Julia a Cardinals baseball cap for her hair, and pulled on his own favorite UNC blue and white. He gave her a grin before slipping on his Oakleys and pulling out.

The twenty-minute drive passed quickly, and by the time they pulled into the Burns' drive, both Julia and Austin were feeling much better. The air had blown the remaining bad feelings out of their heads, and they were laughing as they got out of the car. The front door flew open and Sharon almost ran to grab Julia in a bear hug.

"How's my baby girl?" She pulled back and looked up at Julia. She must have seen something as she narrowed her eyes and said, "We'll talk later. Right now, you two come on back by the pool. Angie set us up there with some of your favorite things and a pitcher of mine."

Sharon reached out a hand and pulled Austin next to her other side. Twining her arms through theirs, she led them around the house and through the gate to the pool. John was already seated, but stood up as he saw them. He opened his arms, and Julia hurried over to grab him up in a bear hug.

"I've missed my favorite decorator. Where have you been?" He, too, looked closely at Julia.

"Blame it on Austin," Julia teased. "He monopolizes my time these days."

Austin stepped up to shake John's out-stretched hand and laughed. "Yeah, yeah, we both know she can't smile without me."

"Barry Manilow! That's one of my favorite Barry Manilow songs—'I Can't Smile Without You,'" Sharon sang. "Did you know that he sang

'Happy Birthday' to me once? Remember John, we were on that cruise for my fortieth birthday, and Manilow was on the same trip?" she looked at the two younger people as she sat down. "I think the man is physically ugly as mud, but can he ever sing." She started humming some tune that Julia was only vaguely familiar with and that Austin had never heard.

"Sweetheart, these kids don't want to hear Barry Manilow songs, and they definitely couldn't care less about his looks. They want to eat," John laughed at his wife. Austin was sure she had to annoy him sometimes, but to look at him, John never seemed to be perturbed by his spitfire wife. He loved her. Looking at Julia, Austin tried to remember if she did anything to really annoy him. He was still trying to think of something when Angie appeared.

"Julia! Good to see you! And Austin, it's *always* a pleasure to see you," Angie liked to tease them both. She set down a pitcher of her red magic juice, as Sharon and Lauren called it, and four glasses on the table. She turned to bring out the food.

"Hey, Angie," John stopped her. "Would you bring a couple of beers out here for Austin and me? We'll leave the jungle juice for the women."

"Sure thing." She started to take back two of the glasses, but Julia stopped her.

"Leave one, please. I hope you don't mind, but Lauren will be here in a few minutes," Julia said, turning to Sharon.

"Oh, boy, my favorite snark buddy," Sharon grinned. "This afternoon just keeps getting better and better."

Angie returned with the men's drinks and a platter of sandwiches, potato salad, and fruit. The food and Lauren arrived at the same time.

"Woo hoo! Just what this gal needs—sustenance!" Lauren grabbed a glass and filled it. She waved off the offered plate. "Food just gets in the way of more alcohol." She took a satisfying swig and turned to look at Julia.

"We just got here, Lauren, and I'm starved," Julia didn't want to come right out and tell her friend to not mention anything yet, but Lauren knew.

They ate and caught up on one another's life. Sharon and John had flown out to New York for Thanksgiving, and Sharon had the latest grandson pictures to pass around. The others described their day with Grandma Bea and the latest gossip from their Scottsdale circle. John and Austin had their heads together, talking sports and business, and Angie brought out another pitcher of drinks and an iced bucket with four bottle necks sticking up from the top. As the conversation started to wind down a bit, Julia looked around the table and decided to let John and Sharon know about Keith's visit. They had never met the man, but Sharon had gotten an earful from Lauren. Granted, Lauren was a bit biased when it came to Keith Landry, but even if she only accepted half as truth, it was enough for Sharon to have her own opinion formed.

Taking a deep breath, Julia said, "Okay, not that I don't absolutely love simply hanging out with you two, we have another reason for coming over." Looking at John and Sharon, she continued, "We had an incident today that has me running to my other mom and dad." At this last, John leaned forward and rested his arms on the table. Sharon picked up Julia's hand and looked at her as if to say *go on.*

"You've heard of my ex-husband…" Julia left out nothing as she related the events of the previous night through that afternoon. As she talked, she could feel Austin tense up beside her and Lauren's face was a thundercloud. Sharon's expression echoed Lauren's when Julia reached the part of her story that included Keith's physical attack and stayed that way until Julia finished. Only John remained stoic on the outside.

"So there you have it. My crummy day." Julia looked around the table and smiled.

"Austin, you should have punched him in the throat. Just one good throat punch. And you," Sharon was on a roll and turned to Lauren. "Have I taught you nothing? Shoot him next time! If he shows up on your doorstep, shoot him and drag him inside."

"Jules," John said softly. "Let me see that arm, please." She reluctantly rolled up her sleeve.

"See, it really isn't that big a deal. I've done worse running into a door," she said. But when she looked again, she saw that the bruises had darkened.

John took out his phone. "May I?" Without waiting for an answer, he gently held Julia's arm and snapped two pictures from a couple of different angles, making sure her face was in both. "My attorney will have these this afternoon, and he'll file the restraining order immediately. Do you want to press charges?"

"Hell, yes, she does!" This came from Lauren who was still steamed she didn't get her pound of flesh from Keith Landry.

Julia smiled and shook her head, "Thanks, but I don't know. What good would that do?" Her face grew somber and she sighed heavily. "I seriously don't think he'll hurt me. As for the restraining order, I guess I need to file one of those if for nothing more than to keep him out of my face and away from my business. You realize it won't go into effect until Monday when a judge can sign off on it and that Keith will already be back in Missouri."

It was John's turn to smile. "I have friends, one of whom is Judge Michaels. I'll give him a call so he'll know to expect the paperwork today." His smile faded and his face hardened. "As for Mr. Landry, I do believe he'll receive a visit from another friend of mine who will expedite his departure. Where did you say he's staying?"

"The Hilton," Austin spoke for the first time. "He claimed to be here for some business meeting, but seldom does anyone conduct business on a Saturday. Who knows where he is now."

"Oh, I'll find out," John assured.

John's face now softened as he looked at Julia. "And Julia? Honey, I'm so sorry this happened to you."

"Me, too, and thanks John. You two always take good care of me." She rose to hug first John and then Sharon.

"Okay," Sharon said brightly, "that's enough of that. My pitcher is almost empty. Let's reload, uh?"

By the time they drove home late that evening, Austin and Julia were feeling considerably better. The cool air refreshed both. Lauren had opted to spend the night with John and Sharon as she'd had more than her share of alcohol, and John encouraged her to drive home in the morning. Julia and Austin enjoyed the return drive down the mountain and into the lights as they headed back to Scottsdale. Julia suggested Austin pull his car into the garage in place of Lauren's so that he could leave the top down. They would enjoy the next day in Tucson where Austin could go through the desert museum. He was trying to get more information on the native flora so that he could incorporate it into his final exam project.

Walking through the door that connects the garage to the entry, they moved a little slower as they climbed the steps. It had been a long, emotionally exhausting day for them both.

"Water?" Julia asked as she opened the refrigerator to grab a bottle for herself. At Austin's nod, she made it two and carried them into the living room. They settled on the sofa and sat together in an easy silence.

Julia broke the silence first. "I know I should call him tonight, but I just don't have the energy." Austin knew who she was talking about. "I'll do it first thing in the morning before we leave. Daddy will be so furious."

"Hey, your call, but you're right. We've had enough for one day. Ready to head to bed?" He looked at her tired face, at those two lines that appeared on each side of her mouth when she was overly tired or stressed out. She was both tonight, and those two lines had been joined by a couple between her eyes. Austin reached out and smoothed the ones on her forehead. As he gently rubbed the spot, he could feel her relax. He moved his massaging fingers from her forehead to her temples. He could feel her body grow heavier against his and her breathing was even. He gently disentangled himself where she'd thrown an arm around his waist and laid her back on the cushions. Austin stood up and, looking down at her, thought again about how she'd handled herself today. He knew that Julia was a strong woman, but he was glad to see that she could also be vulnerable. She knew when to stand alone and when to hold onto someone else.

She's fortunate to have John and Sharon, he thought. As good as his word, John had excused himself and Austin to go into John's study. Austin listened as John called first his attorney, who had him message the photos to him. They talked a while about the restraining order, and Austin thought it odd that all John had given his lawyer was Keith's name. He didn't have a chance to ask as next John was laughing and talking to his friend the judge. When Michaels heard the story, he assured John that it would all be finished by Sunday morning. He asked if John wanted the local sheriff to pay Landry a visit, but neither man felt that would be necessary. With another promise of a golf outing and dinner with the wives, John hung up the phone and looked at Austin.

"I have something to show you." He walked over to a wooden file cabinet from which he pulled a file and handed it to Austin. "I haven't shared this with Sharon or Julia because I don't want to upset them, but I think you need to know who you're dealing with."

Austin looked down at the name on the tab at the top of the half-inch thick file. *Keith Landry*. He looked back up at John, who nodded toward the file and said, "Take a look."

Ten minutes later, Austin was finished. He sat back in his chair, looked at John. "Son of a bitch."

"Yes, he is. It seems that Mr. Keith Landry fell apart after Julia left him. You saw the three sexual harassment suits that were filed against him, the first from the blonde Julia caught him with. The other two are the only ones that made it to court. My man tells me that Landry paid off a couple of other women. Oh, and the paternity suit is an interesting read, too. But the one that bothers me the most is the assault charge. You see that he beat it, no pun intended, only because the woman reneged on her story. I'm sure that cost him a hefty sum."

"None of that surprises me, but the financial stuff is crazy. How can a man who owns his own accounting firm with a hundred employees be broke?"

"There's any number of ways, but when he gave a lot of his assets to Julia five years ago, he evidently didn't alter his lifestyle until he could build it back up. Trips, cars, big house in Lake Saint Louis as well as a new, very nice property on Lake of the Ozarks, where he also has a houseboat bigger than a lot of people's homes. And that's just the stuff we can trace. Who knows what else he's into."

"I'm curious, John, why did you dig into Landry's background?" Austin had to ask. "I mean, all the information you gave your lawyer was the guy's name."

John laughed. "Didn't Julia tell you that I always make it my business to know when it's my family? And before you think I'm some nutcase, I had a feeling about Landry. Julia never really talked about him, but Lauren has given Sharon an earful. Something seemed off, and I always go with my feelings. They've served me well my entire life."

"So...is there a file with my name on it?" Austin had been wondering since John had pulled one out on Landry. Austin admitted to himself that it was bit disconcerting.

John laughed. "Do I need one?"

"It would be rather thin and boring if you did," Austin laughed.

"No, Austin, I don't. After Julia introduced us, I went with my feeling again. And my feeling is that you are a good match for my girl. And she *is* my girl, you know. I'm not her biological dad, and I've only know her a few years, but she has my heart. She also has me around her little finger." John laughed then. "Let's go join the drunken women. I lost count of the number of pitchers Angie has brought them."

"I think they switched to vodka tonics after the last one. Lauren said that the tomato juice was too healthy for her. Can't have that," Austin laughed.

The women seemed to not even notice their absence, but Sharon winked at John when he sat down. Julia had welcomed Austin back with a semi-drunken smile, and Lauren had her attention on her phone.

A car horn from the street brought Austin's attention back to the present. He chuckled as he remembered a conversation he and Julia had early on in their relationship. Julia had joked about John's "connections" and at his finding out things. *Not a joke, sweetheart*, Austin thought. He didn't want to consider John's methods too closely, or he might be as Lauren liked to say, creeped out. This time, however, he appreciated the information. It would seem that Julia really hadn't known the man she'd been married to for ten years.

"I've got your number," Austin whispered, "and I'll be watching."

He picked up a sleeping Julia and carried her back to the bed. He gently pulled her clothes off, frowning again as he saw the black marks that dotted her arm, and tucked her in.

"Aren't you joining me?" she'd curled onto one side and opened an eye to peek up at him.

"No fair, you could have done all of this yourself," he grinned down at her.

"Not as much fun," she mumbled as she was dropping off again. He kissed her on the cheek that was facing up and quietly left the room.

Austin returned to the living room. He couldn't sleep, but he turned off all the lights except the one night light they always left burning in the kitchen. He was stretched out on the chaise and about to doze off when he heard a car pull up outside. He knew that it was probably just the neighbors, but something drew him to the small window that overlooked the drive.

"Son-of-a-bitch," Austin murmured as he turned from the window. "Son-of-a-bitch couldn't stay away."

Austin wasn't about to wake Julia, but he knew that this guy was nuts. He almost wished Lauren and her Ruger were home, but he didn't want to go that far. As he headed down the stairs to meet Landry at the door before he could ring the bell, Austin shot a text to John. *Landry just pulled up. I'm going to keep him from Julia, but it might get ugly.* As soon as he hit the send button, Austin reached the foyer. He turned on the lights inside and out before throwing open the door. The surprised look on Landry's face let Austin know that he wasn't expected.

"What do you want, Landry?" Austin stood holding the door open just enough for him to stand on the threshold.

"I should have guessed you'd be here. Where's your car? Mommy need it tonight and drop you off?" Keith was cocky if nothing else.

"Something like that. Julia's asleep and I'm not bothering her for you. By the way, you may want to stay away tomorrow, too. The restraining order goes into effect in the morning."

"Bullshit. She can't get one of those on a weekend. Besides, Julia would never do that to me." The guy was suffering from a bad case of denial.

Austin decided to educate him a bit. "Actually, she can and did. I thought someone would have already brought that bit of information to you this evening." Austin wondered if John's "man" had found Landry. Obviously, he hadn't.

"Not that it's any of your business, but I've been out. I wanted to apologize to Julia. I'd appreciate it if you'd get out of my way."

"Nope. Not happening. Turn around and go back to where you just crawled from." Austin's temper was rising, and he stepped through the door, pulling it shut behind him.

"I know all about you, Landry. I know about the harassment charges, the assault charges, and your financial troubles. Seems like you fell apart when the best thing to ever happen to you walked out of your life."

"Shut up," Keith was still cocky. "You know nothing, kid, except how to take advantage of a nice, older woman. Hell, she could be your mama. I'll bet she is, isn't she? Is Mama buying you lots of pretty things?"

It was all Austin could do to not knock the man to the ground then, but what he wanted more was to see him gone.

"Yeah," Austin knew where to hit. "We're enjoying spending your money, Keith. Isn't that what you threw in Julia's face today? Everything she has is your money?"

"You stupid, young bastard," Keith was holding on but barely. "She'll get tired of playing house with you, you know, and your little hippie scene here will get old. By the way, is Julia the only one you're playing with, or are you doing the blonde, too? Watch out for that one. She bites."

"I hope you get to find out first hand someday." Austin was finished playing. "Now, walk away, get into your car, and drive off."

"Or what? You're such a kid. Hit me and I'll see you in jail."

"Really? I can't be bullied like you tried to do today to Julia. In fact, did it occur to you that perhaps *you* could be the one sitting in jail?" At Keith's surprised look, Austin knew that thought hadn't crossed his mind. "Of course, with your track record, I'm sure you have an attorney on speed dial."

"Julia would never do that to me," the smug Keith was back. "Wake her up, kid."

With that, Landry tried to pass by Austin, but he blocked Keith's progress. The two stood nose to nose.

"Last time I tell, you, old man. You need to go."

At Landry's smirk, Austin lost it. His fist drove into Landry's middle and before Keith could recover, Austin had caught him in the mouth, sending him to the ground. He stood over him, his fist cocked and ready to take another shot.

"Get up, pussy, get up and fight a real man," Austin was beyond mad. Blood was running in a thin line down Keith's chin, but Austin could have gladly seen more.

Neither one heard the car pull up behind Landry's. It was a dark Mercedes Benz, and two large men got out and ran over to Austin. One put his hand on Austin's arm, slowly lowering it toward the ground.

"We've got this, sir. Please, step back."

"Are you police?" Landry had found his voice. "I want this man arrested. Assault. Look at this," and he wiped the blood from his mouth.

"We're not police, sir, but we'll be taking you to meet some. Get up." By this time, Austin had stepped out of the way, letting the other two take over.

"But you saw him! You saw him standing over me! Oh, I'll be giving the police an earful."

"An earful of what, sir?" The other man had spoken. "All we saw was you trying to attack this man and him defending himself." He looked at Austin. "Isn't that what happened?"

Austin was a good person, but he wasn't that good. "Yes, yes, it is. I appreciate your stepping in when you did. I might have gotten hurt." The other man smiled at Austin and nodded his head once.

"What?! What the hell is going on here? Who are you two anyway?" Keith Landry's smug attitude had taken an abrupt change. "Where's Julia? Julia!" he screamed.

As if in answer to the desperate summons, she appeared in the doorway. She'd pulled on a robe and was rubbing sleep from her eyes.

"What's going on? Are the neighbor's doing something?" She saw Landry then and came fully awake. "Keith? What do you want?" She looked at Austin. "Austin, who are these men? What's been happening here?"

Austin started toward Julia as one of the two men said, "We've got this, sir. If you would, please call Mr. Burns and let him know you're okay. He'll get our report in the morning."

With that, they practically dragged a hysterical Keith away to the black Mercedes. As Austin led Julia back inside and was shutting the door, they could still hear him screaming her name and something about how they'd be hearing from his lawyers.

Julia turned on Austin and demanded, "Tell me what just happened! Who were those men? Where are they taking Keith? Was that blood I saw on his face?"

"Let's go upstairs and talk. I need some ice on this, I think," and he held out his right hand. She could see a split on one bloody knuckle and the whole area was swelling.

"Oh, for heaven's sake. Let's get you fixed up."

While Julia made up an ice pack and cleaned his cut, Austin filled her in on what had taken place in her driveway. When he got to the part where he'd decked the other man, Julia looked at him with one eyebrow raised.

"Don't look at me like that," Austin said. "You weren't there and you didn't hear the asshole. He doesn't know when to shut up, does he?"

"No, I suppose he doesn't." Julia sighed. "But who are those men? Where did they take Keith? Are they police?"

"No, they said they aren't. I believe they're from John."

"John! Why would John be sending people over here?" Julia was struggling to connect the dots.

"I sent him a text when I saw that it was Landry outside. I suppose these are some of those 'men' we've heard about but never seen. I also suppose that they were in the area on John's orders."

They had both sat down by this time and Julia leaned back on the sofa. Her wheels were turning now, but she still didn't have all the answers.

"But why was Keith so belligerent? Why didn't he simply come by the shop Monday if he wanted to talk?"

"Who knows?" Austin wasn't saying much more. "I need to call John and let him know you're okay."

Julia watched him dig his phone out of his pocket with his good hand and punch in a number. It rang but once before she could hear John's voice. Austin assured him that both of them were okay and thanked him for sending assistance. Julia could hear Sharon's voice in the background. She picked up her own phone and dialed her friend's number.

"Honey, are you okay? What the hell, Jules?" Sharon was agitated to say the least.

"Well, I slept through almost all of it," Julia sounded perturbed. "I arrived in time to see Keith hauled away by a couple of men."

"Oh, some of John's security people. I hear they are multi-talented." Sharon laughed. "I would have loved to have seen that!"

"Sharon! You too?" Julia still felt confused. She'd get the story from Austin in a few minutes.

"Sweetie, all I care about is you, and Austin, and that you kids are okay. Now, I'm going back to bed. This old face needs all the beauty sleep it can get. Love you, mean it!" With a couple of beeps from the cell phone, Julia knew the call was over.

Well, that was fast. She knows something, Julia thought. She heard Austin and John arrange to meet the next morning, or maybe this morning she thought as she looked at the clock. Austin turned off his phone and turned to Julia to face the music.

She took one look at his face and couldn't help smiling. "You look so busted," she said. "And you are until you tell me what's going on here. This is more than just tonight, isn't it?"

Austin sighed and settled in to tell her everything. He left nothing out about her ex-husband, and Julia's face was a mix of emotions as she listened. Austin finished with an account of the night's adventure and fell silent.

"Wow...just...wow," was all she could say at first. "Did I ever know him? Where was all of this hiding when we were married?"

Austin knew she'd go there.

"Jules, people change. I've already told you that. Don't beat yourself up for not knowing. Landry is smooth. He's got this charming veneer that doesn't crack easily. My guess is that when you left, he couldn't hold it together anymore." At the look on her face, Austin pulled her onto his lap and cradled his injured hand in her lap. "He's gone, and he's too smart to try to come back again. Ever."

Julia looked at the hand she was holding. "You may want to get that x-rayed in the morning. Does it hurt much? Do you need stitches?"

He took the ice off and looked at the knuckles that were turning blue and purple under the bandage. He flexed his hand and moved his fingers. Everything worked, but it hurt like hell.

"You know, in the movies, the good guy just shakes his hand a couple of times and it's all good. This might take a few days." He looked up and grinned.

"Should we go now? I'll get dressed." She started to get up, but he pulled her back.

"No, I'll go in the morning. Let's just go to bed and try to get some rest. At least we get to sleep late."

They didn't say much more as they turned off the lights and headed to their room. Julia smiled as one last thought went through her mind before sleep overtook her. *Lauren is going to be so pissed she missed all the action and didn't get to use her gun.*

Chapter 26

DRINKING HER COFFEE AT THE patio table and enjoying the beautiful Arizona Sunday morning, Julia found it hard to believe that the previous night had been so awful. *In fact*, she admitted to herself, *the entire day had been crappy except for the few hours spent with John and Sharon.* She looked at her phone lying on the table and tried again to motivate herself to call her dad. Going over in her mind one last time what she would say, Julia punched in the number. Lawrence picked up on the third ring, and Julia smiled when she heard his voice.

Twenty minutes later, she ended the call and leaned back. To say that Lawrence Whitman was not happy was an understatement. Julia had left nothing out, including her mother's role in Keith coming to Scottsdale, the physical attack, John's role in helping them, and Keith's real reason for trying to reconcile—the money he'd given her upon their divorce. By the time she finished, Julia could hear the anger and disappointment in Lawrence's voice. Even though she tried to convince him otherwise, she knew that Keith would be hearing from her dad. As for Dana, Julia couldn't care less about her mother. The woman had been the bane of her existence for years, and Julia had no sympathy. She'd inserted herself into the relationship with Keith and had continued to interfere as much as possible. Her trying to sabotage this relationship had Julia furious. These thoughts were running through her head when Austin stepped out and joined her with his usual bottle of water. She loved seeing him first thing in the morning. His hair was messy and his eyes were still sleepy, but in only jeans and no shirt, he certainly was pretty.

"Hey, baby," she looked over at him, resisting the urge to run her hands over his chest and down his stomach. "How's that hand?"

"Myeh, it's okay. The swelling has gone down and I can move it all okay."

"Are you sure we don't need to get it x-rayed?" She reached out and gently ran her fingers over the bruised and cut knuckles. She looked up, gave him a sad face, and kissed each bruise.

"Nope, a day of that will have it all better." Austin grinned.

Changing the subject before they did something they shouldn't out in public, Julia said, "I spoke with Daddy this morning, and he reacted much as I expected." She shrugged her shoulders slightly. "I suppose with my mother, it is what it is. Daddy asked about Christmas. I told him that I would be staying here in Scottsdale. I have a few holiday parties that I really need to attend, clients and former clients, but he knows the real reason. I refuse to spend time with my mother, and I don't know when I'll be ready to speak to her."

"Want some company for Christmas? Dad, Mom, and Caleb will be coming out in a couple of weeks for my graduation, so we decided to celebrate then. I can't see me flying home again so soon. I was just there."

"Like you have to ask! I'd love nothing more than a low-key Christmas with my favorite person."

"Lauren will be here?" he teased.

"She will! Be a good boy and you can join us," she teased back.

He leaned over and was inches from her face when he said, "Oh, I can be a very, very good boy. But I've heard that I'm even better when I'm bad." He kissed her, and that's how Lauren found them.

"Good grief...you two have a room, you know. Poor Mrs. McDaniel across the way there is getting her jollies from watching you two make out." Lauren had arrived and plunked herself down in a chair across from Julia, who had reluctantly pulled away from Austin. "And what the hell happened here last night? Shit! I get all of my information second-hand these days, and I don't like it. Plus, I miss all the action!"

Julia and Austin filled her in, and the information confirmed what Sharon had told her while adding detail Sharon didn't have. When they finished, Lauren sat looking at them in stunned silence. Her silence didn't last long.

"I knew it! I knew he was a low-down bastard when you were married to him, Julia, but I kept my mouth shut. You seemed to love him, and I'm not that big a bitch. But this?!" She slapped her hand on the table, making the other two jump a bit. "Dammit! If only I'd just ridden with you two last night, I wouldn't have missed my chance." Turning to Austin, "And don't try to tell me that a small part of you wasn't wishing I and my gun were here, Junior." Austin grinned at Lauren and winked before turning his head to look out over the mountain view.

"Thank god you weren't!" Julia exclaimed. "You'd be sitting in jail right now and John would be scrambling around trying to get you out."

"Yep, and he would, too. He loves me." Lauren sat quiet for a few moments before she spit out another "Dammit!" and went into the apartment to get some coffee.

Julia took a deep breath and let it out slowly as she, too, took in the calming view of the mountains in the distance. Austin saw that the lines between her eyes were gone, but the two on each side of her mouth remained. *It's gonna take time,* he thought.

"Hey, you two, I've got something to run by you. I know that we've been one happy little family here, but I think it's time I make myself scarce and move out." Lauren looked at Julia as she said this and gave her friend a hopeful grin.

"Wait! What? Where the hell did this come from?" Lauren had caught Julia completely off guard. "Why would you do that, Lauren? What the hell? We're all fine here, aren't we?" she said and looked at Austin.

"Hey, leave me out of this," he said. "I've still got stuff at my own place, so don't put this on me, Blondie."

"I'm not, Austin, but you two need your privacy, your space. Austin, as much as I hate to admit it, you've been a trooper. Most men would have run away holding their balls if they'd had to put up with me like you have."

"True that," Austin laughed as he said it and covered his crotch with both hands at the look on Lauren's face.

She rolled her eyes and continued. "And Jules, you're my best friend, my sister, and we've been together for how many years now?"

"Too many to count," Julia gave her a half-smile.

"See? It's time."

"For once, I agree with Blondie." Both women turned to look at Austin, Julia's frown let him know she wasn't agreeing with Lauren at all. "Let me finish." He turned to Julia. "Jules, do you remember that meeting I had with Steve Jones last week?"

She nodded, "Sure, to talk about a job, right?"

"Right," Austin replied. "Well, he made quite the offer. Great starting salary plus a signing bonus, so to speak. Enough to set us up in our own house, a down payment." He looked at her with a mixture of excitement and nervousness. "I've been waiting for the right moment to bring it up." He shrugged one shoulder and grinned at Julia. "I guess now is as good a time as any."

"Are you kidding me?" Julia wasn't surprised that Austin had received the offer and job, but she was surprised that he was talking houses.

"Yeah, I'd like to buy a house and have you move into it with me." As he finished speaking, he took her hand.

"Okay, that's my cue." Lauren stood up, kissed her friend on top of the head, turned Austin's face with both of her hands and looked into his eyes. "Be smart, my young friend." She kissed his cheek, turned, and made her way back inside.

"Austin, I thought we were okay with our current arrangement. You've still had your space, we've settled into a routine more or less, you can still help Matt with rent on the other apartment..." she had run out of steam.

Austin looked at her. He thought a few moments and shook his head. "I see, I moved too fast here, didn't I?" At her start of protest, he raised both hands in surrender. "Hey, it's okay, Jules, but I'm still planning on getting my own house. It's time and I have the money. I'd just as soon invest it in real estate as put it in a bank and get nothing. And no, I'm not going to piss it away 'rewarding' myself as Matt suggested."

Julia leaned forward. "Oh, no, sweetie, that isn't it at all! I just never really thought about the whole house thing. I swore when I left St. Louis that I'd never go there again. You know, the house on the cul-de-sac, the yard, the neighbors, kids, dogs—I've been there."

"I know. I haven't." Austin looked away as he finished speaking. He didn't see the stunned look on Julia's face.

Oh, my god, of course he hasn't, Julia thought. *All of this is new to him, and it's an exciting time. And I'm pissing on his dream.* She put her hand on his arm to draw his attention and to look him in the eye.

"Austin, baby, I'm so sorry. Let me think about it? Give me a day or two to get used to the idea, okay?" Julia didn't know how he'd react to this last. "I can have an open mind, at least."

Austin looked down and took a deep breath. He looked at the mountains and thought about his reply before he turned back to her. He almost told her that it didn't matter. They'd just stay in their current situation. Almost. It did matter to him—it mattered a lot.

"Sure, we don't have to decide anything right now, or today, or even next week. We've got time, right?" He smiled and Julia noted that it didn't quite reach his eyes. *Time. It always comes down to time, doesn't it? Who's lived more of it and who hasn't,* she thought.

"Hey, my hand is fine. Let's head to Tucson so I can get that information I need. Do you feel like going?" He looked at her hopefully. They needed to change the scenery.

"You bet! I need to shower and clean up. I can be ready in about thirty." She started to get up.

"No time schedule today, remember? I'll help you with that shower and we'll leave in an hour. And a half." He took her hand and led her back into the apartment. Things hadn't turned out exactly as he'd planned, but like he said, they had time.

Chapter 27

LIFE SETTLED DOWN WITH KEITH'S departure from Phoenix. Julia never knew exactly what had transpired after Keith had left that night, and when she asked John, he only pulled her into a hug and told her not to worry about it. Sharon had agreed and the case was closed. Austin and Julia were busy with work and his school. Austin had been working harder than ever, and he finished with flying colors.

The Sunday of Austin's graduation dawned sunny and warm. December was nice in the valley. Phillip, Natalie, and Caleb had arrived two days before, and the men had played golf all day Saturday. Julia had been busy with Sharon, getting things ready for the celebration dinner although there really wasn't anything for Julia to do. They had decided on Vista Joya at Desert View Resort, one of Julia's favorites, and Austin's family was staying at the resort for their short visit. It would be a small affair with immediate family and friends: the three James, John and Sharon, Lauren, Matt, and Grandma Bea would be joining Julia and Austin.

Sharon had secured one of the private party rooms at Vista Joya, and she and Julia had decided to keep it simple. The only extra decoration was a single banner across the back wall that simply said "Congratulations, Austin" and the tables were arranged in a "u" shape so that everyone could see one another to visit. The restaurant supplied everything, including the actual set up. All Sharon and Julia had to do was select the menu, approve the cake decoration, and show up. Julia laughed at her friend's methods. *Life is just this easy when you have money*, she thought. The party was John and Sharon's gift to Austin even though he wanted nothing, and they enjoyed getting to do at least that for him.

They met at the university, and after numerous pictures outside and then again inside, Austin left them to find their seats as he joined the other graduates receiving their diploma covers. When Caleb heard that was all that Austin would be getting that day, he scoffed and declared the entire ceremony "a crock." At that, Natalie knocked him in the back of the head with her hand, just enough to make her point, and told him to behave. She and Julia had an unspoken truce for the duration, and so far they'd been able to avoid one another. At least they had avoided being alone with one another.

Julia looked down at the program and saw *Austin Phillip James.* She'd never been prouder. Austin had worked hard for this and Julia knew the sacrifices he'd made. Matt and Lauren had their heads together and laughed every so often. Their relationship had evolved into an easy friendship and for that Julia was grateful. She looked at Caleb, who had barely taken his eyes off Lauren. Natalie frowned at the blonde every so often, but she said nothing. For her part, Lauren gave Caleb a sisterly smile when she caught him looking at her and went so far as to engage him in conversation about school, his own graduation in May, and girlfriends. That last made him blush and look away. Lauren didn't take that too far, either. Grandma Bea and Sharon were talking about grandbabies, while John and Phillip chatted about Tiger Woods and speculating on whether he'd ever be "worth a damn" again or not. Julia looked at the people who loved her Austin, and decided that she'd never been happier.

The ceremony lasted all of an hour and a half before it was over. Austin looked over the crowd to find Julia and his family. When he caught her eye, he waved the diploma cover in the air and hurried over. He caught her up in a hug that lifted her off the floor before kissing her quickly and setting her back down. His dad was next, and the others enjoyed seeing father and son shake hands and briefly hug, looking at each other with understanding. They both knew the hard road that had brought them to this point, and they appreciated the moment. Caleb was next as he horned in past his father to give Austin a guy hug and move aside for Natalie. Austin saw the tears in his mom's eyes. He kissed her cheek and said "Thank you" before turning to Matt, Lauren, Grandma, Sharon, and John. As the latter shook his hand, an understanding look passed between the two. They had been semi-conspirators in the Landry situation, and they had bonded, no doubt.

The party was a success, as well. The wait staff was as solicitous as always in Sharon's presence, and she was everywhere, making sure the champagne was chilled just right and that the cake was brought out at just the right moment. It was a perfect celebration.

Austin and Julia finally found the chance to slip out onto the patio to enjoy the views of the Sonoran Desert as the sun was beginning to set. Austin pulled her to him, and they stood there alone for a few moments. When Julia pulled away and looked up at him, Austin leaned down to gently kiss her.

"I am so proud of you, Austin. I know how hard you've worked for this, and I am almost speechless."

"Almost?" He grinned at her in his teasing mood, and asked. "I have to write this down—Julia's almost speechless."

"Yeah, you keep this up and you'll never find out what *my* gift to you is." She met his teasing grin with one of her own. Austin had said no presents, but of course no one paid any attention. John and Sharon's had been the party, which had been impressive to say the least. Grandma had invited him over for his favorite dinner, complete with an apple pie that she sent home with him. His parents had written a sizeable check, which his dad had slipped him before the celebration. From Matt, he had a large bottle of Thomas H. Handy Kentucky Rye Whiskey that Austin was sure to share with his best friend. Even Lauren had gotten on the gift train and had handed him a brightly wrapped package the night before. Not knowing what to expect from the unpredictable blonde, Austin was pleasantly surprised to find a silver Tiffany money clip and matching business card case. At his shocked look, Lauren had only replied, "See, dammit, I can be pleasant." Austin had picked her up and twirled her around the living room. He gave her a brotherly kiss on her red-rouged lips before setting her back down. Lauren had simply smoothed her hair and retorted, "Thank god that's out of the way." Julia had laughed at them both.

"You know you weren't supposed to do the gift thing," Austin grinned at her. Julia remained silent as she took a small envelop out of her pocket and handed it to him. Austin took it and looked at her questioningly. She shook her head that she wasn't saying anything and watched him open it. All he found inside was a white business card that read Karen Meyers, Premier Real Estate.

"Who's this?" Austin asked.

"My friend Karen. I think you met her a while back. As you can see, she's in the real estate business." Julia's smile started at her eyes before making its way to her lips. "I figure it's time you and I started looking for that house."

Austin couldn't have been more surprised. He grabbed her close and hugged her while they swayed gently. Finally, he pulled away.

"Are you sure about this Jules? I love you. I'd live with you in a cave if that's what you want. Just being with you is enough."

"Austin, I thought a lot about this, and I think it's a great idea. Yes, I've been down this road before, but it wasn't with you. You have brought so much into my life, and as we've gone through these past months, you've allowed me to see things in a different light. A new light that's just ours. This house will be us. We'll fill it with our favorite things, our favorite people, and most importantly, our love."

As she said this last, Austin felt a stinging behind his eyes. He seldom if ever cried over anything, but his feelings for this woman were so strong that he felt as if he couldn't contain them all. He leaned down and kissed her softly.

"You have made this perfect day even more perfect, you know."

"Well," she teased, "perfect is what I do best."

They heard someone else coming out onto the patio and turned to see Sharon standing by the doorway and grinning a champagne-laced smile.

"I hate to break this up, but Austin, Matt is taking Bea home and Lauren is riding with them."

"Thanks, Sharon, I'll go say my good-byes." With a quick kiss, he left Julia standing alone with her friend.

"How did it go, Sweet Pea?" Sharon had watched from her spot at the window and had kept anyone else from interrupting the two.

"Very well, thank you," Julia hugged her friend. As they stood with their arms around one another, Julia said, "I feel like I'm getting something right, you know? Like pieces are falling into place the way they're supposed to."

"I do know, Jules, I do know."

Julia left her to talk to Lauren and tell Bea and Matt goodbye. The party broke up when the first guests left, and Austin said good-bye to his family. Their flight would be leaving early in the morning. Austin hugged his brother and father before pulling Natalie in for a kiss and long hug.

"Life is good, Mom, life is good," he whispered in her ear. Natalie looked up and met Julia's eyes. She still wasn't thrilled with her son's choice of female, but seeing him this happy made her feel a bit better. What mother could resist her son's happy face and not feel it with him?

"I love you, son," she whispered back. "Be happy. That's all I want. You happy."

Austin looked into green eyes so much like his own and nodded *yes*. The family left for their cabin then, and John and Sharon were the last to leave with Austin and Julia. They parted on the parking lot with the promise of getting together soon.

As Julia drove her Bimmer back down the hills and into the valley, she could see Austin out of the corner of her eye. Every so often he'd pat the little card he'd slipped into his jacket pocket. She hit the gas, and they both smiled as the little car sped toward the city lights.

Matt and Lauren had dropped off his grandmother, but neither was ready to call it a night.

"Want to go to Remedies?" Lauren had introduced Matt to the bar a few weeks before, and he had decided that he liked it. It was a mix of college kids and older singles like Lauren. Like every other bar in the valley, it had the requisite televisions lining the walls with every sport televised. A small stage was home to local performers every weekend, and Matt knew Lauren enjoyed the music.

"Perfect!" she grinned over at him.

As the weeks had gone by, the two had settled into a comfortable friendship. Matt found himself actually sharing things with Lauren that he usually didn't share with anyone. One of those were his plans when he graduated in the spring. John had told him to come by his office sometime and talk about job possibilities. Matt was a little bothered by the fact that he was using his best friend's girlfriend's second dad to get a job until Lauren put it into perspective for him.

"You see, Junior, here in the real world, that's how it's done. Fathers hire sons. Friends hire friends. You're coming out of that idealistic fantasy world I like to call 'college' where most of the professors have never actually worked outside academia. Yes, you need to know your shit, but as far as the opportunities, you take whatever advantage you can get. Look at Julia and me. Sharon Burns gave us a job, introduced us to her friends, and they introduced us to their friends, and so on. It's how the world works. So get off that high horse and take John up on whatever offer he makes. Yeah, he's probably doing it for Julia. Get over it, okay? Oh, and know that John won't keep you around long if you don't produce."

When she put it like that, it made sense, and Matt looked forward to their meeting. Lauren pulled no punches, and a man like Matt needed that.

They pulled up and saw that Remedies was going to be crazy. Lauren's eyes brightened as she looked at him and smiled. This was her kind of action, and Matt laughed at her expression.

"Come on, Blondie, let's go show these folks how to party!" Matt came around to help her out of the Jeep, and as they walked toward the door of the bar, Lauren asked him a question that had been bugging her.

"Hey, Junior, why do you and your roommate call me Blondie? I have a name, you know."

Matt grinned and replied, "Same reason you call us both Junior, I guess. The names just fit."

Lauren laughed, "Touché."

They couldn't talk once they entered the main room of the bar. The music was blaring, people were dancing, and everyone was trying to talk over the noise. Lauren saw some of her friends sitting in a corner and led Matt over to the table.

"Hey, Lar! I thought you were tied up tonight." The loud voice came from Jackie, one of Lauren and Julia's friends, and she was new to Matt. Jackie looked him over, and when she pulled her eyes back to his, she gave him a slow wink. "But I see that the tying up will be later." She almost purred in his direction.

Lauren's eyes narrowed. For some reason, she wasn't too thrilled with Jackie's overt ogling. As they sat down, she made sure she was positioned between the two.

Lauren leaned over so that only Jackie could hear her, "Down, girl, he isn't available to you." Lauren looked pointedly in the other woman's direction, raised one eyebrow, and made her point. Jackie quickly took the hint. If it came down to it, she was no match for Lauren in the bitch department.

A break in the music came, and Lauren introduced Matt to Jackie and the other two, Lisa and Monica. Matt was enjoying his status as the center of attention at the table of attractive women, and he turned on the charm. He took each proffered hand and laid a light kiss on the back. Lauren rolled her eyes, and when he was finished, sent him off to get them all a round of drinks.

"Start a tab, sweetie, and we'll split it later," she called after him. She looked around the table at her friends, who were giving her knowing smiles.

"What? What the hell's your problem?" Lauren settled back in her chair and gave each a challenging look.

It was Monica who spoke first. "Here I thought Jules was the only cradle robber of our group. Where did you find him, sweetie, the local high school? Does he come with more friends?"

"First, I'm not necessarily robbing a cradle because he's not my date per se. Second, he's Austin's best friend, so he's off limits to you bitches. Third, no, he does not have more friends." She finished and looked around at them. "Geez, get your freakin' hormones under control. You're practically sweating."

The four chatted until Matt came back with a tray of drinks.

"A tray? Who gave you that, Junior?" Lauren shook her head.

"The cute redheaded waitress over there. She promised to pick it up and keep us supplied tonight." Matt was quite proud of himself.

Lauren rolled her eyes again. *I keep this up, and my eyes will get stuck*, she thought. Out loud she said, "Girls, my Matty here can charm the pants off almost any woman." She looked pointedly at him then. "Almost..."

The band started back up and Lauren grabbed Matt's hand. "Let's go show these bitches how it's done!"

They danced and drank until the music ended at one o'clock. Matt had stopped drinking a couple of hours before that, but Lauren had kept it up, knowing he'd get her home. As the musicians started packing up their equipment, Matt, Lauren, and the girls settled their tab. Matt reached for his wallet when Lauren stopped his hand. "You're getting me home, Matty.

This one's on me." He grinned and let her buy. He figured his getting her home safely had been worth a few beers on her tab.

Matt led Lauren out to the Jeep, and as she sat down on the front seat, she looked up at him. Without warning, she pulled his head down and kissed him. Not the sisterly kiss she'd been known to give him every now and then, but a real kiss. When they broke apart, Matt was breathing heavily.

"Holy shit," he whispered. "Where did that come from?"

"A place where there's plenty more, Junior." Lauren laughed and leaned back in the seat. "Take me for a drive, driver. I'm not ready to go home yet. Let's go to the desert! Canyon Lake! I want to feel the wind in my hair and see the stars!"

"You do know that's about an hour from here, right? And on one of the worst roads imaginable?" Matt knew she wasn't exactly thinking straight.

"Drivers don't talk. They just drive. Let's roll." She laughed.

Matt laughed and jogged around to his side. Before he put the car in gear, he leaned over and pulled her seatbelt tight and fastened it. When he raised up, they were face to face. Lauren looked at him in the dim light from the bar parking lot, and he could see her eyes smoldering. Before he could kiss her, she pulled back quickly.

"Thank you," she said and turned her head to the front again.

"Can't have you splattered all over the road, can we?" Matt was a little embarrassed by her rebuff but covered it quickly as he started to pull out. "Besides, anything happens to you and Julia will kill me, literally, using your gun."

Lauren's laugh echoed behind them as Matt pointed the Jeep toward the desert and hit the gas. She leaned over and found an oldies radio station, making sure the volume was turned up. All the noise from the music, the air, and the highway kept them from talking as he turned toward Apache Trail. He'd take her out by Canyon Lake, the same lake Austin and Julia liked to drive out to, and wait for her to sober up a bit. The December night air was chilly, but he turned on the heat rather than turn around. As he drove, every so often Matt would look over at Lauren, but she was looking out the window or up at the passing stars. She'd forgotten to tie her hair back, and it whipped in the wind until she grabbed it in a wad and held it from her face. Every so often she'd let it go, raise her hands into the rushing air, and laugh. When a song on the radio played that she especially liked, she sang along. Her voice wasn't bad, and Matt was enjoying himself. This was a side of Lauren that he'd never seen—carefree, happy, without inhibitions. Usually every move she made always seemed calculating. He found himself laughing with her more than once.

God, she is fantastic, he thought. *Why hasn't some guy landed her? She's smart, sexy, fun.* He wondered then what type of man it would take to finally tame her. *No, I don't want her tamed,* he thought. *I love that spirit.*

The air was much cooler as they climbed the hills, and he looked over to see how she was doing. Obviously, her alcohol still had her feeling no pain. She didn't have goose-bumps on her bare arms, but the warm air rushing from the Jeep's vents was keeping them both warm. Matt didn't stop until they were at the scenic overlook. He cut the engine and looked over at her in the sudden silence.

"Feeling better?" he asked, grinning at her disheveled state. Lauren was always very conscious of her hair, her makeup, and her clothes with everything in place. Tonight, it seemed, she couldn't care less.

"Much. Isn't it amazing how the fresh air can clear your head? And look at these stars! Millions and millions…I never notice them when I'm in town. But out here, they almost take my breath away." She turned to him. "Thank you, Matt."

He was taken aback by her tone but more for the "Matt." It was usually Matty, or Junior, or Babe, or some other moniker.

"You're welcome, Lauren." He returned the gesture by referring to her given name.

"You know that I'm not going to sleep with you, don't you?" she was back to teasing him now. He sighed. She couldn't be serious for too long.

"Nope, I don't." He looked over at her but couldn't see her face in the dim streetlight from the parking lot. Her blond hair was reflecting the dusky light, but her face was in shadow. She laughed a short laugh but sobered at his next words. "I really don't want to have sex with you, you know." From the silence, Matt could tell that Lauren didn't hear that very often, if at all.

Lauren laughed. "I don't believe you, but that's okay. We'll call a truce on that point."

"No, you don't get it. I've had sex with pretty much every kind of girl, and yeah, it was nice while it lasted. That's it, though. It was sex. For the first time in my life, I would like to get it right." His voice had softened. "I wouldn't have sex with you, Lauren, I'd make love to you." He was staring out over the lake and quickly got out of the car. She watched him walk to the wall that surrounded the overlook, lean his hands on the side, and stand there with his shoulders slumped over a bit. Lauren wasn't shocked very often, but his words had left her speechless. The drive out had started sobering her up, and his words pretty much took her the rest of the way to being herself.

Son-of-a-bitch, she thought. *How do I play this?* The last thing she wanted to do was hurt Matt, and that was a change from when she first met him. Somewhere along the line, she'd started to like the cocky kid, and something like this was the very last thing she expected. She paused a moment or two longer before following him to the overlook.

Lauren could tell that Matt heard her because she saw his shoulders stiffen. He didn't turn around when she joined him to lean her arms on the top of the wall and sway gently from side to side as she looked out over the water. She softly hummed the melody to an old Janis Joplin song. "Me and Bobby McGee," Matt recognized the tune. The moon was reflected off the surface, and across the way they could see the dim lights of a campground and boat dock.

"I love it out here at night, don't you?" She stopped swaying and looked at Matt. He still wouldn't meet her gaze, but instead continued looking at the water.

"It's nice. Someday, I wouldn't mind a place on a lake. Build a big deck and just sit beside the water like this, drink a few beers, and enjoy the peace," he said quietly.

They stood in silence a bit longer, when Lauren decided the elephant had to be addressed.

"Matt, I don't know what to say. Mark it down, babe. You left me speechless." She laughed gently, but when he didn't join her, she quickly stopped. "Actually, I do know what to say."

It was his turn to chuckle. "I knew it. You can't stay silent for long. But you don't have to say anything. And don't think that my big declaration up there was some relationship invitation. Matt Hollinger doesn't do relationships, you know."

Lauren raised one eyebrow, but he couldn't see her expression with the light behind her. "Neither does Lauren Reynolds." She leaned against him and twined one arm through his. "So, Hot Stuff, what do we do now?"

She saw his shoulder shrug in the dimness.

"I'll admit. We've had a mutual attraction from the beginning," Lauren spoke first. He turned toward her. "Yes, I'm admitting that it hasn't been all one-sided, Ace. You're a cutie. There, I said that, too. I think you're adorable, actually. But what do I do with adorable?"

"You know what I've always thought," Matt ran a finger up and down her arm and felt her shiver. The desert air held a chill, and she'd left her jacket in the Jeep. "I've always thought that maybe…maybe if I slept with you one time, that one time would get you out of my system. Maybe if I turn all the fantasy into reality, then I can think about someone else. Get you out of my damn head. Sleep without waking up in a sweat." He had kept the slow movement of his hand, touching her soft skin, up and down. When Lauren's silence stretched from seconds into a minute, Matt wondered if he'd made a huge mistake. He didn't want to lose her friendship. He just wanted to stop craving her every time she was in his vicinity.

Finally, she took a deep breath and looked up at him. "You know what, Matty? I think you may be right." She leaned into him. "I'd say your place or mine, but mine is already occupied. Neither of those two would ever understand, you know."

She saw his head nod in agreement before she pulled him toward her. Lauren was tall, and in her four-inch heels, she could look him in the eye. The dark was hiding both of their faces, but she reached around his neck and leaned in. He met her halfway, and she kissed him much like she had in the bar parking lot, but also differently. Matt moaned and thought he was going to lose it when she heard him and pulled back.

"Not here. Let's go back to your place." She took his hand and led him back to the car. She continued to hold his hand as they wound their way through the mountains and down into the valley. Lauren had no idea where his apartment was, but she knew that it wasn't that far from hers. He made the almost hour drive in forty-five minutes, and both were glad that the late hour held no traffic. Neither said anything, and Matt hoped

Lauren wouldn't change her mind on the drive. *Why the hell did we go so far out?* He was mentally kicking himself. As her hand remained in his, he calmed down and focused on getting to his place as quickly as possible.

Matt pulled into the carport space and cut the engine. He turned to look at Lauren and found himself stupidly asking, "Are you sure?" *Dumb, dumb dumb,* he thought, shaking his head in disgust.

In typical Lauren style, she chuckled softly, and he exhaled in relief when she said, "Matty, I'm always sure." With that she disengaged their hands and climbed out of her side without waiting for him to come around. They met behind the Jeep, and Matt took her hand to lead her down the sidewalk and toward the outside stairs. She looked around to get a grip on her surroundings, but all she saw was the parking lot, another building facing the one into which he was leading her, and a grassy open space. She turned her attention back to the stairs and felt the metal under her shoes as he led her to the second level. He stopped in front of one of several identical brown doors and fumbled with his key. She grinned as he finally inserted it, threw open the door, and hit the lights.

Lauren looked around at the typical bachelor apartment. It was messy, but she'd expected no less. Matt was totally unconcerned as he tossed his keys onto the kitchen counter and turned to her. He spread his arms wide and said, "Home sweet home."

"Nice TV," she noted the large set that covered almost one wall. "Bet you have some video games here someplace, too," she teased.

Matt had the sense to not go there. His face became serious as he crossed to her and placed both of his hands on her shoulders. He kissed her, deepening it until his hand dropped to her waist and then her rear. She pulled away.

"Slow down, Tiger, and let's set some ground rules." She looked at his flushed face and blue eyes darkened with his emotions. "I am not one of your usual girls. You aren't calling the shots here." She smiled at his face mixed with confusion and desire. "If you allow me to, I'll make this a night you won't soon forget." He continued to look at her and nodded his head in assent. "Good. Now show me your room."

He led her to a bedroom that was just off the living room, and when he turned on the bedside light, he heard her intake of breath. *Yeah, I do have a mess in here,* he thought to himself. Out loud he said, "Sorry, but I wasn't expecting you."

"You mean it looks like this all the time?" her voice was incredulous. "You seriously bring women in here?" She started to turn away, when he caught her arm.

"We can use Austin's room. I couldn't tell you the last time he was in there, much less slept there."

Lauren raised her chin and looked at him. *Damn, he's cute.* Out loud she only said, "That would be the next room, right?"

Matt turned out the light and followed her the short distance to Austin's bedroom. She found a light switch beside the door and flipped it up. A small lamp beside the bed cast a light that showed a room that looked as if no one lived there. The bed was neatly made and there were no personal items anywhere. Austin had most definitely moved out.

Lauren turned and looked at Matt. She smiled slightly. "Much better." She took his hand and led him to the edge of the bed. Slowly, she reached up to his shirt. He'd worn a button-up, long-sleeved oxford, and Lauren started with the top button. She took her time unfastening each one, enjoying the changing expressions on his face. As she worked her way down, she'd rub down his chest with the back of one finger. He shivered once, and she smiled at him. She'd left her shoes on when they'd come in and they still stood eye level. When she'd undone the final button, Lauren slipped the fabric down, her eyes following her hands as she took in his muscular arms, smooth chest and flat stomach. *Chiseled,* came to her mind. She kissed him, gently nipping his lip a bit before replacing her teeth with her tongue and lips.

Matt started to draw her closer when she pulled back and shook her head no, reminding him that this was her show. It was difficult, but he complied. Next she ran a hand across his stomach and slid her fingers underneath his belt and the button on his jeans. In a smooth move, she had the belt undone and the jeans unfastened. Her head was tilted downward. She raised her eyes to his and gave him a half-grin before lowering her body to slide the jeans down each leg. He helped her by kicking them off the rest of the way until he stood with only the thin fabric of his tight boxer-briefs between them.

"Looks like someone's glad to see me," she smiled and guided him to lie back on the bed. "Let's take our time, shall we? I have a feeling that you have a lot to learn. Let's see what kind of a pupil you are, sweetie."

Matt propped himself on the pillows, put his hands behind his head, and settled in for whatever little show Lauren wanted to give him. This was new to him as most of his experiences had been in a half-drunken state. Now he had all of his faculties, and Matt found himself feeling a bit nervous. He didn't dare look down at himself because he knew exactly what he'd see. Matt wanted this woman like he'd never wanted anyone before. He watched and soon realized that he really had been missing out.

Lauren started with her own top, pulling it over her head and tossing it to the floor, shaking out her hair and lifting her arms to pull it up and let it drop down over her shoulders and back in a soft blond cascade. Her eyes stayed on his throughout the entire motion. *God, she makes that look sexy,* Matt thought as he took in the black lace bra that strained against her skin. That thought had barely left his mind when he watched her slide her skirt down and toss it next to the top. Black lace barely covered her body, and Matt thought he might explode right then. Sensing what was happening to him, Lauren shook her head no and wagged one finger back and forth, sending the same message. She'd left her high heels on, and as she walked across the floor toward him, Matt realized not for the first time, that his dream was about to be fulfilled. *God, this is a real woman,* he thought.

She crawled onto the bed, literally, and moved toward him on all fours until she was face to face. She didn't kiss him, nor did she let him lean into her.

"First lesson, Matty," she almost purred, "is that making love isn't all about you. It's about your partner. Please your partner and you'll please yourself. I'm going to show you how a woman likes to be pleased, and that's what you're going to do, understand? You will not finish until I tell you to." Lauren smiled seductively at him and continued. Her brown eyes were almost smoldering and Matt knew that the desire wasn't all one-sided. "Now, some of this may be new to you, but I get the feeling you're going to be a fast learner." She winked before lowering her head to run her tongue down the side of his neck, and her pulse quickened as she heard his soft moan.

Matt did as he was told and followed her directions until they were both spent. He'd lost all track of time, but he knew that this had been the most incredible night of his life. Her last act before crawling into bed with him was to get a warm, moist towel and clean them both. As she snuggled in against him, Matt kissed the top of her head and wondered, *What in the hell was that? She's more incredible than I had ever imagined.* A few minutes later, Lauren rolled away from him and he could hear her even breathing. He smiled and shook his head. *Most chicks like to do the whole snuggle thing. Leave it to this woman to do that differently, too,* he thought. Matt reached over to snap off the lamp and soon followed her into sleep. For once, he wasn't tormented by hot dreams about a sexy blonde.

Chapter 28

LAUREN WOKE UP FIRST, AND for a few seconds wondered, *Where the hell am I?* It didn't take long for the events of the previous night to come flooding back. She slowly rolled onto her back and turned her head to look at the man next to her.

Oh, shit, she thought. *What did I do? I wonder if I can leave a note and slip out without him noticing. Wait. I have no car. Dammit! I'll go outside and call a cab. Like I've never done that before…*

About that time, Matt rolled onto his side and threw an arm over Lauren. *Well, there goes that idea,* she thought. She wondered how long before he'd be dead to the world and unaware of her slipping away. Lauren felt his eyes on her before she saw his stare.

"You really are here, uh?" He didn't even sound sleepy.

She turned her head to look at him then. *Damn, he's so cute,* she thought, and she smiled at him before replying, "Yeah, I'm really here, Junior."

"You okay this morning? I mean, no regrets or anything?" He didn't even hear the "Junior."

He's worried about me, that I'd regret last night, that I'd be all right this morning. Lauren was surprised. Usually boys—men—like Matt didn't concern themselves too much about the women they took to bed. She didn't want to think too much about why he was concerned. She'd do that later.

"Never better," she assured him. "You?"

"Never better," he echoed her words. He looked at her mussed hair and streaked eye makeup and thought she'd never been more beautiful.

233

Matt usually didn't pay attention to women in the morning, and more often than not, they were gone by the time he was good and awake. He liked seeing her like this, especially when he was the reason for her tousled appearance.

Lauren rolled from under his arm. She sat on the side of the bed and did a morning stretch that had her arms up over her head and her backed arched. She ended with a couple of neck rolls. Finished, she looked over her shoulder at Matt. He'd taken in every movement, and Lauren knew that look.

"Don't get any ideas, kid," she said. "I need to get out of here."

"Why? It's Sunday morning," he looked at her hopefully.

"Damn, it is." She scooted off the bed and started collecting her clothes. Pieces had been flung around the room, and he watched as she bent over to retrieve each item. She didn't know how close he was to tugging her back into bed.

"Lauren, it's Sunday morning," he said again. "Nobody gets in a hurry on Sunday morning." He grinned at her. "Come back to bed and I'll help you find god again. You were certainly calling his name last night," he teased, pleased with himself.

"Don't flatter yourself, Matty, I say 'oh god' for many reasons, sex just being one." She stood in the doorway, looking at his face. His good mood was waning and she saw that her words had punctured his ego. *Damn, why do I say these mean things? Tread lightly, Lauren,* she told herself.

She came back over to the bed to lean down and kiss him. She looked into his blue eyes and grinned. "Okay, I'll admit it. Several of those 'oh gods' were just for you." He grinned back and started to pull her down with him.

"Nope," she was quicker. "I need a shower and food. I know you have the first, but I highly doubt you have the second. Lesson one for today, Matty—learn to cook breakfast. Absolutely nothing sexier than a man who thinks enough of you to make breakfast after a night of great lovemaking."

"It was that great?"

Lauren rolled her eyes and shook her head as she headed for the bathroom. *Leave it to him to latch onto that,* she thought.

The shower looked clean enough, and she found a towel in the cabinet beside the sink. She had no more climbed under the hot spray when the shower curtain opened and Matt joined her.

"I thought you might want some help. You know, washing your back or something."

What the hell, she thought as she handed him the soap. "How about both?"

Thirty minutes later they were toweling off, and she was putting yesterday's clothes back on.

"You know, this is the reason I hate to sleep over." She looked at him, then at her wrinkled clothes, and laughed. "At least the sex was good enough to make the walk of shame worth it."

"So…I'm a good student?" Matt wasn't used to being even a little unsure, and he wasn't comfortable now.

"Yeah, you're a good student." Lauren studied him, her mind working. "But I'm not sure we should do a repeat." She watched his face fall. "Seriously, Matt, I'm seeing a look on your face that is telling me I'm in trouble here."

"What?" he feigned ignorance. "What look is that?"

Lauren cocked one eyebrow and looked at him. She didn't have to say a word. He broke eye contact first and walked to the refrigerator for a bottle of water. He wordlessly offered her one. When she didn't respond, he spoke first.

"You need to hydrate after last night. Oh, and no, I don't cook, but I'll treat you to breakfast before I take you to your place."

"Works for me." She wasn't ready to drop the subject yet and tried to make eye contact with him as she accepted the water. "Matt, I'm serious here. We needed to get all of that sexual tension out of the air, but you should know that I'm not looking for anything else here." She didn't say it, but she was attracted to him physically. Matt was simply too immature in many ways, and Lauren didn't think she had the patience for that.

"Good, 'cause neither am I," He drained the bottle before tossing it into the trash. "Sexual tension has been released. We can go back to whatever that was before."

Lauren was sitting on the sofa, and she looked up at him. *I think he is good*, she thought with relief. *I think this will work out just fine.* She slipped her heels on, noticing that he watched every move, including running his eyes up her legs. When he looked at her face again, a small smile had started at the corner of her mouth. *Yeah, he's good all right.*

"Take your eyes off my legs long enough to drive me home?" she teased.

"Nope, first we eat." He took her hand and pulled her off the sofa. They were face to face and Matt leaned in to kiss her softly. "Thanks for what was without a doubt the best night of my life."

"You're welcome," she whispered. "Thanks for being such a willing pupil."

Not long after they pulled onto McDowell, Matt turned into a Denny's restaurant. Lauren looked at him and laughed.

"What?! Best breakfast around. You said you were hungry, right?" he asked as he eased the Jeep into a parking spot.

"Oh, my, god. I haven't been to a Denny's since…well since college," she laughed and let him help her out. Navigating the Jeep's side step wasn't easy in high heels. "I used to love Denny's," she said, and then almost as an afterthought. "I don't know why we stopped eating here. Jules and I spent many late nights at the one in Columbia." She sighed. "I think it's closed now. Lots of things are different," she said wistfully. "Nothing stays the same, does it?"

He ignored her tone. They had stopped at the door. "Well, get ready to relive the past, lady," he opened the door for her and they were greeted by the smell of bacon, coffee, biscuits, sausage, and everything good.

Forty-five minutes later, they were both full and totally relaxed with one another. They had talked, laughed, and shared a multitude of stories. Lauren had teased him on the amount of food he had put away, and he had retorted that she would eat that much too if she hadn't drunk a pot of coffee. They were winding down when her face took on a serious expression.

"Matty, what do we tell Jules and Austin?"

"Nothing, why?" He obviously hadn't thought ahead. She had.

"They won't be happy. Regardless of whether we do or we don't, they'll notice a change between us. At least, I know that Julia will. Guys usually aren't that perceptive." She grinned at the slight insult to his gender.

"We're perceptive, dammit. Wait, no we're not." He looked at her seriously. "I still don't see why we say anything. It isn't like you're sneaking past Mom and Dad."

"Well, they may not be Mom and Dad, but they're our closest friends," she reminded him. "I didn't come home last night after leaving the party with you. I'm wearing the same clothes—I told you I hate that. And you are dropping me off. I think that will warrant a bit of explaining."

"And you care because…" Matt looked at her. He didn't think Lauren gave a rat's ass about anyone's opinion. *Evidently she cares about Julia's*, he thought.

"I care about what Julia thinks." She reinforced what he already knew about the two women's relationship. "But yeah, she's probably the only one in the world who gets that respect." Lauren looked down at her empty mug and thought about refilling it again. She decided she'd had plenty and looked at Matt before continuing. "See, I promised her that I wouldn't go to bed with you. I don't break my promises to Jules. I suppose I could blame it on the booze. Or say that I got caught up in the moment." She grinned. "Or I could even blame you, and tell her that you seduced me and I couldn't help myself." She laughed at that one. Matt didn't laugh at the joke.

"I get that," Matt said, "but we're two consenting adults. Right?"

Well, one of us is, she thought. Out loud, she said, "We are, and that's what we're going with. We spent the night together. Big damn deal, right?" She echoed his favorite word back at him. "Still friends?" As she thought about it now, Lauren realized that she'd hate to lose Matt's friendship. She also realized that was all she would want from him. *With benefits, though*, she smiled.

He couldn't read that smile, but when he thought about it, he'd like to keep her as a friend, too. *With benefits*, he echoed the sentiment without knowing it.

He looked at his phone. "Shit, I have to be at work in an hour. Christmas season, fa-la-la-la-la, and all that. The store will be a madhouse."

Matt paid and they left for the short drive to her apartment. He pulled in behind Austin's car and stopped. Lauren gave him a quick kiss on the lips, a bit sisterly but not too much, and hopped out. She turned and waved one last time before letting herself in. Matt paused for a few seconds before backing out and heading for work. He was whistling as he sped down the street.

Lauren looked at the time. Eleven o'clock. *Shit,* she thought, *Jules will definitely be up. Well, here goes nothing.* She started up the steps. As she stopped at the top, she saw that both Julia and Austin were sitting on the patio.

"Out here," Julia called.

Lauren tossed her bag on the counter and put on her 'Don't give me any shit' look before joining the two. She plunked down into a chair and raised her chin, challenging them to say something. It took Julia all of two seconds.

"Was that a white Jeep I heard leaving the driveway?" Julia wasn't happy, but Lauren was ready.

"What of it?" She challenged as she felt Austin's eyes take in her rumpled clothes. She'd pulled her hair back into a low pony tail and applied makeup before leaving Matt's. She could do nothing about the skirt and blouse.

"Lauren, did we not have this discussion. You know Matt has this crush on you. Why are you egging him on?" When Lauren didn't defend herself, Julia continued. "You know you're going to break his heart, don't you? Regardless of what you think, he doesn't deserve that. You're only playing with him because guys like him once toyed with you. He isn't one of them, Lar, he isn't. And besides, will it make you feel better to treat him like shit just because others treated you like that?" Julia stopped and sat back in her chair to give her friend a hard stare.

Lauren looked over at Austin. "Next?" she challenged.

"Nope. I told Jules that I'm staying out of this. Matt's a bigger boy than either of you give him credit for. If you break his heart, it's only because he's letting you." With that, Austin left the two women and soon they could hear the living room television blaring the PGA tournament. Austin liked to watch even though it always put Julia to sleep.

"See?" Lauren leaned toward her friend. "If your boyfriend has no problem with it, why do you?" She sat back. "Besides, we're two consenting adults, and I only slept with him last night to get it out of our systems. The boy needed a few lessons, too." Lauren smiled slightly. "Geez, I don't think he's been with a real woman his entire adult life. Obviously, everything he knows, he learned from some porn channel on cable. I swear, Jules, these guys go through life thinking they're so damn good in bed when they seriously suck at it." She winked and smiled widely at Julia. "Let's just say that after last night, I'm thinking Sonny Boy will be much better next time he takes a woman to bed. Hell, the girls should send me a thank-you card and flowers."

At that, Julia sighed and resigned herself. "You're right. It's really none of my business. You're gonna do what you're gonna do. I've never been able to stop you before." She looked at her friend and Lauren's face sobered. "Just remember. Matt is a nice kid, he really is. And when you break his heart, because you will, I think you'll find that yours just might break a little, too." With that, Julia left.

Alone now, Lauren stared out over the mountains in the distance. She always loved this view. Regardless of how she was feeling, a sense of peace settled over her when she gazed out over the desert.

I could use a little peace about now, she thought. *Funny, Julia referred to Matt as a kid when he's the same age as Austin.* She thought about an article she'd recently read that listed the qualities of an immature man: no job, fantasy football enthusiast, beer pong enthusiast, video game enthusiast, watches *Family Guy* and porn. *Well, I know that he's at least half of the list, and I'll bet Austin does none of those things,* she thought. Mulling that over a bit and comparing the two, she came to the conclusion that Austin wasn't typical. *If he had been, Julia would have stayed far away from him. Like I should have done with Sonny Boy,* she thought. *Julia and Austin just don't get it. They've never figured out that men and women can be just friends, share some laughs, enjoy sex if they want it, and get along just fine. Matt and I have an understanding. We're not shopping for a mate. We get each other. They'll see.*

Lauren looked down at her rumpled clothes and heels and laughed softly. She decided that the walk to her room to change would not be fraught with shame. *Lauren Reynolds feels no shame,* she told herself as she made her way through the apartment. Neither Julia nor Austin looked up from their place on the chaise. Lauren was almost disappointed that she didn't get to make her point.

Chapter 29

JULIA AND AUSTIN SAID NO more about the *Matt and Lauren thing*, as Julia called it. They enjoyed a lazy Sunday and decided to drop the subject of their friends' love life.

On Monday, Julia found time mid-morning to call her friend Karen to tell her that she was in the market for a house. Karen had been working on Julia and Lauren, separately, trying to get them to leave the rental world and buy something. If Karen was surprised to hear that Julia was ready, she said nothing, like a good salesperson. Her self-control was truly tested when Julia told her that the house was for Austin and her. Swallowing the many questions she had, Karen suggested Julia sit down with Austin and make a list of what they'd like—size, location, amenities, yard, etc.— and get back to her. She'd plug it all into her computer and see what the MLS had.

"This is a pretty big step, isn't it, Jules?" Their conversation was winding down and Karen couldn't hold back any longer. She figured she was a good enough friend to warrant answers to a couple of questions. It wasn't like she'd be the only one when news of this got out. With Karen, news always got out. "Does this mean you two are getting married?"

Marriage had never entered into the conversation, and Julia told her so. *Marriage?* Julia decided she'd have to take that one out another time and mull it over. They really hadn't even brought it up.

A few minutes later, after some chit-chat that had nothing to do with real estate, the two signed off. Julia sat back in her chair. *Marriage. Austin, we really needed to talk about that one,* she thought. Keith had proven to Julia that a vow meant nothing and a piece of paper was just that—a piece of paper. She really didn't know how Austin felt. He came from a traditional family from the traditional South. Natalie had revealed to Julia just what was expected of Austin for him to stay in her good graces—a career, wife, kids, and home ownership. She frowned at the mental list because out of those, a house was all she could offer. As for that house, it was Austin's as far as Julia was concerned. She'd be living in it with him and lending her professional eye in picking it out and helping him make it a home, but the house would be in his name, not hers. Joint ownership for Julia was next to marriage, and she was finished with that.

We really do have a lot to hash out, she thought. *No better time than tonight before Karen gets rolling on this house thing.* Because he hadn't mentioned getting married, Julia wanted to believe that Austin was committing to Phoenix in his desire to move from an apartment and into a house. With interest rates low and the housing market still recovering, investing in a house made perfect sense to her. In fact, she'd been thinking along those same lines. She and Lauren split the rent, and renting was fine until they decided to make Arizona their permanent home. *It probably is time,* Julia thought, *to put down some roots. Maybe I should think of ownership. And it isn't like I don't have the money.* The women had used the sale of the business in St. Louis to purchase the Scottsdale shop. Along with the profit they'd made the past three years, Touch of Jules was theirs free and clear. Julia still had the cash from the sale of the Lake Saint Louis house, which was considerable, but she simply hadn't thought about using it.

The phone rang to interrupt her thoughts, and Julia didn't have the chance to revisit them. She did on her way home, though, and was still trying to figure out how to broach the subject with Austin when she pulled into the garage. She saw his car sitting in the drive and knew that he'd beaten her home, as he sometimes did. The day had cooled considerably, and she saw that he'd put the top up. She'd done the same, and it made her a little sad to think of warm weather ending.

She went through the garage door, and as she climbed the steps, she could smell meat grilling. They split the cooking, with Austin manning the grill every time it was his turn. Julia liked cooking, and especially cooking for him, so he only got the chance when he arrived home first. As she entered the kitchen, she saw his back as he worked over the fire.

"Smells yummy. Can I bring you something to drink?" she called as she opened the refrigerator door to see what they had.

"Just bring me whatever you're having, babe," he called back. "I'm doing battle with the fire and fatty ground beef." She watched as he doused the blaze with water from a large squirt bottle, cursed the mess, and leaned in to make sure the fire was still going. In his other hand, he held a long-handled spatula.

She laughed and grabbed a couple of Bud Lights. She'd join him for a bit and change clothes later. Julia stepped out onto the deck, set her beer on the table, and reached up to grab his ass.

"No fair," he grinned. "My hands are occupied. You're taking advantage."

"Every chance I get, Ace," she teased. "You want this on the table or in your hand?"

He had the fire under control by then. He set the water bottle and spatula on the grill's side shelf and closed the lid. "Right now, I want something else in my hand," he said as he put a hand on each side of her bottom and pulled her up close. He kissed her.

"Hello, beautiful," he whispered. "How was your day?"

He always left her a bit breathless, and she took a deep breath of air, smelling the smoke that had covered him just a few seconds before. *What did I ever do to deserve this?* She thought before replying.

"Not bad until now," she said, and he pulled back to see if she was teasing. She was.

"Not bad until now," he echoed her words. "So, did it just get worse, or remarkably better?"

"Well, it's improving," she teased before putting both arms around his neck and pulling him back down. Only the sound of sizzling meat brought his head back up.

"Dammit!" he said as he raised the lid to do battle once again.

She laughed. "It's okay, Mrs. McDaniel has come out on her deck anyway. We don't want to get her too excited." He looked over at the neighbor across the way, his face still in a frown over the meat. Julia raised her hand in a friendly wave, and the older woman waved back before settling in on one of her padded chairs.

"Yeah, well, one of these days…" he squirted water from a bottle onto the fire and jumped back as smoke billowed. "I don't know why I put myself through this. I could buy a burger cheaper and with no hassle."

"Oh, there's hassle, babe, especially on 'kids eat free' night," she joked.

"True." He wrapped things up quickly then, and they went inside to eat.

Whoever cooked was relieved from cleaning duty, so Julia sent Austin into the living room as she straightened things up in the kitchen. There wasn't much to do, so she fixed the coffee pot for the next morning, too. She wondered to herself if it was a delaying tactic as she thought about the conversation they needed to have. Austin was watching ESPN. Since it was NCAA basketball season, he paid special attention to the upcoming matchups and rankings. Julia knew that from then until after March Madness, every Saturday and some evenings would find Austin in front of the television. She didn't mind. His basketball obsession gave her time to catch up on her reading. Tonight, though, she'd need his full attention. She waited until *Sports Center* ended before settling in beside him on the sofa. She took the remote from his hand and switched the machine off. Usually she only did that when she was ready for action of a different kind. He was surprised when she simply sat back and looked at him.

"I called Karen today, and she wants us to make a list of things we'd like to have in a house. I've got it written down on that paper on the counter." Austin started to get up, but Julia stopped him with a hand on his arm. "Before we do that, I think we need to talk about some things."

Her serious tone had him frowning slightly. "What's up? You change your mind?" he asked.

"No, but we haven't talked about some things, and we need to do that." She took a deep breath, and jumped in. "First, Austin, you've never really said anything, but I want you to know that this house. This will be *your* house. Of course, I'll move in with you and we'll make it home, but it's still yours."

He looked confused. "That isn't what you said, Jules. When you gave me Karen's card the other night, you said we'd make it ours. 'Fill it with love,' I think you said. I took that to mean joint ownership here. That we'd be in this together." He frowned. "That isn't what you want, is it?"

"I'm not saying this right," she started again. "Austin, Karen asked me questions today that got me thinking. Well, first she asked if we were getting married. I honestly told her that we hadn't talked about it, so no." She tried to gauge what he was thinking, but his face was closed. "She asked if the house would be ours, yours and mine, and I had to think a minute on that one. I don't have answers for her, do you?" She looked at him for help. He was giving her none. "See, I took your buying a house as your committing to living here in Phoenix. You never said anything other than you wanted me to live with you. And your investing makes perfect sense." He still said nothing. "And we really haven't been together that long. What, six months, and in the grand scheme of things, that isn't a very long time. Don't get me wrong, I love you and can't see ever being apart from you. But we are moving a bit fast, I guess."

"Ok," he finally spoke. "Fast according to whose rules? We've always said that what we have works and that we don't have to explain it or justify it. And I just assumed that we would get married down the road." He studied her face now. "That is what you want, isn't it, Jules?" She looked away and he could tell that she was figuring out what to say. His heart beat a little faster as he wondered what was on her mind. *Where is all of this going?* His mind was racing with questions.

"Austin, that's another of those 'been there, done that' things that keep coming up for us." She struggled to make him understand. "I don't talk marriage because I learned four years ago that vows are broken and that a piece of paper is worthless. Oh, I don't hold anything Keith did against you," she hurried to explain what she meant as his eyes started to darken. "It's just that I've learned that love doesn't have to be confirmed like that. Love is between two people, not a group. I don't have to marry you to make society or my mother or my father happy, just as you don't have to marry me for the same reason." She gave a short laugh then. "In fact, nothing would please your mother more than for us to *not* get married." She looked at him to see if he shared the joke. He didn't.

"I've thought about all of that, you know," he said, surprising her a little. "No, we don't have to get married, but if you said the word, I'd drive you to Vegas tonight. And we don't have to be married to share a home. Jules," he reached over to take her hand. It was cold, he noticed, so he took the other one, too, and gently rubbed them. "Babe, I simply want to share my life with you. That means we live together, and we help one another realize our dreams. Yes, one of those dreams for me is my own place." He squeezed her hands as he struggled to make her understand. "You see, that would be *our* home, a place that you and I share alone. It wasn't yours before or mine before. If I want to dig up the yard, I'll dig it up. If you want to knock out a wall or remodel the kitchen, we do it. Jules, it's just another way of sharing. Do you see?" She still said nothing, so he forged on. "And think about it. This would be *your* house, too. Regardless of what you say, that house in St. Louis wasn't really yours. It was Keith's. You simply decorated it, both literally and figuratively. This time you'll share a home from the get-go. Doesn't that excite you, just a little?" He grinned at her and his green eyes sparkled.

Yes, it does excite me, more than a little. She thought. *Here is a man who respects me, sees me as an equal partner, and loves me. Who could ask for more?*

"Ok, but if you put it that way, I think that I should make half of the investment." She knew how this would not go over. He started to protest, but Julia stopped him by raising a hand. "Wait, I know what you're going to say, but if this is truly an equal deal, then it needs to be completely equal. I put in as much as you put in." She watched him lean back and could almost see the wheels turning. After a few moments, he leaned forward again and shook his head "yes."

"You're right, babe," he agreed. "We can get twice the house if we want, or furnish it the way we want, or a multitude of other wants."

She grinned at him, rose, and walked to the counter to bring back Karen's list. "We better get started, hadn't we?"

They decided to take their time. With Christmas coming in the next couple of weeks, things were hectic. Julia had a different holiday party invitation to fill almost every evening, and she was picky about the ones she accepted. Austin was going with her, so she made sure that there were people he would know at almost all of them. She and Lauren split them up so that Touch of Jules was represented and no one was overlooked. As for Austin, Steve Jones threw a company bash that Julia attended with him. He loved to see her dress up and definitely enjoyed showing her off. Whatever room they entered, he noticed that she drew attention. Their favorite one of the season, of course, was the biggest and best party at Sharon and John's. They always reserved the last Saturday before Christmas and opened their Fountain Hills home to their closest friends. John's company had a different party for employees and business associates, so this one was smaller and more comfortable.

This year, Austin would be going with Julia, and she was excited for their first Christmas together. They had arrived early, and as Julia sat on a stool beside the kitchen counter, she watched Austin and John chatting beside the fireplace. *I can't believe how he's grown since last summer,* she thought. His hair was still long, and he kept it tucked behind his ears where it curled around his neck. He was dressed in slacks, loafers, and a dark green sweater, the "uniform" for these functions. But it wasn't his physical appearance that had changed as much as an air of confidence that now surrounded him. He was no longer the college kid, but a valued member of Steve Jones' team. John Burns had welcomed him and shown him respect reserved for men twice his age. And he had Julia. As he had told his dad, she made him a better man, and she didn't even realize the effect she was having on him. Austin had always been mature for whatever age he was, but now no one would question his readiness for whatever life put before him.

It was almost as if he could feel her eyes on him, and as she was thinking about him and staring, Austin turned to look at Julia. They shared one of those looks that true couples do, and he excused himself to walk in her direction.

He's not only more mature, but he's also getting handsomer, she thought.

"Hey, pretty lady, is this seat taken?" He teased her as he took the stool next to her.

"Well, it is, and my boyfriend is an extremely jealous type. We'll have to be discreet." She narrowed her eyes and raised her eyebrows playfully.

"Discreet is my middle name." He leaned over to kiss her playfully on the ear.

"Break it up, you two, you're melting my ice sculpture," Sharon joined them. "Do you know what happens to a Rudolph ice head when it gets too hot? Let's put it this way, those antlers have a mind of their own and are bound to morph into something obscene." She laughed at her own mental picture. She sighed then. "I love this party, but sometimes I wish it were just us, you know? We leave in a couple of days for New York, so don't forget we have a private Christmas dinner here tomorrow night." ·

"We wouldn't miss it," Austin picked up Sharon's hand, raised it to his lips, and kissed the back. They had a long-running joke between them.

"My hottie," Sharon purred. "You know as soon as you get tired of this youngster practically sitting on your lap, I am next in line. And you know what they say about us older women." She wiggled her eyebrows at him and winked. Julia laughed.

"And don't forget, old cat, that hunk over there watching us, well, he's next on my list," Julia teased and grinned at John.

Sharon laughed. "We both have something to look forward to, don't we?" With that she was off to answer the doorbell and welcome the first of the evening's guests. To Austin and Julia's surprise, Lauren and Matt came through the door.

"Whoa, did you know they were coming together?" Austin looked at Julia questioningly.

"Nope, not a clue," she shook her head. "I guess they're friends, you know?"

"Yeah…friends…" Austin rose to do the guy greeting with his former roommate and Lauren looked around.

"Bar's over there," Julia directed her to the station in the corner of the big room where a man in a white shirt and black bow tie was arranging glasses and checking his liquor supplies.

"Catch you bitches later. I have a date with Fifty Shades of Grey Goose." Lauren made a beeline for the bartender. The other three watched her walk away in four-inch heels, hips swaying in the tight black slacks. She had opted for black and a low-cut white sweater. She recognized the holiday with a bright red scarf that came around her neck, the two ends hanging down and outlining her breasts. As they observed the bartender's reaction, Matt, Austin, and Julia all shook their heads and laughed.

"I swear, that girl was born with a make-believe audience," Matt chuckled. Julia looked at him a little closer. Gone was the puppy-dog admiration and the almost drooling reaction. In its place was a look of appreciation that most men wear when looking at a beautiful woman. *Perhaps Matt really is a bigger boy than I gave him credit for,* Julia thought. She looked at Austin, and he'd seen the same thing. He wore an I-told-you-so expression and she childishly stuck out her tongue. When his eyes darkened, she laughed. This was John and Sharon's party. Austin and Julia's party would come later. She joined Sharon to help guests get situated and the rest of the night passed quickly.

The next evening found Julia, Austin, and Lauren back at the Burns', but it was a completely different atmosphere. This was family time, and they all sat around the fire, drank mulled wine, and exchanged small gifts. The others laughed at Sharon's and Lauren's imitations and general ridicule of mutual friends they didn't like. Both were good mimics and complemented one another well. Too soon the evening was passing, and before it grew too late, John asked Julia to accompany him to his den. As she entered, he asked her to close the door.

"What's up, Pop?" Her face was flushed from the wine, and she was still smiling from her friends' antics. "You're too serious."

John looked at the daughter of his heart and smiled at her. "Sharon and I have a special gift for you, and Sharon asked me to be the one to give it to you."

Julia frowned. "But I already love the earrings. That's all you should have gotten me."

"Now, you know how little good it does for you to try to tell my wife anything, or me either, for that matter. No, this is something we've wanted to do for a long time."

John reached into his massive desk and pulled out an envelope. He handed it to Julia and indicated for her to open it. She took out a packet of papers, and as she quickly read over them, she was sobering fast. As she finished, she looked up.

"John, I don't know what to say. This is unexpected and totally unnecessary. I love you two like you're my own mom and dad. And I know you love me. I don't need any of this for you to prove that. What about Johnny? Won't he be upset?"

"Actually, Johnny knows and couldn't agree more. Julia, you're here, and he isn't. If anything should happen to either one of us, it's you we'd turn to. You know that already. And if it's the money you're worried about, we have plenty to go around."

"I do love you, John," Julia looked up with tears in her eyes. "I love you both so much." She came around the desk, put her arms around his middle, and buried her head on his chest. She listened to his strong, steady heartbeat, and prayed that it continued for many, many years to come.

They rejoined the others shortly after, and Austin watched Julia tuck an envelope into her bag. She smiled at him and he knew that she'd tell him later what had transpired. Julia went over to Sharon, hugged her hard, and wished her the merriest Christmas. Angie had prepared a huge spread of their favorites, and they all ate and laughed until it was time to go. As Austin, Lauren, and Julia drove away, Austin at the wheel, Julia turned to see John and Sharon standing arm in arm and waving from the porch.

When they got home, Lauren checked her phone and excused herself. She was going back out, no surprise there. Austin couldn't wait to ask Julia what was up with her and John's visit. She handed him the packet of papers, and after he read them over, he looked up at her and smiled, shaking his head.

"Wow, you've just been made an heiress," he grinned. "I don't know exactly what all is listed here, but from what I can see in glancing over it, you are to have the Flagstaff house, the Fountain Hills house, a townhouse in New York City, and stock shares. Wow…just wow…"

"But you overlooked one major point. In the event of Johnny's absence, look at the medical power of attorney. Me," Julia paused. "Do you realize the love and trust that goes into giving someone that kind of responsibility? I've always known that our relationship is special, but I never expected this."

Austin pulled her onto his lap. As she rested her head in the crook of his neck and shoulder, he ran his hand through her hair, smoothing it back from her face.

"You may feel like the lucky one here, Jules," Austin began, "but I hope you realize just how fortunate they are to have you." He turned his head around to look down at her. "Almost as lucky as I am. I tell myself every day that I have to be luckiest bastard in the world when the last thing I see at night is your smile, and the first thing I see in the morning are those beautiful blue eyes." He leaned down to kiss her, and he tasted salt, knowing that tears had been leaking from her eyes. "Don't cry, babe," he said softly.

"Silly, women cry when they're happy, don't you know?" she laughed then. "If I were any happier, I couldn't stand it." She rose, took his hand, and they headed down the hall. She intended to show him just how lucky they both were, and he intended to show her the same, at least twice by morning.

Chapter 30

WITH THE HOLIDAYS ENDING AND a new year underway, Julia and Austin began house hunting in earnest. They'd added to their list, taken away from it, and changed their minds again. Finally, Julia took the latest list in hand, put it into an envelope, and sealed it.

"There!" she said. "No more. I am weary of this fantasy house we're trying to find. I'll give this to Karen, and we'll see what is out there." She looked at his puzzled face. "Austin, when it's the right house, we'll feel it. All the lists in the world won't matter. If it's meant to be ours, we'll know it. Okay?"

He shook his head in agreement. He'd almost resigned himself to building the perfect house in order to include all that both of them wanted, but Julia had talked him out of that. In the current market, they couldn't build for what they could buy, so buy was what they'd do.

It took Karen all of a day to gather a list of possibilities, and they settled on the next Saturday to spend house hunting. Every evening found Austin and Julia pouring over the Internet photos of houses until they had narrowed it down to their top five.

"I'd always heard that couples who can survive building a house together can survive anything," Austin said one night as they were getting ready for bed. "I think the same can be said for house buying." He was half teasing her, but they had held a rather intense discussion, as she liked to call it, on the virtues of a larger yard and smaller house—Austin's choice—versus the larger house with a smaller yard—Julia's choice. Her arguments were that they didn't have kids or pets so a big lot wasn't a necessity. All they needed was a pool and patio area with a small garage or pool house for storage. Austin wanted the chance to make the outside of his home spectacular, and for that he'd need a big yard.

Julia rolled her eyes at him. "We'll survive, silly. It's just a house. And probably the first of several that we'll own in a lifetime."

"Spoken like a woman who hasn't fully invested herself anywhere," he grinned but then became serious. "I grew up in the same house, and that place is filled with lots of memories. I just want the same for us."

Julia looked at him sadly then. "Sweetie, we won't have kids to fill a house with memories. We only have us. As long as we have one another, we have it all. And if we decide to pack up and go someplace else, I would hope you wouldn't let a house stop you. I've learned one thing—you don't marry a house."

Austin could tell that he'd somehow touched a nerve with her as he looked at her from across their big bed. She continued to pull off the decorative bed pillows, which he never saw the need for, and as she focused on the job at hand, she didn't look up. He came around and pulled her close.

"Babe, we may not have the kids, or dogs, or whatever else the commercials say we should have. We have something better. We have each other." He looked at her intently. "Jules, you *are* my family. And you and I will be making the memories. With our friends and with our extended families." He teased her then. "And you never know. One day I might just come home with a dog. And it won't be one of those ankle biters, either. I'm talking German shepherd or a Doberman. A man's dog."

She laughed. "Whatever. You bring one of those monsters home, you're cleaning up after it."

He knew that the moment had passed and they were good again. Julia still had this hang-up on things she thought he was missing by being with her, children being at the top of the list. Regardless of what he said, she still had reservations. *I'll just have to make sure she knows that she's enough. That we're enough,* he thought.

They met Karen at her office on Camelback Road at exactly ten o'clock that Saturday. As they entered the large lobby, the receptionist came around the counter to greet Julia and meet Austin. *Same old, same old,* Julia thought as she watched the younger woman hold onto Austin's hand just a second or two too long. She grinned at him and turned the girl's attention back to business.

"Melissa, is Karen around? We're meeting her at ten and," she looked at her watch, "it's right at that now."

"Oh, I'm so sorry," the girl gushed and hurried back behind her counter. She hit the intercom button and let Karen know her ten o'clock had arrived. Julia and Austin didn't have time to turn toward the chairs circling the reception area when Karen came rushing out.

"Jules!" she grabbed her friend up in a hug before turning toward Austin. "And Austin! How are you?" She opted for a handshake before leading them to her office. It was a typical real estate agent's space with city maps on one wall, a large bookshelf behind Karen's desk, and a long table against the opposite wall that contained papers and brochures.

"Have a seat," Karen directed them to the comfortable chairs in front of her desk. "Did you bring the list of houses you want to see today?"

Julia took it from her bag and handed it over. Karen perused it quickly and punched the MLS numbers into her computer.

"Okay, four of the five are unoccupied, which means we can definitely take a look this morning. I'll have Melissa call the other to see if it's available and set up a time after lunch. Does that work for you?" She looked hopefully at the two.

Julia looked at Austin who shrugged his shoulders. He'd let the two women make the viewing arrangements. His main interest was in getting started.

"Sounds great," Julia smiled at her friend. "We have been looking forward to this all week."

"Oh, I know!" Karen was in full sales pitch now. "I'm confident we'll find something, and today could be the day!" She spoke the last as she breezed toward the door. "Just let me give this to Melissa and we'll go."

"Let the fun begin," Austin said dryly. "I really hate salespeople and sales pitches, you know."

"Yeah, me too, but if Karen gets too obnoxious, I can always tell her to back off," Julia grinned.

"Thank god," Austin said the last under his breath as Karen came sweeping back in.

They took Karen's big Cadillac Escalade, and Austin was impressed with the way she skirted the busy Saturday traffic. Karen could talk a mile a minute while expertly darting from lane to lane and from street to street.

She only looked down at her map once as they made their way around neighborhoods.

"Here we are!" she said brightly. It was the first house, but it wouldn't be the last. For Julia, whatever they found had to "feel right" and the first one didn't have that feel. Austin wasn't as dependent on how they felt. He was more interested in the brick and mortar of each. The next was okay, but it wasn't what they were looking for. After lunch, Karen took them to the next one on their list. It sat on a cul-de-sac, which made Julia look at Austin and wink—she'd done the cul-de-sac life, and they'd joked about it. As they pulled around the circle drive, however, Julia's eyes lit up.

Austin and Julia stepped out of the car and looked up at the two-story stucco structure. The front held wooden inlay double doors with a small balcony directly above. On the left side, a three-car garage filled one side of the house with living space above. To the right, small paned windows spanned the house from the ground to the second level. Black ironwork stretched along the bottom tier of windows. Directly in front of the window, a fountain trickled water into a pool that was surrounded by evergreens. Julia looked over at Austin, and she could tell that he liked what he was seeing as much as she was.

They entered and found that the living room was home to the soaring windows. The room opened to the second level with a ceiling skylight through which sunlight streamed onto the natural wood floors. Next to the wall of windows was a corner fireplace and along the other wall, French doors opened to a patio surrounding an oversized, oval swimming pool. To the left of the front door, a staircase wound to the second floor balcony.

"You'll find two bedrooms downstairs," Karen said. "The master suite is on this level and is quite roomy with access to a smaller patio. The other bedroom is smaller and could be an office. Upstairs we have two more bedrooms, each with its own bath. Now, we also have a formal dining room, huge eat-in kitchen with island and new appliances, a half bath off the family room/den..." Her voice trailed away as Julia and Austin began looking for themselves. They toured the entire inside before stepping outside to the pool and large yard.

Karen, who had made herself scarce as they toured the inside, followed them outside. "The heated pool has just been re-plastered and has a brand new filter. And look at the two covered patios! The second comes out from the master, but you've already discovered that. And look at this yard! It's like a resort! You have 24,000 square feet of yard space, and I don't have to tell you that's unheard of in this part of Scottsdale and in this price range."

The other two walked away before Karen could get really wound up. Austin was focused on the yard. *Yard has a whole different meaning here*, he thought as he looked at the rock and stone stretched out in front of him. *No grass to mow, at least*, he thought, *but I can change that with an underground watering system. Or not. I like the natural look.*

The outside didn't make a lot of impression on Julia except for the two covered patios and the pool itself. She could picture the furniture she'd put out there and see them relaxing around the fire pit that occupied one corner of the patio. The entire yard was surrounded by a white stone wall, and on the side closest to the pool, Julia saw a small, stucco building, perfect for storing pool supplies but also large enough to be made into something else.

"I'll give you two some time to talk, and I'll just be in the kitchen," Karen smiled, knowing the two in front of her liked what they saw.

Austin came over to where Julia was standing. "Well? What do you think? How are those feelings you're relying on so much?" He smiled at her.

"This feels good." She grinned back. "What do you think?"

"I think we'll walk through again, and I want to see the inspector's report." He was all business now. "This is a lot of money, babe, and I don't want to rush into anything."

"I know, I know." She didn't want to rush either. "But the neighborhood is great. You have your big yard. I have my pool. I absolutely love the flooring and layout. And that skylight in the living room! It's wonderful! You're right, though. Let's walk through it again and sleep on it. It is a lot of money."

They informed Karen of their plans and let her know that it was their favorite. When they parted ways back at her office, Julia and Austin promised they'd get back to her on Monday.

Karen smiled as she watched the two get into their car and drive off. "Bingo! If I haven't just sold a house, I need to get out of the business."

Chapter 31

"GOD, I HATE MOVING!" JULIA was covered in sweat, even in the relative cool of the first day of February. She carried the last box down the stairs and into the small moving van. Since the majority of the furniture was staying, they hadn't seen the need to hire help.

"You?" Lauren was equally sweaty. "Look at me! Thank goodness you're leaving the big stuff."

"Yeah," Matt came up behind them then. "And why you couldn't leave that big-ass bed behind is beyond me." He and Austin had struggled getting the mattress down the stairs and out to the van. The solid wood furniture hadn't been easy either. "Or better yet, why didn't you just call someone to move all of this for you?"

"I didn't want to hire movers," Julia informed him for the tenth time, "because they don't take care of the stuff they move. It always has dings and scratches. And I don't want strangers messing with my personal things, either. Besides, this is nothing."

Austin came out with an armful of hanging clothes and addressed his friend. "Suck it up and help me with this stuff." He turned to Julia then. "Clothes go in one of the cars?"

"Yes, yours. Lay them out across the back seat, and try not to pile them all up and wrinkle everything."

"Babe, it's all jumbled up. By the time we get it to the house, you'll have to take it all to the cleaners anyway." She frowned at his retreating back. Men had absolutely no idea about how to properly handle clothing.

"Lauren," Julia grabbed her friend's arm. "Help me with my clothes. I swear…"

Lauren followed her back into the apartment. She looked back at Matt and mouthed, "Help me…" before she was dragged through the door. He laughed and shook his head. *Damn, I'm glad this isn't me*, he thought. *I have no patience for this shit.* Matt's moves consisted of boxes and a truck crammed with his few pieces of furniture.

An hour later, they were carrying things into the two-story house on the cul-de-sac. Nothing went upstairs since the master bedroom was down. As for any other furniture, Julia and Austin were in the process of furnishing it a room at a time. With the bedroom already finished, their priority was the den. NCAA basketball season was in full swing, and Austin needed a big screen television and comfortable chair. Julia told him that those two items he could pick out himself, but informed him that she would be choosing the rest. "That's my specialty," she'd told him, and he wasn't about to argue with her.

It didn't take long before the four were finished and drinking a well-earned beer. They sat on the patio in the new chairs that had been delivered a couple of days before.

"If it weren't sixty degrees," Matt stated, "I'd be diving into that water right now."

Lauren rolled her eyes. "Big sis. It's a heated pool, and it isn't that cold. Jump in," she challenged him.

Matt raised one eyebrow at her and fixed his blue eyes on hers. "Big sis, uh? That's the best you got?" to which she snorted and took a long pull on her beer.

"Not wasting my time, Junior, and that water's only about fifty-something degrees, wuss," and she rolled her shoulders. "I suppose you realize what a good friend I am, Jules. I'm not used to this physical labor crap." She looked at her friend and grinned. "I need a massage." She looked over at Matt. "Hey, Matty, come here and rub my shoulders."

He obliged, to the surprise of Austin and Julia. Lauren's eyes closed as Matt continued massaging her shoulders and neck. Neither said anything as Matt worked his way around to her side, Lauren's eyes still closed. She never knew what was happening until he picked her up and with her in his arms, jumped into the freezing water. When they came back up to the surface, Matt was laughing.

"Damn! That's cold! Isn't this a heated pool?" he was shaking the water from his head.

"Uh, the heater hasn't been turned on yet," Julia laughed.

"That was not funny!" Lauren was spitting water and making her way to the side. "You are an asshole." Just as she was pulling herself out, Matt grabbed her foot and jerked her back in. He laughed until she dove back under, grabbed his legs, and had him under water again. He came up still laughing.

"It isn't bad once you get used to it," he said.

"Yeah, your lips are always blue," Julia joked.

This time Lauren was able to pull herself out to the aggregate surface that surrounded the side. She was shaking in the cold, and Julia jumped up to get towels.

"Yyy-ou are a boil on the bbb-utt of humanity," she managed to direct at Matt through shivering lips. She was shivering all over.

"Bet you're not hot anymore, are you Blondie?" he had gotten out to stand beside her. Julia came out bearing two large towels.

"You are ssss-uch an asss-hole," Lauren stuttered and she was shivering harder as the cool breeze chilled her even further. Turning to Austin she said, "And ttt-urn on the damn hhh-eater!"

"For heaven's sake, you two are a mess," Julia was rubbing Lauren's shoulders under the towel. "Austin, find Matt some clothes and I'll get Lauren dried."

"I don't know, Jules, he's so much fatter than I am. I'll try to find something with a drawstring," Austin was laughing as Matt pulled off his towel. He wound it up and snapped it at Austin's legs. "Ow! Shit! I should know better than to turn my back on you." Matt wound it up for another blast. He laughed as Austin took off inside.

"Pussy," he said before turning to follow and yell at Austin's back. "And, no, you can't look at my ass. I told you that's over since we broke up."

Julia was laughing when she turned to look at her blue-lipped friend.

"Julia, dd-oo you think they'll ever gg-row up? I mm-ean, seriously, these are the only two mm-en I know who'd do shsh-it like this."

"I know, but they keep things interesting, don't you think?" Julia laughed and led Lauren back inside. "Think of how bored we'd be without them."

Lauren rolled her eyes, "To tears," she snarked.

Austin and Julia had moved into their house the first of February, and Julia's birthday quickly followed. She turned forty-one on February 11, and regardless of what Austin said, she did not want him making a big deal of it.

"Last year was the big one, and I celebrated in Vegas. This year, I only want a quiet evening with my friends."

"I know, Sharon called me yesterday. She's in a snit because she can't throw you a big party, so I told her to buy you something you need. The dining room furniture you picked out last week will be delivered tomorrow."

"Austin!" Julia frowned. "Why did you let her do that? That is too much." She shook her head at the thought.

"Hey, I couldn't stop her. She just kept on and kept on until finally, I caved. Besides, she wants to do something for you, for us, and we've held her off this long." He shook his head. "Has it only been a couple of weeks? It seems longer. Anyway, I thought, what the hell, and told her what you wanted."

Julia thought about it for a few moments. Yes, Sharon had been adamant about buying "the kids," as she called them, something for their new house. She offered living room furniture, a year's cleaning service, china and silver, patio sets, and pretty much whatever she could look around and see missing. John and Sharon had been the first ones besides Lauren and Matt that Julia and Austin had given a tour of their new house as soon as they closed on it and had the keys in hand.

"John," Sharon had said, looking around with her hands on her hips. "The kids need everything. Write Julia a check."

Julia had laughed. "John, do *not* write Julia a check." Turning to Sharon, she mimicked her stance, hands on her hips, and gave her friend a stern look. "Austin and I will put this house together in our own time and with our own money. You are *not* to go out and start buying a bunch of stuff."

It was a stand-off, and John and Austin wisely took themselves out of the room. "John, I wanted to show you…" Austin began as they made their exit, getting out of harm's way.

"But sweetheart," Sharon changed her tactics. "I wish I'd had someone to help me out when John and I bought our first home." She was wheedling now. "Just think of all the *fun* you and I can have, shopping for things to make this the prettiest house. With your decorating style and my deep pocketbook, we can have this whipped up into shape in no time at all. Then you can just sit back and enjoy it, darling." She looked hopefully at Julia, who simply shook her head no.

"But Sharon," Julia continued to mimic her friend, "think of all the *fun* Austin and I will have, shopping together. And it will be truly ours when we pay for it ourselves."

Sharon bit her lip and narrowed her eyes. She was trying to come up with a good rebuttal, but as she studied Julia's face, she decided to admit defeat for now. *Besides*, she thought, *I'll have enough excuses to buy a little at a time and Jules won't be able to argue.* She smiled then. *I know of a birthday coming up in a couple of weeks.* Julia thought the smile was a bit too smug to be one of defeat, but Sharon didn't argue the point anymore.

Julia looked at Austin now and shook her head. She knew Sharon's tactics, and also knew when to give in. *If I have trouble with the woman, poor Austin doesn't stand a chance*, she thought.

She sighed, "I'll call her as soon as it's delivered and thank her. And I promise to sound surprised. I love her dearly, and her heart's in the right place, but she's a load sometimes."

"Ya think?" Austin laughed.

Julia's birthday began with a phone call from her dad. Lawrence missed his girl, and said as much.

"I miss you, too, Daddy. Why don't you come out and see us? We just moved into the new house, and I'd love for you to see it."

"We'll be out soon, baby girl, I promise." He paused. "Your mother sends her love."

"I doubt that," Julia couldn't help herself. "And if it's all the same to you, I'd rather she not come out until I know she's finished trying to run my life." She paused and listened to the silence at the other end of the call. "Has she changed, Daddy?"

"I don't know, Jules. Your mother is a hard one to admit defeat, and she is definitely struggling with your choices right now. She doesn't want to give Austin or you a chance, regardless of what I say."

"Well, that's all I need to know," Julia could be stubborn herself, and her mother's not accepting Austin sealed the fate of repairing any relationship between the two women. "Then you come out, Daddy. I'm sure you could plan a business trip when Mother's already tied up with something else. Just tell her you're going to Boise, Idaho, or someplace you know she'd snarl her nose up at. Then hop on the plane and come to Phoenix." Her tone was excited now. "We'd have so much fun, Daddy! Just you, and me, and Austin. And Lauren! You love Lauren, too! You can stay here with us. You'll love our house. Won't you think about it? Please, Daddy?"

Lawrence missed his daughter, and he would do almost anything for a visit, just to see her and hold her and make sure she was all right. Almost. Lying to his wife wasn't on the list of things he would do.

"Julia, I can't lie to your mom. Besides, she really does love you."

"Yeah, she loves me as long as I'm 'behaving' and she loves me as long as I'm with Keith and she loves me as long as I play mini-me to her Dr. Evil," Julia sighed. "Sorry, Daddy, but I can't forgive her yet. And why should I? Has she ever asked my forgiveness for sticking her nose into my business? God, she acted more married to Keith than I was! I'll bet she's still waiting for me to apologize for the whole Keith thing, isn't she?"

When Lawrence said nothing, Julia had her answer. Lawrence and Dana had had a huge fight once he found out what had transpired in Arizona. By the time he was finished, he had no doubt Dana wouldn't try anything like that again. He'd also visited his former son-in-law to let him know that the restraining order wasn't necessary in Missouri. If the son-of-a-bitch came around his family, Lawrence would make sure Keith was never heard from again. "I don't come from the hills, as you like to call them, and not have an idea of how to make a man disappear. Don't mess with my family and don't mess with me, boy." Lawrence meant every word, and Keith knew it. Julia's voice brought him back to the present.

"Sorry, Daddy. I've come too far to knuckle under her now. Tell her what you want, but I won't do it." Julia sighed again. "I love you, Daddy."

"I love you, too, baby girl. I'll talk to you soon, okay?"

"You better," Julia tried to make light of their situation. "Talk to you later."

"Happy birthday, baby," and he was gone. Julia may be forty-one, but she'd always be his baby.

Austin came up behind her where Julia sat on a stool at the kitchen counter. He rubbed her shoulders and kissed the top of her head. He knew how hard this was on Julia and how much she adored her dad. His relationship wasn't the greatest with his own family, but Dana Whitman had years of trying to control her daughter and had made an art of it. His own mother would never catch up to Julia's.

"How's your mom and dad?" he leaned down and kissed her on the back of her neck.

"Daddy's fine, and Mother is Mother."

"Would a present from me make you feel better?"

She turned on the swivel seat, put her arms around his waist, and looked up at him. "I thought I already had one of those presents," she said, referring to their early morning sex. He loved waking her up, and she was becoming a bigger fan of it herself.

"That isn't a present, sweetheart, that's a pleasure," he grinned before leaning down to kiss her.

"True that," she replied. "So what present are you talking about?"

"This," he said and pulled a small package from his back pocket. She looked up at him and frowned.

"Austin, we've been spending every spare dime on this house, and I did not want you going out and buying me something big."

"It's not big, babe," he assured. "Just open it, please."

She untied the ribbon and ripped off the wrapping. She opened the box to find an infinity necklace of diamonds set in platinum. He'd stuck a note in with it that said, "Forever."

"Oh, Austin, it's beautiful." She started to protest again, but at the look on his face, she changed her mind. "I absolutely love it." His satisfied smile told her that she'd made the right call as far as her reaction.

He helped her remove the velvet wrapping and fastened it around her throat. "Beautiful," he whispered as he looked at the blue eyes he loved.

"Yes, it is," she gave him a half-grin and reached up to pull him down for another kiss. "I do adore you, you know. Forever."

"Yeah, I do," he said before pulling her out of the chair and up into his arms. "Happy birthday, old lady," he teased.

Her smile turned into to a smirk. "Don't push your luck, Junior. Not on an old lady's birthday. We get quite fussy around that time."

They both laughed and started to kiss again when the doorbell rang.

"What the hell?" Austin started toward the door. "Who would be coming by at 8 o'clock in the morning?"

He opened the door to find Sharon on the stoop. Behind her was a large delivery truck.

"Hooty-hoo!" She came sweeping into the house and headed straight for Julia. "Happy birthday, darling!" She pulled her into a big hug. "Guess what I have?"

Austin had told Julia to play dumb, and shook his head no behind Sharon's back.

"I'm almost afraid to ask?" Julia replied. A large man in coveralls with *Karl, The Willow Tree* stitched on his left breast stood awkwardly in the doorway. Julia recognized the name of the exclusive Scottsdale store. It was her favorite.

"Where do we bring it, ma'am?" he directed his question toward Sharon.

"Oh, don't look at me," she pointed at Julia. "Here's the lady in charge."

Karl looked like he doubted that, but nodded his head once in Julia's direction.

"Oh, okay, where do I want what?" Julia played dumb.

"Dining room furniture!" Sharon was like a little kid. "Happy birthday!" She was almost dancing around. "Austin told me what you wanted, and I swear I thought I was going to have to beat it out of him." She grinned in his direction and winked.

Julia addressed Karl and showed him the empty room. He and another man, *Esteban* his coveralls said, got busy. Julia showed them where she wanted the sideboard and mirror, and how she wanted the table set up. Just when she thought everything was in, Karl came back with another box.

"Oh," Sharon said quickly, "Set that down on the floor there."

"We've got three more, ma'am. I think that's all you had in your car," he said, setting the box down where Sharon showed him.

At Julia's look, Sharon quickly explained. "Darling, I know that I told Austin," looking at the man who was standing in the doorway leading to the kitchen, "Sorry, sweetie." She blew him a kiss and then turned back to Julia. "I told him that I was only going to get you the furniture. But I couldn't resist!" She was grinning widely and almost dancing in place. "Now, do you remember that china, crystal, and silver that we saw at Neiman-Marcus that one time, and you said that if you ever had a dining room, that would be what you'd want on your table? Well, I bought it for you. All of it! I just walked in and said, 'Box up the whole table, ladies, I want it all!' They did, and here it is!" She looked hopefully at Julia. "Please don't tell me I've gone overboard. You know how I hate it when people tell me that."

Julia looked at Sharon's hopeful face and at Austin's horrified expression and laughed. She threw back her head and laughed at them all. Soon Sharon joined her. Austin looked at the two as if they were nuts.

"I love you, Sharon, and this is the best birthday gift ever!" She hugged and kissed her friend, looking up at Austin over her friend's shoulder. She touched her necklace and winked. "And tell John thank you for me, too, because I know who wrote the check."

Sharon was wearing her self-satisfied look as she headed toward the door. "My work here is done." She called over her shoulder. "I fully expect to be invited over to use that beautiful room very soon." With that, she was gone.

"For some reason, every time she leaves, I feel as if the air that had been sucked out of the room was released again," Austin did look a bit shell-shocked.

"I know. You'll get used to it after a while. And would you look at this?" Julia was overwhelmed. She shook her head.

"Remind me to never get into a pissing contest with Sharon Burns, okay?" He laughed at the image.

"Oh, sweetie, she'd kick your ass." They both laughed and realized they were going to be late for work. Austin went to call his office and Julia picked up her phone to call Lauren. She was still shaking her head when Lauren's voice came through the speaker.

"Hey, Lar, you won't believe this..."

Chapter 32

LIFE QUICKLY SETTLED INTO A busy routine as both Julia and Austin were working long hours in addition to getting the house in shape. She focused on the inside, downstairs only for the time being, and he spent the March days on the outside, making the back yard a showplace, as he liked to call it. April turned into May. They decided that it was time for a house party so that all of their friends could see their new home. Julia had had a lot of trouble keeping her group of friends at bay. All of them wanted to see what had been keeping Jules from joining them for dinner, drinks, or shopping. She had made excuse after excuse, and Julia knew that they were growing irritated. As for Austin's friends, they weren't nearly as interested except for a couple of friends he'd made at work, and they were tired of hearing all about what he'd done and wanted to see for themselves. They decided to host a barbeque on a Saturday the weekend before Memorial Day, and it was to be a casual party with their closest friends.

May in Scottsdale usually brings the first of consistently warmer weather, so Austin made sure the pool was ready to go. They decided to go with a pool-side barbeque. Lauren spoke up that she would tend bar, and Matt, not to be outdone, would help with the cooking. Julia and Austin had looked at one another as they considered their friends' volunteering because neither could really be trusted. Sharon came to the rescue as she volunteered John to keep an eye on Matt and the grill, and Julia decided to make the bar as self-serve as possible. They both laughed at all the disastrous possibilities and figured it was just their friends, most of whom already knew Lauren's and Matt's weaknesses, and neither of the two could do too much damage.

The day of the party dawned hot and sunny as Julia and Austin worked to get everything ready. Guests would start arriving around three and stay until whenever. Lauren, Matt, John, and Sharon got there early to help set up tables and chairs on the back patio. Sharon smiled indulgently as Austin proudly showed off the work he'd done in setting up a larger seating area around the fire pit, and how he'd set in pavers that connected the two patio areas and short desert grasses that lined each. Next to the wall closest to the pool and house, he'd planted Julia's favorite whitethorn acacia trees. He was far from finished, but as he explained to John, it would be done in small increments. The older couple had wondered about Julia's choice when she first brought Austin around, but the more they were around him, the more they had both come to like him. Sharon now looked upon him as hers, too, and that was an honor she didn't bestow on just anyone.

At 3:00 the doorbell rang, and the first guests started arriving. Julia's crew consisted of her girl friends—Jennifer who brought her husband Jake, Karen, Heidi, and Pam who brought her husband Mark. Austin's friends included his usual crew of Joey, Eli, Dakota who brought his friend Callie, and Ryan who brought his girlfriend Calista. In addition to these, Austin had invited a couple of co-workers he'd become close to while working on a recent project. One was Justin Richards, a thirty-something handsome man whose wife Allison came with him. The second was Audra Martinez, who was Austin's age and had joined the company around the same time as he had. She was a pretty, dark-haired girl whose slender body moved as an athlete's as she crossed the room and stepped out onto the patio. Austin's friends all looked up at her approach, and Julia decided that Lauren would have some competition for the male attention.

By 4:00 the house was full, and those who wanted to were swimming in the pool while the rest lounged on chairs and made full use of the open bar. Lauren kept busy at first, but as soon as everyone had one round and she'd shown them where to get their refills, she joined the rest sitting by the pool. John and Matt were starting up the grill while Julia and Sharon alternated going to the kitchen to check on the food there.

Julia had returned from one of her kitchen trips, and as she stepped up to the bar to refill her drink, Lauren sidled up beside her. Lauren was dressed for swimming in a white bikini with a colorful flowered sarong tied low around her waist. As usual, she was wearing wedges that showed off her long legs. Julia grinned at her friend, knowing Lauren had absolutely no intention of getting herself wet despite the bikini. Julia looked every bit as good in a short white sundress that hit her at mid-thigh, had large violet and turquoise flowers across the bottom, and thin spaghetti straps that wrapped around her shoulders and crossed in the back. Even though it was hot, she wore her hair down simply because she knew that Austin liked it that way. Julia looked at her friend now and saw that Lauren wasn't happy about something.

"I don't like what I see over there." She pointed at Austin, who had taken over the grilling and was standing next to Audra. The younger woman leaned in to peer over the grilling meat, and when she pulled back, she looked up at Austin. He said something that made her laugh. As she laughed, Audra put a hand on his arm and said something in his ear. She stayed close for several seconds. Austin's blond hair contrasted with the dark head next to his, and as Audra moved closer, her body snugged up next to his. Austin pulled away slightly. He looked around, almost as if he were trying to see if anyone was watching. Before his eyes found Julia and Lauren, Lauren spoke up again.

"Jules, either you go over there and break up that little tête-à-tête, or I will. And you do *not* want me to do that." As Lauren finished speaking, Austin's eyes met Julia's, and she could have sworn he looked a little guilty. That look set Lauren off. She plunked her drink onto the bar and started to step away when Julia grabbed her arm.

"I love you, Lar, but I think I can handle this," Julia assured her as she grabbed a cold beer and started toward the two. Over her shoulder, she asked, "Be a dear and send John over to the grill in a couple of minutes, will you?" She had one eyebrow raised as she eyeballed the two in question. She sauntered all the way around the pool and across the patio. Austin had tried to put some distance between himself and Audra, but the woman was not to be set aside that easily. She didn't see Julia coming.

"Austin, sweetie, you look parched. Matt should be doing this," Julia drawled as she approached. At the voice behind her, Audra quickly stepped back but kept her eyes on Austin. Julia took the long-handled spatula from his hand and replaced it with the cold beer, leaned in, and gave him a light kiss on the lips. She then turned to the other woman.

"So, Audra, are you into meat? I mean, are you into grilling meat?" Julia's fake smile stretched across her face. "I notice that you've taken quite an interest."

"Oh, well, I've watched my dad grill hundreds of times, and I wondered if Austin would show me how he likes to cook," the girl's voice trailed off as Julia struggled to maintain the faux friendliness.

"Well, you must be an expert then." Julia thrust the spatula into the surprised girl's hand. "Be a dear and watch this for a minute. I need Austin to help me with something in the kitchen."

Before Audra could protest, Julia had expertly steered Austin away and toward the house. As soon as they were in the relative quiet of the kitchen, she looked at him and burst out laughing.

"If you could see your guilty face," she gasped. "What in the hell was that I just broke up, huh?" she paused. "Should I be worried?" She sobered as she said this last, and she stared him straight in the eye. It wouldn't be the first time Julia had interrupted another woman making her moves. Keith was the perennial flirt, and Julia had broken up more than one huddle containing her husband and another woman. Those encounters had honed her skills. Audra was now on Julia's radar.

"No, you shouldn't," Austin assured her as he looked over her shoulder. Audra was looking at the grilling meat as if it were about to jump out and attack her. John came up and deftly took the cooking utensil from her hand. Seeing that dinner was in good hands, Austin looked back at Julia. "No, you shouldn't," he repeated. "You have nothing to be jealous of, babe. She isn't in your league." He grinned down at her. "But I've never had a jealous woman react quite like you just did. Usually, you women are hissing and circling around one another."

"Oh, sweetie, we were hissing, all right. You just couldn't hear, is all," Julia put her arms around his waist and looked up. "I don't like feeling jealous. But more importantly, I don't like to be put into situations where I feel like I have to stake a claim. I've been there before, and I won't go there again." Her face took on an attitude that Austin had not seen before. This Julia could be hard and determined when she wanted to be. "When two people truly love one another, and those two people are truly committed to one another, then neither should be put into a situation that makes the other uncomfortable."

Her words put him on the defensive. "What could I do, Jules? You saw her, and without being rude, what could I do? She never acts this way at work, I swear." Looking at his face, Julia decided that Austin really didn't know how to tactfully handle the situation.

She sighed. "Austin, some people don't understand anything but rudeness. I think your friend Audra is one of those."

As Austin thought about what she was saying, Julia could almost see the wheels turning. He was trying to remember anything he may have said or done wrong. *He's in a tough spot,* she thought, *but sometimes you have to be tougher.*

He looked down at her. "You're right. And I'm sorry if she embarrassed you, Jules."

She almost laughed again, but at his earnest face, she stopped herself. Instead, she reached up and put her hand against his face. "It's okay. For the record, *she* didn't embarrass me." Julia could tell when her meaning hit him. He started to apologize when she stopped him. Grinning, she decided to lighten things up. She had made her point. "In fact, Little Miss Audra should be thanking me. Lauren was headed your direction first." At his horrified expression, she laughed again. "Now, we have guests to see to and food to put out." They pulled apart and moved to go back outside.

"Austin?" At the sound of her voice, he looked at her. "I trust you completely. Please don't ever do anything to destroy that trust, okay?"

It dawned on him then. Julia had been through this with Keith. Not once, but probably several times, and he could have kicked himself for not seeing it before. He started to apologize again, when she put up a finger to silence him. "It's okay," she said before turning from him and heading outside. He stood there a few seconds more, watching her approach the table where their female friends were seated. Julia smoothly spoke to them and pulled out a chair. He couldn't help admiring the way she could make herself part of any group, and the girls looked at her with respect and appreciation. Lauren came by and sat a drink in front of her friend. Julia smiled up a "thank you" before turning her attention back to the other women.

Before Austin could make an escape, Lauren came in. Making sure the door behind her was closed, Lauren turned back to Austin. Her face was not happy, and she stopped in front of him, close and in his personal space. She crossed her arms and leaned on one leg, her hip thrust out in her "war" stance.

"What the *hell* was that?" Her voice was low but dripped with venom. "If you think for one minute that I'd let you fool around with that little *skank* out there, and under Julia's nose, then you better think again. Julia's too nice to run her off, but I'm not. And by the time I'm finished with her, you can bet there won't be much left for you to admire." Lauren leaned in. She would have been nose-to-nose with Austin but he was a bit taller. "I will *not* watch another man do that shit to her, am I clear? It ain't gonna happen, bud. Not while I'm around. Now you can go tell the little hose-beast to hit the road, or you can stand out of my way while I do it. Your choice, Ace, but she has about two minutes before I show her the exit." Lauren's eyes narrowed and she leaned in closer. "And if you defend her in the least, I will personally see that you pay for it. I will make your life miserable." Lauren was finished. She took a deep breath before letting it out slowly and raised her chin. "Do *not* fuck with Julia, Austin."

"You done?" It was his turn. "First of all, I had no idea Audra would act like that. Hell, she never gave any indication at work that we are more than co-workers because we're not. Now that I know, I can avoid her. I'll even ask for an office transfer if necessary. Second, maybe we're all misconstruing the entire incident. Audra doesn't really know anyone here but me, and maybe she was just being friendly." As Lauren started to speak again, Austin raised a hand and stopped her. "I'm not defending her, just putting it out there." When Lauren remained quiet, he spoke, "Third," he continued, "and probably most important, you should know me by now. You should know that I would never intentionally hurt Julia. I love her as much or more than any of you. I know what her ex-husband did to her, and I'm not Keith." As he took in Lauren's narrowed eyes and furrowed brow, he said again, stressing each word, "I am not Keith." Their stare-down continued.

It was Lauren who looked away first. She let out a deep breath and uncrossed her arms. Some unspoken truce had been set. She looked back at him.

"Just remember, Ace, I am *always* watching. You have no idea of how broken she was when we came out here five years ago. It took time, counseling, and a lot of love, but she reinvented herself and made it through. I have no intention of helping Julia put herself back together again. And I'll do whatever and I'll enlist whomever I have to." Lauren turned and stalked away. Over her shoulder, she reminded, "Get rid of the skank."

Austin felt like he'd just been through a round with Mayweather. "Hell, Floyd Mayweather, Jr. would have his hands full with that blonde," he spoke the words out loud. He looked out and saw that John was still at the grill, but Audra was nowhere to be seen. Just then, she came from around the side of the house and entered through the glass door. She looked up at Austin and smiled.

"There you are! I was wondering what had become of you. I was getting lonely out there. I'm glad I found you in here. So much more private, don't you think?" Audra winked at Austin as she started across the floor toward him. Austin put up his hands, and Audra stopped before she could reach him.

"Audra, I don't know what impression I gave you at work or here today, but I think you've gotten the wrong idea." He looked at her still smiling face and continued. "This is my home with Julia. I invited you here because I know that you're new to Phoenix and could use some more friends. That's the only reason. I'm not looking for anything besides a good working relationship with you. That's it. I'm sorry if you've gotten the wrong idea, but that's all I'll give any woman."

He watched Audra's smile falter before fading completely away. Her beautiful face was hardening into a look filled with distaste. She didn't give up that easily.

"Oh, really?" she started toward him again. "I've seen how you act around me, and I know that you are every bit as attracted to me as I am to you." Her voice took on a more seductive tone. "You may not be ready to pursue this now, but that's okay, Austin." Audra took a step closer to him, her hips swaying. "You'll get tired of your old lady, and by 'old' I mean literally old, and when you do, I'll be around. I'm a patient woman."

He shook his head, and started to say something when Julia came up behind the other woman. She had seen Audra enter and had overheard this last.

"You'll wait a long time, Audra, because I'm not going anywhere." Audra visibly jumped at the sound of the voice behind her and whirled around. Julia was calmly looking at her, one eyebrow raised. This scene had played out before in her life, and Julia had always thought in retrospect how she wished she'd handled things. She wasn't hesitant in the least this time. Austin was almost smiling as he watched Julia, standing in her home and confidently letting the woman in front of her know where she stood. This was Julia's turf. "Now," Julia continued, "I think it would be best for you to leave us, don't you? You've quite worn out your welcome."

"Seriously?" the younger woman laughed. "Here you are, all smug, but let me tell you something. The day will come when someone will wipe that look off your face. It may or may not be me, but trust me. Someone will." She looked around at the comfortable home and then back at Julia. "One day not all the money in the world will keep him around."

Audra looked at Austin and then back to Julia. Austin had come to stand beside Julia, and his arm around her waist spoke volumes to the woman.

"Go," Austin said coldly. "As for work, stay away from me. I will no longer be working on anything with you."

Audra gathered her pride and shrugged her shoulders. She took her bag from those hanging beside the door and made her way out. She didn't say good-bye and neither did Austin nor Julia. As the door closed behind her, Julia released the breath she'd been holding.

"Well, that went better than I expected," she sighed and turned to look up at Austin. "Do you think she'll give you any trouble at work? I know how a woman scorned can be."

He thought for a moment before shaking his head, "Naw, I don't think so. She isn't stupid, and I can't think of a time or place that she'd use to accuse me of anything. And from now on, I'll make sure she doesn't get the opportunity."

They both knew that women crying sexual harassment wasn't unheard of, and Julia didn't know this woman well enough to be sure that she wouldn't play that card. Unfortunately, women who made false accusations made it harder than ever for those who really had a problem to be taken seriously. As Julia and Austin looked worriedly at the closed door, neither of them knew who was waiting beside Audra's car.

"Leaving so soon?" Sharon asked the woman who approached and hit the remote to unlock her car. The look on her face told Sharon that evidently Julia had handled things, but Sharon wanted to put an exclamation point at the end.

"What's it to you?" Audra rudely tried to pass Sharon to get into her car. Sharon deftly held the door and stepped up close. In her heels, Audra had at least four or more inches on the small woman, but what Sharon lacked in size she more than made up for in intimidation.

"I have something to say to you before you go," Sharon had lowered her voice, making it even more formidable. "You don't know who I am, so let me introduce myself. Sharon Burns. Now I know that my name means nothing to you, nor does my husband's, John Burns." Sharon narrowed her eyes and stared at the woman in front of her. "I know women like you. I've seen your kind many times, and I've dealt with women like you for thirty years. Now, I'm only going to tell you once. If I hear that you've tried to pull something on Austin at work, whether it be some trumped up harassment accusation or whether you're simply annoying him, I will see you gone. Not just gone, but your career destroyed along with your reputation."

Sharon's eyes moved from the woman's face, down to her high heels, and back up to end at her dark brown eyes. "Oh, yes, I've seen your kind my entire adult life, and trust me when I say that they never win. Never." Sharon leaned back and glared at the younger woman a few seconds longer. When she believed that her point had been taken, she stepped back. "Drive safely now, dear," she said and smiled. It was a disturbing smile that had Audra fumbling with her keys. She couldn't drive away fast enough.

As the little car circled the drive and pulled onto the street, Lauren came to stand beside Sharon.

"Well played, Sharon, well played."

"I've had to run off more than one woman in my years with John." Sharon shook her head. "A man with good looks, or money, or both always has a target on his back. They think they can take my place." She laughed then. "That one was rather tame, really."

The two women linked arms and started back into the house.

As they came around the corner of the rock wall, Julia looked up and narrowed her eyes questioningly. The innocent smiles of her two friends didn't fool Julia for a minute. While she felt that it was totally unnecessary, she couldn't help appreciating the way the two looked after her. She didn't care if Audra had survived or not.

The rest of the afternoon and evening flowed without incident. Justin and Allison had inquired about Audra, but Julia smoothly gave the excuse of the woman claiming a headache before making her exit. Julia liked this couple, and she hoped that the four could go out for dinner or a movie. When she said as much, Allison was eager to agree. Julia was still talking with them when she looked up to see that Lauren had taken up her position at the bar. She was perched on one of the stools and staring in the direction of the pool. Julia followed her eyes to see what was going on.

On the far side, Sharon and John were holding court with Karen, Heidi, and Pam, and Joey and Eli were filling what was probably their third plate. In the pool, Jennifer and Jake were at one end chatting with Ryan and his girlfriend Calista, and as nothing looked out of place, Julia's eyes roamed across to the other end. *Ahhh*, she thought as she watched Matt toss Callie into the air. Both of them laughed as she came back to the surface and jumped onto Matt's shoulders in an attempt at dunking him. Julia could see that Lauren's mind was in high gear, never a good sign.

As the blonde's brown eyes landed on Dakota, Lauren stepped down from her stool, raised to her full height, and honed in on the young man. Julia started to go over to intercept her. She stopped. *No, Julia thought, I am not getting in the middle of some high school drama. Good lord.* Julia looked around for Austin and found him sitting with Mark, the older man obviously in the middle of a story as his hand gestures helped him describe his tale. While Julia was wrestling with alerting Austin or not, Lauren rose and made her way across the patio to Dakota, who was also watching the pool antics. He looked up at Lauren as she came to stand in front of him, blocking his view.

"Dakota, right?" Lauren turned on her smile, and the young man looked up to see who belonged to the long legs. His eyes rose to take in the curves of her hips, across the flat stomach to her breasts that strained against the white fabric, and finally up to the beautiful smile and dark brown eyes that were fastened on his. Lauren was used to men's attention, and she knew that this one was hooked.

"Mind if I sit?" Lauren pulled out a chair and situated herself to his right, forcing him to turn toward her and away from the water. Lauren leaned in, and Dakota had a hard time keeping his eyes fixed upward. "So, Dakota, tell me about yourself. Are you a yummy college man, too?" At this last, Lauren ran her tongue along her lower lip and looked at him as if she'd just tasted something very, very good.

"Uh, Lauren, right?" the poor man was trying not to stumble over his words. "Uh, yeah, I'm a senior at ASU majoring in accounting."

"Oh," Lauren almost purred. "A man who's good with numbers. I'll bet you're real smart, too." She leaned in closer and rested her hand on his leg. "You know what I've discovered Dakota? Intelligent men make the best lovers. Would you agree with that statement?" Lauren turned on the full charm then as she glanced down to take in Dakota's dark blue and white swim trunks that covered tanned muscular legs, letting her eyes linger just a tad too long before raising them slowly to make their way up his bare stomach and chest, strong jaw, light brown hair that was cut close to his head, and ending at his hazel-colored eyes. Lauren loved to let men know that they weren't the only ones who could undress someone with their eyes. In fact, she liked to think she'd perfected it over the years. Every twenty-four-year-old man likes to think himself experienced when it comes to females, but this woman almost frightened Dakota. He was about to comment when they were interrupted.

"Callie, have you met Lauren?" Matt's voice came from behind Lauren. She winked slowly at Dakota as if to say "We aren't finished yet," before turning around to smile at Matt and the petite blonde with him. Callie looked like some college's cheerleader, and Lauren doubted her ability to drink legally. Until the girl took a misstep, Lauren would play nice.

"Why, yes, I do believe we met when Dakota arrived," Lauren smoothly moved her chair to position it next to Dakota's. "If you're finished with your pool play, why don't you two join us?" She swept her hand toward the empty chairs that were on the opposite side of the table.

"That would be awesome!" Callie dried her legs and arms before pulling the towel around her hips and settling herself on one of the proffered chairs.

Matt wasn't as eager to join the small group, but at the risk of offending Dakota or Callie, he pulled out a chair. Leaning back and stretching his legs out until they almost touched Lauren's red-painted toes, he linked his hands behind his head and looked at Lauren. He knew exactly what she was up to, and she smiled at him, raising that one eyebrow again. She turned her attention back to the girl.

"So, Callie, Dakota tells me he's a senior at ASU. Is that where you go, too?" Lauren could feign interest with the best.

"I do!" the girl's southern voice rose at the end of each sentence as if she were excited about whatever she was saying. "I'm a junior and majoring in graphic design. I'm originally from Memphis, and when my mimi moved out here and I spent Christmas break with her one year, I just knew that I wanted to come back. Isn't this just the best place ever?" She wrinkled her small turned-up nose and fixed her baby blue eyes on Lauren for confirmation. The older woman nodded her agreement. "Oh, and I usually spend summers out here, too. I'm a cheerleader for the Sun Devils. Go Devils!" Her smile actually widened at this last. "We spend the whole summer doing camps for high school kids and getting ready for the next season. Isn't that fun?" Her nose wrinkled up again at this last as her voice traveled up another octave. This was exactly the kind of female that made Lauren's hackles stand up. *Play nice*, she told herself. *She's just a baby.*

"Just precious," Lauren smiled brightly. While this girl represented most of what Lauren hated in the world, she had no intentions of hurting her feelings. She engaged Callie in telling her about what her major involved and her other interests. All the while the girl talked, Matt grinned at Lauren. Dakota's eyes kept moving back and forth between the two women, as if he were watching a tennis match. Neither man joined in the conversation. Finally, Matt stood up and held his hand out to Lauren.

"Come with me. I need a cold beer and you look like you could use one of your vodka concoctions." He looked at Dakota and Callie. "Can we get either of you something?"

Dakota asked for a beer while Callie said she'd like a Coke. "Make it a diet!" she laughed. "Gotta fit in that uniform this fall!"

Matt steered Lauren to the bar and once they were out of hearing distance, looked at her. She returned his steady gaze and said nothing.

"Ok, what the hell was that all about?" Matt began. "For a minute there, I thought you were going to gobble him up, spit him out, and pick your teeth with shards of bone."

"Flattery gets you everywhere," Lauren's smile began at the corner of her mouth before making its way across her lips. It didn't quite make it to her eyes. "Did you enjoy your swim?"

"As a matter of fact, I did," he mixed her favorite vodka and tonic, remembering to put in the extra lime. He didn't know it, but the gesture made her feel good. *He's starting to take note of the little things*, she thought, *but my work here isn't done yet*. He continued, interrupting her thoughts, "You should have joined us, since you were so interested."

"Yeah, not really my style, Junior, but you youngsters go ahead and play."

"What is your style, Blondie? Are you planning a little seduction scene for my friend Dakota there?" he challenged her now. "He doesn't see things like I do. You mess with him, and you may find you have a lap dog for life. Both of us know that isn't your style either, is it?" He opened his beer and took a long swallow. "He doesn't play like you and I do. Dakota takes these things seriously." He looked at her then, his expression no longer playful. "Lay off him, Lauren."

"Or?" She didn't like to be told her business or what to do. "What? You gonna go warn him about the big bad lady who will steal his virtue and leave him a jaded man?" She challenged him now. "Perhaps I like my men jaded. Perhaps I like to mold them into proper lovers." She straightened her back and lifted her chin in challenge. "You never know, Matty, I just might be the best thing to ever happen to old Dakota there." She indicated Callie. "If that's what he's settling for, he needs a little help, don't you think?"

"You know what, Lauren, I've seen you act bitchy, but I never considered you a bitch until right now, right this moment. I don't think that's who you really are, and you don't either." He narrowed his eyes on hers. "What brought this on, anyway? Were you feeling a little overlooked? Not enough male attention to suit you? Feeling the need to sharpen those claws on something?" He paused before his face broke out in a grin. "Or maybe you were a little jealous? Did the green-eyed monster pay you a visit?"

Lauren took a drink of her vodka before giving him a response.

"Oh, Junior, I was a bitch before you were even born. As for your friend over there; I was just playing a bit. He was feeling left out, watching you make eyes at his girl, and I certainly couldn't let that happen." She smiled and looked over at Dakota, who was watching her. "He definitely isn't feeling left out now." She winked in his direction and watched him blush and duck his head before she looked back at Matt. "As for the 'green-eyed monster' you talk of, honey, I tamed him long ago. I also know that before he can appear, one has to feel affection for someone. When it comes to you and me, we're just pals, right? Nothing to be jealous of there, agree?"

She was challenging him, but Matt wasn't sure what it was all about. Was he jealous of the attention she was giving Dakota? Matt turned to grab a beer for his friend, giving him a chance to think without Lauren's eyes boring into his. Did it bother him to see her openly flirt with his friend? Matt didn't want to admit it, but he *was* bothered. Oh, he and Lauren didn't have an exclusive arrangement, but the thought of her with the other man, of her touching and being touched, had him growing angry. He'd promised himself that this would never happen to him. That no female would ever control him like this. By the time he turned back to Lauren, his face was a hardened mask.

"Nope, not a thing, Blondie. You and I are just in it for the kicks. Hell, Dakota's a big boy, and he can sleep with whoever he wants to. You included. Just let him down easy when you're done, okay?"

Lauren wasn't sure what she wanted to hear, but her eyes told him that wasn't it. Her face was also closed off as she walked around him to grab a Diet Coke from the cooler.

"Can't keep thirsty people waiting, can we?" she said over her shoulder as she made her way back to the other couple.

Callie was still talking to Dakota, but his attention was only half on what she was saying. *Damn,* he thought as he watched Lauren make her way back over to him. *If I thought I had a chance with this one...hell, I can't even think. She's the stuff of dreams, for sure.* He grinned widely at Lauren as she reached across him to set the soda in front of Callie. Her breast brushed his arm and he almost jumped. She set her own drink down before turning to settle into her chair. She had turned her back on Matt and didn't see him coming.

Matt swooped Lauren up into his arms and was jumping into the deep end of the pool before she could react. The huge splash they made caused everyone to turn to see what had happened. As they came back up to the surface, Julia looked at Austin and rolled her eyes as if to say, *What the hell...again?* Austin shook his head and laughed. He figured Lauren must have said something to cause Matt to haul her ass into the water. He'd find out why later.

In true Lauren fashion, she came up to the surface and laughed in Matt's face before jumping on his head and burying it under the surface. Julia hoped she'd let him up before he drowned. She needn't have feared because he flipped Lauren up and over before diving under the water to grab her waist and bring her back to the top. They were both laughing by then.

"You are such an asshole," Lauren gasped around her laughter. "Those shoes will have to be retrieved, and I'm not doing it." She swam to shallower water and tossed the wet sarong onto the side of the pool. Her hair was dripping into her eyes, and she went under again to smooth it back off her face.

"Yeah," Matt laughed and started toward her again, "this is becoming a habit, isn't it?"

"You wish, jerk," she was still on the verge of laughing and her eyes sparkled as they looked at Matt.

"Truce?" he put out his pinky.

"Seriously? A pinky truce? What are you, twelve?" Lauren swatted his hand away and barely escaped when he reached for her again. Laughing, she pulled herself out of the water and walked over to the stack of pool towels. She watched as he dove down to retrieve her shoes and toss them onto the side. He pulled himself out of the water, and Lauren handed him one of the towels. They eyed one another as they dried off, and the look escaped no one watching. Julia shook her head and rolled her eyes at Austin. He let out a breath and shook his head.

"Well, Julia," Sharon had made her way over to Julia's side and leaned over to speak into her ear. "That certainly looks like a puma move to me." She raised back to look at Julia and wink.

Yeah, Julia thought, *and I have no idea what to do about it.*

Chapter 33

"Well, that was a success!" Austin closed the door as Lauren and Matt were the last to leave.

Julia laughed, "It was a something, that's for sure. I don't even want to think about what those two are going to do the rest of the night."

Austin pulled her to him and kissed her deeply. He raised his head to smile at her. "Don't worry about them. We have enough to do the rest of the night." He moved in again when Julia pulled away.

"Yeah, like clean up this mess! The patio can wait until tomorrow, but this kitchen is disgusting." She turned to wade into the stacked leftover food and dirty containers. Austin swatted her butt playfully as she moved away, and she turned to laugh and wave her finger at him. "Nuh, huh. Work before play. I won't be able to concentrate if this mess isn't cleared away first."

"Baby, I can make you forget all about this kitchen," Austin's voice had taken on a lower timber as he came toward her.

"Tempted...very, very tempted, but let's do this together. We can finish quickly and have the rest of the night," she looked at him hopefully. He knew how she couldn't stand facing a mess in the morning and resigned himself to work before play. He took the dish towel from her hand and headed for the sink.

Julia was bending over to load more dishes into the dishwasher when she suddenly felt light headed. She gripped the counter and slowly rose, her heart pounding and sweat breaking out on her forehead and beading on her upper lip. Austin was up to his elbows in soapy water washing out a pan when something made him look over at her. He saw her white face and before she could actually fall over, he'd grabbed her and half carried her to a chair.

"What's wrong? Jules? What happened?" He had never seen her ill, and she was scaring him.

Julia put her head down, touching her knees, and focused on taking deep breaths. Soon the bout passed, and she raised her head to look around her. Her vision that had before been nothing but a sea of white was now starting to clear. Austin had kneeled down beside her chair, and as she looked at him, his face came into focus.

"Wow, I have no idea. One minute, I'm feeling fine, and the next minute I'm trying not to fall over." Austin left her a minute to get a cool washcloth, and pushing her long dark hair aside, laid it across the back of her neck.

"That feels good. Thank you, sweetie." She took his hand and gave it a squeeze. His concern was written all over his face, and she wanted to let him know that she was okay. "I'm fine now. A little shaky, but nothing a few minutes sitting here won't cure."

"Are you sure? Should we go to the emergency room?" Austin started to rise, when she pulled him back.

"Austin, really, I'm fine now. I guess I didn't eat enough to make it through the day. In fact, I was so busy making sure everyone else ate that I don't remember exactly what I did have besides one of Lauren's mixed drinks and a couple of diet sodas." She put her hand on the side of his face. "It's all good, sweetie, really."

"If you're sure. You scared me for a minute there. Do you want something to drink? Let me get you a glass of water." He hurried to put ice and water in a glass and bring it back to her.

"Here." He watched her take a sip. "Drink as much as you can. If you didn't eat or drink anything but soda, you need to hydrate. You know what the dry air can do to you."

Julia obeyed. She sat in the chair, drinking water and wiping her face, as he finished up the kitchen. They hadn't much left to do, and he was done within a few minutes. As he wiped down the counter and hung the towel on the oven door handle, he turned to look at her. To his relief, color was back in her face, and Julia was looking much better.

"Can I get you anything else?" he came back over to kneel in front of her again. *His concern is almost too sweet,* she thought and smiled.

Out loud she said, "Not a thing. I'm feeling so much better. I'll bet you're right. When I first moved out here, I'd forget to drink enough water, and I'd feel sick every time. Usually, though, it was more nauseous than faint." She shrugged her shoulders. "Oh well, all better now. And just in time for you to have finished up," she teased.

"Yeah, you played that well, didn't you?" he teased back.

They headed to bed then, neither feeling like doing more than drift off to sleep in one another's arms.

Julia had no idea what time it was when she was awakened by nausea that sent her sliding out of bed and hurrying to the bathroom off the den. She wasn't about to wake Austin and have him hover around her again. Besides, there was nothing he could do but watch her throw up, and she had no intention of anyone watching that. When she felt better, Julia washed out her mouth with mouthwash she kept under the sink for guests to use. She still wasn't one hundred percent, so she curled up in Austin's brown leather chair. Pulling around her a small blanket she took from the sofa, Julia leaned back in the chair, her mind working. She loved sitting in his chair. The smell of leather with just a hint of Austin always made her feel safe and comfortable.

This didn't feel like the times she'd been sick from dehydration. This was a familiar feeling that she hadn't had in years. Her heart began racing as Julia thought back over the past weeks. Her period was never regular, and as far as she could remember, her last one had been more than a month ago, maybe two. A feeling of horror began settling on her. *Oh god, please no,* she thought wildly. *I can't do this again. I won't do this to Austin. I won't do this to me!*

Tears began falling down her face as she worked herself into a real panic attack. Before she could fall apart completely, Julia went into the kitchen to make a cup of tea. Any time she wasn't feeling well or was upset, she would fix herself a cup of chamomile tea with lots of sugar. She took her full mug back to Austin's chair and curled up again.

Calm down, she told herself. *You don't know anything for sure. You could have picked up a bug. Or maybe you do need to hydrate. Or maybe you need to eat.* That thought made her feel almost ill again, so she quickly put it out of mind and sipped her tea. Lauren. She wanted to talk to her friend so badly, but a look at the clock told her that not even Lauren would be up at this hour. She would need her friend and soon. Julia walked to the kitchen where her phone was charging on the counter and took it back with her into the den.

It's 3:30 in the morning, and yes, I'm okay. She typed. *I really need to talk to you tomorrow. Call me when you get this. Please!*

She reread what she'd typed before hitting the send button. It shouldn't worry her friend, but Lauren would get the message that Julia needed her. Julia sat quietly and sipped her tea, her mind running here and there.

What in the hell was I thinking? Yes, the doctor in St. Louis assured me that I couldn't get pregnant, but could he have been wrong? I'm forty-one years old! What the hell! Surely God wouldn't play a sick joke like this on me! What if it's something else? What if something else entirely is going on here? They say that you can tell if your body needs something. I don't think I've ignored any signals. Julia couldn't quiet her thoughts. *Oh, god, what will I say to Austin? I assured him that at my age and with my background, I couldn't have kids. Will he think I've been lying to him all this time? Will he hate me for it?*

Julia set her mug on the table. In spite of her racing thoughts, she was exhausted, and she reclined the chair before pulling the blanket up to her chin. Her mind was still working, but not all of it was negative. Julia thought about a light-haired little boy with green eyes and decided that a baby wouldn't be the worst thing to happen. That was her last conscious thought as sleep overtook her.

"Jules? Hey, baby, are you okay?" Austin's voice pulled her out of sleep. She opened her eyes and looked at a pair of green eyes, just like her imaginary little boy, and blinked a couple of times before his face came into focus.

"Yeah, I got sick last night, and I didn't want to wake you up. I ended up here and fell asleep." She smiled at him. "Good morning, Sunshine." That was her usual greeting for him in the morning.

"You okay now?" His face was full of concern, and she reached out to massage the worry lines from between his brows.

"I'm fine. Nothing a lazy day won't fix."

"What can I get you? You hungry? Can I fix you some breakfast?"

At the mention of food, Julia felt her stomach clinch up. She shook her head, "No, I'll just drink a glass of water."

"What? No coffee this morning? You must not feel well," he teased her a bit before going into the kitchen to get her a bottle of cold water. He opened it before handing it to her. Julia took a long drink and felt better. She smiled up at him.

"Give me a while and I'll be good as new," she assured. "Hey, aren't you supposed to play golf this morning?"

"Yeah," he looked at the clock. "Yeah, I'm supposed to meet John and Steve and some other guy I don't know." He looked at her closely. "I can cancel. They'd understand." He started for his phone when she spoke up.

"Absolutely not. I'm a big girl here, you know. All I need is a hot bath, another mug of tea, and to do nothing. You'll be home before I can get my nap out." She grinned at him. No way was she letting him stay home today.

He was still unsure when an alarm on his phone sounded. He looked down again and said, "My one-hour warning. It will take me a few minutes to shower and get to the course." He looked down at her again. "Are you sure, babe?"

"Go. Get out of here, please. You've not seen me sick before. I always curl up alone and wait for it to pass. Seriously, when I'm not well, I want to be completely by myself. I'll be fine by the time you get back."

He leaned over to kiss her and smooth her hair back from her face. She must have convinced him because he winked and left her to take his shower. Once he was gone, Julia let out the breath she had been holding in. To do what she needed to do today would require his being gone at least the four or five hours she knew it took for him to play a round of golf. She would call Lauren again, take that bath, and get things rolling. She would be on pins and needles until she knew for sure that she was or wasn't pregnant.

Ten minutes later, Austin was back, his blond hair still wet and tucked behind his ears. She looked at him in his khaki shorts and white polo shirt and decided that she loved seeing him relaxed and heading out to have some fun. A quick kiss and he was gone.

Julia grabbed her phone to see that she had no message from Lauren. She pulled up her friend's number and decided to call. Hopefully, she'd have it turned on. Julia listened to the tone of one ring, two, three, and was getting ready to leave a message when Lauren's sleepy voice came on.

"'Lo? This better be good," Lauren wasn't a morning person.

"Hey, it's me. I need your help today."

"What? What's going on? Jules? You sound funny." Lauren was fully awake now. Julia could hear her getting up and figured Lauren wasn't alone. She'd wait until she was in another room before resuming the conversation. "Julia? Are you there?"

"I'm here. I need you to do something for me, and don't ask any questions, please, until you get here."

Pause. "Okay...no questions, but are you okay?"

Julia took a deep breath and released it before answering. "I think so." She paused before forging ahead. "Lauren, I need you to come over here this morning, but on your way I need you to pick up something for me—a pregnancy test."

The silence on the other end stretched out and Julia looked at her phone to make sure the call hadn't been dropped. She was about to repeat her request when Lauren's voice came through.

"Of course. I'll be there within the hour." She paused. "Are you okay, Jules? Where's Austin?"

"No questions, please, but I'm okay and he's playing golf with John. Just get here, please. I need my friend."

Lauren didn't want to hang up on the desolation in Julia's voice, but she had to shower and sneak away from Matt, who was still sleeping in her bed.

"Hang on, sweetie. On my way."

Julia looked at the call ended message on her phone and placed it on the table. She leaned back and took another sip of water. She felt a little better after sharing her dilemma with Lauren, but she knew her problem was far from over. With a mental shake of her head, she got up to take a shower and get ready for her day. *Should be interesting*, she thought.

As good as her word, Lauren came sweeping in an hour later. She didn't tell Julia that she'd left Matt in her bed and Julia didn't ask. Lauren had showered in the other bathroom and left him a note telling him that she'd had to go out. Matt was a topic for another time.

Lauren pulled Julia into her arms and held her for a few moments. When she pulled back, she saw that tears were in her friend's eyes but had yet to spill over. She handed her the white plastic bag from the drugstore and said, "Let's get this over with, shall we?"

Julia nodded and left for her bedroom and bath. Lauren followed her and sat on the bed to wait. They'd done this before, several times when Julia was with Keith, and more often than not, the results were negative. Lauren hoped they would be again. She didn't know how Julia would react to anything other than a negative reading. She was still thinking of her friend's previous disappointments when Lauren's phone dinged. She looked down to see a message from Matt.

What's up? I missed my morning exercise, and you know how I like to work out. Will you be home anytime soon?

Lauren smiled and typed back, *Probably not. I had a thing come up and I have to take care of it.*

It wasn't a minute later that she read, *I have a thing coming up, too. You gonna come home and take care of that?*

Lauren laughed softly and typed, *Sorry. You'll have to figure that out on your own. Lock up when you leave, please.*

Awww…man…you're killing me, Blondie. All right. I have to work today anyway. Later.

Lauren was still smiling when she heard the bathroom door opening. One look at Julia's face and Lauren knew all she needed. Her smile faded and she folded her friend into her arms. They stood there swaying gently and saying nothing. Julia pulled away first and looked up at Lauren.

"Damn" is all she said. Lauren pulled her back into her arms, and they comforted one another.

"Lauren," Julia's voice was muffled on Lauren's shoulder. "What am I going to do? We both know how this is going to end."

Lauren sat Julia on the side of the bed and kneeled down in front of her. Taking both of her cold hands in hers, Lauren gave her a stern look.

"No, we do *not* know how this ends. This is a different time, different place, and different situation. Julia, no pressure. No one expects anything from you this time. You're not performing as a brood mare birthing a prize colt." That last brought about a small smile from Julia's stricken face and Lauren continued. "Sweetie, it's no wonder you lost those babies. God, the burden you carried before…that's gone! You and Austin are so different. He loves you just as you are. You don't have to produce anything for him. Relax…no expectations, no disappointments, nothing."

Julia looked at her friend. Lauren could still see a lot of uncertainty in Julia's face, but she didn't have the words to reassure her friend enough to get rid of it.

"Hey," Lauren smiled brightly. "Think of how much fun we can have! No Dana hanging over your shoulder. Woo hoo! We'll make this the time of your life!"

"Slow down, tiger, we don't know anything for sure, you know." Julia was beginning to return to herself. "I'll call my doctor tomorrow and see how soon I can get in. Once we know something for sure, then we'll make plans." Her face fell again. "Chances are this will turn out just like the rest, you know."

"So? What if it does? Who are you disappointing this time? No one! If it happens, it happens." Julia's head lowered and Lauren's heart was breaking for her. "Please, Jules, don't go there, okay?" Lauren pleaded.

Julia looked at the person who knew her as well as she knew herself and nodded. "You're right. I can't change anything now."

"Nope." Lauren paused. "Jules, does Austin know?"

Julia shook her head, "No. You know my periods. They are so screwed up that we never know what's going on with me. It's a bit of a joke, really."

"Okay, then how did you know to take the test?"

Julia sighed. "I almost passed out last night when we were cleaning up the kitchen. Lar, it was so similar to the last time. Out of nowhere, I felt dizzy, light-headed, broke out into a sweat, and if Austin hadn't caught me, I would have hit the floor. I've had a couple of other episodes, but nothing like last night's."

"And you told him…what?"

"Well, I told him that I probably hadn't eaten enough and only drank soda yesterday. That combination always makes me dehydrated and sick. He believed me, and we went to bed. Sometime in the night, I woke up, threw up, and curled up in his chair. That's where he found me this morning. I told him I'd just rest, drink lots of water and tea, and be good as new tomorrow."

Lauren shook her head and looked at Julia. "Well, are you going to tell him?"

The silence stretched out. Finally Julia spoke.

"I don't think so. Not yet. We went into this with the agreement of no kids. What do I say? 'Surprise! You're gonna be a daddy! Or not!'" Julia shook her head. "I won't do that to him. And should it all turn out like it always does, his knowing will only hurt him when I lose this one, too. And that's provided he even wants it. I won't put him on that emotional roller coaster."

"But Jules, he's gonna see you get sick. He knows you. Are you going to keep telling him you just need water? That you just have a bug? Come on, sweetie, you're gonna run out of excuses sooner or later." She looked down at Julia's flat stomach. "And you always show early. How will you explain that? 'Sorry, babe, but I guess I'm getting fat.' You know that won't work." Lauren paused. "He's not a boy, Jules. He can handle a situation like this. You don't have to protect him, if that's who you're protecting. Seriously…"

"Stop. Just stop, okay? I'm still reeling from the probably pregnant shit. I can't think that far ahead to the protruding belly. And I am not protecting Austin." Julia fell backward on the bed and stared at the ceiling. She could see dust on the ceiling fan blades and thought about how she'd climb up there and clean them off. Or not. She probably shouldn't be climbing up on things, at least for the next eight months or so.

Lauren lay down beside her, both women quiet and dealing with her own thoughts. Almost at the same time, they turned toward one another.

"I don't know about you, preggers, but I'm starved." Lauren grinned.

"Me, too. Let's go find some leftovers."

By the time Austin arrived home, Julia was feeling better physically and mentally. Lauren stuck around to visit a while before making her exit. When it was just the two of them, Austin looked at Julia.

"Are you sure you're okay? You seem to be doing better." She smiled at his worried look.

"Babe, I'm fine." Julia thought quickly. "That's not to say that I won't have another bout, especially if it's a bug of some kind, but for now I feel pretty good."

"Let's go for a drive. You up to it?"

"I'd love nothing more! You pick the direction and I'll grab a jacket." She rose to go when he grabbed her hand.

"Jules, you'd tell me if something was wrong, wouldn't you?" he studied her face.

Damn, he can read me too easily, she thought. Out loud she said, "Of course, you know I would. Besides, what in the world would I hide from you?" She laughed.

"Okay, I believe you, but don't ever keep anything from me, okay?" Austin was serious. Once again, she'd forgotten how perceptive he was.

"Okay..." she gently pulled her hand away and left the room.

Something's up...I know it is, he thought. *Lauren is good at letting on, but Julia sucks at it.* He sighed and got up to grab a hat and his keys. *She'll tell me when she's ready.*

Chapter 34

———

Julia CALLED HER DOCTOR THE next day but couldn't get in until the following week. It would be almost two weeks before she knew anything for certain, and as the days passed she found it was getting harder to keep Austin in the dark. Fortunately, she didn't have any more fainting episodes, but Julia never knew when the nausea would hit her. She thought back to the previous times. With her first two, she'd been sick in the morning only. With the last, she'd been sick almost all of the time. Julia cringed at that thought. So far, she'd been ill late at night, after they'd gone to bed, and as far as she knew, Austin never heard a thing. She had teased him before about sleeping the sleep of the dead, but now she was grateful. She still didn't know why she wasn't telling him, and Lauren wasn't happy with her.

"For god's sake, Julia, just tell the man! Why are you keeping this from him? He won't be mad. Geez…" Lauren would look at her disgustedly over her glasses as they worked at their desks.

Julia was prevented from answering by the ringing phone. Business continued to be good, and both women were busy. Lauren looked at her friend as Julia answered questions and made an appointment for the next day. *I should just accidentally on purpose let something slip the next time I'm with Austin,* Lauren thought. *What's she going to do to me? Beat me up?* The thought made her smile before it faded. Lauren shook her head. *Doesn't she know how much of an emotional help Austin could be? She's still in protective mode from that bastard Keith.* Lauren took a deep breath and let it out slowly. Even the thought of the man made her want to throw something, preferably at his stupid face. Julia finished her conversation.

"That was Mrs. Beckworth. She wants one of us to come out tomorrow and take a look at redoing that huge guest house. She said that they never put guests out there and she needs a studio for her artwork." They both grinned. Mrs. Beckworth's artwork was far from art, unless said art was produced by a second grader.

"You want me to go?" Lauren had worked with her before, but so had Julia.

"Do you mind? I have a doctor's appointment in the morning." Julia looked up and the smile didn't quite reach her eyes.

"Already? I thought we'd be waiting a few more days."

"The office called and they can fit me in tomorrow, so I jumped at it." Julia looked at Lauren. "I can call Mrs. Beckworth back and reschedule. I'm so sorry. I should have asked you first. I wasn't thinking because I don't have the appointment down on anything here or at home."

"Jules," Lauren interrupted her. "I've got this. Stop fretting. You're sounding silly now," Lauren rolled her eyes.

"Sorry, sorry," Jules stopped herself. "I'm so glad it's in the morning because she's doing a bunch of blood tests, too, and I can't eat before those." Julia stopped and stared at the opposite wall. "Crap, I'll have to pretend something for Austin because he always brings me coffee while I'm getting ready. Can't drink coffee."

"Jules, for the love of god, just tell the man. Please. You are driving me crazy with this cloak and dagger shit."

"I will. I promise. When I know something for sure." Julia still didn't want to have that conversation with Austin.

"Sweetie, I see your mouth moving, but I'm not hearing anything that makes sense, nor do I hear anything that I want to." Lauren was disgusted and it showed.

"Let's drop it, okay?" Julia was getting tired of this conversation, too. "I don't want to fight with you."

"I don't either," Lauren said. "I don't agree with you, but I still love you. You big dummy."

Julia grinned, "Love you, too, slut." They were okay again.

The next morning, Julia was sitting at her makeup table and applying the little cosmetics that she wore. Austin had brought her a mug of coffee, kissed the top of her head, and gotten into the shower. As soon as Julia was sure he was busy, she took the mug to the sink and poured half down the drain. She would pour the rest into a travel mug and feign an early appointment to avoid having to drink in front of him. Julia felt bad about the deception, but she shrugged her shoulders. *It is what it is,* she thought. She left before he did, and as she hurried out the door, travel mug in hand, she congratulated herself on her deception. *I should have been an actress,* she thought.

Austin watched her car pull away and rubbed the back of his neck in frustration. Every night for the past week and a half, he'd felt her leave the bed. Curious, he'd followed her one night and stood outside the closed door listening to her retching on the other side. He wanted so badly to go in and look after her, but something stopped him. If she wanted him, she'd let him know. He remembered what she'd said about being sick and wanting to be alone. *I'll respect that,* he thought, *but I'm not letting her off the hook much longer. This is killing me. If she's sick, I need to know. What's wrong with her?* He'd be back in bed and feigning sleep when she'd return. He knew that she kept a toothbrush and mouthwash in that bathroom. She'd always said that her reason was so that guests could freshen up. He knew better now. He thought about calling Lauren, but unless Julia let her, he knew that Lauren wouldn't tell him a thing. He thought about Sharon. She hadn't been around lately, and he doubted Julia had said anything to her.

I'll ask her tonight what's going on, he thought as he turned to get his keys and phone. *She'll tell me one way or the other.* If Julia could have seen his determined look, she would have relented. But for the time being, she was resolute in her ignorance.

Julia had just finished putting her clothes on, when the doctor knocked. At Julia's "Come in" the short, slender, fifty-something year old woman reentered. She had on her white lab coat and the kind, professional look on her face made Julia feel better.

"Have a seat, Miss Julia, and let's talk."

Julia knew what was coming. This wasn't her first rodeo, as she liked to call it. "Well, Dr. Roberts, what's the verdict?" Julia's nervousness was seen only in the way she twisted her hands together, the knuckles white.

Dr. Roberts reached out and patted Julia's cold hands. "It's as you thought, Julia. You are for sure pregnant."

Julia's face registered her shock. She'd held out hope, but that was gone now. "But…how? My doctor in St. Louis said that it would be impossible for me to get pregnant. He assured me it was impossible."

"Julia," the doctor's voice was gentle. "You were in shock and pain at that time. Are you sure he didn't say that you would never carry a child to term? Not that you couldn't conceive?"

Julia thought back to that day. It was so much a blur, and she knew that Dr. Roberts was probably right. *How stupid,* she thought. *I am so stupid. And now I've put Austin and myself in this position.*

All she said out loud was, "I just don't remember for sure. I'm so sorry. I wish I could. You have my medical records from that time. Is there anything in there? Anything to help us know what's going to happen?"

Dr. Roberts studied Julia's face before she spoke. "Julia, I've been in medicine thirty years now, and one thing I can say with certainty is that none of us knows for sure what's going to happen. I've seen supposedly barren women have more than one baby. I've seen women who'd had their tubes tied come in here pregnant. I've seen women try again and again only to give up, adopt a baby, and turn up pregnant." She smiled. "Every pregnancy is different, you know. Now, we have some obstacles here. One is your age. Forty-one isn't too old, but it does put you at a higher risk for birth defects or miscarriage. We'll address both. Another is your history. Just because you haven't carried a child to term before doesn't mean you won't this time. So many factors come into play. Your health at the time. Your emotional state. Your environment. We can't control everything, but we can put you in the best position for success. Now, here's what I recommend…"

They spent the next fifteen minutes talking about what Julia could expect in the coming weeks. Since the best guess on Julia's progress was around five or six weeks, they discussed a possible amniocentesis test, but with Julia's miscarriage history, that decision would be up to her. The doctor said that they'd need to wait between the fifteenth week and the eighteenth week for accurate results. At that time, they'd also do the ultrasound and hopefully know the baby's gender as well as if there were any problems not found with the test.

"Julia, you'll want to discuss this test with the baby's father. It does have some risks, and you also need to decide what you'd do with the test results. If something should be wrong with the fetus, you may consider termination." Dr. Roberts' voice was matter-of-fact, but Julia's breath caught at that last part. Termination—could she consider that step?

"I understand. I have some time until then to think it over and talk to him." Julia still looked almost shell-shocked.

"I have to ask, will the baby's father be a help? Will he be here for you?"

Julia smiled at the doctor's question. "Oh yes, he'll be around." *Unless I don't tell him.* This was the first time she'd seriously thought not when she'd tell Austin, but *if.*

Shortly after, Julia left the office. Dr. Roberts had emailed a prenatal vitamin prescription to Julia's pharmacy and given her a handful of pamphlets and information that she could read on her own. They'd see one another in a few weeks, provided all was well. The doctor didn't see any reason for Julia to curtail any of her normal activities, and she assured her patient that wouldn't be necessary unless something happened.

That's a big if, Julia thought as she made her way out the door. Once in her car, she sat staring out the windshield and tried to wrap her head around it all. *What to do, what to do,* she thought. *I can't think right now.* She felt her breath start coming in short bursts and her heartbeat speed up. Leaning her head down on the steering wheel, she cried. At first the tears trickled from the corners of her eyes, but then they began to fall in earnest. Her shoulders shook, and she couldn't catch her breath. When she'd finished, she sat up and leaned her head back on the seat headrest. She didn't feel that much better, but some tension had been released. She didn't realize the weight until she'd cried it out.

Should I let Austin know, or should I wait? Julia well remembered the toll her miscarriages had taken on the relationship with Keith, and she wanted to avoid that happening with Austin at all costs. *Can I keep on deceiving him, letting him think I have a stomach bug or something?* Feelings of guilt swept over her. She hated lying, whether it was her lying to someone else or their lying to her. Her mind was swirling.

She started the car but stopped. *I can't do this. I can't go home and pretend it's all normal and okay. I've got to think. Figure this mess out.* Suddenly she thought of Sharon. Pulling her phone from her purse, she tried to punch in the number but her hands were shaking too badly. Finally, the call went through. She heard her friend's voice on the other end.

"Hey, Buttercup! What's up?" Sharon's bright voice almost sent Julia over the edge again.

"Sharon?" her voice shook. "Can I come by and get the key for the house in Flagstaff? I need to stay there a while."

"What the hell's going on Jules? Are you and Austin okay?" Julia could almost picture her friend's face as she considered what could be bothering Julia enough to send her out of town.

"Yeah, he's fine. Me? Not so much. Can I borrow the place? Please?"

"Julia, you sound awful." As Julia said nothing, eventually Sharon sighed on the other end. "Yes, of course, you can get the key. Sweetie, do you want me to go with you?"

Julia smiled at the concern in Sharon's voice. "No, but thank you. I just need to get away for a couple of days, that's all. I have a lot to think about and deal with."

"Are you sure Austin didn't do something?" Julia could hear the steel in the other voice. "It isn't that little twit who came to the barbeque, is it? So help me if she and Austin have been up to something...."

"No, no, nothing like that," Julia interrupted her before Sharon could get on a roll. "I'll be by in about an hour to get it. Okay?"

"Of course, sweetheart, and I'll have a bite of lunch for you. I won't send you off on an empty stomach."

Julia was feeling hungry since she'd had nothing that morning. She looked down at her arm and the bandage that was still there from the morning's blood draw. She held the phone between her shoulder and ear and pulled it off.

"See you in an hour then." Julia paused. "And Sharon? Don't say anything to anyone about where I am, okay?"

"Not a word, dear," Sharon assured her. Julia wasn't surprised when Sharon didn't question her further. She knew that would come later, but she'd deal with it then.

Julia pulled into the garage at home, and when she entered the quiet house, it seemed odd for some reason. She shook off the feeling and went into the bedroom. Grabbing an overnight bag from the closet, she threw in some jeans and sweatshirts as well as her favorite pajamas and a couple of t-shirts and underwear. She didn't plan on seeing anyone and decided to go with comfort. In the bathroom, she gathered her toothbrush and other essentials. She tried not to think about what Austin would think when he got home. To think would be to change her mind, and she wasn't ready to do that yet.

I'll leave him a note, she thought. *Yeah, I'm a big coward, but I won't worry him by saying nothing.* She scribbled a quick note and left it on the kitchen counter where he'd see it when he got home. With a look around once more, she lowered her head and walked out the door.

The drive to Sharon's didn't take long, and her friend was waiting at the door. Julia smiled. It almost seemed like Sharon had some sort of radar that told her when Julia was coming. She knew that security cameras were everywhere, but surely the woman didn't sit around watching them until someone came up the drive.

Julia got out of her car. As she got closer, she saw Sharon's eyes narrow as they took in Julia's appearance. She didn't think she looked any different. Her usual work attire of skirt, blouse, and heels didn't scream *different*, but her face must have. Sharon wordlessly put her arms around Julia and pulled her close.

"My sweet girl, I'm so glad you're here. Let's get you something to eat, and you can tell me all about it," Sharon linked her arm through Julia's and led her into the house.

True to her word, Sharon had beef/vegetable soup and grilled cheese sandwiches laid out. Julia's stomach almost growled when she smelled the food. They sat at the counter and perched on the high stools to eat their lunch. Julia attacked her food, and Sharon smiled as she watched her eat every bite in front of her. Only when Julia sat back did Sharon begin.

"Okay, baby girl, tell me what's going on," Sharon looked at Julia and she wore her no-nonsense expression. Julia thought about lying, but she knew Sharon could always tell. She thought about saying nothing, but she knew that wouldn't fly either. She finally settled on the truth.

"Oh, Sharon, I don't know what to do," a tear escaped and rolled down Julia's cheek. "I'm pregnant. Austin doesn't know yet, and I'm trying to figure out how I can hide it from him until I lose this one, too. You know that I can never carry a baby for long, and I don't see this turning out any differently. I'm hoping that if I can spend a few days just to myself that

I'll figure something out." She took a ragged breath. "I will not put him through this. Losing a baby is awful, and the toll it takes on everyone can be impossible. Hell, he doesn't even want a baby as far as I know. Waiting and watching for the first signs of a miscarriage can tear you apart." Julia shook her head, breathing hard. "I will NOT do that to him. If I can just hide it, or go away until it's over, or maybe even just get rid of it now, then I can keep him from being hurt, you know? But I don't know if he'll let me do that. I don't think he will. And if he knew, he'd just get his hopes up only to have them dashed to the ground." She placed a cold hand on Sharon's arm. "So you can't tell him where I am. Promise me you won't tell him." Julia's voice trailed off as she lost steam.

Finally, she's gotten the worst out, Sharon thought. She covered Julia's hand with her warm one. Julia's were always cold lately. She looked her in the eye and took a deep breath. She let it out slowly before she spoke, smiling brightly.

"Julia, sweetheart, I'm so thrilled that you're going to have a baby! You're all gloom and doom here, but I don't see why. You're young, healthy, and you are surrounded by love." Julia started to interrupt, but at Sharon's look, she sat back and remained silent. "Now, what's this nonsense about your not telling Austin. The man has a right to know. You have to tell him and the sooner the better. You're treating this baby like it's already dead, for heaven's sake! That's no way to think! You need to change that attitude and right now." Sharon paused when Julia didn't speak. "And don't even let me hear you talk about getting rid of it. Really, Julia, that is as ridiculous as you running away." Sharon stopped talking as she thought about what to do.

"I just need to wrap my head around all of this before I talk to Austin," Julia's eyes were glossy with tears as she almost begged. "I can't go home and pretend that nothing is the matter. And I don't want to tell him yet. I keep thinking that he won't even have to know if history repeats itself, and with me it always does." At this last, a tear slipped out and slowly rolled down her cheek. "Please, Sharon, please work with me here. I'm only asking for a few days."

The older woman looked at the younger one in front of her and said resignedly. "Okay, I'll let you go to the Flagstaff house, but only for a few days. Longer than that, and I'll come get you myself, and you do not want me to have to come and get you." She took a breath and let that sink in. "As for Austin not knowing where you are, well that's just stupid. What are you some drama queen here? Suck it up, cupcake, put on your big girl panties, and show some intestinal fortitude." She squeezed Julia's hands. "Good god almighty, I've heard some goofy ideas but this takes the cake." Sharon shook her head, but Julia remained silent. She continued, "Now, who else knows besides me?"

Julia sighed. "I called Lauren when I first suspected, so it's just you and Lauren. Why?"

"Just wondering, that's all. Are you dead set on leaving today?" Sharon searched Julia's face, but what she was looking for, Julia had no clue.

Julia nodded, "I think so. I can't see myself going home and pretending nothing is wrong." She began to cry harder. "Oh, Sharon, I didn't mean to but I lied to Austin. I told him that I couldn't get pregnant, and now look at me. Look at us. What a mess..."

Sharon rolled her eyes. "Stop it. Just, stop it. I refuse to listen to this stupid shit. So you were wrong. Big. Damn. Deal." Sharon looked at the woman in front of her, her thoughts churning. She squared her shoulders and spoke. "Julia, I've changed my mind." As Julia started to protest, Sharon raised one hand to silence her. "I will not be part of this goofy plan as far as lying to Austin goes. So here's what I will do. I'll give you the key to the house, but if that boy comes by and asks me, I'm telling him where you are, how long you're staying, and that I think you're a fruitcake. I won't tell him why you've left. That's your news, but I like him too much to lie." She narrowed her eyes at Julia. "And one last thing. You are sadly underestimating that man. You have this stupid mindset that he needs you to protect him or something. My dear, that's the last thing he needs, and it would piss him off to think that you'd do that. Austin isn't a child. Oh, I've joked about his age, and we've had a good time with it, but that's all it is, Jules. A joke! Hell, I call both of you my boy and girl." She was almost finished. "Finally, Austin is not Keith. I am not your mother. All we want to do is love you, sweetheart." Her voice softened. "We just want to love you and take care of you. If you bring this baby into the world, then wonderful. If you don't, that's also okay. I've always said that things work out the way they're supposed to." She smiled. "You weren't supposed to have a child with Keith. Perhaps you are with Austin." Sharon patted

Julia's shoulder and slid off the stool. She walked into the other room and came back carrying a key ring and a slip of paper.

"Here's the key and the security code. I'll call the security guard and tell him to expect you." She handed both to Julia. "Please change your mind."

"I'll be fine," Julia looked at her friend, her second mother. "I really do need some time to wrap my mind around all of this. I'll be back in a couple of days. I promise. I'll call you tonight when I get there. Kiss John for me." Julia kissed Sharon's cheek, slid the key and code into her pocket, and quickly walked to the door. She turned. "I do love you both." With that, she left, softly closing the door behind her.

As soon as Julia was gone, Sharon pulled out her phone and punched in a number.

"John? Yes, everything is fine with me. It's Julia I'm worried about."

Chapter 35

Austin was surprised to see the empty garage as he pulled in from work. Julia usually beat him home, but he knew that she had been busy lately. *Maybe that's why she's not feeling well,* he thought. *Maybe it's stress from work or something.* He let himself into the house and it didn't feel quite right. *Empty,* he thought. He headed straight to the bedroom to change clothes and work in the yard for a while. Normally, whoever got home first started supper, but since Julia hadn't been feeling that great, he noticed that her appetite wasn't good either. He'd let her decide what sounded good, and maybe they'd order out. Almost anything suited him.

As he came back into the kitchen to grab something to drink, the white paper on the counter caught his eye. He picked it up and read it quickly. Once he finished, he sat down on one of the bar stools, and read through it again, slower this time. His head came up, and he looked around, as if searching for something. Almost running into the bedroom, Austin crossed the room and threw open the closet door. He'd just been in there, but nothing had seemed out of place. As he examined her side, he looked at the clothes hanging neatly. Nothing seemed out of the ordinary. He checked the shelf and saw their large suitcases and a couple of smaller bags where they always were. *Her weekend bag,* he thought. *That brown Louis whatever-his-name isn't here.* He searched the floor where many of her shoes were. She'd cleaned the closet, and they'd be either on the shoe rack or lined up neatly on the floor. He smiled as he looked at the mess now. She liked to kick them off and let them fall where they may. He looked for her tennis shoes and found those missing as well as her boots. *What the hell,* he thought as he turned off the closet light. He had no intention of searching her clothes because he had no idea of what all she owned. He was always teasing her about how she really needed a big closet just for her own use. They even talked about adding another. His inspection of the bathroom turned up only her toothbrush and a few other essentials missing.

What the hell, he thought again. Taking out his phone, he pulled up Lauren's number. While the call was going through, he returned to his perch at the kitchen counter and the note she'd left.

"Hello?" Lauren's voice came up on the other end. He frowned. Usually, she saw his name on the caller ID and had some smartass comment that served as a greeting. Her simple "hello" told him that something was different.

"Lauren, what's going on," he didn't even put it to her as a question to be answered. "I know you know, so don't dick around with me. Where's Julia?"

He heard a deep breath on the other end. It was obvious that Lauren was deciding how much or what to tell him. Surely the two had worked all of that out beforehand.

"Well? I'm waiting and not too patiently," Austin's voice was angry.

"Ok, Ace, give me a minute to collect my thoughts here," Lauren began.

"You mean, give me a minute to make up a story," Austin interrupted. "This isn't funny. Julia's been sick for days, she won't tell me anything, and now I come home to find that she's taken off 'for a few days' she says. That's it. She didn't tell me where or why. Just 'it's nothing to do with you' and 'please don't worry.' What the hell is going on?"

"Austin, read me the note," Lauren waited.

He sighed and said, "Okay." Lauren could hear him breathing on the other end and was about to say something when he said, "Here's all she wrote: 'Austin, I'm sorry. Something has come up and I need to get away for a few days. I promise it's nothing to do with you, but I have to have some alone time, time to think. I do love you—please don't worry.' She signed it 'Jules' and that's all. What is this shit? Do you know?"

He heard Lauren let out another deep breath before she began. "Austin, I could feed you a line of bullshit, but I know you'd never go for it. Suffice it to say that she *is* okay and that she *will* be home soon. As to where she is, she didn't tell me. She said that I couldn't be trusted with that because you'd get it out of me. She's right, you know."

"Okay, but why? You know that, don't you?"

"Yes, I do, but that isn't for me to tell, Austin. That's her information. She'll talk when she's ready."

She listened to a string of swearing that made her smile. *Well, well, well, I didn't know that he knew so many colorful words,* she thought. She almost said it out loud but with the foul mood he was in, she figured he'd let loose on her. Then they'd have a big fight over the phone, and this shouldn't be about them.

"Call Sharon, maybe she knows," Lauren knew this was low, but Sharon could deal with him better than she could.

"Oh, I intend to do just that, Blondie," he growled at her. "And if she calls you, tell her that I am *not* okay with this stupid shit and that she needs to call me. Immediately."

"Will do," Lauren said brightly. She knew that sing-song tone always pissed him off and sure enough her phone beeped to let her know the call was ended. Lauren leaned back in her chair and thought about what Julia had told her. She was going away for a few days, and could Lauren cover until she got back. Then something hit her.

"Good god, she wouldn't do that, I don't think," Lauren wasn't sure, but she knew that to Julia, this baby was already dead because she'd said as much. "I've got to call her. Try to find out where she is." Lauren punched in Julia's number but it went directly to voice mail. "Damn!" Lauren got up to pace in front of her desk. "Dammit!" She tried Sharon's number next, but after a couple of rings, it, too, went to voice mail. This time she left a message. "Sharon, I'm afraid our girl might be off doing something stupid. Please call me when you get this." Lauren was ready to head out herself when the shop's phone rang. She stared at it a couple of seconds before answering. *Someone has to mind things here,* she thought as she picked up the receiver. "Touch of Jules," she said brightly. Lauren could hide her feelings with the best of them.

Sharon's phone buzzed, and she looked at the caller ID. Well, she thought. That didn't take long.

"Hey, Austin, what's up?" she answered brightly.

"Don't mess with me, Sharon," he was not happy. "Why has Julia taken off like a teenage girl running away from home? Huh? What's the deal? She wouldn't do anything without telling you, and Lauren as much as said that you know."

Sharon frowned and thought about how she'd deal with Lauren siccing Austin on her. She took a deep breath. "Sweetheart, why don't you come over and let's talk." Before he could interrupt, Sharon continued, "I do know where she is. I do know what she's doing. I do know why. Now, I'm not sure how much of that I'll share with you, but come over and we'll discuss it. Ok?"

He answered almost immediately. "I'll be there in fifteen minutes." Sharon looked at her dead phone and shook her head. *Stupid, stupid, stupid*, she thought. *Is anybody an adult these days?*

Less than fifteen minutes later, she heard a car pull up front. She didn't even make it to the front door when she heard him pounding on it.

"Hold on, for heaven's sake," she said as she opened the door. "Don't knock it down, kiddo." Austin stood there frowning at her. He brushed past Sharon and came into the house. He walked through the living room, the dining room, and started for the bedrooms, when Sharon stopped him.

"She's not here." He stopped and turned toward Sharon's voice. "Her car isn't hiding in the garage, and she's not here. Sit down and let's talk."

They had no more seated themselves on the sofa, when Austin began plying Sharon with questions. She held up her hand and silenced him.

"Now, I told Julia that I would not lie to you, and I won't. But before you go tearing out of here looking for her, hear me out." Austin nodded his agreement, and she continued. "Julia is upset right now. She's had a shock and I really do think that she'll be okay in a few days. At least, that's all the time I'm giving her. She needs to think some things through before sharing them with you, some notion of protecting you or something equally stupid." She looked at his worried expression and put a hand on his arm. "Aw, honey, she's all right, really. If this were something life threatening, I'd have already beaten you to her." Sharon smiled encouragingly at him. "Maybe she needs time alone, maybe she doesn't. That isn't my call. But let's talk, and then if you still want to go to her, I'll tell you all you need to know. Deal?" He nodded again. "Now, how much do you love her?"

"What?" Austin looked as confused as he felt. "That's a dumb question. She's my partner. My everything. My life. Why do you ask? Has something happened to come between us? I can't believe there'd be someone else because that isn't who she is, and besides, I'd know." He wrinkled his forehead in confusion. "I don't think it's her folks or mine because I know that she doesn't really give a damn about what any of them think." He shook his head and leaned toward Sharon. "Sharon, I've been listening to her getting sick every night now for a couple of weeks. Every night, we go to bed and she's fine, and every night she sneaks out to the hall bathroom. I stood outside the door and listened to her throwing up, and I did nothing. She always says that she doesn't want anyone around when she's sick, and I respect that." He looked up at the ceiling. "Maybe I shouldn't have. I should have just barged in and found out what's wrong with her. I keep thinking she has some disease or something." He looked back at Sharon. "She's okay you said. Are you sure? I'm having the stupidest thoughts of what's wrong with her. And why the hell did she just take off? If I wasn't so worried, I'd be super pissed off right now. Who the hell just runs off, anyway?"

"My thoughts exactly!" Sharon was exasperated herself. "I told her I wouldn't lie to you. Ask me a question, any question."

Austin thought a moment. "Where is she?"

Sharon grinned at him. "Flagstaff. I gave her the key to our house up there, and she left early this afternoon."

"Do you know why she left?"

"Yes, she's thinking some things through before she shares them with you." His puzzled look turned to a frown.

"Last one. Does she still love me? Does this have anything to do with our relationship?"

"No, sweetie, she still loves you more than ever. And I've now said more than I should have, but I don't agree with her methods."

Austin stood up and hugged the small woman, picking her up until she swatted him and demanded he put her down. Before he could run out, Sharon stopped him.

"Austin, before you go, please keep in mind that Julia hasn't had an easy road here. She still has some scars and wounds that haven't completely healed. I know that you're mad at her for all this silly keeping-quiet-and-running-off business, but be patient. She thinks she's doing it for you." Sharon said this last softly, letting it sink in.

Austin came back and kissed the older woman on the cheek. "I know. I'll take care of her, I promise." He left, closing the door softly behind him.

Sharon stood there for a few moments before she picked up the phone to let security know that a black Mustang with a young blond-headed driver should be allowed through.

For a forty-year-old woman, she thought, *my girl can be really dumb sometimes.*

Austin didn't even return home, but instead took off on the two and a half hour drive. He was still upset, but now he was getting irritated. *There's no reason why she's doing this*, he thought. *And really no reason why I'm chasing after her. If she wants to go, let her.* Now that he knew there was nothing physically wrong with her, he was getting irritated. His mouth was set in an angry line as he hit Highway 17 and turned north. The desert road stretched out ahead of him, and Austin hit the gas, cruising around eighty-five miles per hour. Driving always gave him time to think, and as the miles passed, he started second-guessing what he was doing. Not quite an hour into the trip, he pulled into a gas station/convenience store parking lot and stopped.

What am I really doing? he wondered. *She asked for time, and that's what I should give her. Hell, if she wanted me to come running, she would have asked me to. She's not a little girl. She can take care of herself.* The car was idling as he sat for a few minutes more. Finally, Austin put the car into gear and pulled back out onto the highway. He dialed Julia's number and this time when it went to voice mail, he left a message. "I love you. Call me." He then called Sharon's number and when she picked up, he kept it short.

"Sharon, are you sure she's okay?"

"Sweetie, John and I are checking on her as we speak," Sharon assured him. Austin didn't question the *how* of that one. He knew they had cameras and security pretty much everywhere.

"Okay. Thanks." He ended the call and hit the gas. He might not have time to get any yard work done before dark, but at least he'd sleep in his own bed.

Chapter 36

JULIA HAD ARRIVED AND AS she walked through the empty house, she began to wonder what she was doing there. She'd driven through a fast food restaurant and picked up a salad for her supper, but that was hours away. She changed clothes and took a walk down the path that led to the mountain views and sat down on the hard rock. Breathing in the clean mountain air, she began to feel a bit better. *Funny,* she thought, *how this place makes me feel better. All I need is a bench. This rock isn't too comfortable.* Julia smiled for the first time since she'd left the doctor's office. That felt good, too. She stayed until the air turned cooler before she started back to the house. The emptiness surrounded her as she set out her salad and fixed herself a big glass of water. She'd found one of her favorite books, *To Kill a Mockingbird,* and stretched out on the sofa to read.

Around ten or so, she decided to go to bed and try to rest but changed her mind. Julia couldn't face sleeping alone in the big bed. Memories of the time she and Austin had stayed there wouldn't let her rest. Turning on all of the lights in the downstairs rooms, Julia found herself wandering from room to room. It was too quiet. She made herself a cup of hot tea and turned on the television, but nothing held her interest. She turned that off and put on some music. Not in the mood for anything upbeat, she smiled when she found Sharon's soundtrack from *Phantom of the Opera.* Julia turned up the volume and the mournful music filled the air. Sipping her hot tea, she snuggled deeper into her blanket. She'd turned on the gas fireplace and the flames danced up as heat poured from the registers on each side. Julia looked down at her still-flat stomach and moved her hand to rest on the area just below her waist.

I guess you're still okay in there, huh? She smiled at she talked to her stomach. *But for how long? A week? A month? We just don't know, do we?* She gazed back into the fire and a tear rolled down her face. *If only I could be sure that you'll still be here, that we'll make it to the end. I'd shout you to the mountaintops, little one. But we just don't know.* She absently stroked the area that held the little life. *You know, this really does feel different. It's like Lauren said, we don't have any pressure to perform, do we?* Her hand continued to move slowly back and forth. *I just wish I knew what your daddy would say. If I knew that he'd not be angry or upset...really, no one else's opinion matters but his.* She looked up like she'd just thought of something else. *And if he is, then he'll either get over it or not, won't he? Maybe I'm just being silly, or should I say stupid like Grandma Sharon says.* Julia laughed at the Grandma Sharon image. She looked down and spoke out loud.

"Well, baby, you and I will just find out, won't we? We'll go home tomorrow and break the news." She sighed. "Regardless of how he reacts, we're not alone, are we? We've got Aunt Lauren, Grandma Sharon, Grandpa John, Grandpa Lawrence, and of course, each other. Yep, we're going to face this mess together. And whatever happens, I'll deal. Your mama's stronger than most people give her credit for, you know." Julia looked up and rolled her eyes. "Sometimes she just doesn't act like it." She curled up on her side then and the warmth of the fire and the blanket pulled her down into sleep.

Austin wasn't sleeping himself. He lay down on the bed, but it was too empty and *big*. He looked across the expanse where Julia usually slept and shook his head. *Why she insists on this big-ass bed is beyond me*, he thought. *Maybe it isn't.* He smiled as he thought about her and how they'd used all of the bed during their lovemaking, but the smile faded. He got up quickly and went into the den. Stretching out in his big chair, he turned on the television and reclined the seat. ESPN was always on, but he couldn't focus on the talking heads. *They are such know-it-alls*, he thought, flipping the stations. He finally found the western channel, and Clint Eastwood's face filled the screen. *Unforgiven*, he thought. *Nope, not tonight.* He couldn't deal with watching one of their favorite movies, not without Julia. He finally tuned in an oldies station and let the music from the surround sound fill the room. Bonnie Raitt's raspy voice was singing about a heartache, and Austin could relate to the music. *Nothing but heartache is the truth*, he thought. *I wish I knew what the hell's going on with Jules. She's never acted like this before. She's always reasonable and ready to face whatever's in front of her. At least, she's always been that way since I've known her.*

He thought back over their conversations, the big ones where both of them bared their souls, so to speak. *The only thing I can ever think of that freaked her out was when she talked about her marriage to Keith. Even then, she wasn't really upset until she told me about the miscarriages. That was a rough time for her, I know.* He remembered her stricken look and the lines that had appeared on her face as she told him about the loss of not one but three babies. *Hell, not even dealing with her mother or mine does that to her. Send her running off.*

His thoughts wandered but kept coming back to the night when they'd talked about her past. She cried, still, when she talked about losing the babies, especially the last one. *She was so afraid to tell me that I'd never be a dad, and I always hope I'd let her know that it's her I want, and not what she can or can't give me. And I know that it can't possibly be another man. There's absolutely no way…but what would send her off the deep end? Upset her enough to act like a silly girl?* He sat thinking if there had been anything lately, besides her being sick every night, that would have her distance herself from him. Suddenly, he sat up straight and looked around.

Holy shit! It hit him. *Naw, she wouldn't run away because of that, would she? Besides, she told me a baby is impossible. Or is it?* He thought back over the weeks. It had been close to a couple of months since she'd had a period and even then they laughed about her being so sporadic. Morning sickness? Nothing there that he could remember. *Dammit!* he thought. *I wonder if women can get sick in the evening? Or at night?* He could still hear her retching behind the closed bathroom door. *And what if she almost passed out not because she needed a drink of water, but because something else is going on.* He stood and paced around the room. *I feel so stupid right now. I can think of nothing else in this world that can upset Julia like babies can. Jesus, is that it?* His phone was lying on the table beside his chair. He'd kept it with him all evening just in case she called. The number he dialed now wasn't Julia's.

"What?" a sleepy voice answered. "This better be good…"

"Lauren, wake your ass up. We're gonna talk." Austin would drive over if he had to, and he knew where Julia kept an extra key to Lauren's apartment, the one the two had shared.

"What the hell, Austin, do you know what time it is?" Lauren hated to be awakened, and she usually turned her phone off at night. She'd left it on in case Julia needed her. She didn't expect Austin to call.

"Yeah, I know exactly what the fuck time it is, it's time for you answer something for me," he wasn't going to lose it on her, but he was close. Lauren heard it in his voice.

"Okay, okay, let me wake up here," he could hear her moving around, probably walking around and collecting her thoughts, or trying not to disturb some poor bastard she was sleeping with that night. "All right, what's your question."

He took a deep breath before starting. "Julia tells you absolutely everything, doesn't she?"

"Sweet baby Jesus, Junior, you wake me up to ask me something so freakin' obvious?"

"Just answer, please."

"Yes, we tell one another pretty much everything. Although I still don't know how big your dick is, but that's for another conversation."

"Shut up. I'm serious here, Lauren."

Any time he used her name, Lauren knew Austin was not kidding, nor was he in the mood to joke. "Ok, sorry. Shoot."

"Is Julia pregnant?"

The silence on the other end of the call stretched out from seconds into a minute. Finally, Lauren spoke.

"Why do you ask?"

"Stop stalling. A question for a question will get us nowhere. Now let me ask again. Do I need to speak slower for you?"

"No, no you don't. Austin, that really isn't something that I can discuss with you. You need to ask Julia that question, you know?"

Austin leaned back in his chair. "I don't have to. I can tell by your voice that I've hit the nail on the head. Julia's going to have a baby, isn't she?"

Lauren said nothing on her end. *Thank god, he isn't an idiot.*

"But why would she take off?" Austin continued. "Why not just sit down and tell me that we need to talk? I don't get it."

Lauren thought before she spoke. "Austin, this is Julia we're talking about here. She's a very independent woman who's fought hard for that, you know. She leans on herself first and others second. Oh, I've jumped in to defend her as have Sharon and John, but honestly, she doesn't need it. You saw her handle that skank Audra. That's our Julia." He heard Lauren sigh before continuing. "As to why she took off, well, she probably needs to collect her thoughts before she approaches you. Whatever's going on, and I did NOT tell you anything and don't say that I did. Whatever's going on, she'll tell you in her own time, okay? Trust her, that's all." Lauren could almost hear him sigh as he took in what she'd said.

Finally, he spoke. "Okay, I'll give her some time, but not much. Are you sure she's okay, Lauren? I mean, you've been through this with her before. Is she doing all right?" The worry in his voice made Lauren smile.

"Yeah, Junior, she's all right. This isn't like any other time in her life, and I'm still not telling you anything here, but she said that this feels different. You and I both know Julia and her feelings about things. Hey, Ace?" Lauren paused, "Don't be mad because she took off. Getting all pissy is something Keith would have done, and believe me when I tell you that man had as much to do with Julia's problems as anything physical." Lauren knew the mention of Keith's name would get Austin's attention. He snarled at any comparison regardless of how minor. She smiled when he spoke.

"Yeah, like I'd be anything like that son-of-a-bitch," his voice changed. "I'll let her have her time and tell me when she's ready. How's that?"

"Good boy," Lauren was back to teasing him. "You just might make a good grown-up after all."

"Yeah, but I'll grow up someday. You'll always be a blonde."

"Good night, Junior."

"Night, Blondie."

Austin laid his phone on the table and leaned back in his chair again. *A baby. What the hell,* he thought. *Not that I'd mind that much, but wow. I'd already made up my mind that a good dog is all we need around here.* He smiled. *I guess now I'll have to go with one that's kid friendly.* He still wasn't sleepy, but Austin knew work would come early. He set the alarm on his phone, turned on *Unforgiven* and watched the rest of the movie. He hoped that Julia would be true to her word and come home soon, or now. He wondered how she'd tell him and if he should let her know that he'd figured her out. *Tomorrow morning I'll call Sharon*, he thought. *I can't let her think I'm a complete dumbass.* He chuckled and turned back to the television. His favorite part was coming up. *Deserves got nothin' to do with it.* He smiled. *Boy, ain't that the truth. I'm a lucky bastard.*

Chapter 37

Wᴴᴇɴ Jᴜʟɪᴀ ᴏᴘᴇɴᴇᴅ ʜᴇʀ ᴇʏᴇs, the sun was streaming in through the patio windows, and she had to think for a moment before she realized where she was. The fireplace was still going, and she realized that was probably all that kept the house from being cold. In the mountains, the nights could drop down to freezing temperatures, and as Julia stood by the window and looked out over the back yard and the mountains in the distance, she saw patches of frost here and there. She turned back to wash up and start her day. Finished, she made her way into the kitchen and a glimpse into the fridge showed her that the house was definitely unoccupied. In a cupboard, she found several brands of herbal tea, so it wasn't long before she was sipping her favorite chamomile. She stood in front of the big window in the front room and felt a calm she hadn't enjoyed for weeks. Finished with her tea, she rinsed her cup, slipped on a hoodie and boots, and headed out for a short walk. The air still held a chill, but the sun was warm as she made her way down the worn path. John and Sharon owned at least ten acres of ground, and they had carved out a walking path that meandered around trees, across a small stream and finally came out on a bluff that overlooked Mount Humphreys and the surrounding mountains. This was the path she'd taken the day before.

Julia sat down on the smooth rock and took out her phone. She saw that she'd missed phone calls from Lauren, Sharon, and Austin, and that she had several text messages. Deciding that she wasn't quite ready to deal with all of them yet, she slid the phone back into her pocket. Pulling her knees up to her chin, she wrapped her arms around her legs and closed her eyes.

The air is so fresh up here, she thought, *and listen to the quiet. Funny saying—listen to the quiet.* She smiled and let her head fall back so that the sun shone full on her face. The worries of the previous day and night seemed so far away. *Up here, I feel as if anything is possible,* she thought. *I can accomplish anything and control my own destiny. It's a good feeling that I've worked hard to find.* She stayed for several minutes before her growling stomach made her realize that she hadn't eaten. She laughed and said out loud, her voice echoing in the surrounding woods, "Eating for two now. That's such a stupid saying made up by women who don't mind packing on the pounds." Julia wasn't one of them and probably wouldn't gain a lot even if she could do so easily. Her mother was slender, and she'd inherited that gene from her.

At the thought of her mother, Julia started to tense up. *Stop,* she scolded herself. *She isn't here, nor will she be. It's just you, your little one, and the people who really love you.* Julia didn't want to think of her dad just yet, either. She'd tell him eventually, but not until she had things figured out, and especially not until she was much further along. She had no intention of letting Austin say anything to his family, either. *No use getting everyone's hopes up for nothing,* she thought. *I've been there and done that.*

Her stomach growled at her again, and she rose for one last look at the scenery and to take a few more deep breaths of the morning air before turning back toward the house. As she approached, Julia saw something sitting on the front porch. She frowned and wondered who had been there as she cautiously approached. Werner's Food Mart was in bold letters on the bag, and the small, white Styrofoam cooler that it sat on was emblazoned with the same. She smiled—Sharon. Who else would have groceries delivered right to her door. She carried her packages into the kitchen and set them on the counter. The bag held bread, a bag of chips, a box of Raisin Bran, and a package of Julia's favorite chocolate chip cookies. Inside the cooler she found milk, fruit, lettuce, ham, cheese, and eggs. She smiled again. Not enough to last more than a couple of days, but good for this one and probably the next.

In no time, Julia had whipped up a ham and cheese omelet and was washing it down with milk. She opened the huge bottle of prenatal vitamins she'd picked up before leaving town, and breaking the foil seal, looked down at the pills. Huge was the only word she could think of to describe them. Big, ugly, yellow, nasty pills. She shrugged her shoulders and dug one out. Popping it into her mouth, she washed it down with more milk.

"Uh," she spoke out loud and snarled her nose. "I really don't like milk. I need to buy some Hershey's syrup to drown out the white."

Finished, she washed up the few dishes and sat down on the sofa. Time to get the phone calls and messages out of the way. She chose Sharon's first. Hitting the voice mail button, Sharon's bright voice filled the room.

"Morning, Glory! You'll find that I've had a little something delivered to you early this morning. Not a lot, but enough for a couple of days. All you'll need. Austin was here and I told him that you're all right. I also told him where you are. He was almost beside himself, sweetie, but he decided to give you your space for now. Jules, don't take too long. He needs you and you sure as hell need him. Call him! Call me! Love you!" Julia sighed and skipped to Lauren's voice.

"Austin is driving me freaking nuts! Calls in the night. Chewing me out because I won't tell him what he wants to know. He's worried Jules. Hell, *I'm* worried. Call him. Call me. Please! Love you, weirdo." She smiled as Lauren's voice echoed in the room. Her smile faded as she looked at Austin's name and the unheard message from him. She took a deep breath and hit the play button.

"Hey, Jules," his voice sounded strained. "I'll be here when you come home. I love you. Call me." She heard his voice catch on that last part, and her eyes filled with tears. Julia knew that she wasn't being fair to him, but she simply wasn't ready to face him yet. She needed to decide how to handle the situation herself, and then she'd be ready to share with him.

Instead of a phone call, Julia decided to text everyone and check in. To Sharon, she thanked her for the groceries and the use of the house, and she assured her that she'd be back in Scottsdale no later than the next day. To Lauren, she apologized for putting her in the middle of yet another relationship. She also had a few instructions for things at the office, and she signed off with the promise of being back the next day.

Her message to Austin was more difficult. She knew that he was upset. *Hell*, she thought, *I'd be upset, too.* She smiled. *No, I'd be pissed.* After a few minutes, she started typing in his message:

Hey, Austin. I wanted to let you know that I'm fine and still here in Flagstaff. Please know that you aren't the reason I left. I had to get away for me. I'm starting to get my head together, and I plan on coming home no later than tomorrow. Sooner, maybe. I do love you. Please don't ever doubt that for a minute. We'll talk when I get back. Oh, and Lauren thinks we're both freaks. Love you!

She reread what she'd written before hitting the send button. It wasn't much of a message, but she had no intention of getting into anything serious in a text message. She'd heard of people doing the weirdest things in messages, and she'd always thought it to be a tacky way of communication, outside of the quick, unimportant note.

Finished, she went back out to the patio and stretched out on one of the lounge chairs. It had been so long since she'd slept an entire night, and her body was ready to catch up. The temperature was rising fast now that it was mid-morning, and the sun felt so good that she soon fell asleep. She didn't notice the security people make their rounds, mainly because they were trained to be unobtrusive. John had called the day before and his people had been keeping an eye on the house and its inhabitant ever since. She also didn't hear the little black car when it pulled into the front drive.

Austin had no more gotten out before a large man dressed in tan khakis and green jacket with Star Security Services stitched over the left breast approached him. Austin noticed the small handgun holstered on one side and radio attached to the other.

"Sir, may I ask your business here?" He didn't actually block Austin's way, but he stood in front of him, hands relaxed but crossed in front of his muscular body. *Relaxed attention*, Austin noted.

"Sure, I'm a friend of John Burns. He or his wife Sharon called the gate security, who let me through."

"One moment, please," and Mr. Security stepped back a few feet and radioed someone who answered immediately. Never taking his eyes off Austin, he nodded a couple of times, and signed off.

"Thank you, sir," he almost apologized. "We have our orders to check anyone who comes to the house. Have a nice day, sir." He walked off and almost melted into the trees.

Whoa, Austin thought. *That was different. John must have had his orders from Sharon No wonder she was so sure Julia was okay last night. She probably had hourly reports coming in all night.* He grinned and shook his head. *Overkill much? You'd think the Queen resided here.*

He started toward the front door, but something drew him around the rock wall and to the back patio. He saw her stretched out on the lounge chair with the sun streaming down on her. *God, she's beautiful,* he thought as he approached. Julia had no idea she was being watched or that anyone had come up. Austin was thankful now for John's tight security. *I should have known that as long as she's here, she's safe,* he thought. He sat on a patio chair that was facing Julia and studied her face. He could see those small lines beside her mouth, but other than that, she looked peaceful.

Jules, why wouldn't you tell me? He looked at her closer, but he could see nothing different about her. *Too soon, I know, but as slim as she is, surely she'll have a bump before long.* Austin had read all that he could on pregnancy the previous night, but he still felt totally out of his league. The entire situation was beyond him, but he intended to learn. He smiled at the thought. Now that he'd had some time to think about it, Austin found himself getting a little excited. He just wished she would share that excitement with him and stop worrying so much. *I suppose if I'd lived through what she's lived through, I'd worry, too,* he thought. He sat and watched her another thirty minutes or more before she finally stirred.

Julia opened her eyes and when she saw the man sitting in front of her, she jumped a bit before she realized who it was. When she did, a wary look crossed her face. She didn't know how Austin was feeling—angry, worried, agitated—and his face gave away nothing.

"Austin. I wasn't expecting anyone," she said as she started to sit up.

"Lay back, it's all good," he knelt beside her chair and gently pushed her shoulders back down. "I'm sorry, babe, but I couldn't stand not knowing what's going on with you. I was missing you. I couldn't concentrate on anything but you, so I thought what the hell and came on up." He looked at her questioningly to gauge her reaction.

Julia had never been so glad to see him. Her smile started in her eyes and soon lit up her face. "I had no idea that twenty-four hours could seem like a week. I'm glad you're here." She reached out to take his hand in hers and brought it to her lips. She leaned it against her cheek and held him there.

"I know. I felt really stupid driving up here, but I had to." He looked at her seriously now. "You ready to talk?"

Julia couldn't read his face, but she knew that it was now or never. She shook her head "yes" and sat up. They looked at one another for a few seconds before Julia was ready to begin. Austin saw that the little lines between her brows were pronounced as she looked at him. He thought about the self-imposed stress she'd put herself under and almost became angry. Not angry with her necessarily, but with the situation.

"Austin, I have something to tell you, but before I do I want you to know how very, very sorry I am." She paused, lowering her eyes as she tried to put her thoughts into words. Her eyes met his as she looked up and unconsciously squared her shoulders. "I deceived you. Well, I actually deceived myself and by association you, too. When I moved to Arizona, I thought I'd left so much behind, and I did. One of those things was a relationship. I was so finished with all of it." She paused for a second and looked out at the mountains. "I'd been burned pretty badly, and I had to learn how to be alone. How to stand alone. It took me a while, but I finally did. Then you came along." She looked back at him and smiled. "There you were, totally different from any man I'd ever been with before. So young, but mature. So handsome. So easy to be with, and to talk to. And best of all, thinking I'm such a catch," she chuckled. "It's no wonder that I fell in love with you so quickly. I suppose that's why I've always heard 'never say never' because you became my never." She smiled at him as she said this last. "When you returned my love, I couldn't believe it. To love and be loved like I have been with you is one thing I'd never experienced before." The smile faded, and her tone grew serious. "But when we entered into this, I had so many reservations and yes, not a few insecurities. I've gotten through them all until now." She paused and Austin almost held his breath as he waited for what she'd say next.

"I want you to know that I didn't plan any of this. What I'm about to tell you came as a shock to me as I know it will be to you. I mean, we had our lives all planned out, or so I thought." She laughed nervously. "Good grief! I haven't been this nervous in freakin' years!"

"Jules," Austin interrupted. "Before you say one more thing, I want to tell you something." He took her hand. "I never really thought about spending my life with anyone. I never thought about what my life would be like someday—wife, kids, house, none of that. But when I met you, and you actually gave me the time of day, I felt like someone had just handed me the world. With you, everything fell into place." He smiled. "Yeah, it's been a little less than a year, but I look at what we've built together in that short time, and I shake my head. I can't believe it." He leaned in toward her to emphasize what he wanted to say next. "I count my lucky stars every single day that I'm with you. I don't know what life will bring us, but I know that as long as we're together, it's all good, you know? It's all good, Jules."

He reached up to wipe the tear that was rolling down her cheek. She took a deep breath and squared her shoulders, a habit that he'd watched her perform any time she had something difficult to say or do.

"Austin, I haven't been honest with you. Yeah, I've been sick. But it isn't a bug, or whatever I've blamed." She paused and met his gaze. "I went to the doctor the other day, and received the biggest surprise I've had in, well, ever I suppose. At first, I thought it was the end of the world. That fate has played a really sick joke on me. But now I'm not so sure it's such a bad joke." He wished she'd just come out and say it, but he wasn't about to push her. Finally, she decided to put it out there. "Austin, we're going to have a baby." She shook her head and looked down. "I know, I know, I was positive that I could never get pregnant, but evidently I can. Now, whether or not I'll carry this baby to term...well, only time will tell us that. I am so sorry. I never intended for this to happen." She still wouldn't meet his gaze, and he could tell that she was struggling.

"Julia, listen, stop apologizing, please. Just, stop. You have nothing to be sorry for. This is life, babe, and life is unpredictable. And regardless of what you think, this is *not* a bad thing." Austin laughed then, stood up, and pulled her up with him. He picked her up and twirled her around, laughing the entire time. When he set her down, she was laughing with him. However, quickly she sobered.

"Austin, I don't think you know..."

"I know enough. And I will not let you sit around the next 7, 8, or whatever months, being all gloom and doom here. Hey, you're gonna be a mom! I'm gonna be someone's dad. Holy hell, Jules! Don't you think that's just a little bit awesome?"

She looked at his young animated face, and had to smile with him. *Yeah*, she thought, *it's gonna be okay I think. I think this is going to be fine.*

Austin reached out and smoothed the worry lines between her brows. As he massaged them out, he could feel her relaxing. When he thought they were gone, he pulled her up against him and held her. *God, she feels so good*, Austin thought, *and I will make this all right for her. At least, I'll do everything in my power.*

Julia pulled back and looked up at him. "Austin, we have a lot to talk about. Some decisions to make…"

"Yeah, we do, but not now. Not right this minute." He leaned down and kissed her. It started out soft and soon deepened into something much more. She ran her fingers through his hair and pulled him closer, leaning in so that their bodies molded together. Austin thought of the roving security team and pulled back. He grinned down at Julia. "Babe, unless we want a very interested audience, I suggest we take this inside."

"What?" she looked around. "What audience? There's no one here." She looked back at him and smiled before running her hand down his back. He caught her hand just before she moved it to the front.

"Babe, John has a security detail that rivals the White House. You can't see them, but they sure can see you."

Julia peered into the trees surrounding the yard, but saw no one. "Are you sure? I've been out here all morning, and I've not seen a soul. Not even when groceries were left on my doorstep."

"Trust me," Austin took her hand and started toward the glass doors.

Once inside, it didn't take them long to resume what they had started outside. Austin couldn't believe how good she felt as he reached under the thick sweatshirt and ran his hands on the soft skin. She was so warm, and he couldn't get enough of her. For her part, Julia's hands were equally busy. She had his shirt pulled out of his jeans and was running her hands across his chest, down his stomach, and farther still. He picked her up and carried her into the bedroom that they'd shared before. After laying her gently on the bed, he crossed over to the window and closed the drapes. In the darkened room, he came back to the bed and removed her boots and socks before moving his hands to unfasten her jeans. They slid easily down her hips and for a split second he wondered at how much weight she'd lost, noticing her slender hips were even more narrow. The thought was fleeting as he brought his thoughts back to the woman lying in front of him. She grinned at him before leaning up to pull the hoodie over her head and sling it in the direction of where her jeans lay on the floor. Now it was his turn to grin. Under the heavy shirt, she wore nothing but the Tar Heel tank top that he'd bought her on their trip to North Carolina. The small scrap of fabric that still covered her hips was a matching blue with the emblem emblazoned on the front. Austin raised an eyebrow in question.

"They made me think of you, babe," Julia said as she shrugged one shoulder. "And if memory serves me, they didn't stay on too long the last time I wore them either."

Austin's smile changed into the sexy half-grin he knew she loved, and he reached out to run a finger along the edge of the lace fabric. His finger continued as he traced the emblem and Julia caught her breath. He pulled back just long enough to strip off his own clothes and return to slip a finger along each side before sliding the fabric down her hips. He tossed the panties onto the pile. For the next few seconds, Austin stared down at Julia before he leaned over and placed a soft kiss on her stomach, right where the little life rested.

Julia laughed before she teased him. "Enjoy it now, pal, because if all goes well, you'll have a lot more area to kiss down there. It will take you a lot longer to cover." At his look, she sobered and blew him a kiss with her lips. One more soft kiss and his mouth traveled down farther. Julia caught her breath as his mouth took her, soon bringing her over the edge. When she could stand no more, she raised up, bringing him with her and kissed him deeply. With a swift move, she had him on his back and was returning the favor. All he could see was her dark hair as it trailed across his body, but he could feel. God, could he feel everything she was doing to him. When he felt himself on the edge, he pulled her up and onto him. They moved together, slowly at first, but as they found their rhythm both gave in to their bodies. He gasped her name just before they collapsed together. Her leg remained over his and she snuggled in under his arm. He stroked her hair as they caught their breath. Suddenly she felt him stiffen.

"Holy hell, Jules! Are you okay? I mean, is it okay, what we just did? Is the baby all right?" he started to raise up, but she held him down. He'd read all about it the night before, but now that he was with her, he couldn't think.

"Austin, it's fine, really. There isn't a thing we do that's going to hurt him, her, whichever." He still looked at her questioningly. "Honey, read up on it, okay? Sex is not going to bother this child one bit." She grinned. "Now, the lack of sex would bother his mother a lot. Don't let that happen, ok?" She felt him relax again.

"Sorry for the panic, babe. I'm the newbie here, you know. I'll trust you to let me know what we can or can't do. Deal?"

"Deal. Now, I haven't slept much lately, and I'm feeling very sleepy right now."

He could hear it in her voice. A quilt was lying at the foot of the bed, and Austin raised up to grab it and cover both of them. He hadn't slept much either. As they settled in against one another, Austin's arms tightened around Julia. He hoped she could feel how much he loved her as he listened to her breath become slower and deeper. *I had my doubts about coming up here, but I'm so glad I did*, he thought. "We're in this together, babe," he whispered before lightly kissing the top of her head and giving in to sleep himself.

A couple of hours later, Julia stirred and looked up at Austin, who was already awake. They grinned at one another, and she raised up to rest on his chest.

"Wow, I forgot how much sleep I need these first few weeks. What's your excuse?"

"Yeah, I live with this crazy, gorgeous woman who drives me insane sometimes. She interrupts my sleep every night when she hugs the toilet, and then she just runs off. It sure takes a toll on sleep."

As he finished that last, Julia made a sad face at him, her mouth curving down. "Poor baby. Maybe she'll break up with that toilet in a few more weeks and you'll have her all to yourself again." She sobered. "Austin, I had no idea that you knew. I tried to be as quiet as I could. I didn't want to worry you. And here I thought you were such a sound sleeper. No fair, you've been holding out on me."

"Hey, I was a sound sleeper until I found a new bed partner. She makes waking up worth it." He kissed her and reached up to smooth the hair back from her face. "You have no idea how hard it was to stand on the other side of that door, listening to you, not knowing what was wrong, and not being able to do anything about it. Jules," he was serious now, "promise me you won't do that again. I understand if you're sick and need to be alone, but don't shut me out. I want, no need, to know what's going on."

She sighed, "Oh, all right. I promise. But I will not wake you up every night so you can listen to me puke. Nope, not doing it. And why I have to get sick in the middle of the night is beyond me. I mean, who does that?" At her expression, he laughed.

"Hell if I know. I only know one pregnant lady." He looked at the clock on the bedside. "Speaking of pregnant ladies, I bet I have one who's getting hungry. I know I am."

Julia thought a couple of seconds and grinned. "Yep. I do believe I am. Wait until you see what Sharon had sent over. She's a such a mess! Just enough food to last me one, maybe two days." She laughed. "Thank god you came up here. She warned me that if she had to come get me that she wouldn't be happy. Have you ever seen Sharon not happy? Trust me, it's scary."

They both laughed at that and Austin got up to retrieve their clothes. He felt eyes on him and turned to see Julia looking at his back side. He tossed her jeans at her.

"Woman, you have the most lascivious look right now. I thought you were hungry."

"Oh, I am," she rose to her knees and pulled him back down with her. "I've been fasting the last couple of days, and it might take a lot to fill me up."

"I think I can help with that," Austin eased himself down on top of her. "I think I know exactly what you need."

When they finally got out of bed almost an hour later, Julia really was starved. She dressed quickly and headed for the kitchen. The package of cookies was lying on the counter, and she tore into it, popping one into her mouth while she took down a glass and grabbed the milk. She washed the first cookie down and had started on another when Austin came into the room. He took one look at her and started laughing.

"What's wrong with you?" Julia mumbled around the chocolate in her mouth. "Haven't you ever seen someone starving before?"

"Honey, I lived with Matt for years. I've seen worse. Just not coming from you. Better move your fingers quicker, or you'll pull back a nub."

"I'd say I'm sorry, but I'm not," Julia had washed the cookie down with more milk. She made a face at the glass and drank more.

"What's wrong? It isn't bad, is it?" Austin looked at the carton.

"No, I just don't think I like milk. Correction. I do not like milk, at all. Remind me to get some chocolate syrup, will you?"

Austin was making a ham and cheese sandwich and spoke over his shoulder. "Put it on my List of Pregnant Lady Preferences. You wanna sandwich or are you just going to eat the whole package of cookies?"

"Sandwich, please. And fruit. I need an apple."

Austin laughed at her as he piled the ham and lettuce onto bread for her. She'd never been afraid to eat in front of him, but her appetite was usually non-existent. *This could be fun*, he thought as he put an extra slice of cheese on top of the mountain of ham. *In lots of ways.*

"Hey, Jules, when do you want to go back?"

"Damn, I suppose we should leave this evening. I have so much to do at work, and I know you don't need to be taking days off right now." He grinned at her disappointed look. "Austin? You do know that I want to keep working, right?"

Austin frowned. "Uh, yeah, but I hadn't really thought about it. I just assume that you'll do what you want to do or feel like doing for as long as you want. Why?"

"Oh, nothing," she turned to the sink and washed her apple. "It's just that before, I always had to fight a battle to keep working." She looked at him. "You have no idea how much that means to me. Your trust. Your knowing that I won't do more than I feel like doing." She exhaled a short burst of air, almost a snort, and shook her head. "Wow, this is awesome." She grinned at him. "And I guess I'll let you take me away from here for now."

"Yeah, we both have responsibilities, don't we? I promise that I'll bring you back up here a lot this summer. Get you out of the heat and let Sharon baby you. And you know that she'll be all over that." They both laughed at the thought.

"Ok. I'll hold you to it. Hey, where are those chips?"

He laughed and tossed her the bag.

Chapter 38

———

"SHARON, YOU'RE SURE EVERYTHING'S OKAY? Julia was really struggling when she left, and I just don't want her to do something incredibly stupid, you know?" Lauren had been worried when Julia hadn't returned her call or text. She hoped her friend wouldn't do anything without thinking it over first, and especially without talking to Austin. "Her attitude was that losing this baby is a foregone conclusion and all she was doing was waiting for the inevitable. I don't want her to hurry that process along."

Lauren heard Sharon's laugh on the other end and frowned. This really wasn't a laughing matter, and Lauren was getting ready to tell her that.

"Lauren, don't worry sweetheart. John and I have been monitoring the house since she got there yesterday. She's gone nowhere and seen no one until this morning. Austin just arrived. By the way, you and I need to talk about your shoving him off onto me yesterday."

"Austin? How do you know all of this?" Lauren usually didn't question her friends' methods, but she wouldn't put it past them to have set up some monitoring or security or something. At Sharon's next words, Lauren shook her head and rolled her eyes.

"Well, first, John's people called him and second, I watched him drive up on live streaming. And don't tell me this is creepy shit. It's called technology and we use it, thank you very much."

"Sorry, but yes, it is creepy. Useful, but weird. I was imagining all sorts of stuff." Lauren's voice became serious. "I know how Jules gets in these dark places, and she was falling there fast."

"Well," Sharon assured her, "she'll be fine now. And I'll bet the Caddy that she'll be coming home with a smile either tonight or tomorrow."

Lauren laughed. "I'll take that bet! Only because I know where that car ranks." Lauren paused before adding, "Thank you, Sharon. You're a good friend, even if you do creepy things sometimes."

"You're welcome, dear. And never question the madness behind my methods. They're effective."

The two hung up and Lauren looked over at the empty desk. She'd come in early to cover what Julia had left. Her phone dinged, and she looked down to see a message from Julia. *Well, crap! She sent this thing an hour ago and I'm just now getting it?!* Lauren shook her head and opened the text. She read Julia's assurances that she was okay, jotted down the few instructions on her notepad, and wondered if Austin's arrival would delay her return. She hoped so only because the two would be completely uninterrupted at the mountain house.

Releasing a deep breath, she said out loud, "I'm burning daylight here," echoing one of Julia's favorite sayings. She pushed her reading glasses back up and started in. Work always made the day pass faster, and Lauren had plans for that night.

After cleaning up the mess in the kitchen, Austin looked at Julia and raised his brows in question.

"Well? Are we ready to head back? I really need to work tomorrow, and I'm sure you have stuff at the shop that needs you."

Julia sighed and shook her head. "Yeah, I suppose we need to. I could stay longer, but I know you've got to get back and I don't want to stay here without you." She laughed. "Even if I'm not really alone." She looked past him to the huge front window. "Are you sure there's men out there? I haven't seen a soul!"

Austin laughed. "Positive. If John hadn't given the okay, I'd be sitting in some locked room about now." At Julia's shocked look, he hugged her close. "It's all good, babe," he said over her head. "When you're rich, you can do things like hire guards and watch people over a camera feed."

Julia pulled back and looked up at him, her blue eyes wide. "What the hell? Seriously? You don't think cameras are in the *house*, do you?"

"Babe, they monitor their properties when no one is supposed to be here. I'm sure John can turn them off or on remotely. And you should know that he'd never invade your privacy. At least, not to that extent."

She looked around. "Creepy. Yeah, let's go." Julia was almost to the door of the bedroom when Austin called to her.

"Jules?" At her questioning look, he continued. "How big a secret are we keeping this? Only three people know besides us. I mean, it probably isn't a good idea to say anything until we make it through this first trimester." At her grin, he defended himself. "Yes, I read. I Googled pregnancy and babies and learned a lot. Well, not a lot, but enough for now. I had lots of time last night."

"Austin, I'm..." she started to apologize again, but he held up a hand and stopped her.

"We're not talking about that again. But I think we need to decide, don't you?"

Julia sighed and looked out the windows again, thinking. When she looked back, she said, "The only other person who may need to know is Matt, and that's simply because Lauren could easily let something out during pillow talk. But other than that, it's just our secret. *No* parents, okay?"

"Oh, hell, no! We can wait until the baby's born before telling them if you want to." She laughed at that and he grinned. He hadn't heard her laugh much lately, and it was good to hear again.

"We have time. Let me get my stuff together, and we'll start back." She stopped at the bedroom door. "Austin? I'm really glad you didn't listen to me and came up anyway. I didn't realize how much I needed you until I saw you. I know that I can be a pain sometimes, but I'll try to make this pregnancy a partnership, okay? I'm not really used to that, so bear with me. And remind me."

He winked and grinned. "Don't worry about that. I'll remind you every day if I have to."

She winked back and left to gather the small number of items she'd brought with her. Within five minutes, she was back and ready to go. They locked up and he walked her to the open garage door.

"Wish I could ask one of the green jackets to drive my car and we ride together. I love this drive with you in the car with me. Without you? Not so much."

Julia laughed. "You'll survive. I'll let you follow me if you want. That way you can watch my ass all the way down the highway. I know how you enjoy that!" she teased.

His response was to swat her on the behind and send her to the little red car. She backed out and Austin hit the button that closed the door. They were heading down the drive when he looked in his rearview mirror and saw a man in green standing in front of the closed house. He was talking into his radio. Austin chuckled and shook his head. "I wonder if John will know when we arrive home, too." Not wanting to think about that one too much, he hit the gas and pulled behind Julia. *Yeah, her little car has a nice rear, but nothing compared to hers,* he thought as they headed toward Highway 17 and home.

Chapter 39

———

ONCE AGAIN, LIFE SETTLED INTO a routine. Julia still got up in the middle of the night with morning sickness, and they joked about the name simply because she was up between one and three o'clock, technically morning. The bouts were getting better as she learned that drinking water before bed kept her stomach from being too empty. Nothing was worse than dry heaves. Austin still fought the urge to follow her and make sure she was okay, but Julia was adamant about that. "You'll get to see plenty later, sweetie. Let me enjoy this on my own," she'd tell him when he'd start to get up with her.

The days turned into weeks, and summer was in full swing. Julia found that she didn't take the heat as well as she usually did, and it was only in the evenings that she and Austin would enjoy their pool. Most weekends they'd head to Flagstaff and stay with John and Sharon, who babied her incessantly. Julia had seen her doctor in July, and Dr. Roberts had seen nothing unusual. The baby's heartbeat was strong and when Julia and Austin heard it that first time, they both had tears in their eyes. Austin couldn't get enough of the sound and even recorded it on his phone. Julia laughed at him, but he couldn't have cared less. She was relaxed and having fun once she decided that the chips would fall where they may. Lauren and Sharon were right about there being no pressure, and Julia was settling into her role easily.

The first time she felt movement, she was sitting at her office desk. She knew that soon she'd feel that flutter, and as she leaned over to look at some new designs, she felt it. Just that small butterfly-wing feeling that most women would overlook, but Julia knew exactly what it was. She sat back quickly and looked around for Lauren, remembering that she was out on a job. Julia started to call Austin, but he, too, was working and she stopped herself before disturbing him. She waited, but felt nothing more until she once again leaned over the desk. There it was! Julia patted the tiny bump and laughed out loud. That evening, Austin sat with his hand on her stomach, but what he was waiting for, Julia didn't know.

"Babe, you can't feel it, not yet. And it's so small that I can barely tell," Julia grinned at his excitement.

"Yeah, I know, but I want him to know I'm here, too," Austin looked at her, his eyes shining. "And later on I'll do all kinds of things to make my presence known." He was involved in every aspect with her, as he wanted to wipe away all the bad memories she had of the past. So far, it was all good. Sometimes when he thought about it, Austin felt like everything was going *too* well, but he shook off the feeling. Not going to worry Jules, he thought. We're going to enjoy this whole experience. He knew that she'd worry at least some until they passed another milestone and still another. They both were concerned that her age would contribute to a premature birth, but Dr. Roberts was optimistic since Julia was in such good health, and the baby was growing on schedule. She wasn't gaining much weight, but the doctor assured them that would change farther down the line.

August arrived and they celebrated Austin's birthday in Flagstaff with just the six of them—John, Sharon, Lauren, Matt, Julia, and Austin. Matt had taken the news of the baby as Austin had expected. One "holy shit" followed by "what the hell, Austin" and he had moved on. Matt was far from ready for the settling down part of life, but if his friend was happy, no big deal. He just hoped they knew what they were getting into. "Anything that smells that bad at both ends isn't for this guy," he'd later told Lauren. She'd laughed at him and let him know that he could smell pretty bad at both ends himself. They were still comfortable with their relationship, if they called it that, and while neither dated other people, they weren't a couple either. They still considered one another a friend with benefits and let it go at that.

The birthday weekend had gone well except Matt and Lauren grew a bit bored. Entertainment consisted of eating, drinking, and talking about the baby. Saturday evening found them sitting on the patio, and as usual Sharon and Julia were talking about the nursery while John and Austin talked about the benefits of Austin adding another room downstairs rather than sell so soon to get a house that would be better for their family. Matt and Lauren were quiet, not joining in on either conversation.

"I swear, if I hear one more baby comment, I'm going to throw myself off a cliff," Matt growled in Lauren's ear. She grinned at him. While Lauren was excited for Julia and Austin, she didn't share in the whole baby excitement. In fact, all she'd seen before was Julia being manipulated and used all in the name of babies. That was until now. Austin was a champ as far as Lauren was concerned, but as much as she loved her friend, she didn't share her enthusiasm. She'd always declared the maternal gene had passed her by, thank god.

"Matt and I are heading out for a bit. Don't wait up for us," Lauren spoke to the group. She took Matt's arm, and led him out to her car. Matt loved to get behind the wheel of her little white Lexus IS. After driving his big Jeep, Matt enjoyed the sports car. It was both a hard top and a convertible, but Lauren usually had the top up on the highway simply because she didn't like her hair mussed. In town, she'd put it down to see and be seen. The August temperature was perfect and Matt immediately rolled down the windows and hit the button. As he watched the hard top fold itself down into the trunk, he grinned at Lauren. He loved playing with all the gadgets and she always let him. He was programming the navigation system, looking for entertainment, when she put a hand on his and stopped him.

"Just drive, babe," she ordered.

Matt looked over at her, slipped his Oakleys on, put the car in gear, and hit the gas, propelling her back into her seat. She shook her head, pulled on her sunglasses in the late afternoon sun, and grabbed a handful of her hair. Such a big kid, she thought as she watched him shift gears and spin the tires on the lane that led to the highway. He slowed down past the security booth, but as soon as he turned onto the county road, he hit the gas.

"Where to?" he shouted over the road noise.

"Into town," Lauren directed. "I'll guide you through once we get there." She sat back and looked at the scenery. The pines rushed past them as Matt accelerated. He loved taking the curves as fast as possible. His Jeep didn't allow him to. They followed Business 40 and soon Lauren had him turn onto Beaver Street. Here they would find several restaurants and bars, many with catchy themes. She guided him into a parking spot in front of the Black Bear Brewery. They could hear music pouring from speakers facing the street, and Lauren grinned at Matt as he helped her from the car. They entered the casual dining room and skirted it to the bar area located on the opposite side. Matt could smell pizza, and even though he wasn't hungry, he found himself wondering if it tasted as good as it smelled. Before he could say anything to Lauren, she'd led him outside where a band was set up and tables surrounded a small dance floor. A waitress led them to a table, took their order, and left them.

"How did you find this place, Blondie?" Matt sat back and looked around at the crowd and the musicians, who were obviously on a break. They mingled with those sitting at the front tables, and their laughter carried across the floor.

"Oh, on one of my excursions. I can only take so much domestic bliss and I'm ready to scream. Not that I don't love Sharon and John and spending time with them. I just get a little bored." Lauren crossed her long legs clad in denim shorts, and Matt watched her. He followed from her wedge heels, up the long tanned expanse of her legs, to the white tank top that was fully stretched across her chest, and finally to her smiling mouth. She was watching him watching her, and she chuckled before turning her attention elsewhere. "I'm glad you're here with me, Matty."

She still called him Matty, or Junior, or Ace, or any one of several pet names. It didn't bother him anymore, but she either didn't notice or didn't care. He leaned toward the latter.

"Me, too, Duchess," he had taken to calling her that simply because it seemed to fit. "If I hear the word *baby* one more time, I might smash something myself. Hell, we're months away from it even making an appearance, and they all act like it's the second coming or something."

Lauren laughed at his disgusted expression and leaned over to pat his arm. "Calm down, Slugger. It will soon be over. Then you get to hear about every burp, smile, pee, and shit." She laughed again as he rolled his eyes in an "oh shit" manner. "Oh, sweetie," she assured him, "it ain't all that bad. Who knows? You might get ideas yourself."

"Ah, hell, no, not this guy. I am far from anything remotely domestic, or haven't you noticed," he grinned at her.

"Yeah, I've noticed, and that's the only reason I let you hang around. At the first sign of serious, I'm out," Lauren finished as the waitress returned with their drinks. Matt was trying out one of the Lumberyard ales and Lauren had opted for her usual, vodka and tonic. He was quiet as he took the first drink and looked at the bottle. *Good stuff,* he decided, and turned his thoughts back to what she'd just said. Lauren never talked about men or what she wanted in a man except for when she was "instructing" him, which she did less and less. He wondered how much he could learn tonight about the woman.

"Yeah, I've noticed," he gave her a smirking grin. "You make that clear all the time." He leaned back then, still looking at her. "Why is that, Blondie? Are you afraid of getting burned?"

One eyebrow shot up as Lauren took in his question. "Seriously? You think that *I'm* afraid of getting burned? Junior, I haven't been burned, as you put it, in a very, very long time." She leaned toward him, exposing more of her cleavage. "In fact, I'll bet it's safe to say that I haven't been burned since you were in diapers." She liked to remind him once in a while just how old she was. He noticed that it was when she was making a point about something. What that point was now, he didn't know.

"You keep track, huh?" he teased her. "Are you sure you can remember back that far?"

Lauren sat back and crossed her legs, knowing he couldn't resist watching. "Honey, I remember everything about my love life." She smiled and winked. "Everything…"

Matt laughed. He could laugh with her and at her now. She could come across as many things—sexy, bitchy, even nice—and now that he'd seen most of her sides, he didn't take her moods as personally as he once had. The only side he had yet to see was a vulnerable side. He doubted anyone but Julia would be allowed in for that one, and even she didn't see it often.

"Yeah, I can't say the same," Matt took another long drink and looked out over the room. Several single females were scattered at different tables, and more than one tried to make eye contact. The man who would have at one time scoped them out and picked one for the night, now found that he wasn't that interested in sex with a stranger. *Damn*, he thought, *when did that happen?* He gave his own answer. *Probably around the time you started hanging around with this one.* He looked at Lauren. She certainly had introduced him to a whole new world in the bedroom. The woman knew what she was doing, and she had upped his game considerably. She caught him staring.

"What?" she frowned. "Is my hair a mess? What?"

Matt laughed. "No, Duchess, your hair is fine. I was just thinking about us, about the last few months. And I was thinking that I've had one hell of a good time with you."

Lauren winked and smiled. "Yeah, I've enjoyed you, too, Matty." She reached out to where his hand rested on the table between them. She laid hers over his and squeezed his fingers. They sat in companionable silence for a few minutes.

"Lauren?"

"Yeah, Matt?" She looked at him, wondering what was on his mind.

He was thinking about how to say it, but finally decided a direct approach with her was best.

"Lauren, where do you see us going? You know, how long do you think we'll keep this up?" He sat back, almost embarrassed. "Shit, that was a chick thing to ask, wasn't it?" He looked at her, but her face revealed nothing about how she had received his question. "Why don't you ever wonder these things?"

Lauren withdrew her hand and stalled for time by draining her glass. Catching the eye of the waitress, she motioned for another round. *Damn,* she thought. *Dammit!* She looked at Matt and smiled.

"No, I don't wonder these things because that isn't the relationship I'm ever in." She leaned in toward him. "Matty, you and I are fun together. We get along, have some laughs, the sex is great—now," she teased. When he didn't return her grin, she continued. "But I swore off serious relationships a long time ago. They never worked out for me, and after a while I decided what the hell. If men can go through life without committing, why can't I?"

"But what about down the road? Do you ever think about winding up alone?"

Lauren narrowed her eyes, "No." She didn't say anything more, so Matt tried another question.

"So it doesn't bother you that here Julia is all settled down with a baby on the way? Or are you satisfied living vicariously through her?"

At that moment, they were interrupted by the waitress, who set their drinks down and looked questioningly at Matt to see if they wanted anything else. He shook his head, and she turned away. When he looked back at Lauren, he could tell that she wasn't happy. Her face was closed off and she wouldn't look at him. Instead, he saw that those brown eyes were perusing the crowd, that one eyebrow cocked upward.

"Hey," he tried to explain. "I didn't mean anything by it. I just wonder about what you're thinking, you know? What plans do you have for next week, next month, next year? You never talk to me about that stuff. It's all either sex, or partying, or hanging out with Julia and Austin."

She looked at him now, that one eyebrow raised and her dark brown eyes cold. "You didn't mean anything, uh? Well, Sonny, maybe there's a good reason why I never talk about 'those things' as you put it. And that reason would be that any plans I might have wouldn't include you. Did you ever think of that?" She leaned toward him. "You and me? We're strictly a temporary arrangement. Got it? We share a few laughs, we drink, we fuck. Every once in a while, we talk. But don't go getting all serious, kid. I don't do serious." She leaned back in her chair, picked up her glass, and drained half of it without breaking eye contact. The lights dimmed and the band started up again. Matt had to lean close to her ear.

"I'm not part of your future, huh? Well, Blondie, news flash, you're not part of mine, either." He sat back, and in the low light she could see the hard set of his mouth.

I've hurt his feelings, she thought. *Well, too damn bad. Feelings are made to be hurt, and the sooner he learns that lesson, the better. It took me long enough to find out.*

Lauren looked at the dance floor. She drained the rest of her drink and stood up. "Dance with me," and she held out her hand. Matt sat and looked at her like he couldn't believe she was even asking.

She wiggled her fingers at him. "Dance with me, Junior, or I'll find another partner."

He knew that threat wasn't an empty one, and he had already seen at least four men who had been watching her since they arrived. Before she could stalk off and grab one of them, Matt took her hand and stood up. She started to turn, but he pulled her into his chest, leaned down, and kissed her. Not just a light kiss, but one that had her legs becoming a little unsteady. When he was finished, he grinned.

"Now, let's dance."

Lauren's legs were a bit shaky as she followed him, but before he'd see the effect he'd had on her, she moved in front of him and put an arm around his neck. The song was one that usually had couples moving apart, but Lauren kept contact, rubbing her body up and down his as the music swelled around them. Matt was used to this from her, and he played along, rubbing his hands down her body when she moved in close and keeping an arm around her waist to pull her in when she'd sway away from him. If they knew that they were the center of attention, neither one gave any indication. Too soon for Matt, the song ended and Lauren stood in front of him, her arms still around his neck. He could tell that they were okay again by looking at her expression. The next song started, a slow number this time, and he found himself wrapped around her again. This time she didn't pull away, but instead moved closer until almost every part of them was touching in some way. Matt felt himself responding to her, and as the song ended, he whispered in her ear.

"Let's get out of here. If we don't, I'm afraid we might make a bigger spectacle of ourselves."

Lauren laughed, a low sexy sound that she knew drove him crazy. "I live for the spectacle, don't you know?"

"I don't. Not tonight."

Without saying another word, Matt led her off the floor and tossed some bills on the table. They made their way back through the restaurant and out the front. He helped her into the car, leaning in close to fasten her seatbelt.

"Time for a ride, Sweetheart," he said, snapping the belt into place. He climbed in behind the wheel and winked at her before starting the car.

"So, where to now, Ace?" she asked.

"We drive." He put the little car in gear and pulled out onto the street. Back on Highway 40, he hit the gas and they left the lights behind them.

Lauren had no idea where he was going until she saw the sign Lowell Observatory. It was late enough that she knew the place would be closed, but Matt kept driving until he turned onto a side road just before the main entrance. He stopped the car. Lauren looked around her at the dark woods and wondered what they were doing here. Matt came around the car to open her door and help her out. Once she was standing, he pulled her to him and kissed her, a kiss much like the one they'd shared on the dance floor. When he lifted his head, her face was in shadows, but he could hear her breathing hard.

"C'mon," he took her hand and started toward the conservatory gates. The gate was locked, but it was made to keep out cars. Matt lifted Lauren over the metal barrier and stepped over himself. He took her hand once again and led her along the paved road, staying in the shadows. They skirted the building and followed a path that led to an opening. Night lights from the building and parking lot illuminated the path enough that they didn't stumble, and Lauren could see that it followed a low rock wall. She felt Matt stop in front of her and almost bumped into his back.

"Good god, Junior, where the hell are you taking me, anyway?" she was asking as he pulled her around and in front of him.

"Here," he whispered.

Spread out before them was Flagstaff, lit up with street lights and house lights, all twinkling through the trees. In the distance, Lauren could see the mountains in the reflection of the moon's light and millions of stars shining above their heads.

"Oh," she breathed. "Wow!"

Matt put an arm around her, and they stood together like that for several minutes, saying nothing. The night air was a bit cool, but neither seemed to notice. Lauren leaned in to Matt and he wrapped his arms around her waist. She rested her head on his shoulder, snug against his neck.

Breaking the silence, she said, "How did you find this place? I didn't even know it existed."

"I took an astronomy class my sophomore year at ASU, and one of the professors had us meet up here for class. After the others left, I did some exploring and found this view. I always wanted to see it at night."

They were both whispering even though not a soul was around. It was a place that demanded quiet, and the two people who loved noise the most respected that demand.

"Hey, Matty? Thanks for bringing me here."

"During the day, this place can get crazy, especially when a bunch of school kids or tourists are here, but like this at night," he paused and looked up, "it's near perfect." She shivered then, and he tightened his arm around her. "Next time I'll bring a blanket."

"No need to wait. I've got two in the trunk of the car." He could hear the smile in her voice.

"Stay put," he said, unwinding his arm and turning back up the path. Lauren stood rubbing her hands up and down her bare arms in the instant chill she felt once Matt pulled away. She could hear the door shut and knew he'd be back soon.

"Here," he came up behind her and put one of the blankets around her shoulders.

"No," she pulled it away and spread it on the ground. "Let's look at the view from down here." She took off her shoes and sat on the big blanket. Laughing, she pulled him down beside her and lay back. He spread the second blanket over them both and put his arm under her head, pulling her closer.

She took a deep breath and let it out slowly. "I can't remember the last time I just laid on the ground and looked at the stars. When I was a teenager, maybe?"

"Yeah, I used to do stuff like this all the time when I was in North Carolina. The air isn't as clean and clear as it is here, but it's still nice." He pointed toward the North Star. "Watching TV the other night, the *Black List* character Raymond Reddington told Liz, 'That's Polaris. The North Star. That's how sailors used to find their way home. When I look at you, that's what I see. I see my way home.' Don't take this wrong, but sometimes, Lauren, when I look at you, I see my North Star."

That is probably the nicest thing anyone has ever said to me. I've never been anyone's North Star. She remained silent as different thoughts swirled through her head.

They didn't speak after that, and soon Matt felt Lauren grow heavier against him. He knew when she fell asleep because her breathing had become deep and even. He smiled at the stars and closed his own eyes.

It could have been minutes or an hour later, Matt woke up to the sound of rustling in the bushes nearby. He gently poked Lauren's shoulder until she, too, was awake.

"Shhh…be very still," he whispered. "We've got company of some kind, and I don't know if it's a skunk, a raccoon, or a bear."

"Bear!" Lauren was far from whispering. "What the hell?! Get me out of here!"

Whatever it was must have been as afraid of her as she was of it because they heard a crashing in the brush followed by silence again. By this time, Lauren was tugging her shoes back on and getting to her feet. Matt laughed and tried to pull her down again.

"Oh hell, no," she shook her head at him. "Nuh, uh…I'm going back to civilization with or without you."

Matt was still laughing when he grabbed up both blankets and followed her back up the path. *Geez, for a chick in high heels or whatever those are called, she can move*, he thought and chuckled again.

"I don't know what you're laughing at back there, Ace, and I don't care. Pick up the pace, Bud, or be left behind."

They stopped at the gate, and Matt helped her over it before following.

"Pop the locks, baby, I'm freezing and not about to become some bear's late night snack," she was almost running to the car now.

Matt threw the blankets into the trunk and by the time he got into the car, she was already fastened in and looking for the seat warmer. He shook his head and chuckled again.

"You do know, babe, that if it was a bear, he's as scared of you as you are of him."

"Bullshit." She could laugh at herself now that they were in the safety of the car and Matt was backing out onto the road. "There is no way in hell that creature was that frightened. Just saying…"

They rode in companionable silence back to Sharon and John's. The big house was dark and quiet as they pulled up to the garage. Matt cut the engine and turned to Lauren.

"Thanks. This was fun tonight."

She smiled at him in the glow from the security lights. "No, Matty, thank you. Who would have ever guessed that you and I would opt for nature instead of closing a bar."

He chuckled and opened his door to come around to her side. As she stood, Matt pulled her closer and wrapped his arms around her in a hug. She rested her head on his shoulder and breathed in the smell of him. They stood like that for several seconds.

Matt could barely hear the words she whispered in his ear.

"You're something special, Junior. Don't ever change."

With that she pulled away and walked toward the door. Sharon had left the side door by the garage unlocked, and Matt watched her disappear. He stood leaning against the car a few minutes more before following her into the house.

Don't ever change, uh? he thought. *It's a little too late, I think, and for what it's worth, I hope you never change either.*

"Hey, Jules." Matt stepped out onto the patio and joined Julia, who was the first one up.

"Hey, yourself." Julia was shocked to see him up and around, especially after what she could only assume was a very late night. Looking at him closer, she could see that he looked tired. "I figured you'd be one of the last up this morning. Have fun last night?" She grinned at him and pushed a chair in his direction with her foot. "Sit and talk to me."

Matt took the proffered chair and slouched down low, stretching his legs out. The sun was above the distant mountains, but barely. Taking a deep breath of the crisp, clean air, he let it out slowly and closed his eyes. He wanted to ask Julia some questions but was unsure how to start. Julia was patient, sipping her hot tea and enjoying the sunshine. Finally, he sat up and leaned his arms on the table.

"Julia? Can I ask you something about Lauren?" he turned his head to gauge her response. The two were as close as sisters, and Matt didn't know how his request would be taken. Julia stared out over the deep green mountains, thinking before responding.

"Ok, Matt," she began reluctantly. "I suppose my answer depends on your question."

"Well…you know that Lauren and me have gotten close." Matt grinned at this but continued. "Ok, really close in a lot of ways. But I can't seem to get through that tough skin of hers. Just when I think I've figured her out, and most of those times I'm thinking 'hell with her,' she says or does something that completely changes my mind again." He shook his head and shrugged his shoulders. "I know, I know, she's older and out of my league in more ways than one, but there's something about Lauren that keeps drawing me back in." He looked away, and Julia figured he was still trying to figure out how to ask his questions. Instead, Matt opened up to share his life.

"Jules, you're the first and only person to know this, but I haven't slept around since that first night with Lauren. Yeah," he chuckled, "hard to believe, but I keep measuring all these other girls against her. And no, they don't stand a chance. I'm not interested in screwing around, and that isn't like me. But as soon as I think she and I are working on something, she blows me off." He didn't see Julia fight back her laughter at the double entendre. She bit her tongue, but it did no good. As she burst out laughing, Matt looked over, annoyance all over his face. She knew the moment he figured out what he'd said because he laughed with her.

"Oh, Matt, I am so sorry, but that was just too good to pass up," Julia was still gasping for air. She straightened her shoulders before speaking. "Ok, I'm good now. Go ahead, hon."

"Well, as I was saying before you so rudely interrupted me," he grinned to take the edge off his words. "She is so damn hot and cold, you know? I've thought and thought, but I can't come up with anything in particular that I've said or anything I did. Help me out here? What the hell made her so tough? So hard? Was she always like this?"

"Have you asked her?" Julia didn't want to intrude in someone else's relationship, but she knew how Lauren was jerking Matt around. She didn't like it, but as Austin reminded her, Matt was a big boy.

Matt shook his head. "No, and I doubt she'd tell me the truth, anyway." He looked at her. Julia felt sorry for him. *So young and so not ready to face off with Lauren,* she thought. *She's chewed up and spit out men much older than this one. Well, I told her to leave him alone, and she didn't listen to me. She can just deal with it.* Her mind made up, Julia pushed her cup aside and leaned her arms on the table with Matt.

"Ok," she took a deep breath and let it out before continuing. "I'm going to confide in you, Matt, and you can never, and I mean never breathe a word of this to her. She'd kill me if she knew what I'm going to tell you. And if I have to choose between you and Lauren, you'll lose that one." She paused to see Matt shake his head in agreement, his eyes boring into hers. "All right, I can tell you a little about her life before we met. Lauren grew up with money, as if you couldn't tell, and after her parents divorced, she was pretty much left to her own devices. She was only sixteen, a rough enough time for a teenage girl, and Joe and Jennie, her parents, took little interest in her. They both found new loves and new adventures, while their daughter stayed in St. Louis and finished high school. Big checks at Christmas and birthdays, but not much parental love and attention. Lauren learned quickly to take whatever was given to her and move on. Oh, she wasn't toughened up yet, and when we met at Columbia, she was still such a sweetheart." Julia smiled slightly. "She wanted a family in the worst way."

Julia's thoughts were taking her back to that time, and Matt saw her face soften at the good memories.

"She and I met in a basic design class, and we became inseparable. Our professor was such a douche, and we kept looking at one another and laughing to ourselves. After class, we found each other in the hall and cracked up all the way outside. We met up for lunch or dinner and spent time studying or just hanging out. At the semester, we moved into an apartment together and became one another's sister. Pretty much everything we had was community property, even guys." Julia chuckled. "Yep, we dated a lot, but soon we were attracted to different types of boys. Lauren went for the bad boys, but I found them to be too much of a hassle." She rolled her eyes. "Yeah, and ended up marrying one. But I digress. Lauren was, and is, beautiful. Male attention has never been a problem, but in spite of being gorgeous, Lauren had many insecurities. She would latch onto some guy, usually some bastard who was using her for money or sex, but she'd fall in love and listen to no one. I often wonder if part of her search was for that missing love. Someone to fill that hole that her parents' abandoning her caused." Julia shrugged a shoulder. "Dime store psychology at its best, here, but that's what I've always thought. Anyway, in our senior year, Lauren met David, a pre-med student who was at UMC.

He was gorgeous, equally wealthy, intelligent, and seemed to really think a lot of Lauren. I thought she'd found someone who could see past the beautiful face and body and find what lie beneath." Matt saw Julia's face tighten, and he was almost reluctant to listen to more.

"They spent most nights together, attended every fraternity bash he wanted to go to, and Lauren was the perfect arm ornament for David. I had a bad feeling about him—you know me and my feelings—but I held my tongue. I really did think he loved her, and I definitely wanted him to love her. Graduation came, and Joe and Jennie decided to get along just enough to throw Lauren a big bash. Everyone was there, our friends and many of theirs, but David wasn't. All evening, Lauren watched the door and kept looking at her phone." Julia chuckled. "Yeah, we had cell phones, but nothing like today's. No texting, no voice mail. Pretty simple. Anyway, by the end of the evening, Lauren was almost beside herself. She'd kept up a façade all night, smiling and talking and carrying the party, but as people started leaving, she was frantic. I suggested she call David's mom, since he obviously wasn't answering his phone." Julia sat straighter in her chair, and Matt watched her face harden and her eyes turn an icy blue. *I hope to god I never make her angry,* he thought, *because this Julia is scary.*

Julia's voice brought Matt back to the story. "Guess where dear old David was? The Virgin Islands. And not alone. His mother took great pleasure in telling Lauren that the golden boy was off with a family friend. And not just any friend, but David's fiancé. It seems that she was a perfect match for David, with her pedigree, well-connected surgeon father, and a shared history. Lauren learned that the two had an understanding that dated back to their high school days. David would be marrying this girl as soon as he finished medical school, and her daddy would be setting him up in practice." Julia shook her head. "Lauren was heartbroken, of course, but I'm afraid something else was taking place. After that, she began using men just like she believed they had used her. Oh," Julia assured him, "I tried to talk to her. I did everything I could to get her to see a counselor, talk to someone, but she shrugged her shoulders and told me there was nothing a goddamn counselor could tell her that she didn't already know."

Julia took a drink of her now-cold tea, made a face, and shoved it away. "At first she wasn't the pro at man eating, but she's honed her skills over these last eighteen or so years. And when I married Keith, she wasn't happy, but she said nothing." Julia smiled. "Oh, she had plenty to say once I discovered what an asshole he is, and man, did she unleash on him. Talk about venom! The man would practically run before facing Lauren." She chuckled again. "That was almost fun, though. And I really don't know if I'd had the guts to leave Keith and do what I did without her. At times, I do believe Lauren had a lot of fun at his expense." Julia sobered and looked at Matt. "So now you know what in her life caused my beautiful, good-hearted, loving friend to develop her bitch from hell persona."

Matt had taken in all Julia was telling him, and once her story ended, he nodded his head and sat back.

"Yeah, I get it," he sighed. "But does she have to lump us all into that category? Will she always see us all as users?"

"Uh, Matt," Julia waited until he looked at her. "You do realize that before Lauren *you* were a David? That you used girls like the one Lauren once was?" Matt's blank stare told Julia that he hadn't thought of himself in that way. "Sorry, bud, but you belonged to that 'category' as you called it. So don't pull some 'I'm being wronged' shit with me."

Something in Julia's tone kept Matt from defending himself. *Well, hell,* he thought. *She's right. I would have used her, showed her off to my friends, and probably broken it off without another thought. And she'd only gotten that much because she's fucking sexier than anyone I've ever seen in my life.*

"So Matt," Julia's voice broke into this reverie. "Before you play a victim, give it some thought. I'm not saying that Lauren's treatment of you or holding you at arm's length is right because I don't know enough about your relationship. But now you know the source of her feelings." She put her hand on his arm. "Matt, I will tell you that you've gotten beyond Lauren's veneer better than men twice your age and experience. But don't get your hopes up. Others have tried and failed. The only thing you have that they didn't is a base—friendship. She likes you, Matt, or she would have already sent you packing. Now my question is for you. Do you want a relationship with Lauren? How hard do you want to try?" Julia paused. "And do you think she's worth it? Because until you decide that, you don't stand a chance."

"Hey, what's going on here?" Austin walked through the door and watched as Julia removed her hand from Matt's arm. He leaned down and kissed her neck before rising up to look at the two questioningly.

"Good morning, sweetie," Julia's face lit up as she looked up at Austin. "Matt and I never get the chance to talk by ourselves, and we're taking advantage of it this morning."

Austin took a seat opposite the two and frowned at them. Matt seemed lost in his own thoughts, and Julia was smiling at him, just happy to see him. *I'm sure this has to do with Lauren,* he thought, *and I sure as hell don't want to be involved in that drama.* He looked up as Sharon joined them, followed shortly by John. The only person absent from the scene was Lauren, but that wasn't a surprise. She was always the last person to get up. Austin didn't get the chance to ask, and by the time he did, he decided that he really didn't care.

Chapter 40

ON THE NEXT VISIT, JULIA'S doctor wanted to do an ultrasound, and if they wanted further tests, this would also be the visit for those. Calculations put her around twenty weeks along, and Austin and Julia still hadn't decided for sure on the amniocentesis. Since the results wouldn't matter as far as terminating the pregnancy or not and a slight miscarriage risk still existed, they decided not to do the test. Julia called her doctor's office to tell the nurse their decision, and after confirming their appointment, there was nothing to do but wait. That evening, when Austin asked her what to expect the next day, Julia tried to describe the procedure.

"I'm excited," Julia grinned. "Dr. Roberts said that she's going to order a regular ultrasound. You remember our first one, right? It will be pretty much the same thing. I'm sure she's encouraged by my not needing to see her except for the checkup. Hell, *I'm* encouraged!" She reached down and patted the growing bump. She opted for clothes that didn't cling simply because she still wasn't telling anyone. As slender as she was, Austin knew that wouldn't last much longer, either. Anyone who knew her well could see a difference in her body. "Austin," her voice brought him out of his thoughts. "Do you realize that we're probably almost half-way there? Can you believe it?"

"No, I really can't. But if you don't let Sharon get started on the nursery soon, she may explode."

Julia laughed. Sharon had not said a lot, but as Julia continued feeling good and the baby was okay, Sharon was finding it hard to not push her young friend.

"I told her that if we find out if we're having a boy or a girl this trip, I'll let her know and we can begin. I swear, she may be out of control, you know."

"Yeah," Austin nodded. "I've seen her in action." He looked around their house and noted the many small things Sharon had "picked up" for them. All of it had been either mentioned by Julia or by him at one time or other. They soon learned to say nothing or said item would be delivered.

"She means well, sweetie, and as John says, 'If it makes her happy, what the hell.'"

"Now that doesn't surprise me a bit."

The day of her doctor's appointment dawned and Julia was up early. She left Austin sleeping soundly since they'd both taken the morning off. She carried her tea out onto the patio. The morning sun was hot, but as she sat in the shade, she thought about what they would need to do to make the pool and yard kid safe. Her mind began to wander and soon she found herself thinking back to six almost seven years before. *I'm in such a better place,* she thought. *No one keeps looking at me like something bad is about to happen. Austin is absolutely wonderful. And I feel like this is so right.* She placed her hand over her bump and smiled.

Julia could hear Austin in the kitchen and smiled knowing that he was probably fixing her breakfast. He loved cooking for her and watching her eat. She grinned at the thought. He came to the open door.

"Hey, babe, I made you pancakes with fruit. You want to eat out here?"

"I'd love to, but let me help you," Julia started to get up, but Austin put a gentle hand on her shoulder and guided her back down.

"Nope, I live to serve," he said in her ear before heading back into the house. Not two minutes later, he came out balancing two plates and two glasses of milk, hers dark brown with chocolate. He set it all on the table and pulled a bottle of water out of his pocket and placed that in front of her. Julia laughed and dug in. Now that she was no longer sick, she enjoyed eating again. She finished the last bite and washed it down with water before sitting back to sip on her milk. She took the first drink and snarled her nose at the glass. Austin laughed. She went through this ritual every time she drank milk, but she decided that it was only for a few months and she'd survive.

"I'm a little nervous this morning," she looked over at Austin. "I know that everything is okay, so maybe the better word is anxious. No, excited." She laughed. "Whatever. I can't wait to know if we have a little boy or a little girl in here." Austin leaned over and rested his hand on her bulging stomach.

"I couldn't possibly care less," he assured her. "I'd like a little boy to throw footballs to, but then I'd also like a little girl to make me a tea party." He smiled and looked around. "Before too long, though, I need to figure out how to child-proof this patio and pool." At Julia's laugh, he looked at her questioningly.

"I was thinking the same thing this morning. And we really do need to decide if we want to stay here or not. We have the two bedrooms downstairs, but I don't know if I want a second level. Right now it isn't a big deal, but as soon as the baby is mobile, we'll have to secure the stairs." She chewed on her bottom lip until Austin extended a finger and rubbed it gently.

"Hey, one thing at a time. Let's get the little James baby here and decide that later," he replaced his finger with his lips.

"Deal," Julia grinned. She stood and started gathering their dishes. "Now, I need to clean this up and get dressed. We're burning daylight."

Julia felt the cold gel the nurse swiped onto her stomach, and the doctor began moving the transducer. She and Austin stared at the screen, but neither of them could figure out what they were seeing, even though the technician pointed out the different images of the baby. They could see the head and face, little arms and legs, but nothing was clear.

"Oh, now I'm seeing if we have a little boy or girl," she teased. "But I promised Dr. Roberts that I'd let her tell you that herself."

Julia wrinkled her nose up at Austin, "Crap, I was hoping she'd let it slip." Austin laughed and looked back at the screen.

Julia felt the fullness of her bladder, but so far it wasn't painful. Soon the technician was finished and the nurse was handing Julia wipes to clean the gel from her stomach. Once they left, she dressed and used the restroom. They waited for Dr. Roberts, who entered about ten minutes later.

"Well, everything looks great!" the doctor patted Julia's arm. "I'm setting your due date for January 1, but you know that it could be two weeks either way. Now," she paused for effect, "do we want to know the gender?"

"Why wouldn't we?" Austin could barely contain himself.

"Well, some couples want me to keep it secret so that they find out at a reveal party." She looked at the two in front of her. "But my guess is that you two are wanting to know now, am I right?" She was smiling at the couple in front of her. No, they weren't her usual pair, but Dr. Roberts could see that they were a good couple.

"Please," Julia leaned toward her doctor. "We really want to know. We're not into all the 'reveal party' stuff that others enjoy."

"Okay," Dr. Roberts' smile was even bigger. "You're the proud parents of a little girl. Go buy lots of pink!"

"A girl," Julia sat back and Austin could see that her mind had kicked into overdrive. The fact that she was twenty weeks pregnant with a daughter didn't escape him. He reached out and took her hand, squeezing gently.

"Thank you, Doctor," he said, looking up at the older woman. "And everything looks good with the baby?"

"Neither I nor the technician saw anything wrong. Everything looks good," she assured him. "Now, I'm going to leave you two. Julia, make another appointment before you go, and call me if you have any questions at all."

Hearing her name brought Julia back and she looked up at the doctor. "Yes, of course. Thank you so much."

Dr. Roberts left them alone and Austin came to kneel in front of her, taking both of her hands in his. Her face was closed off, but Austin knew exactly what she was thinking.

"Jules, don't go there," he said gently. "How many times over the past few months have you said that this feels different, that this isn't the same, that this feels right? Baby, you're fine. Our baby girl is fine. Please, don't go there, sweetheart."

Julia heard him, but she needed a few moments to pull herself together. Austin was right. She did feel fine. Knowing she was having a little girl was a jolt Julia thought she'd prepared for. Evidently, she hadn't. She looked at Austin, at the love on his face, and felt better. *He's just so awesome*, she thought, *and I know that everything is going to be fine.*

She smiled, and he visibly relaxed. "I'm back. It was just a moment I had there. I'm good now, and I am so excited, aren't you?"

Austin laughed and rose to his feet, pulling her up with him. He wrapped his arms around her and they stood holding one another. He kissed the top of her head.

"Babe, I have never been so excited in my life. I'm gonna have a daughter." When she pulled back to look at him, Julia had to wipe a tear that had started down her face. He finished wiping it for her before replacing his hand with his lips.

"Let's go home," he said. "We have some anxious people to call, and Sharon is at the top of the list."

Julia laughed then. "Oh. My. God. She will be out of control. I can see it now. The baby's room will look like the house vomited Pepto Bismol."

They were still laughing when a nurse knocked and entered the room.

"I have some still images here that I'm sure you two want," she said, holding the envelope out to Julia. She took it and smiled her thanks.

"How much can we see?" Austin asked, taking the envelope from Julia.

"Oh, lots! I think you'll love them!" she said, exiting the room.

Austin pulled out the small pages. Julia looked around his shoulder at the black sheets of paper with the white images. They could clearly see the side view of a little head and face, the tiny nose and mouth visible in one. They could also make out a small arm and what appeared to be a leg. Austin took his phone from his pocket and snapped a picture. Julia laughed.

"What?" he asked. "My baby girl's first photo shoot, and I want my own copy."

Julia winked at him. "Me, too! Send me that picture, please. And let's get out of here before they come back and kick us out."

"I'm ready." Austin put an arm around her as they walked out. She stopped to make the next appointment, and they headed to the parking lot and her car.

Unlocking the door, Austin was still grinning. "Babe, we may need to trade one of our cars, you know. I can't see a car seat fitting well in the back."

She looked down at the tiny back seat. "You're right, of course. And I do not want to get rid of the Mustang. So this one is history!"

349

"You plan on looking for a minivan?"Austin teased. He knew she detested all minivans and couldn't resist teasing her.

"Oh, hell no," Julia shuddered. "I refuse to drive one of those big-ass things."

"Babe, the reason we are buying a bigger car is to fit everyone in it."

"Yeah, and that's why I want a Tahoe," Julia grinned and raised her eyebrows. "With a third-row seat, DVD player, sun roof..."Austin's laugh stopped her. "What?"

"Jules, that's as much a big-ass car as a minivan," he said.

"Totally different," Julia insisted as she lowered herself into the passenger side of the little Bimmer. "Vans are lame. SUV's are cool."

Austin laughed and got behind the wheel, watching as she fastened herself in.

"Well, heaven forbid you drive anything 'lame' sweetheart."

"Yeah, well, don't tell me you actually want to drive a minivan, either. Just think what that would do to your 'cool' image. Man, would your buddies ever have fun with that! Of course, Lauren and I used to make fun of the Tahoe Hoes, as we called them. I'll have to rethink that one." Julia's laugh echoed in the car as he eased into traffic. He looked over and winked.

"A girl!" Sharon almost squealed as Julia pulled the phone away from her ear. "I have to call John! Shit! I have so much shopping to do. Jules, you have decided on a theme for the baby's room, haven't you? Are you going with animals? Or perhaps one of the popular kids cartoons? Or Disney?"

"Sharon, calm down," Julia's voice was soothing, trying to keep her friend under control. "No, I haven't decided, but as soon as I do, you'll be the first I call."

"Promise me," Sharon's voice took on the no-nonsense tone that Julia had come to love.

"Promise."

Lauren wasn't nearly as ecstatic as Sharon. Julia waited until she was in the shop to tell her friend and show her the picture. Babies weren't Lauren's thing, and Julia knew that. She also knew that regardless of her personal preferences, Lauren would be a great aunt.

"Oh, isn't she…cute," Lauren looked at the black and white image and handed it back to Julia, who burst out laughing. "What? What did I say that was so funny? I thought I was being nice."

"Lauren, sweetie, you are too much. I know that you can't make out much from this thing, but aren't you just the littlest bit excited?"

Lauren looked at Julia and saw her glow. *Julia is a beautiful pregnant lady, but no surprise there,* she thought. *And even though I think babies are a pain in the ass, literally, I'm happy if Jules is happy.* Lauren pulled her friend in and hugged her tight.

"Jules, I think your baby girl will be beautiful, especially if she looks like her mama. And this *is* my excited face." She pulled back at Julia's peel of laughter and smiled at her friend.

"Well, Lar, I think it's time we broke the news to our circle of friends, don't you?"

"Yep. I'll arrange a little get-together, and you can bask in all the attention."

Julia chuckled and shook her head. "Yeah, like you ever share that."

"Hey, I can share…just not all the time." Lauren winked and they both went back to work.

That evening, Julia and Austin were relaxing in the den when he looked over at her.

"Jules?" she looked up. "Don't you think it's about time to tell the parents?"

Julia sighed. "Do we have to? You have no idea of how much I've enjoyed this being just our thing." She thought for a few seconds. "I'd like my dad to know. He'll be so excited. And if I knew I could swear him to secrecy and keep my mother out of the loop, I would have already called him. But we both know that he'll tell her, just like he always does. Dammit."

Austin felt sorry for her, but he really wanted to share his good news with his family. "Jules, I understand, really I do, but I *want* my family to know. I want them to be excited for us and as happy as we are." At her noncommittal look, he continued. "I know that you and my mom have your differences…"

"Differences? Is that what you're calling it? Austin, she hates me. She resents my presence in your life, and she'd love nothing more than for you to kick me to the curb. You heard her when you didn't come home

for Caleb's graduation, even though I begged you to go. She blamed me."
Austin remembered well the scene on the phone. Natalie had cried, begged,
and finally attacked Julia for keeping her son from her. Austin had ended
the call as soon as Natalie brought Julia into the conversation, and he
hadn't spoken to her since.

"Jules, I talked to Caleb on the phone more than once, and he was fine.
Hell, he said that he was jealous and would have gotten out of it himself
if he could have. He's coming out here next week before he starts college.
Caleb and I are good."

"Yes, but you and your mom, and maybe even your dad, aren't. But
let's stay on the subject. When do we tell them? You decide when to tell
yours, and I'll decide when to tell mine."

"You're serious, aren't you?" Austin wanted to present a united front,
and to do that, he needed her on board. "Babe, when we give them this
news, and it will be *we*, I want you by my side."

Julia sighed. *He's right, dammit.* "I know, I know. And your family
doesn't cause me nearly the stress that mine does." She rolled her eyes and
grinned at him. "Get your laptop and contact Caleb. We'll do, as my dad
calls it, the Skype. We'll tell them together."

Austin jumped up and leaned over her as she lounged on her chair. He
looked her in the eye and said, "I do love you, woman."

Julia smiled, "And I do love you, man." He kissed her and hurried to
get the laptop set up on the dining room table. Julia slowly got up and
followed him. "All wonderful things must end, I suppose. But I'm not
telling mine yet. Not yet."

Chapter 41

~~~~~~~~

Austin sat at his desk and looked out over the city. The corporate offices of Coast to Coast Industrial and Commercial Landscaping occupied the top three floors of the ten-story office building in downtown Phoenix. Austin's small office contained a desk, two chairs, bookshelves along one wall, and a large window that overlooked the city. As he stared out, his eyes weren't really focused on anything as his mind wandered back to the previous night.

He and Julia had contacted his family via Skype, and together they had broken the news of the baby. Phillip was as excited as Austin had seen him in a long time, which surprised Austin. He'd never thought of his dad as one to look forward to being a grandpa. Caleb was disconnected, neither happy nor excited. Austin chuckled at his brother's expression of distaste and remembered himself at that age. Babies weren't high on his list of "awesome" either. As for Natalie, Austin sighed as he thought of his mother's shocked and not-happy-at-all face. She'd held her tongue on what she really wanted to say and her congratulations was stiff. Julia, Austin smiled to think, handled herself well, promising to send them a copy of the baby's picture and to keep them updated on her progress. Shortly after that, they had all signed off. Julia had felt like it all went well, but Austin knew better.

He waited until she was asleep to call his mom on Natalie's cell phone. He knew that she'd be up, stewing about a situation over which she had no control. The conversation had been brief and unpleasant.

"Austin, just what in the world are you thinking? Tying yourself to that woman with a *baby!*" They had barely said their hellos when she'd started in on him. "Look at how *old* she is! It's almost like *me* having a baby at my age! Good Lord! Why, it's hard telling what kinds of issues that child will be born with." She barely paused before starting in again. "Oh, and please tell me that you aren't going to marry her now out of some sense of obligation. I mean, really Austin, it's bad enough to share a child with her, but to make things worse by marrying her would be the worst thing you could do. And here I had such high hopes for you to marry a nice girl, a girl your age, settle down..."

Austin waited until his mother ran out of steam, quietly listening while she talked. He'd been expecting nothing different, so she didn't say anything that surprised him. Only after she'd gone silent did Austin speak.

"Are you finished, Mom?" Austin waited a couple of seconds before beginning. "You know, growing up I never saw this side of you. Oh, I remember you having strong opinions on a lot of things, but I don't remember this hatefulness. Have you always possessed it, or has it come out since I left home?" Natalie tried to break in, but Austin stopped her by continuing. "Just stop. Stop talking. It's my turn." His voice hardened. "You don't like Julia? Too damn bad. And what you've just said about my daughter is beyond ridiculous." He gave a short, derisive laugh. "Really, Mom? You find out that you're going to be a grandma for the first time, and all you can think about are the kinds of 'issues' my daughter may have?" He was getting wound up himself now. "Has it occurred to you that that little girl is half mine? She's part of you? That she's not some mistake that I've made?" He tried to maintain control. "You're not happy? That's too damn bad, too, because *I* couldn't be happier." His voice tightened in his resolve. "Let's get something clear. You are to do nothing to upset Julia, you hear me? She doesn't handle stress well right now, and I won't have you causing her problems. You are not to call her or contact her in any way unless it's to talk to the both of us. If you do, I swear, I'll cut you out of my life completely." He ignored the gasp of surprise from his mother's end and continued on. "Your total lack of respect for me, for the life I've chosen, and for the woman I've chosen to share it with me is crazy. I love you, Mom, but right now I don't like you very much."

"Austin, that simply isn't true," Natalie tried to justify herself. "Of course I look forward to your children, and Caleb's, and yes, even this baby..."

"Even *this* baby? Would you listen to yourself?" Austin interrupted her. He took several deep breaths before speaking again. "Mother, whether or not you're part of my life is totally up to you. You know exactly what you have to do to be included in my family, and until you're willing to do that, there really isn't anything else to say." He paused. "To be honest, this is one of the best times of my life. I have never been happier. I have a job I enjoy, a new house that's mine, and someone to share my life with who's made me a better man, a better person than I ever imagined. I'll ask you to do one thing—to not ruin it for me." He took a ragged breath. "In fact, I hate to say this, but don't call or contact me until you're ready to make amends, Mother, and that means accepting Julia. And for the love of god, don't put Dad in the middle, or Caleb either. Leave them out of it."

"Well," Natalie's voice was full of tears. "I never thought I'd hear my son talk to me this way. I only love you and want the best for you. For you to be happy."

"Then show me, Mom. You say the words but they're meaningless. Make the effort. Try to see this from my point of view." Austin shook his head. "You're such a drama queen. Well, right now, I don't need or want your drama. And I think we're done here for now." At Natalie's protest, he interrupted her. "No, we're done. Remember what I said, Mom. Leave Julia alone. I mean it."

"But Austin…."

"Tell Dad what I said or not. That's up to you. I've got to work tomorrow and I need to sleep. Bye Mom."

He had hung up on her tearful "Austin!" and sat in the darkness, wondering what would provoke a parent into acting the way she was.

In his office, a knock on his door startled Austin and brought him back to the present. At his "Come in," Austin heard the door open and he turned his chair around to see who it was. Audra. The woman had avoided him conspicuously since the barbeque, and he was surprised to see her now. They weren't working on any of the same projects, and he frowned at her approach.

"Leave the door open, please," he said as she started to close it. Audra tilted her head and smiled at him before crossing the small distance to stand in front of his desk. "What do you want, Audra?"

"Oh, nothing personal, I assure you," as she smirked in his direction. "Ray asked me to drop off the designs for the stadium project in Ohio. I didn't know you were working on that, too."

"I wasn't until last week when Roger had to help out with the new airport expansion in Houston." He looked at her and frowned. "Don't tell me you're on the team."

"Why, yes, yes I am, and I suppose we'll be working together on occasion," the woman sat down and crossed her legs. "You don't have a problem with that, do you, Austin? I mean, my being around won't bother you, will it?" She leaned toward his desk, and before he could stop himself, Austin pulled back in his chair. The slight movement didn't escape Audra, and she leaned back into her own seat.

"Not in the least. It's just a job," Austin assured her. "By the way, you should be congratulating me."

"Congratulating you? For what?" she narrowed her eyes to look at him. *Yes, he's as handsome as ever*, she thought, *and looking quite pleased with himself. Oh shit*, as it hit her. "You're not getting married are you?"

Austin laughed. "Nope, something better. I'm proud to say that Julia and I are expecting a baby girl the first of January. I'm going to be a dad!"

If he'd told Audra that he was taking over as CEO of the company, she wouldn't have been more surprised.

"No shit," she just looked at him. "That's the last thing I would have expected. So you and the old...I mean Julia...are having a baby. Wow! I didn't see that one coming." She shrugged her shoulders. "Whatever floats your boat, I suppose. Oh, yeah, congratulations." She uncrossed her legs and stood up, Austin also rising. Audra extended her hand. Austin looked at it and then back to her. "I won't bite you, for heaven's sake. I just wanted to wish you the best. Oh, and Julia, too, of course."

Austin reluctantly took her hand and felt her slightly squeeze his before he pulled away. "Yeah, I'll extend the wishes to Julia. I'm sure she'll appreciate them." Austin smiled and said no more, his silence dismissing the woman.

"Oh, Ray wants you to get back to him on that," she indicated the paperwork with her head, "as soon as you can." Audra walked slowly to the open door and turned to look at him again. "Just remember, if you ever get tired of the domestic life, give me a call." Before he could respond, she slipped out the door.

"When hell freezes over, and probably not then," Austin said out loud to the empty room, as his phone rang. He looked at the caller ID and saw that it was Matt.

"Hey, man, what's up?" Austin hadn't talked to his buddy in a while.

"What's up with you? I swear, you knock up a female and I never see you anymore," Matt laughed to take the edge off his words.

"Yeah, well, at least I can get the job done," Austin laughed. It was good to joke with Matt again. "Whatcha need? You never call me during the day. And you don't bring me flowers. You don't sing me love songs. I never see you anymore. Hell, you never call me, period."

Matt laughed at the other end. "Well, Period, why don't you meet me for lunch? Since the old lady has all of your time monopolized, I figure I'd better grab you when I can."

Austin looked at his calendar. "Sounds good. Meet me at The Dinner Fork at 11:30. And don't forget the flowers loverboy." He ended the call before Matt could reply. Austin sat back and wondered what this was all about. Matt never called to invite him to lunch. Maybe for a beer after work once in a while, but even then it didn't happen often. *Oh well*, Austin shrugged his shoulders. *I'll find out.* He opened the new file on his desk and focused on work.

The restaurant wasn't too crowded at 11:30, but Austin knew that by noon the place would be wall to wall people and loud. The small café specialized in what he had always called blue-plate specials and was one of the few he knew that served a decent open-face beef sandwich. He entered and looked around for Matt. His friend occupied a corner booth and waved him over. Austin slid into his side and grinned.

"Hey, man, how's it going?"

Matt grinned and raised one shoulder. "It's going. Work is work, as they say." He leaned his arms on the table. "John is one helluva big deal around here. I had no idea until I went to work for him. Son-of-a-bitch is demanding, but so far I've been able to keep up with it all." He leaned back and stretched his legs under the small table. "He sure does pay well, though. It's nice to leave Dick's Balls behind, that's for sure."

Austin felt guilty that he'd never really inquired about his friend's new job. He knew that Matt had graduated and started working for John, marketing if he remembered correctly, but Austin had done little except attend a graduation party for which Julia had bought him a gift. *Shit, I don't even know what we got him,* Austin was stunned to realize.

A young waitress, *Anna* her name announced on the tag fastened above her breast, came over to take their orders. She flirted just enough to let them know that she was interested, but when the two gave no response, she politely wrote down their choices and left them alone. They had barely started talking again when she brought two sweet teas and a pitcher for refills. She set the pitcher down, winked, and made her way back to the kitchen.

After filling one another in on work, Matt fell quiet. Austin knew from the silence that something was on his friend's mind. He started to ask, but decided not to. Matt had called him. Let him lead the conversation. After Anna brought two plates of steaming food—bread piled high with mashed potatoes, roast beef, and gravy—they had both dug in, and neither one spoke much for the several minutes it took for them to clean their plates. At the last bite, Austin pushed his plate away and shook his head.

"Damn, that's good stuff," he said before washing the last down with a long swig of tea. He poured himself another glass and pushed the plate away. Matt followed suit and the two looked at one another.

"Well?" Austin raised one eyebrow.

"Well, what?" Matt raised his own back. When Austin said nothing, Matt leaned back and put a hand to the back of his neck, rubbing and rolling it around. Austin knew his friend always did this when he was stalling. He still said nothing.

Matt stopped and looked at Austin.

"I'm confused on something, and I need your advice," Matt looked at Austin, his face serious. Matt wasn't serious very often, but this was one of those times. Austin nodded for him to continue. "You know that I've been seeing Lauren for a few months now." Austin resisted the urge to tease him with a "no shit" and nodded his head for Matt to go on. "Man, that blonde has me tied up in knots. One minute she's all sexy and fun. The next she's a bitch from hell. And I never know which one is going to come out, so I'm always ready for either one." Matt was getting agitated talking about it. "I mean, what the fuck, you know. I like her, a lot, and every time I think we're starting to get closer, she pulls back. But not before busting my balls for one thing or another. It's like she's watching for me to say something wrong or act in a certain way, and BAM! She's on it. We'll cool it for a few days, and then one or the other of us comes back. No apologies, just mind-blowing make-up sex, and we're back to normal."

Austin frowned. "I'm confused, here, bud. Isn't sex what this whole Lauren thing is all about? I mean, isn't that what you're in it for, man?" At Matt's silence, Austin leaned back and crossed his arms. "I told you what kind of woman she is. You didn't listen. You said that it will be a good bang and that's it." Matt looked up at him. This wasn't easy for either of them. *Hell*, Austin thought, *this should be chick shit.*

"I thought I was okay with all that, but I guess I'm not," Matt shook his head. "I just need to vent a little, I guess. I talked to Julia, you saw us, and she told me some things in Lauren's background. All that did was screw with my mind even more. Now that I know more about why she does these things, it only makes me more likely to keep going back. Julia told me to ask myself if I think Lauren's worth it."

"Well?" Austin looked at his friend. "Is she?"

Matt shook his head and mumbled, "I don't know. I just don't know."

"Man, she makes you miserable. What female is worth that? Dump her and move on," Austin was sure that's what he would have already done.

"Yeah, you're seeing the miserable. You have no idea of how good it can be when it's good. I find myself stopping to wonder what Lauren would think when I have a tricky decision to make. Funny thing is, when it's a serious subject, she'll give me good advice and even be nice. As for my seeing anyone else, I'll meet a woman and immediately compare her to Blondie." Matt grinned. "I'm okay. Like I said, I needed to let off some steam. Fuck it. As long as the sex is good and the good times outnumber the miserable ones, I'll hang in there."

Austin grinned back. They both left money on the table and rose to leave. That evening Austin shared with Julia the conversation he'd had with his buddy. She filled him in with the same information that she'd shared with Matt. Austin could see why Matt was so confused. *Thank god*, Austin thought, *Julia isn't like her friend.*

Chapter 42

———

"**I** KNOW, DADDY, ISN'T IT EXCITING?" Julia had phoned her dad to give him the good news about the baby.

"Baby girl, I couldn't be happier for you, you know," Lawrence's voice was almost tearful as he reacted to hearing about his granddaughter. "Are you sure you're feeling okay? I know you said that all the doctor's tests are good, but how are you feeling? And Austin? How's my boy doing?"

Julia laughed. "He's fine, too. Seriously, Daddy, this is so different from the other times, and I know this time will work out."

Lawrence knew all about his daughter's feelings—he liked to call it trusting her gut—and if Julia assured him all was well, then he breathed easier.

"Daddy, I know that you'll tell Mother, but please, please don't let her come out here," Julia was almost begging. "You know how she is. All she'll try to do is run things. Heck, just the thought is making my stress levels rise." Julia could feel her ears turning red at the thought of how Dana would react. "Plus, she doesn't like Austin, she doesn't like our being together, and she definitely won't be happy about my out-of-wedlock pregnancy."

"Julia," she knew her dad was serious as soon as she heard him call her by her name and not Baby Girl or a host of other endearments. "I won't keep this from your mother, regardless of how you think she'll act. That said, I will do everything in my power to keep her from rushing out there. That much I promise you."

Julia sighed. "I know. She's a load, but we love her." She paused. "Yes, I love her but I don't have to like her." Julia rolled her eyes at her father's

360

laugh on the other end. "Well, I *don't* like her very much, Daddy. You saw how she was with Keith, then the way she treated Austin like crap on the sole of her Gucci, and you know she won't be any better now."

"Jules, you may be surprised," Lawrence replied. "She's had a lot of thinking time since the whole Keith episode. Once you get this little girl here, you'll know what I'm talking about when I say that you'll do anything and everything to protect your child."

"You're right, I will, but I won't try to dictate her life. I've learned the hard way how much that can hurt."

They chatted a few minutes more about their work, the house, and life in general before signing off. Julia promised to send them the photo of the baby with the additional promise of letting them know about her progress. Lawrence had warned his daughter that if she didn't, nothing would keep him from flying out to Phoenix.

Julia laughed, "I love you, Daddy."

"I love you, Sweet Pea." Lawrence hung up and Julia sat in Austin's chair, thinking about what he'd said.

I guess he's right about one thing, she thought. *I do know that I'd do anything to protect my little girl. Little girl...we really need a name here.* She laughed, the sound echoing in the empty room. *I'll talk to Austin about that tonight.*

Time continued to march along. Julia's little red convertible was traded in not for a Tahoe but for an Escalade. It had all the bells and whistles Julia had insisted on. As August gave way to September and then October, Lauren and Julia hurried to finish up the usual summer work load. In the middle of it all, Julia and Sharon began working on the baby's room as her friend kept after her to give "that sweet baby girl" a name. After much discussion and many suggestions from her friends and Sharon, Austin and Julia decided on a name for their daughter, but it hadn't been easy.

"Well, I think it's safe to say that Dana and Natalie are out." Austin laughed. They were discussing names, and so far he wasn't coming up with anything productive.

"I know," Julia sighed and rubbed her growing belly. "And I don't want the usual names. Not that there's anything wrong with them, but right now everyone's naming their babies either Emma, Ella, Olivia, or Isabella. I don't want our daughter to share her name with two or three other little girls in her class at school."

Austin was little to no help outside of going through the baby name book with her, and even then he didn't last long. Just when he was ready to give up and go with whatever Julia decided, he grinned at her.

"What?" she looked at him. "You've thought of something, haven't you?"

"I think I have. What about your favorite smelling tree, acacia?"

"Acacia…" Julia tried it out. "I love it, Austin!" She thought a few moments before adding, "Elise. One of my dear childhood friends was Elise. Acacia Elise James." She grinned and patted her growing stomach. "I love it!"

Austin looked to the ceiling and sighed, "Thank goodness. I was ready to go for Baby James, you know, like that movie you and Lauren always like to watch. Patrick Swayze and what's-her-name."

Julia laughed, "No, I refuse to name my little girl Baby. And in the movie Baby was just a nickname. I think we have the perfect name."

Julia called Sharon later to share their decision. "Acacia Elise James, and we'll call her Caci, spelled C-A-C-I," Julia said proudly.

"I love it," Sharon declared, making the name official. "Now, let's get to work on that pretty pink room!"

"Sharon," Julia warned her friend, "We are not going with some sickening sweet pink that makes me want to scrub my eyes when I leave." Sharon laughed, totally unaffected by the veiled insult.

"Oh, sweetie, when I get too bossy, just slap me down, okay?" Sharon was having fun, and Julia wasn't about to spoil it for her. She also wasn't about to give in either. The interior decorator had her own ideas, but Sharon was insisting on furnishing the nursery regardless of how much Austin and Julia protested. Finally, John had come to Julia.

"Jules, I know that this is an imposition, but will you please let Sharon at least buy the furniture? She's so excited. I haven't seen her like this since little Johnny was born. Don't do it for you. Do it for her. Make her happy, please?" John chuckled then. "Besides, you know she'll drive me crazy unless you keep her busy."

Julia laughed. She and Austin had talked it over, and just like they had done with the house, neither would talk much about the nursery with Sharon around. They didn't want cribs, changing tables, and high chairs magically appearing on their doorstep.

"John, I tell you what I'll do. I'll design the room. Austin will do the painting, and I'll let Sharon do the furnishing. You think that will make her happy?"

"Immensely," John hugged her tight. "More than you know."

Surprisingly enough, it was Lauren who came up with the final design. She had come by to look at the room, its dimensions, window locations, and other factors. The next day at work, she tossed a manila folder on Julia's desk.

"Don't say I never gave you anything," Lauren said, before returning to her own desk to settle in.

Julia took out the several pages. Taking her time, she looked at the colored drawings of a beautiful nursery. Two walls were colored a soft white with the other two in a soft yellow of two varying shades. The furniture was drawn in brown with soft pink and multi-colored bedding and cushions. The wall that contained the window was white, and Lauren had painted light brown shutters with Tinker Bell perched on the top of one. Next to the little fairy was a dragonfly painted in bright colors. The yellow walls were striped in the two shades of the color, one a matte finish alternated with the glossy finish, and interspersed on both walls were more dragonflies and brightly colored daisies. In the middle of the white wall where Lauren had drawn the bed, the name *Acacia* was painted in curling brown letters with bright butterflies scattered across the wall, flying from the tail of the last "a."

Julia finished and looked up at her friend, tears swimming in her eyes.

"Lauren, this is beautiful," she said, as Lauren raised her head to smile at Julia.

"I also volunteer to do the artwork, oh and that two-tone wall. I do not trust Austin to get that right. As for the furniture or other stuff for the walls, I'll leave that to you and Sharon," Lauren got up, but Julia was already heading toward her side of the room. She pulled her unpredictable friend close.

"Lauren, you are a mess. Here I didn't think you cared about Caci or her room or anything to do with, well, any of this," Julia pulled back to look at Lauren, unconsciously putting a hand on her stomach.

"Hey, I care," Lauren insisted. "I just don't live it, you know? Besides, I refuse to let you and Sharon do some pinky pink and black or whatever nightmare. At least this isn't too pink."

"It's perfect," Julia assured her. She laughed. "What I can't wait to see is you and Austin working together on this project." With that she laughed even harder. Lauren thought about being irritated, but seeing Julia so happy at her expense had her joining in the joke.

"Ha, I'll have him straightened out in no time. Hell, I may even get old Matty in on the fun," Lauren's face lit up at that thought.

"So, how are things going with Matt?" Julia seldom broached the subject, never knowing what Lauren's reaction would be.

Lauren shrugged her shoulder. "Myeh, it's going. Probably nowhere, but we're having fun, you know?"

Julia looked hard at Lauren, who refused to meet her eyes. "Lauren, stop wasting the man's time. If you aren't interested in anything lasting, tell him. That way he has the option to move on. You're older and more experienced than Matt. And I fear that you are going to really hurt him."

"Oh, stop worrying, Mom. We both know the score, so to speak, and we're still having fun. Besides, it will end soon enough when the 'man' in him rears its ugly head," Lauren turned away and Julia watched her saunter back to her desk. After regaining her seat and pulling her reading glasses onto her nose, Lauren looked up, challenge in her eyes.

Julia put her hand up in surrender. "You win. I just don't want you to end up alone."

Lauren laughed. "Me? Alone? I'm not that old yet, Jules. Hell, I don't even know anyone that old." At Julia's frown, she rolled her eyes. "I. Am. Fine. Okay? Just because you're all nesting and shit doesn't mean that's for me." Her shoulders moved in a mock shiver. "Ugh, no thank you. I'll live that life vicariously through you, thank you very much." She'd unconsciously repeated what Matt had accused her of doing.

Julia let it drop, knowing that to Lauren the subject was closed. *I'll always worry about her, but I can't change anything for her. I'll just love her.*

Chapter 43

"I REALLY DON'T WANT TO GO," Austin was pouting as he watched Julia neatly fold his clothes and tuck them into the small suitcase. "You're getting closer to the baby coming, and I know Steve would understand if I begged off."

Julia stopped what she was doing long enough to give him The Look. *She really is perfecting that expression,* he thought as he took in her no-nonsense stance. *Poor Caci won't stand a chance.*

"Austin, you'll only be gone three days, and the baby isn't due for another five or six weeks. Save the big favor for when we really need it," Julia stepped back and motioned for him to finish. "Now, I have the shirts folded so that they won't wrinkle, and your pants are under them. As soon as you get to the hotel, take them out and see if they need to be pressed. If so, call the front desk and they'll send someone to pick them up."

"I know, I know, sweetheart. I have travelled before," he grinned at her fussing over him. Lately, she'd been fussing over everything, including him. "I'm just glad the nursery is finished and that isn't hanging over my head."

Austin and Matt had knocked out the wall painting in a weekend, supervised by Lauren every step of the way. It took her a week of evenings and two weekends to complete the artwork, but the finished project was spectacular. Julia thought the sketches were good, but the completed room was unbelievable. Sharon had kept her distance until it was ready for the furniture, curtains, and other furnishings. She and Julia were in the shop pouring over swatches of fabric until they narrowed it down to two. Things stalled as the two couldn't agree and Lauren stepped in, picked something that was totally different but worked perfectly, and smirked as she went back to what she was doing.

In typical Sharon style, the curtains were finished and hanging, the nursery furniture was in place, and the crib was outfitted with the matching ensemble, all within a week. She'd even had the rocking chair and ottoman cushions upholstered in matching fabric. Julia stood in the doorway and took in the magical room. The only difference between the real room and the drawing was the additional Tinker Bell that Lauren had painted beside Acacia's name. It looked as though the little fairy was using her magic wand to release the butterflies that flew across the wall. Tears filled her eyes.

"It's really happening…I'm really having a baby," she whispered.

"I certainly hope so," Austin whispered in her ear as he came up behind her, "because if you aren't, we really need to get you on a diet and exercise program. Not to mention return all of those gifts you've been getting."

Julia turned and smiled, shaking her head. He wiped the tear that had escaped and kissed her gently. "It's really happening, sweetheart." As if to punctuate his words, Acacia chose that moment to kick, almost hitting Austin's crotch. They both laughed. "I know there's a joke in here somewhere, but I don't know what it is right now," he said, putting his hand where the little limb had been. "Watch it, little girl. Daddy needs those parts."

He looked around the room. "It really does look fantastic, doesn't it?"

Julia took a deep breath and released it slowly. "Like a dream. I couldn't ask for anything more perfect than this, you know?"

Back to the present, she was still thinking of that time when Austin's voice brought her around. She shook off her thoughts and focused on the job at hand.

"I still don't want to go. Are you sure you don't want to come with me?" he asked hopefully.

"We talked about this, and I really am not up to flying, not even if it is to Miami Beach. I've always wanted to go there, but not when I'm as big as a whale."

"Baby, you are far from whale size," he came toward her and she recognized that look in his eyes. Their sex life hadn't slowed down at all, and Julia was hoping it wouldn't until Acacia was born and then not for long after that. "But just in case I'm missing something, let me take a good look." He put his arms around her and kissed her slowly before moving his hands up her back and unfastening the zipper on her short dress, sliding it down her back. Julia closed her eyes at his touch, and when she opened them, he could see the blue had deepened. Her hands did some traveling of their own as she unbuttoned his shirt, smiling up at him as each came undone. They were heading toward the bed, when the mess stopped them. Julia laughed at Austin's disgusted look as he tossed the suitcase onto the chair. It was a mess now, but she didn't mind. This would be worth packing again.

Austin gently laid her on the bed and finished undressing her, pulling his own clothes off before joining her. He looked down and his eyes took in her enlarged breasts and swelling stomach. She'd never been so beautiful. As for Julia, she joked about her size, but she knew from his look that he still found her desirable. She rolled toward him, running her hands across his muscled chest, down his flat stomach, and still lower. He groaned as she touched him and his mouth found hers. His hand cupped first one soft mound of breast as his mouth soon followed. He trailed kisses down and across her stomach where his baby girl rested. As if on cue, he felt her roll around and kissed the little bump that could be a leg or arm. The baby may interrupt them later, but not now. He grinned and moved still lower. As Julia moaned under him, he rose and took her then, trying to be as gentle as possible.

"Please, more," he heard her whisper as he stopped holding back. He felt her release just before his own and collapsed onto his side, lying by her. He patted her stomach.

"Good try, little girl," he laughed. "Someday you'll be successful at interrupting, but not yet."

"Yeah, well, if I have anything to say about it, she won't be successful then, either," Julia's voice was soft as she rested beside him.

They lay a few minutes longer before she raised up, struggling a bit until he gave her a push on the back to help her along. She smiled her thanks and went into the bathroom. He heard the water running and soon she was back with a warm moist towel to clean him up. He lay back, hands linked behind his head and watched her as she worked over him, her long hair brushing his legs.

"You're going to miss this, you know," he reminded her.

"No, *you're* going to miss this," she grinned and left him to return to the bathroom. Austin sat up and looked for his clothes that were scattered around the floor. He shook out his shirt and pants, decided they were still okay, and dressed. Julia had wrapped her robe around her, tying the belt above her stomach, which protruded beneath.

"Let me help you get this suitcase lined out again," she grinned as she started to pick it up to put it back on the bed.

"Oh, no, you don't," Austin nudged her aside. He rarely let her carry anything and was diligent in watching her go up or down stairs. She laughed at his protectiveness, but he was so cute about it that she let him boss her in that respect. It was his contribution to the cause, so to speak, and she indulged him.

A few minutes later, his things were straightened out, and she zipped up his suitcase. Austin stood looking at her a little longer. He pulled her close as they stood holding one another.

"I really don't want to go," he was whining again, and she laughed.

"God, you're such a whiny baby. Three days. That's all. I'll text you all day, and you'll return my texts. We'll talk all night, every night, and before you can even miss me, you'll be home. And somewhere in all of those texts and talks, you'll get the job done. Deal?"

She heard his sigh and pushed him away. His eyes met hers, and he wasn't happy. Julia shook her head.

"Austin, please. Go. I'll be here waiting when you get home Friday night. I promise."

"I'll hold you to that, woman," he grinned then and stepped back to grab his suitcase.

After another kiss at the door and another at the car, Julia watched him drive away. She stepped back to close the door, leaning against it with a sigh. "I already miss him," she whispered before shaking her head and starting for the bedroom to bathe and change clothes. "At least Sharon and John will distract me tonight." She grinned at the thought.

Chapter 44

———

THE BRIGHT LATE NOVEMBER SUN reflected off the ferns and flowers that surrounded the patio and pool area of the Hilton as Austin sat in the shade of an umbrella, several pages of the proposal spread on the table in front of him. He was officially finished for the day, but a couple of things were bothering him about the site, and he wanted to have them firmly in mind before the next day's trip to the location. He looked down at his phone, but Julia hadn't returned his text yet. He smiled as he thought about her running around in her new SUV. She had been right about the "cool" factor.

He was lost in thought and didn't notice the brunette who came up to the table. Audra was clad in a black bikini and had a pool towel draped over one arm. She moved next to his chair, and when he still didn't look up, she cleared her throat. At the sound, Austin looked up and stared at Audra a couple of seconds before it registered who was there. She took his extended gaze as interest and sent a sexy smile his way.

"All work and no play, you know," she said, taking in the papers spread out in front of him. "Why don't you put those away and join me for a swim? The water looks almost as good as you do."

The woman and her meaning finally registered in Austin's head as he looked away from her and back down to his phone. This was exactly what he didn't want, her attention. Shuffling the papers on the table, Austin tried to decide what to say to get rid of her.

"Yeah, the water does look good, but I wanted to get some of this straight in my mind before tomorrow." He looked up and smiled. "And I'm expecting Julia to call me soon. We've texted off and on but there's nothing like hearing her voice, you know?"

"No, I don't know, but I'll take your word for it," Audra's voice had lost a little of its friendliness but she wasn't giving up just yet. She came around the back of his chair and leaned in to see what was on the table. As she did, her breast came to rest on his shoulder. As soon as he felt the touch, Austin pulled away, his chair scraping on the stone patio.

"You'll enjoy your swim," he said, dismissing her. "Looks like a fun crowd gathering over there. You'll fit right in."

"Oh, I will," Audra drawled, leaning in toward him. Before she could make contact again, Austin moved his body away and turned his head back to his phone, pointedly ignoring her.

You're strong, my handsome friend, but I'm patient, she thought.

"Well, I guess I'll just head that direction and see what's happening. Sure you won't join me?" At his negative nod, Audra turned and sauntered toward the water. Austin didn't even look up. His attention was back on his paperwork.

Neither of them had seen the woman sitting in one of the lounge chairs, but she had seen them. Karen was just far enough away to be unable to hear what was said, but she certainly knew what she saw. She noticed Austin only because of the brunette who had first walked past her on her way to his table. *Skinny bitch,* Karen thought as she watched the woman stop beside a handsome man with blond, curly hair. *Isn't that...* she thought and when he looked up at the woman standing beside his chair, Karen caught her breath. *It's Austin!* As he continued to stare at the woman in front of him, Karen took out her phone and snapped a picture. Why, she didn't really know, but something told her to record all of this. She watched as Austin looked back at whatever he had on the table and said something to the woman, who leaned over, resting her breast on his shoulder. Karen snapped away and was looking at her phone when Austin pulled away and turned his attention back to something on the table. She watched as the two talked together a few more seconds, and the brunette turned toward the pool. He didn't look her direction and hadn't seen Julia's friend yet.

I know where I've seen her, Karen thought. *At the barbeque that day! She works with him or something. But that certainly didn't look like work.* She gathered her own things and walked to where Austin was sitting.

"It's a small world!" Austin turned at the familiar voice, and recognizing Karen, smiled at her. "What are you doing down here, Austin?"

370

"All work and no play," he replied. "What brings you here?"

"Oh," Karen laughed cheerfully. "I have a convention for realtors that I never miss. I have to admit that we are mostly play and little work." She laughed and he chuckled with her. They chatted about Julia and the baby, how the extra downstairs bedroom of the house had been transformed into a nursery. Karen was getting ready to make a sales pitch for a more kid-friendly house when Audra returned.

"Austin, who's your friend?" She extended her hand and Karen took it reluctantly. "You didn't tell me you knew anyone else down here this week."

"Audra, you met Karen at our barbeque, you just don't remember," Austin was gathering things together as he talked. "And now, I'll leave you ladies to the sun and water. Karen, good to see you. Audra, see you at dinner." He turned and walked toward the building, both women watching him go.

"Isn't he something?" Audra crooned as she kept her eyes on the man until he disappeared inside the hotel. "Handsome and smart."

"And taken," Karen raised one eyebrow in Audra's direction.

Audra turned and smiled at Karen, as if she held a secret that the other one hadn't figured out.

"Not for long. Doubt even a baby will help Julia hang onto him." She leaned closer to the astonished woman. "Not if I can help it. He warms up to me a little more every day." She straightened up, her breasts thrust in Karen's direction. "It's just a matter of time now."

Karen had been speechless at the woman's candor, but found her voice. "Don't be too sure."

Audra laughed. "Oh, I'm very sure. Now, you'll excuse me. I'm meeting Austin for dinner and need to shower. Caio."

With that, Audra walked away toward the building and the door Austin had disappeared through.

"Oh, we'll see how sure you are, Miss Skinny Bitch." Karen looked at the photo on her phone, wondering what to do. Should she send them to Julia? *Tempting*, she thought, *but until I know for sure that Austin is sleeping with the bitch, or even considering it, I don't want to bother a pregnant Julia. She's so sweet and doesn't deserve to be treated like this.* She thought of Lauren. Karen's fingers flew over her phone as she typed a message to her other friend, attached the photo, and hit send. She waited a few minutes, but when Lauren didn't reply, Karen grew more worried. *Well, I won't do nothing, that's for sure,* Karen thought. *I'll be keeping my eye on those two. I've got your back, Julia!*

The table at dinner that night held the five co-workers, and Austin made sure Audra was seated first before he took a seat out of her line of vision. He wasn't really worried, but he knew that he'd have to meet the problem head on before long. Not that he was tempted—nothing was further from the truth—but he was growing tired of having to fend off her advances at every turn. Austin smiled at the thought. *Reverse harassment,* he thought. *Things have certainly changed in the workplace.* He turned his attention to the conversation and enjoyed the rest of the meal without giving Audra another thought.

As they finished up, Austin looked at his phone and noted the time. This was when he always called Julia, and he excused himself to return to his room. The others were headed for the bar, but Austin begged off. He ignored the jests about his being an "old man" and laughed as he turned and walked away. He made it to his room and hit the speed dial.

"Hey, Jules, god I miss you," he closed his eyes and could almost breathe her in. Almost. "How are my girls tonight? Or is it afternoon there?" He referred to Julia and Caci as his girls these days.

Julia laughed at the other end. "We're both fine, and both of us are getting bigger as we speak." He loved hearing her laugh, which she did again. "I swear, I am eating all the damn time! I hope to god this changes in a few weeks, or you'll be glad we have that big-ass bed!"

They both laughed, and he asked about her day. Julia had finished telling him about a Mrs. Harcourt when someone knocked on his door.

"Hey, babe, someone's at the door. It's probably Roger or Stewart. Can I call you before bed?"

"You better," he could hear the smile in her voice. "Go do your thing, sweetie, and hurry home!"

"I can't get there fast enough. I love you more than life," he said, and ended the call. The knocking came again.

"Hang on, I'm coming." Austin opened the door.

"Hey, party pooper!" Audra came striding through the door, bottle of wine in her hand. "I figured I'd bring the party to you!" She closed the door behind her. Waving the bottle in front of her, she smiled.

"Audra, you have to leave," Austin strode toward the door, but he stopped when he felt a hand on his arm. He looked down to where Audra had hold of him and back up at her, his eyes hard and unfriendly. "Do you mind ?" he said, looking pointedly at her hand. She reluctantly moved it and smirked at him.

"Really, Austin, I don't know what the hell your problem is. I've been nothing but nice to you. I've kept my distance like you asked, and I've tried to be professional at the office." She took a step toward him, her voice lowering. "But we're not at the office now, are we? No one else is here. No one else need ever know a thing. Not the others, not the boss, not Julia."

At the mention of Julia, Austin had had enough. He opened the door and stood there holding it.

"You can leave on your own, or I can toss you out. Your call," Austin's cold voice and hard eyes let Audra know that he meant what he said. "I am so finished with you and your games. Take your wine, take your unwanted offer, and go."

Audra straightened her shoulders and sauntered past him, pausing at the door.

"You know that…"she began, but he interrupted her.

"All I know is that I want you to leave," he stated, "now."

The woman walked into the hall and after hearing the door shut behind her, stalked away in a very unattractive gait. She was angry and she didn't like not getting her way. Audra smiled as she thought, *Tomorrow is another day*, and headed to join the others at the bar.

Neither of them had noticed the woman who watched the first part of their meeting. She had followed the brunette from the bar and had hidden in front of a recessed door a few yards down. She could hear everything, and as soon as Austin opened the door and the brunette from the pool hurried through, closing it behind her, Karen flew toward the elevator. All she had heard was "I thought I'd bring the party to you!"

"Ohmygod, ohmygod," she texted to Lauren. "Lauren help! You won't believe what I just saw, you won't believe it…" The rest of the text was a replay of what she'd seen. What Karen didn't see was Austin tossing Audra out of his room and the woman's angry reaction.

More than two thousand miles away, Lauren heard her phone ding and looked down. *Karen,* she thought and rolled her eyes. *The cow loves rubbing it in when she's in Florida. Like I give a shit.* Lauren saw that she'd missed an earlier message. While she usually ignored Karen's messages, something caught her eye. As she read, Lauren's eyes opened wider. *Son-of-a-bitch!* She thought when she finished the first round of texts. As the photos came through, Lauren lost it. She stalked around her living room, cursing a blue streak. Her mood didn't improve, just the opposite, after she read the last message regarding the hotel room and wine-bearing woman.

"That miserable bastard! That asshole! Oh, he had me fooled all this time. And Julia," Lauren stopped in mid-stride, her breath coming in deep heated bursts. "My sweet Julia, pregnant out to there, and that bastard is off screwing around. I knew he was too good to be true! The assholes always show their true colors eventually. *Damn it!*"

Lauren sat down hard on her sofa and glared into space. She looked back down at the phone and read again the most recent message relating Austin's hotel room visitor. Lauren's eyes narrowed and she felt the heat rising up her neck. *Not on my watch, you asswipe,* she thought. Lauren punched in a search that gave her the number of the airline. The soonest she could get a flight to Miami Beach was nine o'clock the next morning. "I'll take it," her hard voice assured the ticket agent. Lauren gave her credit card information and wrote down the confirmation information even though the agent would email her all she'd need. She had no sooner ended that call than she texted Karen: "Do NOT tell Julia. I'm on my way and will handle this. I repeat DO NOT tell Julia! She's too close to delivering this baby and we don't want to worry her. I'll see you tomorrow."

Lauren sat on the sofa, and she was thinking back over the past. She envisioned the men in her life who had betrayed her, David being the last. She thought about Keith and all the pain he'd caused Julia. She recalled the long road her friend had taken to get back to a good place with Austin, but he was a jerk, too. Finally, she thought about Matt. He was probably just like the rest of them. Hell, he'd already shown that he was, with his parade of young women coming and going from his bed. She failed to acknowledge his monogamous relationship with her. Lauren sat like that for at least an hour before throwing a pillow against the fireplace. That was followed by another pillow, a magazine, a book, and finally the remote control, which shattered as it hit the marble surface. Hearing the sound brought Lauren around somewhat. She was breathing hard, trying to regain control.

Julia, she thought. *Dammit.* Lauren took out her phone and punched in a message to her friend. "I won't be in the office tomorrow and maybe not the next day. I'm caught up on everything, I think, and I thought it would be a good time to get some R and R. I'll call you. Love you—mean it!" She hit the send button and immediately felt guilty for lying to her best friend. *The truth would be too much, and I'm not about to be the cause of yet another baby disaster. I'll handle this myself.*

Damn that Austin, she thought. *Damn him to hell where I hope his ass burns hotter than the hottest cinder. And when I get there, I'll make sure he suffers even more.*

Austin was oblivious to the drama that was unfolding on his behalf. The following day, he refused to look at Audra throughout the meeting, and on the trip to the project location, Austin rode in front with the driver so that he wouldn't have to sit anywhere near her. They returned in the late afternoon, and Austin was determined to not have a repeat of the previous day. He excused himself and went directly to his room. He was getting ready to shower off the day's heat and humidity when someone knocked on his door. *Dammit,* he thought. *I will not go through this shit again.* He threw open the door, a look of annoyance on his face.

"Lauren!" he exclaimed as she pushed past him and barged into the room. She stalked into the bathroom and checked all around before whirling on him.

"You lousy, no-good, two-timing son-of-a-bitch!" She was just warming up. "Oh, you had me fooled. Hell, you had us all fooled! Playing Mr. Sweet and Nice while the whole time you were just biding your time to make your move. God *damn* you! Julia's home, pregnant with *your* baby, and here you are screwing some hosebeast from the office." She looked like she'd like nothing more than to put her fist in his face. "Really, Austin?! You didn't think anyone would ever find out? How long have you two been at it? Since the barbeque? She certainly tried then." Lauren was stalking back and forth in the room, and Austin was too stunned to interrupt her. "Well, you're not doing this shit on *my* watch, you hear me?! Not on my watch! I've seen it all before, and you're no different from the rest." She turned and her eyes bore into him. "*Pigs*! You're all a bunch of *pigs*, and if you think you're going to break Julia's heart like Keith did before, you better think again. I think I'll kill you first and do the world a favor, you no-good bastard...you have no idea how lucky you are right now because if my gun was in my hand, I'd blow your ever-loving brains into next week. *Dammit!*" Lauren stood glaring at Austin, her hands bunched on her hips like she'd just as soon punch him in the throat. He looked at both her hands, making sure she didn't have one of her guns with her. She was that mad.

Austin took a deep breath. "Are you finished?"

Lauren took a breath, ready to start again, but Austin raised a hand. "Wait a minute. If I knew what the hell you're talking about, I might be able to answer some of this crap you're throwing my way. I honestly have no idea. Now, if you can calm down enough, will you tell me what's going on?"

Lauren dropped into a chair as if the air had been let out of her all of a sudden. She took out her phone and showed Austin the text messages from Karen, the photo, and what Karen had seen the previous night.

"So there, hot shot," she glared at him. "Let's see if you can talk your way out of this one. And don't try to bullshit me, Junior. I won't have it."

"No bullshit, Blondie, but you're wrong. Karen's wrong." He explained the events of the previous day and evening, his avoiding Audra throughout the day, and ended by explaining how he was ready to let management know how the woman was hounding him. As he finished, he shrugged his shoulders. "And that's the truth. Believe me or not, that's it."

Lauren sat staring at him. She was still mad, furious, but as she took in his explanation, she decided that perhaps Karen did have her story wrong. *It wouldn't be the first time*, she thought. The more she thought about it, the angrier she became, not at Austin but at Audra.

"Well, it looks like I need to have a little chat with Miss Audra. Do you know where she is?" Lauren was rising to search for her enemy.

"No, I don't, and I don't want you doing anything to her. I think it's time that I had the pleasure of setting Miss Audra, as you call her, straight."

Austin sat in the chair facing Lauren's and his face was set in concentration. After a few minutes, he pulled out his phone and scrolled through his contacts. Finding the number he needed, he hit the call button.

"Hello, handsome," he heard the voice at the other end drawl. Lauren could hear her, and he had to wave her back before she could say anything.

"Hey, I was wondering if you wanted to meet me in the bar."

Lauren was frowning at him, her brows making a deep V in her forehead.

Audra's excited voice echoed in the room. "I'd love nothing more! When?"

"How about now? Thirty minutes?" Austin's calm voice betrayed none of the emotion he was really feeling.

"See you then. And Austin, I can't wait," Audra almost purred before signing off.

"Oh, my god, I'm going to scratch her eyes out and feed them to the seagulls," Lauren was storming around the room again. "What the hell was that all about, anyway? And don't think you're meeting her alone. Oh, when I see her in that bar..."

"Lauren, you can't be there. Well, you can," he corrected as dark brown eyes zeroed in on him, "but I don't want her to see you. Sit close where you can hear, but keep your back to her. She won't be looking for you, so I don't think she'll notice." He went on to explain what he planned. As he finished, Lauren's face broke out into what Julia always called her scary smile.

"I love it," she said. "I've got your back, but if she pushes me, get out of the way."

Austin shook his head. "I'd never dream of coming between you two."

They left soon after and hurried to put themselves into position. Lauren ordered a drink that sat untouched in front of her and spoke over her shoulder.

"Say something, Austin. I need to know that I can hear you."

"I can't. She's coming in," Austin said.

No problem. Heard that loud and clear, Lauren thought. She wanted so badly to turn around and physically attack the woman who was striding to Austin's table. She clinched her hands together and bit down on her bottom lip. At the woman's first words, Lauren visibly fidgeted in her chair.

"I knew you'd see it my way. I don't know what changed your mind, but I'm so glad you did," Audra took the chair closest to Lauren but facing away from her and leaned in closer to Austin. "I promise you won't regret it."

Audra looked at Austin's face and pulled back. His eyes were hard and his mouth was set in a line.

"My only regret, Audra, is that I didn't set you straight a long time ago," he began. As she started to speak, he stopped her. "No, you hear me out. Julia told me months ago that some people only respond to rudeness. My beautiful girlfriend is also very smart. I should have never been as polite as I have been, but my mom did a good job of raising me with southern manners. No more." He leaned his arms on the table and moved closer to emphasize what he was about to say. "Audra, I've had it with your sexual innuendos, your unwanted attention, and pretty much everything that is not work related. I am not interested in you, nor will I ever be interested in you." He looked at the woman in front of him with nothing but contempt. "I love Julia. We're having a baby girl, and we are happy together. Move on, Audra. Go find someone else who actually wants your attention."

Audra's pretty face was quickly transforming from radiant to hard. She sat back and glared at the man in front of her. Austin could almost see the wheels turning, and he decided to beat her to the punch.

"Oh, and before you can cry sexual harassment on me, know that I've already started the papers charging *you* with harassment in the workplace." It was a little white lie, and he inwardly chuckled at Audra's shocked look. "Yeah, harassment goes both ways, or didn't you watch the training videos?"

"You have no proof," Audra was regaining her control.

"Oh, I think I do. Lauren?"

Lauren had held herself in check throughout the conversation, and now she rose from her chair, pulling herself up to her full height. She towered over the still-seated woman.

"His proof is *me*!" Lauren leaned closer so that her words wouldn't carry across the room. "Fuck off, you little bitch. You're done. And don't think this will end here." Lauren smiled. "I remember overhearing a little conversation that you had with a dear friend of mine, you may remember. Sharon Burns?" As Audra raised one eyebrow and glared at Lauren, the latter continued. "Oh, it may not be next week, or even next month, but you'll feel the full wrath of that woman. And trust me, Sugar, I wouldn't want to be in your shoes for all the money in the world."

At that, Audra jerked to her feet, glaring at Lauren and then Austin. She grabbed her bag from the table before she turned and huffed out of the room. Lauren grinned at Austin.

"Damn, that was fun! Let's celebrate with a drink, shall we?"

Austin let out the breath he had been holding. He wasn't sure what Lauren was going to do and had been ready to pull the two women apart had the need arisen. He shook his head.

"Make mine a double. This drama shit has made me very thirsty."

Lauren laughed and called the waiter over. He'd been watching Lauren since he'd first taken her order, and he was eager to fawn over her now. Lauren took the vacated seat and laughed. Both decided that it had been an exhausting day, but now it was all over. They had no idea of what Karen had been up to.

Chapter 45

KAREN WAS WORRIED ABOUT JULIA. She hadn't heard from Lauren since the previous night, and she didn't know if she should call Lauren, Julia, or what to do. She didn't want to worry Julia, but if it were Karen, she'd sure as hell want to know what was going on. With that thought, she pulled out her phone and started typing. She read again her account of the events she'd witnessed the previous day and night, and attaching the photos of Austin and Audra, she hit the send button. *Wow,* she thought, *that's a load off my shoulders. I hate keeping secrets like that.* It was but a few minutes and she heard her phone ring. Looking down, she saw that it was Julia.

"Oh, Julia," Karen answered, "you have no idea how sorry I am to be such a bearer of bad news."

"No, I'm sorry, Karen, but you must be wrong. I'm certain you've just misunderstood what you saw."

Karen sighed. "I wish I were wrong." She paused. "Call Lauren. She's down here right now confronting Austin and Audra. She'll confirm my story."

A couple of seconds passed before she heard Julia's reply. "Thanks, Karen. I'll get this all straightened out. You're a good friend. Talk to you later."

"Love you, Jules," Karen started to say more, but Julia had already ended the call. She sighed, hoping she'd done the right thing.

Still in the bar, Austin and Lauren were laughing about the day they'd painted the nursery when Austin remembered that he needed to call Julia.

He reached into his pockets, but couldn't locate his phone. He thought he'd laid it on the table and was looking around when Lauren asked what he was doing.

"My phone. I can't find it, and it's past time I always call Jules. What the hell…"

"You said you laid it on the table?" Lauren asked, understanding dawning on her. "What do you want to bet that hosebeast picked it up?" She shook her head.

"Dammit! Come with me and let's get it back."

They said nothing as they made their way to the elevator and up to the floor where Audra was. At Austin's knock, she opened the door, holding his phone.

"Looking for this?" she asked sweetly. "I accidentally picked it up and was getting ready to take it to you." She looked around his shoulder. "Oh, I see you still have the guard dog with you."

Lauren growled in her throat and glared at Audra. The sound startled her and she pulled back.

"Well, here you go. No harm, no foul. Later." Audra shut the door.

"God! I hate that woman," Lauren turned to start down the hall, but Austin was lagging behind.

"I don't see anything from Julia. If we don't call by this time, we always text one another. I hope everything is all right."

"Don't go looking for trouble, Ace. I'm sure it's all fine. Call her now."

Austin hit the speed dial number and listened to the tone at the other end. Julia's voice came on, directing him to leave her a message.

"Hey, Jules, it's me. I'm sorry I didn't call before, but I was busy. Call me when you get this. Love you." He hit the end button and stared at the wall in front of him. "Something's off, Lauren. I feel it."

He so seldom used her name. Lauren turned back and put her hand on his arm. He really was worried.

"Hey, Aus, it's okay. I'll try." She punched in Julia's number, and her call also went to voice mail, this time directly. She was getting a bad feeling, too. Julia always answered Austin's calls and seldom did she ignore Lauren's. She wouldn't normally react, but in Julia's condition, Lauren wanted to be safe rather than sorry. She scrolled through her contacts and hit another number.

"Sharon? Hey, it's Lauren. I'm worried about Julia. Will you go check on her?"

Austin could hear Sharon's voice loud and clear. "Of course! What's wrong? Lauren? What's happened? Something's not right. I can hear it in your voice."

Lauren tried to assure her. "Everything's fine now, but Julia isn't answering either my calls or Austin's. Just check on her, please. I'll answer questions later."

The silence stretched out a bit before Sharon came back on. "Of course I will. And, Lauren, you will tell me what's going on." The no-nonsense tone left no room for argument.

"Yes, you know I will. Now, go look in on Julia, please, and call either me or Austin."

"Good as done. Later." Sharon's call ended.

Lauren looked at Austin's face and smiled, squeezing his arm with her hand.

"Hey, it's all okay, okay? Julia's just in the tub, or on another phone, or something."

Austin nodded. "Yeah, you're probably right, but I still have a bad feeling."

Lauren wouldn't admit it, but she did, too.

Chapter 46

⟋⟍

J ULIA SAT ON THE EDGE of her bed and thought about Karen's call. She remembered Lauren's telling her that she was taking off for the day and remembered thinking it odd but not totally unheard of for Lauren to take off unexpectedly. It was the photos that Karen sent her that had Julia frowning. Karen was the worst of gossips, but more often than not, her information was accurate. And if Lauren was there, Julia was convinced that something wasn't right.

Well, only one way to find out, she thought, *I'll go to the source.* She dialed Austin's number and listened to the ring at his end. She was ready to leave a message when a female voice answered.

"Hello?"

Julia recognized the voice. "Audra? What are you doing with Austin's phone? Is he there? I need to speak to him." She felt the heat rising up her neck at the thought of the other woman.

Audra laughed, "Oh, I'm sorry, Julia, but Austin can't come to the phone right now. He's in the shower. Can I take a message?"

Julia was shocked, but she found her voice. "No, no message because I doubt you'd give it to him anyway. I'll try again later."

"Ok, I'll…" the beep of the phone letting her know the call had ended stopped Audra from saying anymore. She smiled and spoke out loud, "Well, that couldn't have gone any better. I wonder what Queen Julia will have to say to lover boy." She looked down. Quickly, she erased the last call and checked his text messages. Not seeing anything that would alert him, she turned off the phone and waited. She knew he'd eventually figure out who had it. Sure enough, not ten minutes later, someone knocked on

Audra's door. Looking out the peep hole, she saw an irritated Austin with Lauren close behind him.

Following the exchange, Audra closed her door and leaned against it. *Well, I may not have made any inroads to Austin, but I've certainly made life uncomfortable*, she thought and laughed out loud. *Very uncomfortable.*

Julia still sat holding her phone, feeling numb. The baby rolled around and gave her a kick. Julia reached down and rubbed a hand back and forth over the protruding area. She was as confused as she'd ever been, and hurt. *Once again*, she thought, *I'm the last person to know what's going on behind my back.*

Climbing up onto the bed, Julia wrapped her arms around her stomach, the phone still clutched in one hand. She didn't know how long she lay there when she heard Austin's ring tone. She stared at the picture of his smiling face that always came up when he called. This time she didn't smile back. Instead, she turned the cell off and closed her eyes. She really wasn't in the mood to talk to him. With the phone off, Julia didn't know that Lauren was trying to reach her, and that John and Sharon were calling from their car as they drove over.

Julia's mind was racing. She couldn't imagine Austin going behind her back. Their relationship never warranted her to even consider he might be unhappy. Yes, the baby was unexpected, but Austin seemed as excited as she was now. Their sex life hadn't slowed down a bit, and if anything, he was more loving than ever. *So why is he hanging around Audra?* She wondered. *And if he was in the shower, why in the world would that woman be in his room? Answering his phone? None of this makes sense.*

Of course, none of Keith's activities had made any sense, either. He'd kept his phone locked so she never knew who was calling him or what calls he was making. He took several business trips without her, but she never thought anything of those either at the time. And when she finally caught him with his mistress, Julia had been mortified to realize that everyone else had known except her. *Please, don't let this be a repeat*, she pleaded. *I don't know if I can take it again.*

Julia was still lying in the same position when she heard the doorbell. *My door, and I don't feel like answering it*, she thought. The insistent ringing was followed by someone pounding on it and yelling. She thought it sounded like Sharon, but she couldn't bring herself to go check. *She has a key*, Julia thought, *she can let herself in.*

Sharon's voice echoed from the living room. "Julia! Sweetie, are you here? John, check the garage for her car. I can't imagine why she isn't answering...." Sharon stopped at the bedroom door and saw Julia lying on the bed.

"Sweetheart! Are you all right? Jules! Why didn't you answer me?" Sharon came around and sat down beside her. She took in the pale face, messy hair, and arms clutched around her stomach. "Julia?" Sharon's voice was soft. "Honey? Are you okay? Baby, what's happened?" When Julia didn't answer, Sharon reached out and smoothed her hair back from her face. John came in.

"Oh, good, you found her," and at Sharon's worried expression, he, too, came around to the side where Julia lay. "Baby girl?" He sometimes used the same term of endearment as Lawrence. "What's wrong? Are you and the baby okay? Are you hurt?" At the sound of his voice, Julia's eyes filled with tears that spilled over and ran onto the pillow beneath her head.

"Oh, honey, it's okay." Sharon pulled her up and into her arms, cradling her there. She looked up at John, who was standing beside her, and mouthed, *What the hell?* To which he shrugged and shook his head. When the younger woman had cried it out, Sharon softly asked again. "Now, will you tell me what's going on? I know pregnant women have raging hormones, but this isn't a hormone thing, is it?"

Julia's red, puffy eyes looked at Sharon, and she shook her head no. "Sharon," she started to speak, her voice raspy, "I just don't know. Karen sent me pictures, Lauren lied to me and left, and Austin," her voice broke, "I think Austin is with another woman in Miami Beach. She answered his phone, said he couldn't talk because he was in the shower. It's that Audra he works with." Tears leaked out of her eyes again. "What am I going to do?"

Sharon was shocked into silence. She looked at John as if to tell him to get on it and find out what the hell was happening. It was as if he could read her mind because he pulled out his phone and was getting ready to place a call when Julia cried out.

"Oh!" She pulled out of Sharon's arms and clutched her stomach. "Oh my god, it hurts!" She looked up at John and her frightened eyes pleaded for him to do something. "It's coming again...ahhhh..."

Sharon put an arm around Julia and looked at her pale face, twisted in pain. "John we've got to get her to the hospital. Should we call an ambulance? Drive her? What do you think?"

John immediately went into action.

"I'll drive," he said. "I can get her there faster myself," and John slipped an arm under Julia and picked her up. He strode through the house as Sharon ran ahead. As he carried Julia out the front door, Sharon had the back door of the car open for him to slide Julia in. Sharon slipped in from the other side and cradled Julia's head on her lap as John got behind the wheel. They heard him on his Bluetooth, talking to someone as he started the car.

"Yes, I need you to alert St. Luke's Mercy Hospital and tell them that I have a woman giving birth, I think. She's in a lot of pain, and I'm rushing her there myself. And if you could get a patrolman to meet me at the 101 Loop and help us get there faster, that would be great. And call Dr..." He looked back at Sharon for the name. Julia said, "Roberts," and John continued giving orders. He stopped long enough to listen a few seconds before they heard his voice rise. "No, damn it, I do *not* want an ambulance to come get me. I'm on my way! You people figure it out!" He hit the end button and accelerated the big car. They were in Sharon's Cadillac and as Julia's cries became louder, Sharon urged him to go faster.

When they barreled up to the emergency room door, they were met by EMT's with a stretcher. Two men with radios were on either side of the entrance, and they hurried to assist with the doors. John was already out of his side, and he tossed the keys to the one closest. "Just park the damn thing anywhere," he said over his shoulder as he watched the team lift Julia onto the stretcher and hurry through the door. He and Sharon followed.

Julia disappeared down the hall as John and Sharon were directed to a waiting area. He put his arm around his small wife and felt her shaking. A receptionist came out to collect Julia's personal information. John followed her into a small office, but it wasn't long before he was back. He pulled Sharon close to his side and held her there. She was still shaking.

"It's okay now," he whispered. "We got her here and the doctor will take good care of her."

"John? We need to call Austin. He'll want to be here. And Lauren. But John, you heard Julia tell us the strangest thing back at the house.

I couldn't make out half of what she said, but part of it was that Austin was in Miami Beach with another woman! Surely she's mistaken. I can't imagine Austin doing something like that, can you? I know Julia's all emotional with the baby, but she usually doesn't overreact like this. Will you call the boy? And get him on a plane? Oh, and Julia said that Lauren is with Austin, too. Have you ever heard the like? I am totally confused."

John left his wife to step outside where he could use his phone. One of the security men was waiting. John simply nodded at him and held up his hand. He'd talk to him in a minute. He scrolled through his contacts and found Austin's number.

"John? Did you get hold of Julia? What's going on there? I still can't reach her." John could hear the worry in the younger man's voice. He hated to make it worse, but he had no choice.

"Austin, now we don't know what's going on, but Julia's here at the hospital. Sharon and I drove her. We found her in bed, almost in shock, and she managed to explain a little to Sharon before she started having pains." At Austin's shocked interjection, John calmed him down enough to continue. "Son, she was talking about you in Miami Beach, some other woman answering your phone, saying something about how you couldn't come to the phone because you were in the shower, something about pictures, and that Lauren is gone, too. What's going on in Florida, Austin?"

"Nothing is going on in Florida, for god's sake, except a big load of crap. Good grief! John, I can explain everything, but right now, I want to get home. I need to get off here and try to book a flight. Lauren is here, too, and we need to get home." If John was surprised, he hid it well.

"I'll take care of everything. You pack and tell Lauren to do the same. I'll call you back in a few minutes to let you know when you're leaving. And Austin?" John paused in the silence. "You better have a damn good explanation for all of this." His voice had turned stone cold, and Austin didn't have to see the look on his face to know that John was not happy.

"Yes, sir, I do. But right now, all I want to think about is Julia. Are you sure she's okay?"

"No, I don't know because they took her back and I've been outside making calls. I'll have Sharon look in on her and call you. Now, get busy because I don't think it will take me long to set things up."

They both hung up. John immediately dialed another number and started giving orders to whoever was on the other end.

Austin couldn't move fast enough. He was on the phone with Lauren while throwing things into his suitcase. After he signed off with her, he dialed Stewart to tell him that he was leaving immediately for Phoenix. The other man wished him well and promised to take care of Austin's responsibilities there. When he'd done everything he could from Miami Beach, Austin sat down heavily on the bed and stared at the door. In a few minutes, his phone rang, and he saw John's number.

"Yes, John, I'm all ready to go."

"That's good. I've called in a favor from a friend of mine who owns a small jet. He's getting all the flight registration taken care of and he said that you should be able to leave in about two hours. A car will pick you and Lauren up at the hotel and take you to the airport. They have your number and will call when they get there. We should see you sometime late tonight."

"John? How's Julia? I haven't heard anything from Sharon. Hell, she probably doesn't want to talk to me, am I right?"

She didn't, but John wasn't about to tell the man that. "The doctor has put Julia on a medication that should stop the contractions. She said that the baby is fine and that Julia is, too. Now, if that little girl decides she wants to be born, there isn't much anyone can do about it except let her. I'm trying to get you here as quickly as I can."

Austin sighed. "Thanks, John. I'm going crazy here. I wish I could do something, anything, but just sit and wait." The older man could hear the uncertainty in the younger man's voice. "Hey, John, will you find out if I can talk to Julia? I'd really like to hear her voice, let her know that I'm coming home."

"I'll check on that for you. Just hang tight. You'll be here before you know it." John hung up and looked at the phone in his hand. He turned and headed down the corridor and to Julia's room.

As he entered, Sharon looked up. She was holding Julia's hand and watching the baby's monitor register the fast heartbeat. On another monitor, Julia's vital signs were being recorded. John saw that an IV had been started and two bags hung from the stand. One he knew was the saline solution and he guessed the small one was the medication. Julia had her eyes closed but her faced was pinched with either pain or nerves. John hoped it was only the latter. It was a few weeks too early for the baby, and no pain was a good sign. He pulled up a chair and joined Sharon as they watched the girl they both loved. John didn't know who or what had caused this for Jules, but when he found out, things would get ugly fast. Sharon looked at his face and smiled. She knew exactly what he was thinking, but this wasn't the time for it. They needed to be positive and loving right now. Time for the other would come later. John relaxed his tense shoulders and winked at his wife, reading her thoughts. She was right, as usual.

"John?" Julia's voice was still raspy. "I'll bet you've been running around, barking orders, and getting everybody all in a tiz." She opened her eyes, and he could see that she was better. Her eyes weren't snapping blue like usual, but she seemed calmer.

"You know me well, don't you?" He winked at her. "Yes, I have things in motion. You're right, Lauren is in Florida with Austin, but they both will be here in a few hours." He came to her bedside and took her free hand in his. "Jules, Austin is beside himself with worry. He wants to talk to you in the worst way. Do you feel up to speaking to him? It's totally up to you. Say the word and I'll make it happen."

Julia sighed and closed her eyes. When she opened them, he could see that the worry was back.

"I don't know, John. I can't be upset right now because that's hard on Acacia. I need to do everything I can to prolong this pregnancy and give her a chance to get bigger and stronger. Stress has always done strange things to me, you know that. If I knew that the conversation would be civil and calm, I'd like nothing more than to talk to Austin. But John, what if it isn't? What if he has to lie to me and I'll know it. Then what?" She shook her head. "I'm sorry. He's a big boy. I need to worry about me and my baby now."

"I'll explain it to him. Don't worry about any of it. You're right. He is a big boy, and he'll just have to deal, won't he?" John patted her hand.

The doctor came in, and she smiled at Julia and introduced herself to John and Sharon. As they both shook the woman's strong hand, they felt better about the situation.

"It's nice to meet you, John, Sharon." She turned to Julia. "Now Miss Julia, the baby's vital signs are good, and even if she decides to make an appearance soon, I think she'll be fine. Small, but nothing indicates that we'd have a lot of issues other than the usual..." She went on to describe what Julia could expect, and as her patient relaxed, Dr. Roberts nodded her head.

"And you, Mom, you're doing okay, too. Those contractions could have been a false alarm or they could be warning us of something else. I'm going to keep you here at least overnight. If you don't have any more pain, then I'll assume the medication did its job and we've bought some time for little Acacia to stay put. You rest and I'll look in on you before I leave for the night." She patted Julia's hand and left. Julia looked at the worried couple.

"You two go home. I'm fine. I'll sleep here in a minute."

Sharon was shaking her head vehemently. "No, absolutely not. You're here. I'm here. Period." She looked at her husband. "Now, John, you should go on home. I'll stay right here and if I have to I'll sleep in that lounge chair tonight. I'll call you if anything changes." She smiled at him. It was too early for him to be tired, but he needed to take care of a few things. He thought a couple of minutes before nodding his agreement.

"Jules, get some rest. That's an order. I'll be in early in the morning." He kissed her forehead, and he and Sharon walked out into the hall.

"John, call Austin and tell him that she's not able to talk to him right now." Sharon looked at her watch. "It's still early, and you think they'll be here when?"

"Last I heard, the plane took off at seven o'clock their time, which is three hours ahead of us. So our time, their plane should land around ten o'clock. I'm sure he and Lauren will come straight here. I'll have a car waiting for them."

"Do you think that's a good idea? What if he upsets her again? John, we don't know what went on in Miami Beach. I know what we want to think, but we've been around long enough to not be surprised by anything."

John hugged her, and they stood there for a few seconds. He pulled away and looked down at the worried face of his wife. "Sweetheart, I'm going to trust Austin. I spoke to him, and he's as upset as I've ever heard anyone." He paused. "In fact, *I'll* meet their plane and get the story from those two before I ever bring them here. If I don't hear what I want to hear, I'll dump them off at home."

Sharon shook her head. It was the best they could do. She kissed him good-bye and promised to call if anything changed. Looking into the room, her heart broke for the dark-haired woman in the bed. *Audra,* she thought, and her eyes narrowed. *I don't know what you've done, but my guess is that I won't be happy. And you don't want me unhappy. As my daddy used to say, you've shit and fallen backward in it. Big time.* She straightened her shoulders and went back to sit by Julia.

Chapter 47

⎯⎯⎯

THE FLIGHT LANDED ON TIME, and Austin couldn't get off the plane fast enough. Even Lauren picked up her pace, and the two were almost running into the airport. They stopped short when they saw John. He wasn't smiling.

"John! Oh. My. God. Am I ever glad to see you!" Lauren ran up and threw her arms around his neck. She pulled back. "How's Jules? We haven't heard a thing up in the air. We need to get to the hospital."

"John," Austin came up and started to reach out to shake the man's hand, but he pulled back his own once he saw the look on John's face. "I don't know what's been said by Karen, Audra, Julia…all I know is the truth and that is I've done nothing to be guilty of. Ask Lauren here."

Lauren vigorously shook her head. "He's right. I had some misinformation from Karen, dumb bitch, and flew down, ready to go to war. Oh, I'm still not happy, but not at Austin. Seriously, he's innocent. But why the hell that stupid Karen called Julia, I'll never know. What was she thinking?" They started to walk toward the parking lot.

"I've arranged for your luggage to be delivered to your houses. I've got my car outside, and I'll drive you to the hospital. I'll expect you both to give me the full story." He looked at Austin. "Julia does not need any stress right now. For some reason, stress sends her body into a spin. She's calm now, and the medication has stopped the contractions. Both she and the baby are doing well. You be thinking about what you're going to say, but keep that in mind." Austin could hear the warning in his voice, but his eyes were gentle.

Austin nodded his head. "Yes, sir, I know. We'll talk about all of this eventually, but tonight, I just want to be there with her. I've come two thousand miles and that's all I want."

They pulled onto Highway 10 and John eased his Mercedes into the traffic. He usually cursed the busy highway traffic, especially the trucks, but tonight he was listening to the story Lauren and Austin shared. He wasn't happy, but now his displeasure was directed at someone other than Austin. They made the trip in good time, and after giving them the room number, John dropped Lauren and Austin at the door and drove off to find a parking space.

It was a quiet ride up the elevator and to Julia's room. They both paused at the door and took in the site. Sharon was still sitting beside Julia's bed, and her head swiveled around at the sound of their footsteps. She motioned them in.

Austin felt his pulse quicken at the sight of the IV tubes and all the monitors that were silently recording their information. He looked at the dark-haired woman lying with her eyes closed and wished none of the past two days had ever happened. He wished more than once that he'd followed his instincts and stayed home. But that was done. He couldn't go back. He squared his shoulders and quietly slipped into the room. Julia needed him to step up, and that's what he intended to do. Sharon vacated her spot beside the bed, and Austin came forward to take Julia's hand. It was cold and he put both of his around hers to warm them up. She stirred and opened her eyes. Those beautiful blue eyes, Austin thought. He smiled at her, relieved when she returned his smile.

"Hey, baby," he whispered. "I leave for a couple of days, and my girls wind up in a hospital." She started to speak and he shook his head. "No, I've been worried literally sick since John called me this afternoon, I've been waiting with no word and no way to talk to you, and I've come a couple of thousand miles. Just let me look at you." A tear slid down his cheek, and Julia reached up with her other hand to brush it away. He turned his head and kissed the hand, being careful of the tube that was running into it.

"It's all my fault, you know," she whispered. "I should have known better than to pay any attention to Karen. I worked myself up into a frenzy, and Caci didn't like it." She smiled at him. "I was too fast to think the

393

worst, and I am so sorry, Austin. I've had several hours to think, too, and I can't believe I let my trust slip, even if for a short time. For an intelligent woman, I can be pretty stupid sometimes."

"Shhhh, baby, it's all stupid shit. I'm here and we'll do what we need to do to keep Miss Caci where she belongs. At least for another two or three weeks." He leaned over and kissed her then, and rested his head on her shoulder. "God, I just love you so much. It hit me so hard when I was flying across the country." He lifted his head and grinned. "Dumb jet wasn't fast enough."

She chuckled and he felt a sharp kick hit his arm. He rubbed the spot where he could see a little ridge on her stomach, and it soon receded. They looked at each other, and it was all good.

"Excuse me," Lauren came creeping up behind Austin. "Make room for me, too." She came around to Julia's other side and leaned over to kiss her cheek. "Do not scare me like this ever again. Look at me. I look like a damn extra for the *Rocky Horror Picture Show*." Julia grinned at her friend's appearance, taking in the messy pony tail, the smudged mascara and shiny red nose.

"Honey," Julia teased, "you're scaring me right now. Have you looked at yourself? Didn't the plane have a bathroom mirror?"

Lauren shook her head. "You're not getting rid of me that quickly. Right now for the only time in my life, I really don't care. I simply don't give a shit." Lauren rolled her eyes. "By the way, you really know how to make a girl feel good about herself." Lauren kissed her friend's cheek and whispered in her ear. "Don't scare me like this. I love you, you know." When she lifted her head, Julia's answer was a weak smile.

"Ok," Sharon stood at the foot of the bed. "I'm heading home to sleep but I'll be back bright and early." She pointed at Lauren. "You, come with me. You look like hell and I'm embarrassed to be seen with you. We'll have to find some way to erase the security footage before it's posted on YouTube for Halloween." Lauren rolled her eyes again and kissed Julia once more before walking to the door.

"I love you, Ju-Ju!" Lauren knew Julia hated that name, and she laughed when Julia stuck her tongue out at her. "See you tomorrow. I'll be at the shop all day, but whether you're here or at the house, I'll be by." She blew Julia a kiss. "Love you—mean it!" Julia blew her one back.

"Now, you," Sharon pointed her finger at Austin. "Take good care of my girls. I'm tagging out for the night. And call me if anything changes, do you hear me?" Sharon came around to hug his neck. As she did so, she whispered in his ear. "Do not upset this girl, or I will personally gouge out your eyes." She pulled back and smiled, but it didn't quite reach her eyes. Sharon hadn't heard Lauren and Austin's story and was still upset. To Julia, she pointed a finger. "You and Caci behave yourselves tonight." She leaned over to give Julia a hug.

"Thank you so much," Julia whispered. "You and John. I know what you did for me, and I love you two more than anything."

"I know, baby," Sharon whispered. "Love you more." She reached down and patted Julia's huge belly. "And you, Miss Acacia, had better be good. Do not make me come back here tonight."

With Sharon and Lauren gone, the room seemed to have a little more oxygen. Austin pulled a chair closer, and once again covered Julia's free hand with his. He was so tired, and he soon rested his head on their joined hands. Julia gently pulled her hand free and ran her fingers through his hair. She leaned her head back and sighed. Her world felt right again. Julia closed her eyes and felt herself slide into sleep.

Chapter 48

N<small>O ONE EVER SLEEPS IN</small> a hospital, so when the doctor came in the next morning, Austin and Julia were eager to learn if they'd be going home or not. Austin had moved from his chair by the bed to the recliner and back again. He was operating on fumes, and he looked it.

"Julia," Dr. Roberts was looking at the chart on her laptop. "Last night you and the baby did great. You haven't had any more contractions." She looked at her patient over her reading glasses. "I think you can go home today." Before they could celebrate too much, the doctor had some strict instructions for them both. "But Julia, you must remain stress free. Understand? Do normal activities, work if you want to, exercise; you know what to avoid. And you," she looked at Austin. "Your job is to make sure she behaves herself. Like I told Julia last night. Even if the baby came today, I really do think she'd be fine. Small, perhaps some lung issues, but nothing out of the ordinary for a preemie." She closed the computer and let her glasses hang free on the chain that wound around her neck. "Okay, if I don't hear from you in the next week, I want to see you in my office." She smiled at them both. "Don't worry. You're doing beautifully." With that, the doctor swept from the room.

Julia and Austin looked at one another. It had been a horrible twenty-four hours, and Julia was ready to put it all behind them.

"Well," she sighed. "As soon as the nurse gets in here and unfastens all of this electronic stuff, I'll be ready to go home. Will you find my clothes? They took those from me as soon as I got in here, and I was so out of it I have no idea of where they are."

Austin looked around the room and saw a small storage locker. He opened the door and saw a dress on a hanger. Her shoes were sitting neatly below and a bag contained what he assumed were her underclothes.

"Yeah, it's all in here, but I can't see getting it out until you're ready. Hospitals aren't known for being in a hurry." He came over and sat on the edge of her bed. "Jules, let me know when you're ready to talk, okay? I can't tell you how bad I feel about all of this." He motioned the room with his head, including the host of monitoring equipment.

Julia closed her eyes and sighed. "Austin, I told you last night that I don't blame you for anything. It was a series of misunderstandings and too much jumping to conclusions. If I could have talked to you, things would have been very different. Or if I hadn't over-reacted. Or if I hadn't..."

"Stop. Please, just stop. Babe, you're right. We can point fingers all we want, but the bottom line is that it's turned out okay. Not perfect, but okay. I only brought it up because I know that you have a lot of unanswered questions. But trust me, once you know everything, you'll only get all fired up." He chuckled. "Let's leave that to Blondie and Sharon, okay? Right now, I would not want to be Karen or Audra." He frowned. "That reminds me. I need to make a phone call. I'll be just outside." He was pulling his phone out of his pocket and walking toward the door. He looked down and saw that the charge he'd given it on the plane had held.

"Hey, Austin," he turned back at the sound of her voice. "I really love you." Julia's smile was the one he loved most.

"Love you more," he grinned at their usual routine.

"Love you most," she winked. Austin turned the corner and she couldn't see him. She took a deep breath and released it slowly, feeling a calm that a cleansing breath could bring. Julia didn't want to know the whole story just yet. She was embarrassed at her role in the mess, feeling like such an idiot. *When will I get it through my head that Austin is not Keith*, she scolded herself. *But that isn't important anymore. He's home and Caci is fine.* She rubbed the little ridge that she knew had to be an arm or leg. In a few seconds, it disappeared and she felt the baby roll around. Austin soon came back.

"Everything okay? I assume that was work," she was a little curious.

"Yep. I needed to check in and let them know that I won't be in until tomorrow, if then." He was frowning. "I also had to talk to someone in human resources. I've got a little harassment paperwork to file. In fact, I will probably run by later today and get it all completed." He ran his hand through his long hair in frustration. "I kept thinking it would all just disappear, I guess, but you always knew, didn't you?"

Julia raised one eyebrow and tilted her head in a silent *Well? I tried to tell you*. Out loud, she only said, "Baby, live and learn. This is one time my age is an advantage. Women like Audra are a pain in the ass, and you usually only get rid of them through extreme means. She's still young, relatively speaking, spoiled, attractive, and not used to hearing the word *no*. I don't know how much of a pain in the ass she'll be to you at work, but my guess is that her days at Coast to Coast are numbered. And did I hear correctly that Sharon knows about her little stunts?" At his nod, Julia laughed. "Oh boy, that could be an interesting confrontation because I know Sharon, and she *will* find the opportunity to have a little talk with Audra." She grew quiet, thinking before she spoke again. "My wish is that the woman will simply leave town quietly, but I don't see that happening."

Before Austin could respond, a young, pretty, red-haired nurse came almost bouncing into the room. She didn't give Austin a second look, and Julia grinned at him and raised her eyebrows as if to say, *Losing your touch?* His smirk made her chuckle.

"And look at you all in a good mood!" Kindsey, her name tag read, almost chirped. "And why not? You're going home, I hear." All the while she was talking, Kindsey was expertly removing Julia's IV and bandaging the small hole. She continued to chatter as she removed the monitors from Julia's stomach and chest. Soon Julia was a free woman, and she was eager to get dressed and head home. With a startled expression on her face, she looked at Austin.

"Hey, sweetie, if John and Sharon drove me here, and John drove you here, how are we getting home?" she laughed at the confused looked on his face. The thought hadn't occurred to him, either.

He dug his phone out of his pocket and soon had Sharon on the line. Julia could hear her laugh clear across the room. Austin grinned as he turned off his phone and walked over to get her clothes out of the locker.

"Yeah, you heard her, I guess. She's on her way."

"I never doubted she would be," Julia grinned. Austin closed the door and helped her dress. He was helping her with her shoes when her stomach gave out a huge growl. He looked up and laughed.

"Yeah, well, you saw me send back almost all of that meal the hospital calls breakfast." Julia shrugged her shoulders. "So I'm spoiled. I have this ridiculously handsome chef who makes my breakfast. The hospital's idea of eggs isn't my idea, you know?"

"Uh, yeah, I do, and I'm right with you," he finished what he was doing and stood. "I'll go finish up whatever paperwork you have to fill out and Sharon should be here by then." He kissed her and she watched him walk away.

Cutest butt in the world, she thought and grinned. *And I've missed it lately.*

Julia sat on the edge of the bed and waited. About ten minutes later, Austin came back, accompanied by a sour-faced older woman. The look on his face wasn't pleasant either, and she wondered what this was all about.

"Jules, it seems that since I'm not your legal spouse, I can't do anything regarding your insurance, release papers, whatever. This is Mrs. Snotgrass."

"That's *Snod*grass," she shot a venom-filled look at Austin before turning her attention back to Julia. "Ms. Whitman, I explained to Mr. James that the only reason I even talked to him about all of this is because you have him listed for us to share information about your care. HIPAA, you know." She looked at Austin and shook her head. "Really, your little outburst wasn't necessary, young man, and yelling at me does you no good."

Austin raised one eyebrow in Julia's direction. "She thinks I yelled at her," he said.

Before either of them could get into it again, Julia reached her hand out for the folder. She half listened to Mrs. Snodgrass as she looked over the paperwork, signing in several places. With a final flourish, she closed the folder and handed it all back to the woman. Austin was slouched in the chair and looked like he wanted to say something, but didn't. He watched as the women exchanged pleasantries. Mrs. Snodgrass left the room with not a backward glance in his direction.

"Sorry, babe," she apologized. "I should have known the hospital would need my signature on things."

"It's all good," he wasn't convincing her one bit. Before he could say anything more, Sharon came in followed by a nurse with a wheelchair.

"Well, look at you! Hey, Austin! Let's get out of here, shall we?" She looked around. "Jules, did you bring anything in here with you?"

Julia felt empty-handed. "Uh, no, I guess I didn't. How did the hospital even admit me? I have no ID, no insurance cards, no phone, nothing." She looked at Sharon's raised brow. "Never mind. I'm sure someone we love and adore took care of it all, right?"

"Duh," Sharon looked at Austin. "Let's go. The Caddy is parked illegally, and I don't want some Barney Fife security man making a big damn deal about it."

The trip was brief, and Julia was thrilled to be home.

"Oh, my god, I need a shower in the worst way! You two do whatever, and I'll be cleaning myself up." She kissed Sharon's cheek. "Thank you for rescuing me, both yesterday and today. I love you."

Sharon patted her cheek. "S'nothin' darlin'."

Austin watched Julia make her way down the hall before turning to Sharon. The older woman had a fist on one hip and her eyebrow was arched as high as it would go.

"Well? I think it's time that I got this whole messed up story, from the beginning to the end. And leave out nothing. I got Lauren's version, but I want to hear yours."

By the time Julia had showered and rejoined them, Austin had finished filling Sharon in with the details. The look on Sharon's face told Julia that her friend was privy to everything.

"Hey, you two! Let's eat! I am starved and so is Caci. She wants a big juicy hamburger loaded with lettuce, tomato, mayonnaise, and pickles. Lots of pickles." That's all it took for Sharon to jump up and head to the kitchen. She was followed closely by Austin, and between the two of them they had Julia's requested meal fixed up in about twenty minutes. They sat together eating and chatting. Julia smiled. This was her normal, and she liked it. Austin loaded the dishwasher and turned to Sharon.

"Will you stay a while with Jules? I need to run by the office," his face was serious again, and Julia knew what it was all about.

"Absolutely," Sharon replied. "Take your time and get everything lined out. We'll be here when you get back." She hugged his neck and slapped him on the behind as he turned to go to Julia. "I'm still next in line, hot stuff," she said before leaving the two alone.

Austin sighed. "I need to get this over with." He looked at her. "Any advice, old wise woman?"

Julia laughed. "No, just go kick some ass. But don't you want to clean up some first? You look like you slept in those clothes, babe."

Austin looked down at his rumpled jeans and shirt. "Yeah, I didn't even think about that. This won't take long."

She joined Sharon in the den, and the two of them talked about everything her friends had given Julia at the small baby shower they had thrown for her the month before. Julia pointed out that with the shower gifts, everything she and Austin had bought, and all of the things Sharon had been bringing in, Caci lacked nothing.

Austin came in to kiss Julia good-bye and wink at Sharon. They heard his Mustang roar down the drive. Julia took a deep breath and let it out. She was tired, and Sharon could see those little lines on each side of her mouth.

"Baby girl, you go lie down for a while. You obviously didn't get any rest in the hospital, and you need all that you can get."

Julia got up slowly, feeling the weight of her protruding belly. "I'll have to agree. I'll leave my phone with you if you don't mind. I'm beat, physically and mentally."

Two hours later, Sharon was bustling around the kitchen, baking Julia's favorite lemon pie and straightening the refrigerator. Since a cleaning service came in once a week, there wasn't much for Sharon to do, and she was getting bored. She had just set the pie on the counter, admiring the golden brown meringue, when she heard Austin's car. He came through the door, and Sharon could tell that his afternoon had been stressful.

"Well? How did everything go? Does John need to make a phone call?"

Austin grinned. "No, but thank you. Here's the thing. According to HR, unless I've got something physical—photographs, emails, stuff like that, then there isn't a lot they can do. It's a he said/she said situation. I told them that Lauren overheard our last conversation, but since Lauren and Julia are such close friends, Audra can simply cry foul on that and say Lauren was just lying." Austin ran his hand through his hair and rubbed the back of his neck. "They offered to give me a transfer. See, Audra isn't my supervisor, so they are hesitant to take any action against her."

"What?!" Sharon's face started out in disbelief that quickly turned to anger. "Do you mean to tell me that little bitch can pretty much do whatever she wants and no one will do a thing? And *you* would be transferred?!"

Austin shrugged. "It's still relatively new waters we're navigating here." He smirked before continuing. "Yeah, it's like men are supposed to be receptive—who in his right mind turns down a willing female, right?"

By this time, Sharon was up and pacing. Austin missed the image she made—a shot of fireball that was ready to launch—because he was in his own thoughts. Suddenly, she stopped. Austin had sat down heavily on the bar stool and stared at the pie, not really seeing it. He shook his head. "I just don't get it. Why do people have to be so damn dumb, you know? Here's Audra…young, attractive, educated, talented…and she does shit like this." He looked at Sharon, his eyes troubled. "The company isn't happy with her, at all, and as much as I'd like for them to give her walking papers, I feel guilty about that. I never wanted to cause someone to lose her job, especially over stupid shit that is so juvenile."

"Whoa…wait right there, what happened last night was NOT juvenile—it was evil," Sharon was angry. "That woman is a boil on the butt of Coast to Coast." She shook her head. "If it hadn't been you, she'd have picked out someone else. Sorry, handsome, but that's how these women work, so don't flatter yourself too much. And you wouldn't be so eager to feel sympathy if you could have seen what her actions did to that girl in there." She nodded her head in the direction of the bedroom. "I'm telling you, if Julia hadn't pulled through that last night…And if anything had happened to that baby…" Her expression was a bit frightening.

"I know, I know." Austin looked almost as tired as Julia had earlier. Sharon's face softened as she looked at him.

"Sweetie, go lie down with Jules. You're every bit as beat as she is. Are you planning on going to work tomorrow?" He nodded that he was. "Well, don't worry about our girl. I'll be here around 9:00 in the morning and stay until you get home."

"That would be great," Austin smiled. "Julia will argue that she's fine and that you don't have to do that, but deep down, we both will feel better knowing you're here."

"Good. Now, I'm going to take off and you get some rest. I've fixed up a chicken casserole and a salad in the fridge. All you have to do is heat the oven and bake it about an hour at three hundred fifty degrees. Oh, and you need milk. And chocolate. That girl goes through more chocolate syrup these days." She laughed, picked up her purse, and kissed his cheek before heading out the door. She stopped, one hand on the doorknob, and looked back at Austin.

"Austin, I don't want you worrying about this anymore, okay?"

He shook his head, "Yeah, maybe just my bringing it to the company's attention will make her back off. God, I hope so."

"Like I said, you stop worrying about that. You've got all you can say grace over keeping Julia in line." Sharon grinned at him. "Go check on her, enjoy your dinner, and I'll see you tomorrow." She blew him a kiss and stepped through the door, closing it gently behind her. He heard her car start up and listened to it disappear down the drive. He really was exhausted.

Julia was still sleeping soundly when he crawled into bed beside her. He pulled the blanket over both of them and grinned when she snuggled in closer to him. He put an arm around her, his hand on the baby, and closed his eyes.

Julia's stomach awakened her, and she was surprised to feel the big warm body next to her. She was able to slide from under his arm and was almost to the bedroom door when he opened his eyes.

"Sneaking away so soon?" he grinned and rolled over onto his back.

"Yep, I'm hungry. Again." She laughed and came back to climb onto the bed with him. "Just a couple of minutes and I really do need to eat. Every time my stomach gets too empty these days, I feel nauseous." He pulled her close and enjoyed the moment. Too soon, Caci gave them both a swift kick, and Julia laughed as she pulled away and got up again. She looked at his frustrated expression.

"You realize, sweetie, that this will happen all the time in a few weeks. We'll be one of those couples who's always looking for private time." Julia shook her head. "Lauren and I used to make so much fun of them." She raised her eyes and looked at him. "Now, I've joined the pack. Damn!"

He laughed and gave her Sharon's instructions on the casserole. He closed his eyes for what he thought would be just a few minutes more only to snap awake an hour later. He could smell something wonderful coming from the kitchen and joined Julia there. They ate and were lounging on the patio in the warm sun when Lauren came by.

"Food! I smell yummy stuff!" She breezed into the house, and the sounds of dishes could be heard. Shortly after, she came out to join them, a plate piled high, mainly with salad, in one hand and a beer in the other.

"Well, look at the picture of domesticity," she said before taking a big bite of food and moaning in pleasure. "Surely you two didn't cook this. I'm tasting a Sharon creation. Especially with the pie. That thing looks like a picture."

"It tasted even better," Austin grinned. Since the Miami Beach incident, Austin and Lauren had developed a different bond. Having a common enemy had brought them together, and Julia liked seeing her two favorite people not only getting along, but actually liking one another.

"Jules," Lauren looked over at her friend. "I swear, you look like you ate a small child. Girl, if you go another four weeks, you will be bigger than Myra Wilson. Remember her?" They laughed at the shared joke.

"Austin," Lauren continued. "Myra was the most obnoxious woman we've ever worked for. She was as big around as she was tall and mean as a snake. She was always lurking everywhere, as if anyone the size of a small bus could sneak around, and she always thought she was really smart. She always had the idea that people were cheating her. I'll bet she counted the nails every night when the work crew would leave for the day. One time…." Lauren kept them entertained for the next hour, mimicking several other clients. Austin didn't have a clue who they were, but seeing Julia laugh made him laugh, too. Not long after, Matt dropped by and joined them on the patio. He had a huge slice of pie that he was washing down with beer.

"Ewww…." Lauren snarled her nose. "How can you eat that delicious pie and chase it with Bud Light? Such a kid combination." She shook her head. Matt laughed at the intended insult.

"Hey, Blondie, don't knock it until you've tried it. Beer goes with everything, or didn't you know that?"

"Don't disagree with him, Lar, or he'll be tossing you into the pool… again." Julia laughed.

"Oh, hell no, he won't," Lauren looked over at Matt and raised one eyebrow as if to say she'd shoot him first. "I have been there, twice, and it's not happening, bud." Her warning look was met with a grin.

"You can't, Matt," Julia broke into their staring contest. "She's wearing my silk shirt. And aren't those my Prada shoes?"

Lauren looked down and back up to Julia. "Yep. You're too fat for the shirt these days, and the heels on the shoes are too dangerous, you know. You're too top-heavy for stilettos." At Julia's look of outrage, Lauren backtracked. "Not that you aren't just the most beautiful pregnant woman in the world, but seriously, hon, you can't possibly wear anything in your closet these days."

"Hey, Lauren," At hearing her name, she looked at Austin. "I'd just shut up if I were you."

Lauren's mouth snapped shut, and she gave Julia her "I'm sorry" look. It was so ridiculous on the beautiful face that Julia laughed.

Lauren and Matt stayed until around ten, when they all called it a night. As Julia and Austin made their way to bed, going through their nightly routine, Austin felt her eyes on him.

"What?" he asked.

She shook her head. "Nothing. I'm just thinking about how perfect my life is. I love you."

"Love you more," he grinned.

"Love you most!"

Chapter 49

IN ANY OFFICE, REGARDLESS OF its size, the atmosphere changes when something is afoot. Austin felt the change around ten o'clock that morning. He saw several people passing back and forth in the hallway outside the offices, and as hard as he fought it, his curiosity got the best of him. Austin hated office politics, but this had people buzzing. Four of them shared one secretary, and Austin tried to seem nonchalant as he strolled to her desk in the outer office.

"Hey, Elaine," the older woman looked up. "What's going on around here? I've seen a ton of traffic out in the hall. Did I miss cake in the break room or something?" he was teasing, but Elaine's face remained serious.

"Well, it seems that the big boss, Mr. Jones, has been here meeting with Mr. Horton, and they were joined by Mr. Barton of HR. None of them looked too happy." She peered around Austin to get a better look at the hallway leading to the main lobby. Lowering her voice, she continued, "It seems that somebody's head is on the chopping block. Audra Martinez, I hear." She sniffed. "Good riddance, if you ask me. That female is no good. I know. Women know these things."

At the name, Austin looked uncomfortable but covered it well as he thanked Elaine for the information and headed back to his office. *Hmmm…*he thought. *I wonder how much Sharon Burns has to do with all of this. She wasn't happy last night, and I wouldn't put anything past her if she's angry.* His office phone rang, and he didn't have another chance to think about Audra until much later. When he did, the office had quieted down and Austin worked through lunch in order to get home early. He and Julia had texted a couple of times, and he knew that she was doing fine. With Sharon there, he wasn't worried.

Sharon and Julia were spending the day working in the baby's room, putting wall hangings up and organizing things. Every time Sharon came over, she brought more baby paraphernalia until Julia had to put her foot down. "Really, Sharon, I'm going to run out of room for the baby!" Sharon always laughed, declared "Nonsense!" and kept on going. This day, Julia was in the rocking chair with her feet propped up on the ottoman while her friend centered a growth chart on the closet door. At the sound of the doorbell, Julia started up, but before she could get to her feet, Sharon had motioned her back down.

"I got this," she declared. "It's probably a salesman or something. Stay put." Julia smiled and relaxed again. As Sharon hurried toward the front door, her face changed. She had a very good idea of who this could be, and she'd be damned if Julia would be disturbed.

Opening the door, Sharon wasn't surprised to see Audra on the front stoop.

"Oh, I should have known Julia would have one of her guard dogs on duty. Where is she? We need to talk," Audra tried to maneuver past Sharon, but it wasn't happening. She pulled the door shut behind her and physically backed Audra off the porch.

"What could you possibly need to say to Julia?" Sharon crossed her arms in front of her and stared at the dark-haired younger woman. Audra was beautiful, but not this day.

"Oh, I have all kinds of things to talk about, mainly her little boy toy. I'm sure she'd just love to know what he's been up to the last couple of days."

Sharon arched an eyebrow and glared at the woman in front of her. *Yep*, she thought. *I've seen this type more times than I care to count.* Sharon took a deep breath and let it out slowly before she spoke.

"That's where you're wrong, honey, but you've been wrong for a long time, haven't you?" As Audra raised her chin in a defiant move, Sharon shook her head and continued. "Let me see if I have all of this correct. You flew in early this morning and were called directly to the office. Once there, you were told by some secretary to report to one of the boss's offices, and there you met with none other than Mr. Steven Jones." At this,

Audra frowned, her face confused. Sharon continued. "Mr. Jones made a special trip to sit in on the meeting. That meeting, I'm sure, was called to tell you that you need to pack your bags because you're needed elsewhere. Let's see, I'm thinking that your talents are needed up north somewhere… Alaska, right? And you're needed immediately, so the company will supply movers to get your things all packed up and shipped to your new home. Anchorage, right? How am I doing so far?" Sharon smiled then, the expression not reaching her eyes. They remained hard.

"How do you know all of this? Who talked?" Audra's mind was working, but the older woman was way ahead of her.

"How do I know? I told you, sweetheart. I've dealt with women like you before." Sharon took a step closer, forcing Audra back. "Now, here's the rest of the story. Be sure to correct me where I'm wrong. Mr. Jones is none too happy with your unprofessional behavior not only on this trip but on other occasions, and he's given you two options. One—try to stay in Phoenix, file whatever trumped up shit you want, and fight to work at a place where no one wants you. Eventually, you'll leave but not before you've been exposed for the whore that you are. Or two—go away quietly. Take your new position in Anchorage and prove to Steve that you're worth the trouble. Screw up there, and you're history. The second option will allow you to start over someplace else without 'baggage' while the first, well, let's just say that word will leak. Your inappropriate behavior will follow you wherever you go."

"You seem to know so much, but you have no idea of what I've gone through and all because of your precious Julia." At the mention of Julia's name, Sharon's hands balled into fists that she held at her sides.

"You are not to even say her name. I've been patient with you, but you've worn out your welcome," Sharon's voice was low. "Not only are you stupid, but you're one sick little girl, aren't you? Nothing has happened that wasn't brought on by your irresponsible behavior and poor decision-making. Nothing." Sharon leaned in closer. "Oh, I've checked you out, sweetheart, and you are nothing more than a spoiled brat who has finally met someone who tells her no. And I have to wonder if you're really attracted to Austin because he's quite a catch or because he's off limits." She smiled. "I suppose only you would know that." Sharon leaned back and her chin rose. "We're all finished here. You can leave on your own, or I'll get you some assistance. You will not come within five hundred feet of this house or its inhabitants. Do so, and you'll be hiring yourself a lawyer." As Audra started to say something else, Sharon raised her hand to silence the woman.

"Say nothing. Go. The company can't legally do anything about the poor behavior you've exhibited, but I'm not part of the company and I've never been known to follow rules." Sharon fixed her eyes on Audra. "Don't cross me, Audra Martinez. You'll regret it." Sharon paused to let what she had said sink in. "Now, it's time you go. And don't even think about trying to bother Austin or Julia again. I warned you once before that I won't have it." To the surprise of the younger woman, a man in a green shirt came from the side of the house.

"Is everything all right, Mrs. Burns, ma'am?"

"I think so, Mike. This woman was just leaving," Sharon smiled at Audra. "Make sure she does, please."

"Yes, ma'am," he said as he crossed massive arms across his chest.

Audra snarled her nose and almost spat at Sharon, who had turned her back and was going back into the house. "You people are fucking crazy, aren't you? Hired goons? What the hell?"

Sharon turned to smile. "Crazy? Yeah, I've been told that by more than one person." Her eyes glittered. "And now, I'm done with you. Do drive safely, dear. I'd hate to see you get into an accident," and this time when she smiled, Audra felt uncomfortable. Sharon turned her back and disappeared into the house. As Audra got into her car, she took one last look at the now closed door and the big man standing in front of it. *Fucking crazy*, she thought. *What a bunch of nuts!*

Sharon closed the door and heard the car pull away. She looked up to see Julia standing by the kitchen counter, her arms crossed in front of her and resting on her huge stomach.

"What?" Sharon asked as she crossed to the kitchen to get a bottle of water. "It was no one important."

Julia watched her take a long drink before she spoke. "Oh, I know that wasn't anyone important, but really Sharon, did you have to pull one of the goons out of the bushes? Good grief! Who does that, anyway?"

"I do, that's who," Sharon shrugged her shoulders and moved onto one of the stools. She motioned for Julia to join her. After Julia had settled herself on the chair, Sharon looked at her.

"I know that it always seems a bit overboard, but honey, you have no idea of the types of people that are out there. John is a wealthy man, and he's gotten there by dealing with some interesting characters, especially early on. Anyway, to protect our homes, businesses, and other interests, John started a security company about fifteen years ago. They take care of us, of course, but John has expanded it until the company has several wealthy clients now. Some want body guards. Some want home security. Some want surveillance. Some want it all. John's company provides the services, both full-time and part-time." She took another drink and smiled at Julia. "This woman who just left is devious. She's manipulative, and in this day, who knows what else? John will have her watched until she leaves town, just like he did with Keith. And aren't you glad that worked out like it did?"

Julia wasn't quite sure how to say it without offending her friend. "Sharon, you realize this all sounds like something out of some dime-store novel, don't you? I mean, you have these security people who 'take care' of things. That's a bit weird."

Sharon laughed. "Don't I know it! But I've gotten used to it now and I forget how others may see it." She sobered. "Please, honey, don't be uncomfortable. John never does anything that he thinks would make you feel uneasy. And today was just a precaution only because of the baby." She gave Julia a small smile. "He loves you, baby girl. Like he loves me, Johnny, and the rest of his family. Mike will stay outside until he hears that Audra is gone. He'll be gone then, too. I promise."

Julia thought back to when she had stayed alone in the Flagstaff house. Now it made sense why Sharon and John had never been worried about her. The more Julia thought about it, the less she felt weird. *It is what it is*, she thought. And if having John and Sharon look after her involved unconventional methods, then so be it. Julia thought of something.

"By the way, Sharon, what did Audra want? I know that was her because I peeked out the window. Was she looking for Austin?" Julia's blue eyes darkened at the thought. Austin had told Julia the entire story the night before, and Julia's dislike for the woman had intensified greatly.

"No," Sharon admitted. "She wanted to talk to you, but that wasn't happening in this lifetime." Sharon looked at Julia's worried face. "Now, sweetie, I don't like that look. Don't worry." She put a hand on Julia's.

"Audra is leaving for Alaska. She won't be causing you or Austin any more trouble, I promise."

Julia burst out laughing. "Alaska! Sharon, you didn't!" At her friend's closed lips and self-satisfied expression, Julia shook her head. "Thank you, Sharon. I'm so glad you were here to run interference with Audra. I seriously hate that woman for what she did to Austin. And what she tried to do to me. I'm glad she's gone. I have bigger things to be concerned about." Julia's hand moved to her stomach and rested protectively.

"Yes, you do, and we have more stuff to put on the walls of that nursery. Are you up to supervising?" Sharon jumped to the floor and took Julia's hand. They were laughing as they entered the baby's room.

Crisis averted, Sharon thought smugly. *As always.*

Austin found them still piddling in the nursery when he arrived an hour later. He shook his head, wondering what in the world was so intriguing about the room that the two women could spend hours in there. *Must be a woman thing,* he thought as he stuck his head around the corner. He saw Julia in the chair with her feet up and Sharon standing on a dining room chair. She was trying to get a small basket level against the wall. Sharon hammered in a nail to hold it up and stepped down to examine her work.

"Well, it will have to do," she determined.

"Sharon, it looks fine, really, and it looked fine the other two times you put it up. Seriously, this room will have more holes than a sieve."

"Hey," Austin said, coming in to join the women. "I painted those walls, and holes weren't part of Lauren's plans. Blondie will have a cow if they outnumber her butterflies or dragonflies, or whatever else she paints in here." He leaned over and kissed Julia before perching on the ottoman at her feet.

"Yeah, well, I'm covering them up, Ace, so it's all good," Sharon winked and picked up the chair to take it back to the dining room. "And since you're here, I'm going to head home. I left Angie a list of what I wanted her to fix for supper, but who knows if she'll get it right."

She came back shortly and bent down to kiss Julia's cheek. "I won't see you tomorrow, Jules. It's Saturday, and I know Austin will be here. If you need anything, call me." She blew a kiss in Austin's direction as she headed toward the door. "Bye, Handsome," and she was gone.

Austin turned around on the ottoman, leaned back, and rested his head on Julia. She rubbed his temples and felt tension leave him.

"Rough day?" she asked.

"Not as rough for me as for others," he replied. "I guess you heard. Sharon has a direct line to everything, as we well know. My guess is that she and John orchestrated most of what happened."

"Yeah, I heard. I had a visitor today. Well, an almost visitor."

At that, Austin raised up and turned to face her. He was frowning, his eyes troubled. "Who was that?" he asked guardedly.

Julia rolled her eyes. "Who do you think? The woman scorned, of course." As he started to get agitated, Julia put her hand on his arm and stopped him. "She didn't even make it to the door. Sharon met her there, and my guess is they reached an understanding." She smiled at the word. "And, get this, one of John's security men was here! Can you believe the overkill?" She laughed and watched Austin's face turn to confusion. Julia filled him in on what Sharon had shared that afternoon.

"I don't know whether to be disturbed or in awe," Austin said, shaking his head. "So John owns the company."

"Yep," Julia replied. "And I asked Sharon more about it while she worked in here, and it really is something. John hired this ex-military man who was some major or something, and he knows all about self-defense and security and stuff like that. Anyway, he runs the company. He hires other former military and they do all kinds of stuff. Like provide security for celebrities and stars. And rich people. Just all kinds of people. Oh, and they do home and business security stuff, too. Evidently, it's a lucrative business. Kinda cool, when you think about it."

Put like that, Austin could see that it wasn't all as clandestine as he'd originally thought. He said as much to Julia. They let the subject drop, but Julia could tell that Austin had something else on his mind.

"Hey, Jules, I've been thinking about something." At her confused look, he took her hands. "Hear me out before you say anything, okay?" She smiled at him, but her eyes were narrowed in a question. He continued.

"Remember at the hospital, when the old bitch wouldn't let me do any paperwork for you? Well, that bothered me." His eyes met hers. "You know how much I love you, and you know that what we have works for us—living together, sharing life. But legally, we have no say-so over anything. It hit me yesterday. And then I was thinking. If you and I were married, would Audra have been so eager to make a move on me? Would a ring have deterred her, and could we have avoided all of the shit we've put up with? Would the hospital have treated me like an unwanted bother?" He took a deep breath. "I guess what I'm trying to say, and not very well, is that I want to marry you, Jules. As people say," and he picked up her left hand. "I want to put a ring on it." He kissed her hand and grinned up at her.

Julia was speechless. *Whoa, I didn't see this coming*, she thought. She looked at him, her thoughts racing. When she spoke, she was hesitant.

"Austin, we talked about this. It's just a piece of paper," she stopped as he interrupted her.

"I know, I know, but to the world it isn't just a piece of paper. It's how the world knows that we are together. That we are joined, so to speak." He paused. "And Jules, it's more than a piece of paper to me, too. I've never made a big deal out of it because I know you've had a bad experience. But, babe, we've proven more than once that we're different. I'm tired of referring to you as 'my girlfriend' and I really want to be able to call you 'my wife.' To let everyone know that." As her silence stretched on, he spoke again. "Julia, will you marry me? Will you share my name and my life? We already share everything else, including a child. Will you share this with me, too?"

Julia looked at his eager face. *He looks so young*, she thought, *and I haven't thought that in a very long time. And he's right. We do share everything else. But does he really want to be joined to a woman who will one day leave him a very young widower? To a woman who will continually look more like his mother than his wife? I can't ask him to do that.*

"Austin," she was carefully choosing her words. "You realize that you're asking me to spend the rest of our lives together." She paused before continuing. "While we haven't talked about it in a very long time, you do remember that I out-age you by almost sixteen years. When I'm fifty, you're thirty-four. When I'm sixty, you're only forty-four. And when I'm seventy..."

Austin interrupted her. "No, I'm too young for all of that upper-level math," he replied sarcastically. "So, you think that down the road I'll want to jump ship because of what, a wrinkle you have that I don't?" His face took on a pained expression. "Wow, I thought you knew me better than that by now. What the hell, Jules? Does it always come down to my damn age with everything?"

She leaned back and sighed. "No, of course not. I'm not saying this right. Let me try again. I don't want to tie you down."

He snorted and looked at her. "Seriously? We own a house together. That's not 'tied down' as you put it? We're having a baby. That's not 'tied down' either? Good grief, Julia, listen to yourself." He pushed off the ottoman to kneel in front of her and lean over the chair. "I love you more than life. Marry me. Tell the rest of the world to go to hell and marry me."

Julia found herself being pulled into those green eyes and before she could think, shaking her head yes. She grinned. "Yes, Austin Phillip James, I'll marry you." He kissed her before pulling her up into a bear hug.

"Yes!" he laughed, twirling her around, both of them laughing.

"We have a problem," Julia stopped him. "We really need to wait until this baby comes because I don't think wedding dresses come in maternity sizes."

"That won't be a problem," he grinned. "If I know you, you won't want a big wedding, right?" She nodded. "Then how about we get married now and celebrate with a reception later. After Acacia gets here and you're back to one hundred percent." He sobered. "Jules, I want you to have my name before the baby is born. Please?"

She thought about what he was asking. *Why not?* She thought. Out loud she said, "You're so right about the big wedding, even though I don't think your mom will appreciate not getting her moment in the groom's mother spotlight." She grinned. "Of course, I don't think a wedding with me in it would be a spotlight she'd want anyway."

Austin grinned back. "I didn't know we were asking her to come. In fact, I'm thinking more along the lines of Matt, Lauren, Sharon, and John. I'm sure John can pull a few strings and get us a judge for Sunday, don't you?"

Julia grinned. "I think that would be entirely possible. Let's do it here. In the yard. And no frills. We'll all go out to dinner afterward. How does that sound?"

"Perfect. Now, let's call Sharon and John together, and then I'll call Matt and you call Lauren." He grabbed her up and whirled around again. "We're getting married!"

Julia laughed and shook her head. She followed Austin out to the living room where they would place their phone calls. It was going to be a busy weekend.

Chapter 50

WHILE JULIA AND AUSTIN WOULD have liked the wedding to happen immediately, Julia's body had other ideas. She soon realized that any time she stood for too long, she began to feel the now familiar ache in her lower back that signaled more pain that would work its way around her body. Rather than take a chance on hurting either Julia or the baby, they decided to postpone the wedding for at least two weeks. Austin was still hoping they could make it official before Acacia's arrival, but Julia had her doubts. She had no intention of short-changing their wedding by her being laid up.

Julia looked at his expression as they sat on the patio and enjoyed the December sunshine.

"Austin, stop pouting, please," she laughed. "We will get married. But I don't want to just say the words in front of a judge and not have a party." She shook her head. "I intend for this to be your only time and my last time to do this, and I want to do it right."

"Am not pouting," he mumbled. At her laugh, he looked over and grinned. "Maybe a little. I hear what you're saying and I agree, but I had my heart set on making it all official."

"And you know that while the rest of the family won't be here for the ceremony, they all want to be here for the baby's birth, don't you?"

"Yeah, well, that may or may not happen, you know," he looked out over the yard. Sharon had insisted they call their families to tell them that Julia had been in the hospital but that now everything was fine. Julia's father had wanted to come out immediately, and only Julia's insistence that she didn't want Dana there yet kept him home. While Natalie and Phillip had talked about coming out, it didn't take Austin much to convince them to stay put until the baby arrived. Natalie was still struggling with it all, and as soon as she had started in on Julia, Austin had to enlighten her once again.

He thought back over the conversation and shook his head at how that had gone. Things hadn't ended well the last time Austin spoke to his mother, and he hoped she had had time to think things through.

"Austin!" he could hear the happiness in her voice. "I wasn't expecting a call from you. How are you darling? When are you coming home?"

Not "How's Julia" or How's the baby?" He shook his head, took a deep breath, and let it out slowly before speaking.

"I'm fine and Julia's doing good now. We thought Caci was going to make her appearance last week, but after a night in the hospital and medication, the doctor was able to stop the contractions. Julia's been pretty much on bed rest ever since, but she's doing great now. Both of them are."

"That's nice, darling," Natalie was still reluctant to acknowledge that Julia still came first for Austin. "So how have you been?"

"I'm good, Mom," he almost sighed. "I'm only calling because I thought you would want to know about our close call. The doctor says that the longer Julia can go, the better the chances Acacia will be bigger and stronger. We're almost out of the woods on that now."

"Well, that's good," Natalie still didn't respond with the excitement of a new grandmother. Austin wondered when or even if she ever would. He brought himself back to attention as he heard her continue. "I know that Christmas is in a few weeks. Were you planning on coming home? If you get here the Saturday before, you'd be able to make at least the club party." She ended on a hopeful note.

"Mom, listen to yourself. You honestly think that I'd take off and leave Julia here alone just so I can make the Christmas party rounds with you?" Austin's incredulous voice echoed the expression on his face. "Did you even hear a word I said? Julia has to rest, take it easy, not move around a lot, and definitely not get excited or stressed. And you're talking parties?"

"Now, Austin, you know that isn't what I meant," her voice took on an air of aggravation. "Of course, I'm concerned about Julia, but I thought maybe you could get away and fly out here for a couple of days. Forgive me for wanting to see my son."

Austin's patience was thin enough without this.

"I tell you what, Mom, I'll call you when the baby comes, and if we don't make it happen before, you can make it out here for the wedding. Maybe combine a baby visit with a wedding. How does that sound?"

Why did I just say that? he thought. *Like I want her here for either right now.* He shook his head. *What is it about her that makes me want to always shock her?*

"W-w-what did you say? Wedding? What wedding?" Natalie stumbled over the words.

"Mine. And Julia's. I've wanted to get married for months, and two weeks ago Julia agreed to marry me, but we postponed things until she's back on her feet. We'll probably have a private ceremony and a bigger reception later." He felt mean, but he figured she deserved a little meanness. "I'll let you know when it all goes down."

His words were met with silence on the other end. After a brief pause, Natalie found her voice.

"Yes, please, you let us know, son," Natalie was struggling. "Are you sure about the wedding? I mean, are you sure you don't want anything big?" She laughed hesitantly. "I know you don't want anything big, but really, Austin, you and Julia should have done this months ago. But it's a little late now, I suppose." She paused and continued, "And Austin, I do care about the baby. I'm not that much of a horrible person, you know. And of course, when you and Julia marry, we'd love to be there. And I'm hurt that you think I don't care about Julia or the baby."

"I know, Mom, but you never call to ask or act like you give a rip. We've been through all of this before. I've said it once, and I'll say it again. You don't want me to choose between my family and you. You won't win, Mom."

"Austin, I've never asked you to choose…"

"Don't. Please." Austin wasn't getting into this again. *Geez, what a stubborn woman,* he thought. Out loud he said, "I've got to go, Mom. Please tell Dad what's happening out here and tell him that I'll call again next week or sooner, if anything happens."

"All right, son," Natalie's voice held tears, but Austin was immune by now. "Tell Julia hello for me. I love you, Austin."

"I'll tell her, and I love you, too. Bye, Mom," Austin ended the call before she could say anything else.

He didn't like to admit it, but these conversations with his mom took it out of him. He loved her, very much, but until she could accept his life choices, her role would be limited. He shook his head. He never expected her to react this radically to Julia and especially not to his daughter. He had hoped that she'd relent and come around by now, be excited for the newest member of the family. *Maybe when she holds her granddaughter,* he thought. *Maybe then she'll realize what she's missing.* As he thought back over the conversation, he had to admit that she was a bit more receptive than he'd heard until then. In fact, Austin was feeling a bit bad that he had cut her off so quickly. His phone had rung shortly after he'd hung up with Natalie, and he enjoyed a visit with his dad. Phillip was excited to learn about the upcoming wedding, but he was more concerned about the recent scare.

"Son," Austin could hear the concern in his dad's voice, "if this happens again, you have to call us immediately. Promise me you will."

Austin shook his head and remembered that his dad couldn't see him. "Sure, Dad, I'll make sure you know. And I'm sorry I didn't call you before."

"It's all good," Phillip assured his son. "I'd like nothing more than to be there when my granddaughter makes her entrance," he chuckled.

Austin smiled. "You bet, Dad. I'll talk to you later," and they had ended the call.

Julia's voice now brought him out of his thoughts. "What do you want to do about Christmas, babe?" She looked at him.

"Christmas?" Austin had almost forgotten about the holiday. Lauren had come over and helped them put up a tree in the living room. Julia had insisted.

"It's our first Christmas in our house, and I'd love to have our friends over. What do you think?"

Austin looked over at her and saw that she really was excited about the holiday. "Whatever you want, babe. Whatever you feel like doing." He was still concerned that she'd overdo things, but so far she'd behaved herself, as he liked to put it.

"Well, I talked to Sharon yesterday, and she said that instead of the private family party at her house, they would bring the party over here. What do you think?"

"I think that would be great," Austin pretty much gave her whatever she wanted these days.

"And…I was thinking…since we're less than two weeks from my due date, why don't we combine the Christmas celebration with a wedding."

At his shocked expression, Julia laughed.

"See? I hadn't forgotten how much it means for you to be married before Caci arrives. And when else would we have such a good opportunity?"

Austin had come over to where she was sitting and knelt down on the floor in front of her. She looked at his beautiful eyes and then at his big smile.

"I would like nothing better," he took her hands.

"Well, that's a good thing," she continued, "because I've already asked John to get his friend Judge Michaels over here Saturday night, and we're going to get married."

"December 19," Austin looked at his phone calendar. He looked at her and smiled. "I can handle that."

"Well, you need to call Matt and we need to get a license tomorrow. I've already asked Sharon and she's working on dinner." Julia grinned. "I have the easy part. I make one phone call, and my pint-sized friend springs into action."

"Works for me," Austin leaned over to kiss her. It was more difficult as Julia was all stomach these days. Having never been around pregnant women before, Austin didn't realize how large a woman's baby stomach could get. From the back, no one would ever guess that Julia was almost nine months along, but once she turned sideways, her middle protruded and Julia looked like she couldn't grow any bigger. He leaned back and looked at her face. Austin could always tell her moods or how she was feeling just by looking at her. He saw slightly darker circles under her eyes but not the two worry lines that appeared beside her mouth any time she was under stress or worried.

He couldn't stop smiling. *I'm getting married.*

Chapter 51

SATURDAY DAWNED BRIGHT AND SUNNY, which was the norm for Scottsdale, Arizona, even in December. By the afternoon, it would be an unusual eighty degrees, perfect for an afternoon wedding. After the phone call with their friends, things seemed to happen quickly. Sharon and John, of course, had gone into action. John called them back about fifteen minutes later to let them know that his friend Judge Michaels would be there at two o'clock to perform the ceremony. Since Julia was feeling so well, they decided to have the ceremony at the house and then go out to eat. Sharon had secured Vista Joya for the small reception party, and she would be by with Calista Freeman, whose maternity shop carried nothing but the best. Calista would be bringing several outfits for Julia to choose one. Julia started to protest, but decided that Sharon would wear her down anyway.

Matt and Lauren were shocked, but both agreed to stand up with their friends. Lauren volunteered to pick up flowers while Matt agreed to be on time. Austin and Julia had decided to go with simple platinum bands for the ceremony. Austin wasn't happy, but Julia reminded him that he'd already have a gift idea for their first wedding anniversary—a diamond ring. A trip to the jewelry store didn't take long and they were set.

"No dressing up," Julia declared. "I know that Sharon is springing for some dress, but honestly, I wish she wouldn't."

Austin looked at Julia closely. "Babe, you're not too tired, are you? I mean, this isn't all too much, is it?"

Julia laughed. "No, silly. I'm fine. Stress-free, you know!" He laughed with her, but when she turned away, concern was back on his face. He had to fuss with Sharon a bit to keep her from draping the entire yard and patio with white flowers, but as soon as he mentioned Julia's need to keep things simple because of her health, Sharon immediately changed her mind.

"Absolutely," she assured. "You are so right, Austin. Simple is the word. Although it goes against my natural instincts." Austin laughed at her and assured her that it would be fine. Once the baby arrived, they would plan a big reception celebration with all of their friends and families. He promised Sharon that she'd have the fun of planning that party, which prompted her to throw her arms around Austin and declare her love. He laughed.

At a quarter to two, Judge Michaels arrived to join the rest of them. Matt and Austin were dressed in slacks and button-down shirts with no ties. Lauren had opted for a short navy dress that for once didn't display too much cleavage. Julia had gone against the suggestion of Calista and Sharon, who wanted her in white, and chosen a satin short dress with a low scooped neckline and long draped sleeves. It was in Austin's favorite shade of blue, and on Julia, it brought out the dark blue of her eyes. They all gathered beside the acacia trees, and the judge performed the brief ceremony.

As Lauren watched Julia promise to love, honor, and cherish Austin, she couldn't help comparing this small gathering to the big sideshow of Julia's first wedding. While no one likes a big show more than Lauren, she couldn't help preferring this ceremony. Lauren smiled at her best friend and had to admit that Julia had never looked happier or more beautiful. As for Austin, he was happy to be marrying the love of his life. Matt felt the whole thing was a bit surreal. His buddy was getting married, and for him that seemed almost like an afterthought. In Matt's mind, Austin had gotten hitched the moment he and Julia moved into the house together. But his buddy was happy, and if this was his choice, then Matt would be happy for him.

In a matter of minutes, it was all over. Julia and Austin each had a new ring and after the ceremonial kiss, they accepted the hugs and congratulations of their friends. After offering the couple his best wishes and securing their signatures on the paperwork, the judge excused himself.

The six of them piled into the limousine John had waiting, and the drive into the mountains was filled with champagne for all but Julia and a lot of laughter. Once they arrived, the staff at Vista Joya welcomed them into a room smaller from the one in which Austin's graduation party had been held. This room was more intimate, but every bit as beautiful with a

French door that opened onto a balcony that overlooked the mountains. Austin took Julia's hand and led her out to the view. They both held champagne glasses, hers with club soda. Once they were alone. Austin gently tapped his glass to hers.

"Here's to a wonderful future," he sipped his drink. "Just when I don't think I could love you any more, I do."

Julia took a sip, closed her eyes, and smiled. "I tell myself every day that I have to be the luckiest woman in the world." She cupped his face in her hand and gently stroked his cheek with her thumb. "What's that line from the Tom Cruise movie—'You complete me.' I always thought that had to be the cheesiest thing I'd ever heard. Until I fell I love with you. Now it just fits."

Austin slipped his arm around Julia, and they stood together looking out over the mountains. Soon Sharon came looking for them.

"Hey, you two, I hate to break it up, but we have food. We all skipped lunch, and I'm starving."

Julia laughed, "I never skip a meal. I ate, remember? But I'm ready again."

Austin laughed with her, "She's worse than a teenage boy with a hollow leg, as my mom always put it." At the mention of his mother, Austin sobered.

"We'll call everyone tonight, okay?" Julia wanted him to call them before, but Austin refused. In his mind, this was all about them, and he really didn't want to listen to the drama that was his mother. Julia didn't want to tell Lawrence and Dana before Austin had the chance to tell his family, so they waited. Neither side would be happy, but nothing would deter from Austin and Julia's day.

Austin nodded, "Yeah, we'll call them tonight. Or not." He grinned.

"Well, whatever," Sharon broke in. "Let's eat, please."

Austin and Julia let themselves be led back into the dining room where the chef stood behind a cart filled with silver-lidded dishes. On a separate table, a two-tiered wedding cake was surrounded by flowers.

"Sharon," Julia scolded, "a two-tiered cake? We'll never eat all of that."

"Sweetie, the top layer is to freeze for your first anniversary. Remember?" Sharon rolled her eyes and shook her head. "As for the leftovers, we've all seen you and Matt eat cake. It isn't a pretty site."

"Hey," Matt defended himself, "I'm still a growing boy. I don't know what her excuse is." He faked defending himself against Julia as she stuck her tongue out at him.

"Yeah, well, Junior, you're not too many years from growing out instead of up. Then we'll see where all that cake settles," Lauren had switched from champagne to vodka. She took a sip and winked at Matt.

"We'll see…if you're still around," Matt teased. "You aren't getting any younger and may keel over by then from one of your massive eye rolls." Lauren rewarded him with one of her best before draining her glass. A waiter immediately sprang to refill her drink and she rewarded him with her signature sexy smile. Matt cocked an eyebrow at the man and smoothly moved between him and Lauren as soon as the glass was full.

"Children," Sharon broke in. "Please. I'm about to pass out."

They were finishing the third course when suddenly Julia stopped and sat straighter. Austin was immediately aware of the movement and leaned toward her.

"Are you okay?" he whispered. "You are as pale as that cake."

Julia sat still for a minute before shaking her head. "I don't think so. My back has been aching all afternoon, and that didn't feel like an ache just now."

Austin's eyes widened. "Are you okay? What do you think it is? I should have never insisted on the wedding…"

"Austin," Julia interrupted him. "I'm fine. But I do think that we need to go. This ache is turning into a cramp. One that occurs about every ten minutes."

"John?" Austin got his attention. "Is that limo outside?"

John heard the odd tone of Austin's voice and looked at Julia.

"It is. Do we need to go somewhere?" He was already signaling for the attendant to alert the driver.

"Julia? Are you okay?" Sharon had risen and was coming over to look at her eyes. "What's wrong, sweetie?"

Matt and Lauren both froze, their eyes widening. They looked at one another and each could read the other's thoughts. *Holy shit! She's gonna have that baby right here!*

"I'm okay, now, but my back has been hurting for a while, and I think that was a pain." Julia grinned at the faces surrounding her. Austin's was stunned, John's was all business, and Sharon's was concerned. Matt and Lauren looked shell-shocked. "Hey, it's just a baby. But I think we need to be going now." She turned to Sharon. "Have the chef box up that cake. I have a feeling that I won't get any until tomorrow."

With that, they all sprang into action. The wait staff assured Sharon that the cake would be delivered to her the next day, and they all made their way to the car. Austin had gotten over his shock, and his birth training classes kicked in. He hadn't noticed the time of the contraction, but he had his phone out, ready for the next. It came once they were all in the car and heading back to the valley. At this point, no one knew except for Julia's hand clinching Austin's as he checked his time. After about a minute, she relaxed and smiled at Austin, who grinned back.

"Uh, people," Lauren spoke up, "isn't this baby coming a bit early? We're awfully calm here, don't you think? I mean, personally, I'm freaked out over here."

Julia looked up to see Lauren's big brown eyes were even bigger as if she expected the baby to come popping through Julia's stomach like in the *Alien* movies. Julia laughed at her friend. Lauren knew better, but after champagne and vodka, her mind wasn't working well.

"Lauren, it's okay. Yes, we're a couple of weeks early, but Dr. Roberts assures that it's all okay. Calm down." As if reading Lauren's mind. "Caci won't come popping out the top of my stomach."

"They can do that?" Matt had been quiet, but spoke up at the image. "I mean, that was the old *Alien* movie, right? Babies can't really do that, can they?"

Disgusted, Austin looked at his friend. "Didn't you pay any attention in health class? Good grief."

"Uh, no. And ruin my image of women forever? Dude, I don't want to think about that nightmare, and what happens to one of my favorite parts of a woman's body. I mean, man, those images stay with you."

At this point, John and Sharon began laughing, and they all settled down for a few more minutes until Julia clinched Austin's hand again.

"How far apart?" Sharon asked.

"Far. Ten minutes," he assured. He looked at Lauren and Matt again. "Guys, Julia won't have the baby in here, okay? If we were home, we wouldn't even be heading to the hospital yet."

"We weren't worried about that, were we?" Lauren looked at Matt for affirmation.

"Speak for yourself. I'm a little freaked over here," Matt's knee was jiggling up and down. Lauren leaned over and placed a hand on it, stopping the motion.

"Honey, you're shaking the car. Don't shake the baby out," Lauren teased and sat back satisfied at the horrified look on Matt's face. She'd gotten herself under control and was back to her confident self. She glanced over at Julia who gave her a warning look. "What? Can't I have a little fun here?" Lauren rolled her eyes and looked out the window.

Julia had another contraction before the stretch limo pulled up outside the emergency room. As attendants rolled a stretcher toward the car, Julia waved them off. Out of the corner of her eye, she saw a man with a radio attached to his lapel standing beside the door. She almost laughed at the thought, but sobered quickly as another pain took over. She stopped, Austin gripping her hand with his other arm supporting her. In a few seconds, it passed, and they made their way into the hospital.

John and Sharon followed close behind, John turning to the remaining two.

"The limo is yours the rest of the night," he said. "I see no need for the two of you to hang around here unless you just want to." Matt and Lauren looked at one another. "Trust me, it will be boring for hours. Go have some drinks and come back later. I insist."

"No, I want to be here in case Julia needs me. I will, however, take you up on the car offer to go to their house and pick up her bag. Let me run back to ask where she keeps it and get Austin's house keys." With that Lauren hurried after Julia and Austin. In less than five minutes, Lauren was back.

"She's good. The nurses assured me that it will be hours yet, so let's take off. I want to change clothes and get back," Lauren grabbed Matt's arm.

The two climbed back in, and John watched the car disappear before he turned to go into the building. He stopped to give instructions to the man at the door. That done, he found Sharon waiting for him. They headed toward the elevator and the maternity ward, where they would be waiting out the night.

"John, I'm worried. This baby shouldn't be here for another two weeks. You don't think this wedding had anything to do with Julia going into labor, do you?"

John's frown answered her question. Sharon started pacing. "John, I don't know what those kids were thinking. She should be resting, not getting married. And John, should we call anyone? I mean, Lawrence and Dana, or Phil and Natalie? We need to ask Austin as soon as we can."

"Calm down, sweetheart," John stopped her in mid-stride. "You go see what you can find out. I'll be here." He knew that she had to do something or she would be driving him crazy.

Sharon came back, concern on her face. "Austin will be out to talk to us and make his calls. John, Dr. Roberts is on her way, and they've called the pediatrician for the baby. I don't like this."

John chuckled, and quickly sobered when his wife shot daggers in his direction with her narrowed eyes. "It's been too long, I suppose. This is all standard procedure. You don't remember how it was when John Junior was born? And we didn't get there for Johnny's birth until after the fact." He patted the seat next to him. "Sit, get yourself under control, please."

They looked up as Austin came out to fill them in.

"The nurses are getting her undressed and hooked up to all the equipment. We're in a birthing room down the hall and around the corner. You can come back and stay with us for a while if you want to. If everything goes all right," and here his voice became more nervous than excited, "the baby will be born right there."

"Austin," Sharon stood up to walk to him. "Hon, do you want us to call your parents or Julia's? They need to be told, don't you think?"

Austin ran his hand through his hair, a sign of his thinking. "Yeah, I guess I need to let everyone know we're here. It isn't as if they could be here or anything, but they'd be mad if I don't at least keep them posted." He looked at Sharon. "If I make this first call, will you keep them updated after that? I'll need to be with Julia."

"Of course I will!" Sharon hugged him and sent him outside where he'd have some privacy.

Ten minutes later, Austin came back in looking a bit tense.

"Well, that went as well as I expected. Everyone except Caleb will be on airplanes heading this direction as soon as possible." He looked at

Sharon and John. "If they all pile in here before the baby arrives, will you keep them occupied and out of Julia's hair? I mean, I'm sure they will all mean well, but she really doesn't need that kind of excitement, especially if anything unusual is happening with Caci."

"You bet we will," John stepped up. "I'll call Lawrence and Phil and offer to have a car to pick them up. They can sort out rentals later."

Austin grinned his relief. "That would be great. Thanks."

A nurse came out and motioned to Austin. "Mr. James, you can come back now." With that, he excused himself and hurried back. Then he remembered and stopped to speak to the other couple.

"Hey, you two come back now and help us pass the time. Usually mothers aren't even here yet, but I suppose Dr. Roberts is taking precautions."

An hour later, John and Sharon returned to the waiting area. John had spoken with Phil and Lawrence and had already notified his car service when and where to pick them up. Julia was doing okay, and Dr. Roberts had already been by to check on her. John sensed something in the doctor's face that he didn't like. She took a lot of time looking at the baby's monitor and listening to the heartbeat. While the baby wasn't coming early, the doctor evidently had some concerns. She also studied Julia's monitors longer than usual. Before John could mask his thoughts, his intuitive wife looked over at him.

"What? John, what are you thinking?" Sharon took his hand.

He took a deep breath and let it out slowly. "I don't know, Shar. I just sensed something in the doctor's demeanor. She didn't say anything or at least not anything that I overheard, but I think she's keeping an eye on something."

"Well, of course, she is," Sharon smiled. "Julia's a couple of weeks early, that's all. Now, I need some coffee. Isn't there a Starbucks downstairs by the front door? I'll run back and tell Austin where we are and see if he needs anything."

Chapter 52

THE REST OF THE NIGHT was spent back and forth from Julia's room to the waiting area. Lauren had returned. After going back to see Julia to make sure her friend was all right, Lauren had settled on a short sofa and fallen asleep. John and Sharon dozed off a couple of times in the reclining chairs, but as soon as one or the other would drift off, someone new would enter the room, making enough noise to wake them up. In the early hours of the morning, John's phone rang, a driver confirming that Dana and Lawrence were on their way.

"I'll go back and let Austin know," Sharon slowly stood. She stretched and her back popped loudly. John grinned at her and she reminded him that his turn was coming. She was soon back, grinning from ear to ear.

"The doctor says that she thinks Julia will be fully dilated soon and that we could have the baby here in the next couple of hours!"

"That's great!" John had stood and was walking around to limber up and awaken Lauren. The three had just returned from another Starbuck's visit when Dana and Lawrence came rushing in.

"John," Lawrence shook the other man's hand, "Sharon, we got here as quick as we could. How's Julia?"

Dana remained quiet except to accept Sharon's outstretched hand and give her a brief greeting.

Sharon jumped in to answer his question. "Well, it's been a very long night, but the doctor thinks we could have a baby before too long. Isn't that exciting?"

Lawrence's smile covered the lower half of his face, but Dana's face was strained. She murmured something about that being nice, but fell silent again.

"Do you think we could peek in?" Lawrence asked.

"You'll have to go back and ask the nurse," Sharon replied. "Things could be happening as we speak, and since the birth will be in her room, I don't know. I suppose that as long as it's all going okay, we can do nothing but wait here." She gave them an encouraging smile.

At the mention of the things happening immediately, Sharon saw Dana's face grow pale. *Yep,* she thought, *pretend all you want, you old hag. You're as worried as the rest of us.* Out loud she shared that from everything they were told, it was standard procedure.

Lauren came sweeping in from the ladies' room. She didn't look worse for wear even though John knew that she and Matt had enjoyed a couple of drinks before she returned to spend the night with them at the hospital. She almost ran up to Lawrence, threw her arms around his neck, and wrapped him in a giant hug, which he returned. Her greeting to Dana was much cooler, no physical contact, but she did tell her hello and inquire about the flight.

Lauren insisted on checking in on Julia. "I'll only peek around the corner," she assured. She came back to report that she didn't get to see anything before a nurse ran her off. "Can you believe that crap?" she wasn't happy. "Like I wanted to stick around and watch, but the least they could have done is let me say hello." She looked around for somewhere to sit and settled on a vinyl-covered sofa. After settling in, she looked around and declared, "I hate hospitals, don't you? I mean, this is supposed to be the happy ward, and look at us." She made a face. "Lighten up, people. It's all good."

Lawrence shook his head, smiled, and joined Lauren while the rest settled in around them. Another hour passed, and still no word came from the birthing room. John rose.

"I'm going to go ask how things are going. You all sit tight." He disappeared down the hall and around the corner, the others all watching his receding back. He returned shortly with a white-faced Austin. He was still in the hospital scrubs that were required for him to be in the delivery room. The two men were looking at the floor as they walked toward the small group. Lauren stood up first and grabbed Austin's arm.

"What? What's wrong?" she demanded.

Austin looked at Lawrence and Dana, registering that they were there and looked back at the others. He shook his head.

"Julia's in surgery," he sounded shell-shocked. "Caci was born, and she's perfect," he feebly smiled, "I got to hold her briefly before they took her off to the nursery to check her lungs and stuff. But Julia," his voice broke. "Julia started hemorrhaging. I've never seen so much blood. Dr. Roberts has rushed her into surgery and no one's told me a thing since." He sat down on the sofa that Lauren had vacated, and Sharon and Lauren settled on either side of him. "She was so pale. One minute we're celebrating our daughter, and the next she's passing out on me and I'm being shoved aside and the doctor's barking out orders. The next thing I know, I'm outside and they've taken her through another door. I guess it goes to the operating room."

Just then someone began sobbing. They turned to see Dana with her head buried in her husband's chest, her shoulders heaving. She calmed down enough to speak to Lawrence.

"I told you she shouldn't be having a baby at her age! I told you! And now she could die! That girl never thinks. She never listens to me or anyone! She always just dives into things and never gives anyone or anything a thought." Lawrence stood there patting his wife's back as she continued to cry. She looked at Austin. "And you—it's all your fault that she's in this mess! What you're doing with Julia is beyond me…"

Austin's eyes came to rest on Dana as his face registered both shock and guilt. Was it his fault? Could he have done something to keep her safe? And how was his little girl?

Lauren looked at Dana with no sympathy, but as she took in Austin's expression, her eyes narrowed and she started to say something. Before she could, with a shake of her head, Sharon motioned for her to remain where she was.

Sharon approached the two. "Dana, let's go find you a bathroom where you can clean up. Julia will be out of surgery soon and in recovery. You don't want her seeing you like this, now do you?" She took the other woman's arm and guided her down another hallway and through a door. The others looked after them in stunned silence. Austin still looked to be in shock, and Lauren took his hand in hers, gently squeezing it. Lawrence and

John looked at the door through which their wives had disappeared. After a few seconds, John led the other man over to sit. Both were on the edge of their seats, staring at the floor. Austin and Lauren remained where they were—Austin gazing down the hall from which he'd come and Lauren absently patting his arm and assuring him that everything would be okay.

Sharon let the door close behind her before she whirled on the woman with her.

"What the hell was that!" she demanded. "Really! Your own daughter is in surgery, and you have the audacity to stand out there and criticize? To attack your own child? This isn't all about you and your little *feelings*, you know." Dana had stopped crying and was wiping at her eyes. Sharon leaned closer to get the woman's attention. "You should be celebrating the birth of your grandchild, for heaven's sake! You should be praying that Julia is okay. You should be comforting your son-in-law. Instead, you're grandstanding a big scene."

Dana stopped wiping her eyes to look at the other woman. She remained silent.

"You know, I always wondered what in the world could make a woman break off her relationship with her only child. Now, I know." She came closer, lowering her voice. "You are a self-centered, spoiled, and yes, sometimes wicked woman. You have no idea of the beautiful, loving, and sweet daughter you so casually toss aside. Well, let me tell you, lady, you're making a horrible mistake. And if you think for one minute that I'm going to let you say those awful things in front of her husband, who's beside himself with worry, then think again. I really don't give a damn about your feelings. And if Lawrence wasn't such a good man, I'd personally run your ass right out of here." Sharon took a breath and paused. Dana still remained silent. "If you can't behave yourself, then save us all the distress and go find a hotel. I'll have the driver take you myself."

Dana had been quiet until Sharon finished, but as the words sank in, a new expression came over her face. Dana glared at the woman in front of her. "Her husband? My son-in-law? Are you telling me that my daughter married that boy in there? When?"

"Yesterday, and I can completely understand why she left you out of the loop," Sharon crossed her arms in front of her chest.

"Well, I suppose she's done it this time." Dana looked at Sharon. "And I guess you're just all hunky-dory with all of this? I suppose allowing someone else's child make monumental mistakes doesn't bother you in the least."

"First of all, Julia isn't a child. If you haven't checked lately, she's forty-one years old, a successful business woman, and a wonderful friend. As for the 'boy' as you call him, I haven't met too many forty-something's who are in his league as far as maturity and integrity. But we all know your choice in men for Julia—Keith? That womanizing abuser?" Sharon snorted in disgust. "Yeah, you're choice is excellent Mommy Dearest."

"I don't have to listen to this," Dana started to push past Sharon, who reached out to grab her arm.

"Julia is in surgery. We don't know if she's going to be okay. That man out there is beside himself with worry, as are the rest of us." She leaned closer again. "Keep your mouth shut unless you have something encouraging to say. If you upset him in the least, I *will* have you removed, and don't think I won't."

"What are you the boss around here?" Dana glared.

Sharon smiled, "No, I'm simply the mother to Julia that you refuse to be." She chuckled. "I also protect those that I love, and I use whatever methods I have to as long as the job is done. You probably shouldn't forget that," Sharon released her arm and stepped back. The other woman raised her chin and turned to leave. Once the door shut behind her, Sharon leaned against the sink. She was exhausted and that scene had taken it out of her. She heard the door open and looked up to see Lauren enter. They smiled weakly at one another.

"By the look on her face, I'd say Cruella isn't too happy right now. What did you say?"

Sharon rose and straightened her spine. "Nothing that shouldn't have been said a long time ago. Now, let's go check on that baby and Julia. Surely we can learn something by now."

As the two women made their way back to the waiting area, a nurse was just coming in. She was smiling, a good sign, and motioned for them to follow her to the nursery, where Acacia was waiting for her daddy.

"Your daughter weighed in at six pounds and twelve ounces, and she's eighteen and a half inches long." She stopped at the door. "I can only let two of you come in at a time. Dad, you come in, of course, and one more."

Austin hurried in and the rest simply looked at one another. Sharon and John didn't want to jump in ahead of Dana and Lawrence, who still appeared to be shell-shocked. Finally, Lauren spoke up.

"Well, hell, I'll go in!" and she quickly followed Austin.

The others looked through the window as the pink bundle was placed in Austin's arms. His face softened as he leaned over to look at every feature. They could see one little arm waving in the air, and Austin gently took the tiny hand into his. Sharon's eyes filled with tears, and she looked over at Dana. She, too, was fighting tears as they all stood at the window.

"Well, I'll take my turn in a bit," Lawrence spoke up. "I need to know how my girl's doing." He turned to look for a nurse.

Soon Austin handed the baby to Lauren and hurried back to the others. His face was a mix of wonder at his daughter and worry for his wife.

Austin looked at Sharon and Julia's parents. "You go check on the baby, and I'll be there in a bit. I want to be with Julia when she wakes up."

As if on cue, Dr. Roberts came around the corner and stopped beside the small group. She was still wearing scrubs, but she was smiling.

"I think we got the bleeding stopped, and Julia's being taken into recovery."

"Doctor," John spoke for them all, "what happened? Could she start hemorrhaging again?"

Dr. Roberts shook her head, "I don't think so. What happened is the placenta failed to completely separate. Placenta accreta is what it's called. I was looking for this to happen since the condition is possible whenever the placenta is implanted over a previous uterine scar. Given Julia's miscarriages, the possibility of scar tissue was great."

"But is she okay now?" John gently prodded.

"Absolutely," Dr. Roberts put a hand on Austin's shoulder. "Why don't you go on back and see her. She'll be in recovery for the next thirty minutes or so, and then I'll have the baby brought back to you both."

Austin shook the doctor's hand, "I don't know how to thank you. Where is she? Which direction?"

The doctor pointed him to the nurse's station and assured him one of the staff would take him to Julia. With a last look at the baby in Lauren's arms, Austin turned to find his wife. The doctor excused herself, and the others turned back to the nursery. Lauren looked up and motioned for one of them to join her. Dana and Lawrence walked through the nursery door, and they all watched Lauren place the baby in Dana's arms. She came out to join Sharon and John.

"What's up with Julia? Is she okay? I saw Austin leave," Lauren had missed it all. John filled her in, and they all turned back to look through the nursery window once again.

Dana couldn't believe the small miracle in her arms. She leaned over and took a deep breath, smelling that unique baby smell. "Our grandbaby," she whispered. Caci had lots of dark hair, and when she opened her eyes, they were a dark blue. Dana could see flecks of green, but it would be a few months before Acacia's eyes turned to their permanent shade. Lawrence was grinning as he leaned over and inspected his newest baby girl.

"Acacia Elise," he said softly. "I like that name."

Dana started to sniff, but when she looked back down at the tiny face, she changed her mind. "I think it suits her," she admitted.

The two held her a bit longer before Lawrence looked up to see two others who were anxiously waiting for their turn.

"Hey, hon, let's see if we can find out something on Julia. John and Sharon can take a turn at holding the little one here."

Lawrence returned to the others, and Sharon hurried in to take his place. The two men watched as Dana reluctantly handed the baby over to Sharon. The two women were soon absorbed in the baby, which allowed them to ignore one another. John soon joined them and Dana came out. She looked at Lauren, who raised one brow as if to say, "Well?" Dana said nothing but pointedly turned her attention to the nursery window. Just then they were joined by a new pair.

Phillip and Natalie came rushing up to join the group. They hadn't met their new in-laws and didn't even know that they were recently related. They stopped as both recognized Dana as Julia's mother by the family resemblance.

"Excuse me," Phillip smiled. "Are you Julia's mother?"

Dana looked at the two newcomers before replying, "I am. May I help you?"

"Dana," Lauren stepped forward, "this is Austin's mom and dad."

Lauren made the introductions before excusing herself to check on Julia.

"So," Phillip spoke first. "You're Julia's parents. It's nice to finally meet you." He extended his hand to Lawrence, and the two men began chatting. Dana and Natalie looked at one another, and it was Dana who spoke first.

"We just held the baby, and she's perfect. I'm sure you're eager to meet her, too."

Natalie looked around Dana's shoulder to peer into the nursery, where Sharon was gently rocking the baby in her arms. Sharon looked up to see the newcomers and said something to John, who came out. He introduced himself, and Natalie and Phillip went in to take his and Sharon's place.

"The nurse said that as soon as Julia's in her room, we can all go back and visit," Sharon said. She looked at her watch. "It shouldn't be too much longer now, I wouldn't think." She looked at her husband. "John? Why don't we go get some coffee? We'll join the others later."

After asking if anyone wanted anything, they turned to make their way to the hospital lobby. Starbuck's was their favorite, but they were getting tired of the place. After having nothing but Starbuck's for hours, it was getting old.

Lawrence watched them disappear before turning to his wife.

"Well, it seems that all is going to be okay, doesn't it?" he smiled at his wife.

"Really?" Dana looked at him. "You don't know, do you?"

"That the kids got married yesterday?" At Dana's shocked expression, Lawrence laughed. "John told me. Lighten up. Isn't this what you always wanted? Julia's happily married and she has a new baby. You should be smiling, hon."

Dana crossed her arms over her chest and looked back into the nursery. Lawrence knew that she wasn't there yet, but he had hopes that his wife would soon see past all of the disagreements and arguments and hard feelings. He wasn't naïve enough to believe that his wife and daughter would ever enjoy a close relationship, but he hoped that they would at least set aside their differences for the family's sake. For Caci's sake. She would need both of her grandparents.

They turned at approaching footsteps as Lauren walked up. In the confusion of Phillip and Natalie's arrival, no one had noticed that Lauren had disappeared.

"Julia's in room three seventy-four, or she will be shortly. She's still pretty groggy, but she's awake. I think they'll take the baby in soon." She hesitated. "How about we all go grab some wonderful hospital breakfast food and give Mom and Dad some alone time?"

"That's a great idea," Lawrence smiled at Lauren. They all looked through the nursery window to see the nurse take Caci from Natalie's arms and place her in a small bassinet. She wheeled the baby through a different door from the one that Phillip and Natalie now came through.

"Isn't she perfect?" Phillip grinned from ear to ear.

"That she is," Lawrence replied. "I don't know about you, but we were up all night and really didn't eat anything. How about we get some breakfast before checking on the kids?" He turned to Lauren. "Lauren? Do you want to come, too?"

She looked from one couple to the other before shaking her head. "Uh, tempting, but no thanks. I'll just grab some coffee and make a few phone calls. I know that Matt will be wondering how things are going around here, and I have a few others to call. Thanks anyway." With that, she turned on her heels and quickly walked toward the elevator. She turned back to see the four looking after her as the door slid closed.

Good lord, that would be a fresh hell that I am definitely not up to, she thought as she rolled her eyes.

Chapter 53

———

Austin had no idea that his parents had arrived. He walked into the recovery room, although why it was called a room he didn't know. It was more of a recovery cubicle. Taking in the pale face, Austin felt his chest tighten. *She looks so vulnerable,* he thought. In addition to her pale complexion, her dark hair had been pulled up under a paper cap. Sitting beside the bed, he reached out to take Julia's cold hand in his and gazed at her peaceful face. *She's been through so much today. God, I've never seen anything like childbirth, but she took that in stride. It's what happened afterward that I can't believe. One minute we couldn't be happier and the next...* Julia frowned a bit in her sleep before relaxing again. Austin reached up to smooth her forehead and her eyelids fluttered before closing again. A nurse came in, took her blood pressure, and listened to her pulse. She smiled at Austin.

"It won't be long now and she'll wake up," she assured him. "Everything looks good."

The nurse left them, and Austin went back to holding Julia's hand and looking at her. She had scared him to death. He was thinking about her, the baby, and what he would have done had he lost her when she stirred. Julia opened her eyes and tried to focus on the room and the man beside her. He knew when it all registered because her eyes focused on his, and she gave him a small smile.

"Hey, baby," he whispered and leaned over to kiss her gently. "Welcome back. You left me for a while, you know."

"Why? What happened?" she whispered. "Where's Caci?"

Before she could become agitated, Austin assured her the baby was okay, just in the nursery for a while. He gave her a brief explanation of what had happened and told her that she would be fine.

"I want to see my baby," she leaned her head back on the bed. "When?"

A nurse came in, followed by the doctor. Another check of Julia's vital signs and a brief examination from the doctor ensued. At the conclusion, Dr. Roberts motioned for Austin to follow her out into the hall.

"It looks like everything is fine, but Julia's blood pressure isn't as high as I'd like to see it. She lost a lot of blood, and we had to give her a transfusion. I'm hoping to get it back up to normal soon."

Austin asked, "Are you sure? There's nothing else going on here, doc?"

"I am. And now I'm going to see about getting her into a room and settling you two in with the baby."

She turned to the nurse's station and left Austin standing outside the small room. The nurse came out, smiled brightly, and motioned for him to return. Austin resumed his spot by Julia's bedside, but she was dozing quietly. Lauren stuck her head in the door, and Austin grinned at her.

"Hey, Junior, how's the patient? Everybody's down at the nursery making goo-goo eyes at the baby. Good news!" Her voice took on the false excited tone that Austin knew would be followed by anything other than good news to Lauren. "Your mom and dad arrived! Yah!" She ended with a false smile.

Austin chuckled. "Oh, I'll bet that scene is playing out in fine dramatic fashion."

Lauren came in to lean over and look intently at Julia, who had closed her eyes again. "I wouldn't know. I made some introductions and fled. I left the four to have at it." She looked back at Austin and grinned. "Yeah, I'm a chicken shit, I'll admit it."

That brought a small laugh from Austin, who looked back at Julia in time to see her smile.

"Is that my best friend I hear calling herself a chicken shit?" her voice was still low and she spoke slowly.

"Hey, Jules," Lauren leaned closer to speak. "I just came from holding the most beautiful baby in the whole world, but she isn't happy. She wants her mamma." Lauren took Julia's other hand.

"Mamma wants her, too," Julia whispered.

A nurse came in with the paraphernalia used to draw blood. Lauren raised an eyebrow at Austin.

"That's my cue to wait outside. You all just do whatever it is you're going to do…" her voice trailed as she started back out the door.

"Oh, you can wait in her room, if you want." The nurse spoke as she looked down at a chart. "She'll be in room three seventy-four, and as soon as she's settled, we'll bring the baby in."

Lauren looked at Austin. "You stay with Jules and I'll go inform the crowd. In fact, I'll see what I can do to get you kids some alone time. Something tells me you won't have much of that as soon as they all descend."

Austin smiled his thanks, and as the nurse put the tourniquet on Julia's arm and patted the skin to find a vein, the blonde scooted the rest of the way out and gently closed the door behind her. Austin grinned and watched the nurse's adept hands. Soon after she finished, two others came to wheel Julia to her new room, Austin following behind. A short elevator ride later, they exited onto the regular maternity floor. Austin could hear babies crying and as they passed a large cart overflowing with flower arrangements and balloons, he mentally reminded himself to order some flowers. Daisies, he decided with a grin. Julia once told him that roses reminded her of a funeral.

It didn't take much for the nurses to have Julia transferred from the wheeled bed and onto the room's bed. It was a comfortable room with a small sofa along one wall, a rocking chair, a recliner, and a nice television affixed to the far wall where it could be seen from either the bed or the recliner. The nurses had just finished getting Julia settled in when a young girl carried in a huge bouquet of fresh flowers. She handed Austin the small card. *All our love, John and Sharon.* Austin smiled and showed the card to Julia.

"Leave it to them to be the first," he shook his head.

"They probably had the florist on stand-by, knowing them," Julia chuckled. Her voice was still weak, but she was looking better.

They both looked up as the baby's bassinet was wheeled in, and a smiling nurse picked her up and placed her in Julia's arms. While Julia and Caci stared at one another, the nurse showed Austin where all the diapers, wipes, and other items were located in the cabinet beneath the bassinet bed. He was patient but kept looking over at the bed. As soon as the nurse made her exit, he came over to his wife and daughter. Julia looked up to smile.

"Hey, Dad, isn't she something?"

For a moment, Austin thought that his heart would burst. "You two are the most beautiful sight in the world," he whispered. He looked at Julia. "I love you more than life, baby."

She smiled the smile he loved most and replied, "I love you more."

He grinned. "I love you most."

Julia moved over to make room on the bed for Austin, and the three of them stayed that way for several minutes. Caci had closed her eyes and was resting on her mother. Every once in a while she'd let out a small squeak and her tiny pink lips would move in and out. It wouldn't be long before she'd be ready to nurse. Julia and Austin sat staring at the little face they already adored.

"Who's here?" Julia softly asked.

"According to Lauren, everybody," Austin replied.

"Everybody? As in your mom, my mom, our dads," she looked at him questioningly.

"Yep, the gang's all here, but I haven't seen any of them except your folks. I guess mine arrived in the middle of the excitement."

"Then let's enjoy our quiet while it lasts. They'll all be swarming in here soon, I guess."

They grew quiet again, and Julia spoke first.

"Austin?" he looked up as she continued. "I know that a baby wasn't in our plans, and I've felt guilty about that ever since we found out we were expecting." Austin started to interrupt, but Julia stopped him. "Wait, please, let me talk. I want to apologize for so many things." She gave him a small smile. "For sometimes making a big deal out of our age difference. I know it's meaningless, but it's taken me some time to get past that. I'm sorry my mom is a pain. I'm sorry that I haven't found a way to make amends with your mom, and I promise to start working on that as soon as I can." She paused and looked down at the baby, who had made a small noise before settling down again. She looked back at him. "But most of all, I'm sorry for not marrying you sooner. I was being selfish and thinking only about how I was feeling. If we were doing what I wanted us to do. And I've learned something over these past months." She paused to take a

441

deep breath and smile weakly at him. "I am my happiest when I've made you happy, if that makes any sense. And I've learned to trust you, to trust us." Her eyes had started to fill with tears. "I love you Austin Phillip James. I'll love you forever."

Austin smiled as she finished speaking. He gently kissed her upturned face before leaning over to gently kiss the head of their sleeping daughter. He put an arm around Julia and they both settled back together.

"Life is all about learning, babe, and I've learned as much or more than you have." He lightly touched the silky hair on the baby's head. "Something tells me that I'll be learning a whole lot more in the future." He kissed Julia's soft hair, too. She loved it when he kissed her head, and she usually would look up for another. This time she didn't.

Austin noticed her arms and body becoming slack.

"Julia? Jules!" He tried to get her to respond and when she didn't, he took the baby from her arms and pushed the red button on the side of the bed. Clutching the small infant in one arm, he used his other to try to shake Julia awake, all the time calling her name.

"Julia? Come on, baby, say something! Jules!"

A nurse came rushing in and pushed him aside as she hurried to Julia. Another soon joined her. As they surrounded the bed, Austin could do nothing except cling to the baby in his arms and watch helplessly. The nurses were soon joined by more and all Austin could do was watch them work on his wife.

"Julia," he whispered, still clinging to the infant. "Don't leave me, baby, please…"

Chapter 54

THE WARM SUN BEAT DOWN on his head as Austin sat on the bench that overlooked the mountains in the distance. John had put the bench there for Julia after he'd heard her say that she wanted one. In his arms, Austin cradled his daughter. Like her daddy, she liked nothing more than to be outside, even if the air contained a chill. He had bundled her up with a one-piece snowsuit, attached baby mittens that she kept losing, and a hat with the snowsuit's hood tightly fastened. A heavy blanket covered her and him.

"Well, baby girl," he spoke gently to the baby. "Today's the day. I wish I could be doing a lot of other things besides this, but life doesn't always give us what we want." At his voice, Caci waved her little arms and squealed. Austin brought her up until their faces were inches apart. He grinned and green eyes met blue-green ones. Natalie was sure that within a couple of months, Acacia's eyes would turn even greener, but Austin hoped not. He would love for her to have a combination of his green and Julia's blue. Father and daughter stared at one another until the baby grinned and spit bubbles at him. Austin laughed and kissed her cheek. She was still warm, he noted, so he decided to stay outside a bit longer. He continued the one-sided conversation.

"Yep, your Grandma Nat has finally seen things our way, hasn't she? I knew she would. And even Grandma Dana has learned to behave herself. Isn't that something?" He laughed as he thought about his in-laws. Dana still wasn't warm and fuzzy, as Julia would have described it, but she was civil. And she was crazy about the baby he was holding. Austin continued talking to Acacia. "Your grammas will always try to run our lives, but we won't let them, will we? Now, let's hope they can keep it civil today, right?" He smiled at the thought of the possible drama that was always waiting to bubble up when Dana and Natalie were involved.

"Your mommy definitely wouldn't let them run things, would she? She always put her touch on everything, making it hers."

His thoughts travelled back to all the people Julia had touched, most of all Austin himself. He gave her credit for all the wonderful things and people in his life: John and Sharon, a beautiful home, his dream job, confidence in himself and his abilities, love, and most all, his beautiful baby girl. As if she was reading his mind and knew he was thinking of her, Acacia gurgled and reached out to grab her daddy's nose. Austin laughed and indulgently let her hold on, all the while kissing the little hand that was attached to his face.

"Touched by Jules, that's what we all are, aren't we, baby girl?" Austin continued talking to the infant.

They both turned at the sound of someone approaching. Lauren came down the path and plopped down on the bench beside Austin.

"Wow, I can see why Julia wanted a bench put here. This is such a gorgeous view." She paused and looked out over Mount Humphreys. "I still don't know why in the world you'd want to come up here this time of year. April is still a suck month, you know. This warm day, if you call this warm, is totally a freak." Even as she spoke, her face turned toward the mountains bespoke calm. She lifted it up toward the sunshine.

Austin looked over at Lauren, who had a red hat pulled down over her blond hair. She'd made it known that coming up to the mountains wasn't her first choice, but this wasn't Lauren's call.

"Hey, Lauren." At his voice, Lauren turned her attention to the man beside her. Austin had stepped up big time in the being-a-dad business, and Lauren appreciated him all the more for it. He continued. "I want you to know how much I've appreciated all of your help these last three, four months. Things haven't been easy, but you've been a good friend. And a great aunt for Miss Acacia here." At her name, the baby looked up at him from where she'd been working his coat button with a small finger.

Lauren reached over and put her finger out for the baby to grab onto to. Caci reached her little arms out for Lauren, who could never deny her anything. Austin shook his head as he handed his daughter over. Acacia seemed to know who would spoil her the most and deny her nothing. Already the baby's closet was crammed with clothes she'd never be able to wear and her room with toys she'd never be able to play with. He knew that would always be the case with Lauren and Sharon in her life.

"Well, Ace," Lauren spoke to Austin even though her eyes were on the baby, who was reaching for the bright blond hair barely out of reach. "I was just thinking about how you've stepped up to be a damn good dad. Of course," she cut her eyes over to him, "I'd kick your ass if you weren't, but that's beside the point." She laughed and made funny baby noises while pulling Caci to her for a kiss before lifting her into the air and away from her.

Austin shook his head. *Who would have guessed Blondie has a maternal instinct?* he thought. Even his buddy Matt had become more interested in the baby. Not at first, Austin recalled, but as Caci responded to the people around her, Matt had taken more of an interest. Austin smiled as he remembered the first time Matt had received one of the baby's big smiles. That was it. Matt's heart was taken by a two-month-old female.

All three looked up as Sharon approached.

"There you are! Good grief, you two! I have a house filled with people, Austin, your mom and dad are looking for you, and Lauren, I've needed your help. Here, give that baby to Gramma Sharon, and you two go back to the house." As Sharon finished up, her voice had taken on the baby-coo that it so often held these days. Caci smiled as Sharon took her from Lauren and walked her back up the path, stopping often to point something out. The baby would look at the leaf, or the bird, or whatever Sharon was pointing to, and she seemed to understand what Sharon was telling her. Sharon looked up at Austin.

"Smartest baby on earth, bar none, I tell you," she laughed and continued up the path. As they all stepped onto the patio, Sharon directed Austin to the French doors leading to the bedroom. "You need to change, and I'll take care of this one. Lauren, I think Matt was looking for you. He's in the den." She looked at them both. "Let's all meet in the great room in about thirty minutes, shall we?"

They went their separate ways, but met as Sharon had requested. Austin looked around the room. Matt and Lauren stood to the side, heads together as they spoke in low voices, Caleb joining them. *Probably planning their getaway later*, he thought. John, Phillip, and Lawrence were standing beside the big fireplace where they were talking to another man. Sharon, Natalie, and Dana were on the sofa where Caci was the center of attention, as always with the three women. A tentative truce had been established between Dana and Sharon, and they were almost smiling at one another, Austin noticed. He looked around, but the one person he really wanted to see here was absent.

No sooner was the thought out of his head than they all turned to watch Julia enter the room. She was wearing a long tight-fitting, white satin dress and her hair was long and curling past her shoulders. Her eyes found Austin's and she looked down at his black suit and green tie, the green bringing out the same color in his eyes. He crossed the room and took her hands.

Looking at Julia now, Austin thought of that day when he'd almost lost her. He'd been beside himself as he remembered the horror of watching the doctor work over her before he had been run out of the room. The baby had been taken from his arms before Austin stumbled into the hallway. Those next hours had been torture, but Julia had fought back. She'd come back to him. To all of them.

Austin continued to gaze at the face he loved most as he thought about everyone else who had almost lost Julia. They were gathered here now. Lauren and Matt stood with Caleb. Sharon stood beside John, his arm wrapped possessively around her. Phillip now held Caci, who had been dressed in a pink and white ruffled dress. He had one arm under her bottom and one around her chest as she faced the room. She was kicking her legs and waving both arms to the adoring audience who watched. This included her Gramma Nat. After seeing the devastation on her son's face at the prospect of losing his wife, Natalie had a change of heart. She'd come to accept Julia and the marriage because she knew that her son's happiness lay with his little family. Lawrence also gazed at the new apple of his eye, and had already informed his wife that they would be spending a lot more time in Phoenix since he'd retired.

As for Dana, she'd undergone the biggest transformation of them all. It had never entered her mind that she could lose her daughter, and as Julia's life hung in the balance, something happened to Dana. As she'd later told her husband, the worried mother had pleaded with God that day and made Him a promise: If He'd save her daughter, Dana promised to respect Julia's choices and stop interfering in her life. That promise wasn't easy to keep, but Dana was trying hard.

The family needed a celebration, and this day would give them that opportunity. Since half of them had missed the first wedding, Julia and Austin had decided to renew their vows in front of them all. This is what had brought the family to the Flagstaff home at Julia's request.

"I know that we've already been through this, but are you ready to do it again?" Austin grinned at her.

"Absolutely. After all we've been through, I think nothing is more appropriate than this, and with our entire family this time."

"Oh," Austin said, pulling a small box from his jacket pocket. "I didn't want to wait a whole year for this." He opened it to take out a beautiful diamond solitaire set in platinum with smaller diamonds surrounding the bigger stone and trailing down both sides of the ring.

Julia gasped and stared at the beautiful ring. "Oh, Austin, it's beautiful." She reached a hand toward it, but Austin pulled it back.

"Not so fast! This stays with me until we make it all official—again," he teased.

Julia laughed softly and leaned in to kiss him. She pulled away, but not before whispering in his ear. "I should make you get down on one knee and do this properly." Glancing at Lauren and Matt, she continued in a whisper, "But you'd never live it down."

Austin laughed and shook his head. "Never. And I thank you for that."

"One thing, though," Julia grinned at his puzzled look. "Now you'll have to come up with something bigger for our first anniversary."

Austin laughed. "I think I can handle it." He sobered and held out his hand. "Are you ready?"

"Baby, for you I was born ready," she grinned.

"I think we're all set to do this, Father." Austin looked over at the man talking to his dad. He looked back at Julia.

"I love you," she whispered and smiled.

"I love you more," he spoke as he took her hand and led her to the cleared space beside the windows.

"I love you most," she grinned as they all took their places, and the minister began speaking the age-old words of promise: to love, honor, and cherish.

THE END

About the Author

CONNIE DUNN HAS TAUGHT LANGUAGE arts to high school juniors and seniors and college freshmen for almost thirty years. Touch of Jules is her debut novel. She and Kevin, her husband of thirty-six years, make their home in southeastern Missouri, where she continues to teach part-time at the local junior college.